Seladiënna

TILL NOEVER

FIRST EDITION

ISBN: 1-4116-5605-9

Copyright © 2005 by Till Noever.

All rights reserved. Reproduction or utilization of this work in any form, by any means now known or hereafter invented, including xerography, photocopying and recording, and in any known storage and retrieval system, is forbidden without written permission from the copyright holder.

Cover design by Till Noever.
Sword designed and crafted by Greg Wilson, of Dunedin, New Zealand.
Woman's face rendered using *Poser 6* for Macintosh, and DM's 'Alina' character.
Photo on back page by author, taken in Okefenokee.
The title font is 'Amiante', which was created especially for the Vance Integral Edition (www.vanceintegral.com).

Seladiënna is a work of fiction. Any resemblance between the characters depicted herein and any persons living or dead would be coincidental.

www.owlglass.com

*To my wife and daughters,
for everything...*

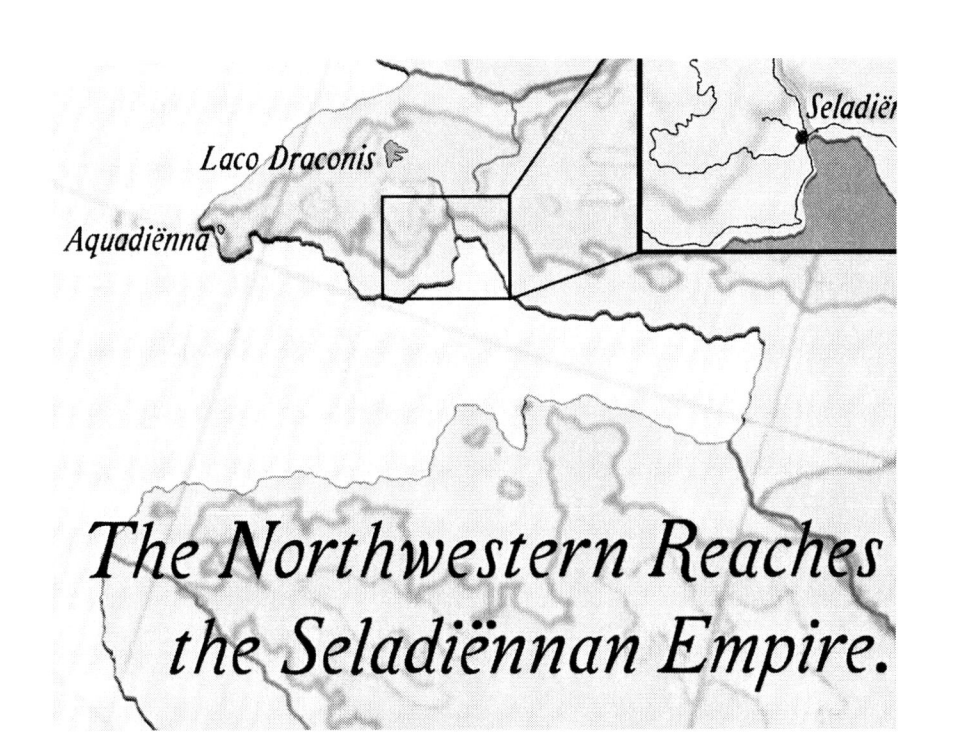

The Northwestern Reaches the Seladiënnan Empire.

1

In Sam's considered opinion Otto Leap would never fly a helicopter. He might fly planes, but every dimwit could do that. Just like everybody could drive a car. Do this and do that and Bob's your uncle. Not so here. An anonymous wit once noted that flying a helicopter was like trying to screw a rolling donut. Otto Leap probably couldn't even do it with a stationary one, let alone one in motion. And he definitely shouldn't ever again touch Suzie's controls!

A pity, really. If ever Otto advanced to the stage of obtaining a license, he would probably end up flying for only a few hours—maybe minutes!—before killing himself; which would be a convenient way to dispose of yet another fascist swine. The perfect murder: teach Otto enough to pass the tests and then let him commit suicide–by–incompetence. Nobody would ever know. Another jerk from ADLER six feet under, making the world just that little bit safer.

Sam sighed and set the MD-500E down with precision and a deftness of touch born out of years of experience and an innate feel for—maybe even a union with—the machine whose brain he was. His conscience fought a brief battle with his sense of vengeance. Conscience won. As the blades started to spin down he turned to Otto Leap.

"It won't work."

"Huh?" Otto's high forehead crinkled as his narrow eyebrows went up.

"You," Sam said. "You and helicopters. It's not what you might call a 'winning combination'."

"What?"

"Take my word for it."

Otto's mouth gaped open. "Just because…"

Sam shook his head. "No, not 'just because'. You suck at this. You always will." He shrugged. "I can tell."

Otto Leap's florid face flushed. He jerked the earphones off his head and flung them against the canopy. "What kind of a stupid-fuck instructor *are* you? You think you know everything, huh? Just because you used to be some hotshot sonofabitch…"

He fell silent as Sam raised a hand.

"Get out," Sam told him. "Go home and shoot yourself some non–Aryans, or whatever it is you lunatics do for entertainment. Just don't make the skies any more unsafe than they already are."

Otto Leap's right hand twitched. Sam allowed himself a thin smile. "Don't even think about it."

"Or *what*?"

Sam just stared at Otto. He could take this jerk out without even blinking. All he needed was a nice, clean reason. Maybe that's what he was waiting for.

Otto glared at him. "You stupid fuck!" But he didn't make a move and the moment passed.

Sam sighed. "Get out—before I change my mind and take us up again."

He saw that the guy didn't get it. *Surprise, surprise.*

"Ever tried to jump from a few hundred feet without a 'chute?'"

Otto, his face mottled with fury, fumbled with the latch, finally got the door open and tried to get out—only to be restrained by the belt. He hissed an obscenity and undid the buckle, got out and, shielding himself from the down–draft of the still–whirling rotor blades, stalked off to his car.

Sam looked after him.

So, ADLER had finally come to New Mexico. They'd been in Texas for decades of course, reeling in those who couldn't forget the Alamo or whatever imagined grievance. Still, up to now New Mexico seemed to have been spared. It couldn't last forever. ADLER's continued expansion was inevitable. One hoped against hope: as it turned out, in vain. And the global terrorist menace, as if not enough of a threat in itself, only fueled and advanced the philosophical corruption endemic in Western societies. Loony Left or ADLER; atheist anarchists or religious fundamentalists. Tomato, tomato.

The truth was that Otto Leap had been in clear and present danger of death-by-a-long-drop from the moment he'd revealed his motives for wanting to learn to fly helos. Of course, Homeland Security didn't check on the likes of him; he didn't look Arab and hardly would have made it onto a watch-list already cluttered with bogus threats. Just as well he'd ended up in Sam's lap.

Why?

The gods only knew why Otto had picked Sam to be his instructor. There were dozens of helo-schools in the phone book! Didn't the guy read the papers? Or did he just have a memory shorter than your average cockroach? Or—and this gave Sam pause—had he *known*?

Sam sighed and shook his head. Paranoia had its place, but maybe he was taking it too far.

Maybe.

Sam waited until the blades had spun down, then did post–flight on the helo, whose name was 'Suzie', and who was a woman in more ways than one. Satisfied that all was as it should be, he closed the clamshell access panels and headed for his office, squinting in the glare, despite his wraparound polaroids, as the New Mexico sun beat down with merciless abandon from a crisp blue sky.

The office was a cubicle in the pre–fab hangar, now just about at hot–oven temperature. The same hangar also housed Meg, Suzie's twin: another ex–army MD-500E, this one still adorned in somewhat tattered camouflage colors; with patches of newer paint, where Sam had brushed over those spots where the old insignia had been crudely removed, probably with a wire brush. Meg was a work in progress: fully functional, but not yet quite as well refurbished and tidied up as her sister.

The sweltering air in the office occasioned an immediate outburst of uncontrollable sweat. Sam looked around himself. A desk, two chairs, a phone, a computer, an appointment book, a tool–box, a trash–can, a sideboard with tools, testing instruments, grimy service manuals he didn't need but was obliged to have. Near one corner of the desk, an aluminum–framed picture of Katie at the age of eight. Sam looked at it; looked away again; felt his viscera crawling with nauseous loathing of the likes of Otto Leap—and the sense of something ineffably precious gone forever. After more than ten years it still hadn't abated—and today it was worse than usual. Otto Leap's presence no doubt. Maybe he *should* have made that guy live up to his name!

Sam looked at the appointment book, though he didn't have to in order to know that Otto had been his last client for the day.

What now?

Same question every day. And in the evening—unless Rita came over and kept him occupied—it would be the same. Probably worse.

He stared at Katie's picture and he could *hear* her talking to him. He could see her face. Trusting completely. A trust betrayed by a dumb mistake. It never left him: wondering if she'd actually been conscious of her father's betrayal.

Sam left the office, closed the sliding hangar doors, and locked them with a couple of heavy padlocks. He activated the burglar alarm with a remote and walked back to the helo outside. One of these days, when he finally had enough, he'd run Suzie or Meg and himself full speed into the side of Jonesy's Break.

Boom.

But not yet. Plenty of time to do the irrevocable. Right now he was just going to fly home. As the rotors spun up again Sam reflected that normal people went home in cars.

Sam owned a cellphone, but he kept it turned off: a futile symbolic gesture against the electronic umbilical gaining ubiquity. But he did have an answering machine on his phone at home, and he communicated by email with a variety of people, far and near.

Arriving home—a small ranch-style house on a five-acre spread at the outskirts of Albuquerque—he found two messages on his answering machine and eleven in his email inbox. He attended to the email first, disposed of nine junk messages, briefly replied to Joshua Eisenhaupt in New York and Candice Porteus in Phoenix, then turned his attention to the answering machine.

A message from Rita, wanting to know if he was still picking her up at eight as arranged. Sam grimaced. Rita *knew* he would have forgotten! She didn't seem to mind though—which was a strange thing, and probably indicative that she was quite serious about him. He'd have to deal with that sooner or later. Maybe sooner was better. Rita had a life to get on with, and the earlier she was rid of him the better for her. Women in love tended to ignore it if the guy they're with was a losing proposition—usually until it was too late and they'd wasted too much of their life on him.

Rita was too good for that. He mightn't be in love with her, but they'd had some good times, in and out of bed, and she was his friend. She deserved to get a life and a suitably devoted boyfriend and father for the children she definitely wanted. Sam had been a father once, but he really didn't think he could ever be one again.

The other message was from Harry, asking Sam to call him back. Sam dialed Harry's cellphone, only to find it engaged. He left a message and went into the shower.

When he came back into the lounge, stark naked, he found two people sitting in the low armchairs around his coffee table.

"Whoa!" Harry slapped his leg with one hand and raised a can of Bud in Sam's direction. "Here's to the *man!*"

"Screw you, Harry!"

The head of the other person in the room, one Helen McCormick, confirmed pain-in–the–neck– and–lower–down and Harry's girlfriend for about a year, turned around slowly enough for Sam to jerk back behind a door jamb and out of sight. With Harry's laughter ringing through the house he slipped into a pair of jeans and threw a T–shirt over his head. He came back into the lounge and gave Harry the finger.

Harry grinned from ear to ear. "I tried to call! Honest!"

As Sam went over to them, Helen turned her head. She gave him a cool cursory inspection from a pair of inscrutable dark–brown and quite remarkable eyes, set in a face that would have been beautiful, if only the owner hadn't been such a total bitch. Sam ignored her and kept an indifferent mien—though inwardly he felt like punching Harry out cold and kicking him and Helen down the front steps.

He slumped down into a chair opposite Helen and pretended that it all wasn't so. From his peripheral vision he noticed that she was studying him with furtive intensity. Probably wondering what she could say to add to his discomfort. Helen always had a barb at the ready. Surprising really that this time it took her so long.

"Sorry to intrude on your ablutions," Harry chuckled. "But you really should turn on that cellphone occasionally."

"If he knew how," Helen muttered.

There it was. Thank you, Harry!

Harry laughed. "Shush! Be nice! Remember what we came here for!"

"You mean you didn't just come here to piss me off?"

Harry shook his head. "Would I do that?"

"I know *some* people who would," Sam said darkly.

Helen's mouth twitched but she held her peace. Small mercies.

"Well, I'm not one of them," Harry declared.

"I'm glad."

"How was your day?"

"All right—if you ignore the Nazi asshole this afternoon."

"Nazi?" Harry narrowed his eyes.

"A jerk from ADLER, would you believe it? What is it with the world? There's only one of me and maybe a thousand of them and they find me without fail! This asshole wanted to learn to fly helos so he can chalk up another point on his organizational scoreboard. Maybe go and buy a helo and hunt for the inferior races or some shit like that."

Harry was silent for a moment. He glanced at Helen, who evinced no disposition for snappy comebacks. Mark the day in the calendar!

"What did you do?" Harry wanted to know.

"I didn't kill him."

"That's a relief."

"I thought about it."

"Not too much, I hope!"

"Enough."

"When are you seeing him again?"

"I'm not."

"You're not?"

"I told him his flying sucked—terminally. He wasn't impressed. He protested. I threatened to drop him from a great height. He chose to forego the experience."

Chapter 1

"Nice going." Harry obviously didn't approve, but he seemed relieved. He glanced at his girlfriend, then back at Sam.

"It makes it all the more urgent."

"What?"

Harry grimaced. "Reason why I came here: to invite you on a journey of discovery."

"Huh? You booked on an expedition or something?"

Harry wagged his head. "Close." He sat straight. "Sam," he said firmly, "you and I know that you need a vacation. So does Rita. I need one, too. So does Helen—who, you'll be glad to know—and you're the first one, too! has today consented to marry me at an unspecified date in the hopefully–not–too–distant future."

Sam glanced at Helen, who stared back defiantly.

"You gonna *marry* her?" he asked Harry.

" 'Her' is here!" Helen snapped. "If you don't…"

"Children, children!" Harry broke in, half laughing, half exasperated. "Can we just be nice? Just for today? Or maybe just half an hour?"

To Helen: "Let the man get used to it, all right?"

To Sam: "Maybe you could do what prospective best–men usually do when they find out their best friend is getting hitched. At the very least commiserate. Or you could do something really outrageous: like congratulate me on my good fortune maybe?"

Sam took a deep breath and got up. He looked from one to the other.

"Congratulations, Harry."

Forcing it out in her direction. "And you."

You're getting the better deal. He bit back the remark.

"Best man?" he asked Harry.

Harry shrugged. "Who else?"

Sam issued a lopsided grin. "Yeah." He glanced at Helen again, who was studying him with an odd kind of intensity. Like she was asking herself some serious questions.

What about? If he was going to make trouble? The thought of him as Harry's best man wouldn't enchant her. Their dislike was mutual. Oil and water, and who knew who was which?

"Of course," he said to Harry. "Shall we drink to it? Let me get another couple of cans from the fridge."

He turned away to go into the kitchen, then stopped on the spot. "How does *Rita* come into this? And what's this 'journey of discovery' shit?"

Harry grinned. "Rita's a co–conspirator. Sorry, Sam, but that's the way it is. We're all going to take a two–week vacation and you're going to come with us."

"I can't leave! I've got clients."

"They can live without you for two weeks."

"Who's going to look after the hangar?"

"Do you know how many security firms are in the yellow pages?"

"Where are we going?"

"Cornwall."

"Cornwall?"

"Cornwall. King Arthur country."

"Oh." It all made sense now. Harry's long–planned pilgrimage to the holy land of his hero.

Sam stood, thinking. "Rita's wanting to go?"

"If you are."

"She's got work to do as well."

"Not during *those* two weeks."

"You've been plotting this?"

"Ah–yep."

"Screw you, Harry!"

"You're welcome."

"I'm going to kill Rita for this. She should've told me."

"I think she would prefer a night of hot, sex with you expressing your undying gratitude for her complicity and knowing better than you what's good for you."

"Shut up." One day Harry would get himself punched out: buddy or not.

Sam waited for the inevitable sequitur from Helen, but it didn't come. He hesitated, thought it over for a few seconds, then decided that it didn't really matter a damn one way or the other. It would make Rita happy and give them both a break. He hadn't had a vacation for years. Maybe trudging along after Harry as he explored the haunts of his fixation was just the thing to do. Maybe the time away would give him a chance to figure out what to do about Rita. Maybe, as unbelievable as it sounded, this was exactly what he needed.

He went into the kitchen and returned with another round of beers for them and a Coke for himself. Sam didn't drink anymore. He had tried the path of boozing himself out of his skull on a regular basis and found it wanting. He didn't have the genetic makeup to become an alcoholic; and getting drunk was an unpleasant effort, which invariably ended in bad hangovers on the following day—and why should anybody subject himself to that? Besides, it almost was a betrayal of Katie's memory. How would *she* have felt about her father if he'd become some pathetic drunk? And if he bowed out of life—as surely he would one day, there being little reason to carry on forever a pretty pointless existence with nothing to justify it—when the day came, he was going to do it not because he'd been heading down some steady slope to extinction, but with eyes wide open and aware of his choices until the very last instant of consciousness.

Choices. That's what it was all about. Nobody and nothing else but yourself to blame for your actions and their consequences. Anything else was a cop–out.

"So, tell me about the Nazi," Harry said when Sam had plonked himself down in his chair again.

Sam grimaced, and provided a brief summary.

Harry shook his head. "I know how you feel about these assholes, but you've got to be more careful."

"What can they do to me they haven't done already?" Sam was going to say more, but then remembered that Helen was here.

Harry, insensitive as usual, didn't know when to stop. "Call Frank Ricci. He'll take care of it."

"Who's Frank Ricci?" Helen asked, looking from Harry to Sam and back again.

Sam gave Harry a dirty look. Even Harry picked it up—which meant that Helen would have, too. Sam avoided looking at her and stared out the verandah window, across the arid New Mexico landscape outside. The afternoon sun shone from a clear sky, reflecting off Suzie's canopy, standing on the concrete pad just off to the left: a monstrous insect; a living creature of metal and plastic, poised to leap into action at any instant.

"Someone who owes Sam a favor," Harry said evasively.

Sam expected a follow-up question from Helen, but it didn't come.

An uncomfortable silence fell. Sam got up.

"We were thinking of dinner," Harry said, "in the company of good friends. Think Rita would want to come?"

Sam hesitated. He really didn't feel up to a social evening in the presence of Helen. But then again, the occasion meant something to Harry, and if Rita was game…

"Sure. Where'd you want to go?"

"Who's Frank Ricci?"

Now that they were alone, driving back from Sam's place, Helen felt free to ask and this time, freed from Sam's presence, she intended on getting an answer from Harry.

"I told you…"

"No you didn't."

"A guy who owes Sam a favor."

"What's the big secret?" she prodded.

Harry's squirm was almost physical. There *was* a secret here. Something to do with Sam and his murky and occasionally tragic past. Something that had gotten him so tense that it almost punctured that damn thick layer of control, and nearly allow a glimpse at the real person underneath. Not that she expected to find much that was edifying. In fact, probably just more of the same. Pride. Cynicism. That biting sarcasm of his.

So, what was she looking for? Weakness maybe? Something redeeming?

What for?

What could you hope to find in some obnoxious, eccentric bastard who thought it was cool—or maybe he didn't even *think* about it any more, which made it even worse! to drive home from work in a helicopter, rather than doing it like ordinary humans, who had the good grace to stick to cars.

"Could we *not* talk about this?" Harry begged.

Helen shifted in her seat and looked at her fiancée: the guy she was going to marry one day, though just exactly when was quite up in the air. A good man, Harry was; though here, too, she sensed that things remained concealed, which one day would no doubt bubble to the surface. As long as they didn't come to bite it was all right. Everybody had some muck in the bilge of their souls, and that was all right, too. Let the one who wasn't damaged goods fire the first shot.

"Harry," she said, carefully, because she was going to know what she wanted to know, "we are engaged, are we not?"

"Yes." She heard the defeat in his voice.

"Sam's going to be your best man. He is, you've told me a thousand times, your best—maybe your only—real friend. I think I have a *right* to know something more than his name and his official record."

Harry grimaced sourly and, as she'd known he would, surrendered to her insistence.

"Frank Ricci is the father of one of the men Sam—we—saved from that boat."

Helen waited.

Harry made a fretful sound. "You know the story, right? Hell, the whole damn world knows it after they made it into a movie."

"*Eagles in the Storm.*"

"The one and only."

"What about it?"

"There was some...artistic license..."

"Don't tell me. Sam wasn't the hero they made him out to be."

Harry shook his head. "I wish. But he was. He took us out there when they told him to can it because it couldn't be done. He pretended that the radio had crapped out, ignored orders, and went ahead and risked our lives—and a multi-million dollar helicopter; which *really* pissed everybody off! to save a few drug-running scumbags from drowning in a shithouse storm."

"He really did?"

"Yeah."

"Why?"

"Because," Harry shrugged. "Shit—who knows? Who knows why Sam does what he does? Ever since Katie...and then Frances..." Harry fell silent.

Helen gave him a few moments.

"What about the 'artistic license'?"

"Remember the ending? One of the guys was made out to be a DEA undercover operative. So, rather than face the music, they suppressed all the names. Everybody sworn to silence. Nobody ever saw their faces or knew their names. The coast-guard was told to cease its internal investigation of Sam's insubordination. He resigns anyway, and becomes a flying instructor and resolves to live happily ever after with the woman he loves."

"Who was she?"

"Nobody. Sam had a brief fling with someone at the time, but she didn't matter a damn. Nobody has since Katie died and Frances left him. Except maybe Rita, and even that..." He shrugged. "Anyway, the critical difference between the Hollywood version and what really went down is that in the real version there was no DEA involvement. Every single one of those fuckers was a bona fide drug-runner. One of them was a kid, barely eighteen. Tony Ricci: son of one Frank Ricci, who's a big crime cheese in the New England region..."

Helen nodded thoughtfully. "So, Sam didn't resign, but was told to leave."

"Most definitely. Especially since Tom, our navigator, chose to open up about Sam's radio-crap-out bullshit."

"Everybody covering their asses."

"Exactly. Tom wanted a promotion. Got it, too. The coast-guard felt it wouldn't look good if they spent their efforts and looked they were risking valuable equipment trying to save scumbag drug runners; so they made one of them into undercover DEA. Still Tony Ricci—that's the kid—thinks the sun shines out of Sam's ass; as does his dad. He phoned Sam later. Told him 'Anything you want, consider it done. Anything.' Seems like family, especially your own kid, still has this blood-debt shit associated with it. I'm sure if Sam called Frank today and asked him to clean out ADLER on a nationwide basis, Frank would go and do it. He'll probably manage to make some kind of profit out of it as well—but do it he would, and could."

" 'ADLER'?"

"The 'Aryan Defense League for European Races'. They must've worked hard to get the acronym right."

"It actually *means* something?"

"It's German for 'eagle'. Which just about pins them down. Bunch of neo–Nazi jerk–offs with shit for brains and itchy trigger fingers. You know, the ones who…"

"Yeah…" Now she remembered. It had been all over the news; almost decade ago when Sam's daughter died. The juvenile lunatics who'd decided to 'purify' their neighborhood by trying to get a school with too many 'Jews' closed down by taking a class of third–graders hostage, and then—when it all went wrong as it had to, and they should have known if they'd had even a single brain between them—killing several, among them Katie Donovan…they had been ADLER. So the cops determined afterwards, when they identified the attackers' corpses.

Ten years later, and they still existed?

"What is it with Sam and ADLER?"

She didn't realize that she'd said it out aloud until Harry answered.

"Yeah," he said thoughtfully, "it's like bad karma."

"You really think that Frank Ricci guy would do this for Sam? Why hasn't Sam asked him? What a way to get even!"

"Nahh. Not Sam."

"Why not?"

"Ask *him*."

"I'm asking *you*."

"No idea. Sam's Sam."

"You think if he'd known…Would he have done it different?"

"That they were going to fire him?" Harry grinned. "No way."

"No? If he'd known these guys were drug runners?"

Harry snorted. "He did. We all did. That's why we were told to abort the rescue. We would have been expected to risk our lives for upstanding citizens of the United States—but drug–running trash? No way."

"What did *you* think?"

Harry was silent for a few moments. Helen glanced at him sideways, to find an oddly tortured expression on his face. It faded the moment he noticed her regard.

"The truth? I don't know. Risking five good men—not including himself—for the sake of three criminals? What kind of a deal is that?"

"Anybody argue with Sam?"

"You don't argue with the pilot, especially if he also happens to be the ranking officer. That's like mutiny."

"Even if he goes against orders?"

Harry chuckled. "He's also got control over the aircraft."

"You were his co–pilot."

"Not in that kind of weather, thank you. I was damn good, and I knew it. But Sam and helos…they're like…" He made a curious gesture with one hand, expressing his apparent inability to formulate the concept on his mind.

Helen stared out the windscreen at the road ahead. The western outskirts of

Albuquerque were closing in around them. Traffic was thickening. People going about their business, oblivious of each other's lives and their joys and tragedies. She tried to get her mind off the subject, but in her mind two scenes from *Eagles in the Storm* kept playing over and over again. One was the actor who played Sam holding his dead child in his arms. The other: in the cabin of the helicopter in the storm, as Sam turned off the radio and told his crew that he didn't give a shit about who or what these people were, and that it was his job to save their lives. That's what they'd signed up for and that's what they were going to do, and damn the bureaucrats and the chain of command. Period.

Hollywood had come along and done its thing to capitalize on a news item that had caught the public imagination for more than just the usual fleeting moment. And Sam had gone along with it. Profited handsomely, if the truth be told; making money out of his misery. Not quite the hero Harry made him out to be. Tragic, maybe. That affair with his daughter was terribly sad; but pathetic as well: how he'd become the stand–offish jerk he was.

No excuse for that. A person *chose* who they became. Life's vicissitudes seldom provided adequate excuses for its mismanagement. If she had allowed herself to be unduly influenced by the fact that she had been an orphan, left behind as a baby on the doorstep of a Manhattan church, her own life would not have been as it was; a guy like Harry would not have asked her to marry him; and she probably would not have been a fast–rising star in the ranks of Keeler and Associates either. Her ads had won several prestigious industry awards and been described as some of the most imaginative and ground–breaking material to burst onto television screens in the last year.

Of course she had also learned some of the less pleasant things about life: her mother had abandoned a perfectly healthy baby; and if such a thing was possible then so were a good many others—and one never knew *what* people were capable of.

With Harry it was different. Harry she knew well. They had been going out for just about a year now, and though they had not actually lived together—but would soon, this being the sensible thing to do under the circumstances—she had him pretty much figured out. Not a mental or emotional giant. Quite an ordinary guy in many respects, though he owned and ran a multi–million dollar software company. Not some damaged entity like his buddy Sam. Loving, and definitely needing, her.

Needing wasn't a bad thing, contrary to what psychologists told you. Not every 'need' implied co–dependency. The fact that Harry had asked her to marry him proved only that he was in this for the long haul. By contrast, Sam and Rita wouldn't last out the year, if that. God only knew what she saw in him. Why a good–looking girl like her was wasting her time with a loser like Sam was one of the great unsolved mysteries of the universe: right next to the origins of jokes and human stupidity. Maybe Rita's infatuation with Sam was just a testimony to the lack of judgment even in people who should have known better.

Rita should! She was, after all, a professional psychologist, though maybe not trained in all the right specialties of her profession.

Harry said something, interrupting Helen's ruminations across the spectrum of people figuring in her current existence.

"What did you say?"

Harry glanced sideways at her. "Thinking hard?"

She shook her head. "Just tired. I need a break."

Harry chuckled. "You'll get it. End of next week."

Yeah, sure. With Sam around it was going to be real fun…

Why would anybody risk his life—and those of people under his command—to rescue three low–life drug–runners? What if they'd been ADLER members and he'd known? What then?

"If it were me," she said thoughtfully, "I would let Frank Ricci do his job."

She felt Harry's sideways look. "Bother you, huh?"

"I just don't understand the guy."

"Who does? But I tell you one thing: if there's anything to know about ADLER, Sam probably does. He's got a few gigs of stuff on them. It probably surprised him to no end that they'd started up in New Mexico without him knowing about it." He chuckled mordantly. "There's some weird shit going on with these guys. Did you know that two of them—and their wives—disappeared without a trace some years ago? Seems like they went on some hush–hush neo–Nazi convention to Europe—and *Cornwall* of all places! One day two of them just vanished. *Poof.* Sam's says that hell probably swallowed them up. Only place that would have them.

"If Sam gave the info he has to Frank Ricci, ADLER could be a greasy historical footnote by the end of the year. But he won't—though I wouldn't be surprised if one of these days he decided to go and do a bit of the good work himself."

"He'd go and *murder* people?"

" 'People'?"

"They're human!"

"Barely."

"I'd still be murder."

"A moment ago you said *you'd* set Frank Ricci onto them!"

"That's different."

"How? Because you hire someone else to do it?"

"It's different," she said with finality.

Harry was wise enough not to push the issue. She was glad about that because he was right.

"Would Sam really do that?" she asked as they pulled up in front of her apartment.

Harry turned off the engine. "I don't know. Sometimes I think he might. Wouldn't you—if they murdered *your* kid? I tell you, I have no idea what's going on in Sam's head. He keeps it all in—as you may have noticed. But I tell you one thing: he loved Katie—and Frances. But Katie above all. And he never forgets—and this one he ain't gonna forgive either."

"Is that why he never smiles?"

"Yes he does! Just not at you. Probably because he doesn't like you. Which," he added, "is totally beyond my comprehension."

She smiled. "You do know to say the right things." She leaned over and kissed him hard, making it an affirmation of her…

…what?

Commitment?

Love?

Why had she agreed to marry him?

She didn't want to go there right now and dismissed the question, which would surely be answered one day when the time was right.

Or it'll come back to bite me when I least expect it...

"See you tonight?" she asked him.

"Seven–thirty sharp."

"I'll be waiting right here."

She got out of the car and waved as he drove off.

⁓⁓⁓

Sam didn't know what made him fly back to the hangar. He rationalized it by arranging with Rita to meet him here, rather than at his place, which was farther from her own, lying, as it was, at the opposite side of Albuquerque. They could go to the dinner from here, then come back here and take the helo back to Sam's where they'd spend the night. In the morning Sam would drop her here again, and Rita would go off to the university.

Such were the overt reasons why Sam returned to the hangar. He admitted to himself that others lurked just beneath the surface. These were, however, not as limpid. Most prominently figured the vague unease which had taken hold of him sometime after today's lesson with Otto Leap. Those Nazi freaks had no sense of humor at all, and now that they were in New Mexico—and how come he hadn't known about that? they were right in his backyard again. Just like they had been when they murdered Katie.

So, who was it going to be this time?

Rita?

Harry?

Or maybe Helen. Even she deserved better than to get caught in the cross–fire of ADLER's twisted machinations and deluded activities. Besides, Harry loved her; so that was that.

As the helo cruised above the rolling expanse of Dale Ashburn's ranch Sam pondered the few people still figuring in his life. None of them really, truly mattered—the way Katie and Frances had mattered. Still he felt vaguely responsible for their welfare. If he'd pissed off Otto badly enough, and if Otto thought that maybe he should get his own back...

If he organized his buddies to show this deviant Sam Donovan just who was who around here and that they deserved some fucking *respect...*

How had they gotten into New Mexico without him knowing about it? He thought he knew all an outsider could possibly about these jerk–offs. It was part of his weekly routine to update his database by searching the web and especially some select pay–sites for the latest updates on ADLER's activities. It was a worry all right!

Sam suddenly remembered that Otto's license plate was in the database at the hangar, together with the usual details about his students. From a number plate to just about every other 'official' detail in the man's life was a smaller step that most people dared to admit to themselves. Which of course implied that ADLER probably by now knew more about Sam than he did about them. They were nuts, but not dumb.

The thought gave Sam pause. The question as to whether Otto had *known* who Sam was before coming to see him—if he'd followed up Sam's background far enough to know about Katie...

Had he?

Sam felt the intimations of a chill. The notion of being targeted—for whatever twisted reasons or purposes—by these lunatics was novel and frightening. Katie's murder had been a random event. Nothing to do with Sam personally, though in many ways it had been his fault and he knew it.

But what about *this*? Sam thought back to his conversations with Otto; especially the last one. Was there anything here to suggest that Otto *knew*?

Without being conscious of it Sam increased the Suzie's speed.

The hangar stood on a twenty–acre section of fenced land on Dale Ashburn's land, which he'd leased to Sam on a long–term contract and for a ridiculously low rent. It had been surveyed and accorded a separate title; and Dale had recently told Sam that if he wanted to buy it he was welcome to do so. The price he'd mentioned was nominal and Sam was sorely tempted to agree to it. He could build a house beside the hangar and live there. There was even a well taking care of the major problem associated with dwelling this far from the city's water supply.

But the hangar was an eyesore: an old corrugated–iron barn of Dale's, which he'd used for storage of feed and vehicles, and which Sam had cleaned out, patched, painted, and converted into something moderately respectable and protective of his valuable helos. Still, it remained an eyesore and Sam by far preferred his house where it was now. He'd probably take Dale up on his offer—if he could scrape together the cash without having to oblige his bank by taking out a loan and paying them interest they didn't deserve. But he wouldn't choose to build a house there: not as long as he could take the helo home without neighbors complaining.

Sam pulled Suzi higher to clear Lazy Hill and swooped into the indentation beyond. In the rapidly fading light he hangar appeared ahead. Sam squinted his eyes. A car was parked on one side. Not his, which he'd left inside. Not Rita's either.

Sam reduced speed as he scanned the area. Just the car. The hangar door, as far as he could discern, was closed. Sam circled the hangar. Nothing. He hovered above the car, a non–descript Chevy that had once been black, but now exhibited patches of paint dulled and faded by lack of attention and long exposure to the New Mexico sun. Not Otto's either. Not the one Sam knew about anyway.

If anybody was inside the hangar—which was almost certain—they'd know Sam was here. The helo wasn't exactly quiet.

A motion near the hangar door, caught in his peripheral vision.

Crack!

A webbing spot appeared in armored plexi–glass of the canopy.

Sam jerked on the stick. Suzi rose and peeled off sideways as Sam pulled her out of the shooter's range.

Bastard!

Someone ran toward the car. Suzi turned and swooped. The figure raised an arm, pointing in Sam's direction. Suzi swerved right, and left again. The man's arm jerked with the recoil. Sam used the second required to bring the gun back in line to pull Suzi around and head straight for the guy—who panicked, as Sam had hoped. He lowered his gun and started to run back for the hangar. The helo came down in a dizzying arc. The hangar loomed close. The left skid caught the guy in the back and threw him to the ground. Sam jerked on the stick. Suzi did a sharp turn; the rotor blades missed the hangar by inches. Sam completed the turn, swooped around and set down hard.

He killed the engine, opened the door, and, as he jumped out, jerked the Beretta from its holster underneath the pilot seat. He raced toward the guy, who was scrabbling to get up. Hearing Sam approach, the man rolled around and scrambled for the gun on the ground beside him.

"Don't!" Sam shouted, pointing the Beretta.

The idiot was too dense to appreciate his predicament. His hand closed on the gun. He pointed it at Sam, who threw himself on the ground, skinning his elbows in the process. A shot rang out, sharp and thin in the open air. Far too high. The guy brought the gun down from the recoil and lowered his aim. Sam fired. An instant of frozen motion as the bullet struck. The instant passed. The perp's gun–hand continued on down until it hit the ground. Sam brought the Beretta into line again and waited. After a few breaths he got himself up and sidled up to the body. He kicked the gun out of the man's reach and bent down. A rattling breath. Sam straightened and ran for the hangar, slid open the big door and found a light switch.

For a few indecisive moments he stared at the office phone. Decisions, decisions. A cop he'd known in San Diego once told him, not entirely jocosely: "What's the point of letting these fuckers live a to have another go at you? I they don't try to kill you, it's their lawyers suing you for doing your job!"

If the GSV here was ADLER, letting him die would be doing the world a favor in more ways than one.

Sam fought a brief battle. Then he dialed 911.

Officer George Malone was a corpulent man in his forties, with a bulge of fat hanging over the equipment affixed to his belt. How he could possibly reach it in a hurry, especially his gun if the need arose, was an interesting question. However, Officer Malone was very sympathetic as he interviewed Sam. The doctors had assured him that the perp, a young man barely twenty–five, name of Jerry Polhem, would live: mostly thanks to Sam's decision to heave him into the helo and fly him into hospital without delay. Sam might have shot the guy, but he'd also saved his butt.

"Gotta confiscate the gun," Malone said apologetically, "It's evidence, you know. You gonna get it back, of course. Seems pretty clear–cut what happened." He peered at Sam. "Any idea what the guy wanted? You got anything in that place except the other chopper and stuff?"

Sam shook his head.

"Think he was trying to steal the chopper?" Malone wondered, making notes on a pad.

Sam shrugged. "Maybe."

Hardly.

"We'll need your statement," Malone told him. "If you could come down to the station…"

"The helo was still on the hospital's pad. I don't think they like it much."

"Shit! I forgot!" Malone shook his head. Then he grinned. "How about this? You take the chopper back to your place. I go with you for the ride. Gotta do it, you know. Until I have a statement, you're…well, you shot the guy…"

Chapter 1   15

"No problem," Sam assured him. "I'll drive you back into town."
He'd be trimming Suzi all the way back to the hangar!

On the flight back to the hangar Officer Malone enjoyed himself hugely. Classic reaction to a first–time helicopter ride: it either scares the shits out of you or you'll get hooked beyond hope of recovery. Riding a bike at a hundred miles an hour came close. Charging along on a fleet horse was another. Great sex might have been the only thing better.

Officer Malone was hooked. He also knew who Sam was and was therefore positively disposed toward him; so the ride to the hangar was pleasant. Malone alighted from the helo and watched open–mouthed—and from a distance—as Sam opened the door and then *flew* Suzi inside. It was a stunt that could go seriously wrong, but then again, *anything* could go wrong.

"That was some serious shit," Malone said, clearly in awe. "You do this all the time?"

Sam laughed. "Only when I feel lucky."

He did a very brief post–flight, then drove out the car and slid the door close. It couldn't be locked: the guy had wrecked the latches. Sam waved aside Malone's objections. He was quite sure that nobody undesirable was going to pay another visit tonight. Not for a few hours anyway. When the cops were done with him he'd come back and fix the door.

He drove Malone into Albuquerque, where Sam underwent a brief and comparatively painless debriefing. While this was going on, he received a call from Rita, who wanted to know if he was all right. He calmed her down and told her to phone Harry and cancel the dinner. Sensibilities or not, he didn't feel up to it tonight.

The cops kept the Beretta for forensics, but officer Malone insisted that it wouldn't be a problem. The perp had three priors: one for drunk and disorderly conduct, once for B&E, another for beating up an geriatric rabbi—in that order. Nothing said 'ADLER' in so many words, but Sam knew the profile. Another loser with an unspecified grudge, needing somebody to blame for his own uselessness.

Sam thought of communicating his suspicions to the cops, but refrained. Let them think it was simple B&E. He'd take care of the other angles.

He wondered what the kid had been after.

The answer came to him later after he'd returned to the hangar. The hose leading to the av–gas tank outside the hangar was not in its usual place. Looked like someone had taken if off and then dropped it in a hurry; probably when he heard Suzi.

So, what was this? Some weird initiation rite? Send the kid to blow up Sam Donovan's hangar? Show that he's a man who can do shit just like the rest of them?

Whatever; these guys wasted no time. Not much for careful planning though.

Sam wheeled up the arc welder, plugged it in and welded a small steel plate over the damaged area of the door, then re–attached the loop for the padlock. He wheeled out Suzie again, fueled her up and, after locking the hangar with a spare padlock, did pre–flight and started up the engine. As the helo lifted off the concrete he reflected that the time of assuming that nothing was going to happen at the hangar was definitely over. Tomorrow he'd get started with installing some serious security systems.

When he approached his house the lights were on and Rita's red Mazda convertible stood in the driveway. She came to meet him as the rotors spun down. She gave him a tight hug and a hard kiss.

"I was *worried*!" she said emphatically.

They went inside. Rita was a good listener. She heard him out without interruption, briefly expressed her concern and told him to *please* be more careful—then told him that she was as randy as hell.

Sam gaped at her.

Rita chuckled huskily, then turned serious. "I just want to be close to you. Maybe so I know I haven't lost you after all."

She slid her hands under his shirt, down his back, and under his belt.

"I think I need a shower," he told her.

"Not now," she assured him and did her best to shut him up.

Later.

"I meant what I said."

"I'm gratified."

"Not that, silly!" She dug her thumbs gently into his ribs and wriggled them.

Sam squirmed. "Stop that!"

"Then stop teasing."

"You didn't mean it, huh?"

"I *did*...oh, you know what I'm talking about."

"Maybe. Tell me anyway."

"I *was* worried! You really got to be more careful. I don't want to lose you, Sam."

He was silent for a few moments. He looked at her face above his, the blonde hair framed by a halo of light from the almost full, curving skylight set into the bedroom's ceiling.

"You know," he said gently, "you could do better."

"I don't think so."

He stroked her hair; his hand came to rest on the side of her head, against her cheek. She pushed against his palm.

"I love you, Sam," she murmured. "If I can do better I can't imagine how."

"I love you, too," he said, and meant it, though not the way she would have wanted it. It was the truth and yet it was equivocal. He loved Rita. She was a great girl, a good friend, a devastatingly passionate bed–partner, beautiful and warm, the closest thing to a 'lover' he'd had since...

Whenever. A long time ago. Very long.

Rita was good for him; kept him from walking too close to the edge, and did so without being cloying, clingy, or demanding. And she was patient: very patient; but ultimately she was hoping for a future; preferably a long–term one. Something he couldn't guarantee. And she knew that and still she stuck around.

"I know," she said and kissed him; and he felt bad and guilty because he was terribly fond of her and yet he didn't love her: not like he should and like she deserved. Somewhere, deep inside him, something remained untouched. He didn't know what or how or why, but he knew that it mattered. He wished it weren't so, but that's how it was, and no matter how hard he tried—and try he did—it didn't seem to matter.

"What're you doing with a loser like me?"

She stiffened. "Don't say that! You know it's not true."
"Some people seem to think so. Can't say I blame them?"
"Who?"
Sam chuckled softly. "Maybe I'm one of them."
"Don't listen to Helen!" she advised. "Screw her!"
"I think I'll leave that to Harry."
Rita laughed huskily and nibbled on his ear. "You'd better."
"You're crazy."
"Maybe. But I'm on top and I'm not done with you yet."

Dale Ashburn was livid.

"Those bastards! They went across *my* land to do *this*? I'll be damned if I…"

"I'll take care of it," Sam assured him.

Dale, a lank individual in his sixties, with a leathery epidermis battered by sun and wind, and a pair of bright blue eyes that missed nothing, waved the comment aside.

"No way! You're not hiring nobody! I've got over a hundred thousand acres and ten hands working for me full–time. They'll be doing shifts at the hangar every night you're away—*with* Jackie or Mannie. I'm gonna have no fucking neo–Nazi sonofabitch violating my property or that of my friends."

Sam bit back a grin. He should have known Dale wasn't going to take this crap lying down. Jackie and/or Mannie, huh? Those Dobermans should put the fear of the Lord into just about anybody. Dale's ranch hands also were not exactly the wimpy kind. They couldn't afford to be. Dale's spread was big; some of the best land around here. His cattle were good stock, and rustling was not entirely a dead art form as yet. Dale's minions were a tough lot. They'd do a better job than any security firm or electronic alarm.

Still, Sam felt vaguely guilty.

"Don't!" Dale told him. "I'm not *just* doing this for you—or your dead kid." Dale was one of those who knew; and, while not effusive about it, evidenced a measure of true compassion and empathy; probably because he'd also lost a kid to a random act of fate—and the thing had wrecked his first marriage just like Katie's death had Sam's.

Sam stretched out his hand and Dale shook it.

"Thanks, Dale."

"Don't mention it. Go and have a holiday. Get away. Look at the world. Screw your girlfriend until she can't walk with her legs together." He laughed when he saw Sam's face. "I wish someone like that wanted to hog my bed."

"I'm sure Maddie gives you a run for your money," Sam said, referring to Dale's second wife, a vivacious woman whom Dale had married only about five years ago, with Sam as the best man.

Dale chuckled. "Well—yes…"

Sam grinned and left. He flew Suzie back to the hangar and from there he called his current crop of students and advised them that he was going to be away for two weeks starting the coming Friday. All but one took it well and wished him a good vacation. The last individual, however, made a song and dance about it, so that in the end Sam told him to shove a spiked pole up his ass and go somewhere else. With a final invective the guy slammed down the phone. Sam reflected that maybe he had to work on his people skills. He was getting just a tad crotchety and impatient.

Next he got onto the web and logged onto the usual search engines—some of them specialized and requiring payment—and tried to update his database on the most recent ADLER news. Nothing, oddly enough, about New Mexico. Maybe the foray was still too new—or too clandestine?—to have made it into the various databases. He logged onto his anonymizer account and spent some time searching under different key–words, logging onto various 'Aryan' web–sites, some of which provided enough links to keep a person busy for days on end, surfing the web for the apparently endless evidence for some of the most base and dismal of human proclivities.

Finally, sickened as wading through this crap always left him, and none the wiser for having done it, he gave up. Whatever ADLER was doing around here was as yet either too insignificant or too novel to have made it into cyberspace. Or maybe there was nothing about this expansion but the natural progression of things. Growth or decline. There seemed to be no middle way. Stasis was not a natural condition.

Officer Malone called. He told Sam—very confidentially, of course—that the D.A. had decided not to lay charges against him in connection with the shooting last night. The perp however, who was well on the road to recovery, would be charged with B&E and aggravated assault. Some lawyer freak had poked around and made enquiries about the shooting. It sounded like the perp—or whoever sent the lawyer—wanted to have a go at Sam himself, but Malone didn't think he had much of a case.

Sam enquired about the lawyer's name: just in case, he told Malone, he was contacted. That way he knew.

Malone told him. One Theodore Howard from El Paso. Sam thanked him and Malone wished him good luck. Maybe one day soon, when he had some extra cash, he could take up flying lessons. Sam said, "sure, just come on up", hoping that it would never happen; but if it did he'd take it from there. Keeping on the good side of the cops could not hurt.

He hung up and pondered the significance of the existence of Theo Howard from El Paso. He made a new entry in his database: under 'ADLER: New Mexico'. The first snippet of information. Hopefully there would be more soon. He backed up the database over the internet to an off–site location, and did another backup to a re–writable CD which he took with him as he flew home.

At loose ends for the rest of the day, he called Rita, made a date to meet at *Capers* in downtown Albuquerque, then called Harry and invited him and Helen as well.

"Make up for last night," he told Harry.

"Gotta tell me all about it," Harry insisted.

"Of course."

"See you at eight."

Sam hung around the house for a while, strangely uneasy, but unable to place the cause. He felt like there was *something* he should be doing, but couldn't figure out what. Finally, in despair, he flew back to the hangar and immersed himself in servicing his helos. Halfway through this exercise the phone rang. Sam wiped his hands and went into the office cubicle to pick it up.

"Donovan Flights."

At the other end a silence. Sam frowned and opened his mouth to say something more. He hesitated and listened.

Breathing.

"We're gonna get you for this."

The man at the other end hung up.

Sam stared at the receiver.

Yeah, and I'm so scared.

Maybe he *should* be scared.

He picked up the phone and dialed a four-digit code. On the LCD display appeared a phone number.

These jerks were living in the dark ages. Had they never heard of caller tracing? Or were they just plain dumb? The possibility was real. You wouldn't have expected it from paranoid bipolar morons like that but there it was: incontrovertible evidence that you could, indeed, never tell.

Sam sat down and logged onto the web again. Five minutes later he had the name and address of the caller. He shook his head when he saw it. Even now, with the evidence staring him in the face, he refused to believe that Theodore Howard from El Paso could possibly that stupid! Still, that's where the call had originated.

Sam hesitated and looked at the address again. 'Theodore Howard'? Sam made a couple of calls. No such person was or had ever been listed with the New Mexico bar. Not in El Paso or anywhere else.

A private address? Was there something so devious about this overt stupidity that he was completely missing it?

Sam added the address to his database and returned his attention to Suzie and Meg.

⁓⋅⁓

The atmosphere at *Capers* was very un-New-Mexico. Cosmopolitan. Almost 'continental', without being too affected about it. Something about the way Giovanni Garbini had arranged it. None of the usual prissy, pretentious crap. Just a nice ambience, mooted light, a theme of amber and brown wood, nice personnel, and excellent food. Giovanni's recipe had born fruit: *Capers* was booked out every night of the week, with long queues lining up to go there. To get a table without booking weeks ahead was almost impossible: unless you were a friend of Giovanni's, which Sam was. Giovanni, like Frank Ricci, owed Sam: at the very least a few hundred bucks—probably his health, and possibly even his life.

In the early days, when *Capers* was just starting off and was still located in a somewhat unsavory district of Albuquerque, there had been an attempt at robbery. It had been late and the place just about empty. Sam, who at the time had a brief fling with Jane, one of Giovanni's two waitresses, came to pick her up after closing time—only to run right into the holdup.

Giovanni, seeing which way the wind was blowing, was cooperating and meek, but the two perps, high on some designer-dope, were aggressive and hyped, shouting and waving around their guns and generally having their version of fun. One of them was pawing Jane, who had been cleaning up and waiting for Sam; the other was threatening to blow Giovanni's head off unless he revealed the location of his great stash of cash—

which existed only in the perp's imagination, but what the heck.

Sam, looking in through a break in the curtain behind the glass of the door, adjudicated the situation, concluded that there was no time to call the cops. He retrieved the Beretta from his car—the same one that had recently nailed Jerry Polhem—and returned to the shop—only to find the situation had gone from bad to worse. One perp was kicking Giovanni, who lay on the ground, squirming, while the other had the gun pushed up against Jane's neck and his other hand under her blouse, doing things there she really didn't seem to be enjoying much. The two of them were shouting and screaming and laughing hysterically, all at once.

Sam took another look along the street, found it mostly deserted and no cop in sight. He pushed at the door, which opened with a creak. The perps saw him, forgot all about their victims and, without much ado and whoops of delight, opened fire. Sam dived into cover behind a table. The perps, leaving Jane and Giovanni behind, converged on Sam's position with guns blazing. Regular cowboys. Unfortunately they were too doped to count their ammo, and by the time they got to him they had emptied their guns. They also weren't very coordinated physically. Sam suffered only a minor bruise and never had to fire a shot: basic SDT had been sufficient to lay them out cold.

The cops arrived in due course. Sam's non–use of lethal force and his background got him out of this one with a nod and a wink. Jane was so worked up from the whole affair that she not only screwed the living daylights out of him that night, but also developed acute symptoms of co–dependency—which in due course led to a bitter breakup between them, with her making at least one half–hearted attempt at suicide afterwards, and then, when the ruse proved to be ineffectual, moving away to the other side of the country. The whole thing left Sam with the uneasy sense that maybe rescuing damsels in distress wasn't all it was cut out to be. The sex afterwards was great, of course—but the other bits?

Thanks, but no, thanks.

Giovanni and his wife—who'd been terminally pregnant at the time, and therefore at home and completely unaware of the whole affair until she'd had her baby three days later, after which event Giovanni finally told her—expressed their undying and eternal gratitude to Sam. *Capers* always had a table when Sam wanted it, and payment was never required. Giovanni also made it quite clear that he would be deeply offended if Sam did not avail himself of this offer on a regular basis. Sam chose to oblige, though he thought that Giovanni had probably 'paid' his imagined debt many times over. But Giovanni would hear none of it. His sharp Sicilian features creased into a grimace of dismay when Sam even hinted at it—meaning that it was never raised again, and that on this evening, after yet another emergency of sorts, Sam and his three prospective travel–companions were enjoying *Capers*' hospitality at a specially arranged table at the window, whence where they could watch the traffic flow past through one of Albuquerque's older districts, whose colonial leftovers lend it a picturesque air that was absent from most of the rest of the city.

As he retold what happened the previous day, Sam, who was doing it with only half a brain, contemplated the three others. His traveling–companions–to–be: if all went as planned. The prospect of being stuck with these people for two weeks without interruption cast novel aspects on his interaction with them. It had been many years since he had been in the company of anybody as consistently as he would on this trip.

He might learn more about them than he really wanted to.

With Harry of course that was not an issue. Sam knew him well enough. After his separation from Frances they had even shared an apartment for a few months. Harry was, therefore, a known quantity. A slob to live with—one of the reasons why Sam found his own apartment soon enough—but basically honest and reliable. No hero; certainly not given to impulsive bouts of recklessness. A Republican, who couldn't understand Sam's indifference to and cynicism about, all politics. A good pilot, but with none of the true *empathy* for the machine that would have made him into a brilliant one; a much better businessman: with a good nose for what to do and how and when to do it. A silly fool, too, with his soft side for that frump, Helen.

Helen.

And Rita.

The two juxtaposed quite naturally in his mind, sitting, as they did, beside each other in his field of view: Helen opposite Harry, Rita opposite Sam. A Harry–thing. He liked to look at his dates across the table. Normal people liked to snuggle up. Everybody had his quirks.

Rita looked stunning—as usual. Devastatingly sexy, but not blatantly so. She just couldn't help it. With looks like that, a voice the could melt the polar ice caps, and a personality that made her into just about the nicest person Sam knew…no wonder she made Helen appear insignificant. Or maybe that was the wrong word. Maybe just less glamorous. Inside and out. Helen could have helped the matter if she'd turned on that smile of hers for anybody else but Harry. But she didn't; and the one time he caught her glancing in his direction—an action she avoided as much as possible—her face had become a mask. The expression before that… Sam wondered what it had been. Intent observation maybe. A sizing up. Like she was having the same thoughts: *Will I be able to stand being with this person for a whole two weeks without a break?*

The topic of what happened the previous night died an unnatural death, starved of oxygen by Sam's pronounced lack of enthusiasm to dwell on it. Harry produced a map of Cornwall and propounded on his plans. They'd hire a Range Rover at Heathrow and make their way west, following Harry's carefully worked-out schedule, working their way toward Land's End, and then straight back to London and home.

Two weeks in a car with Helen? Their eyes met across the table. A silent staring match, lasting maybe a second or two and unnoticed by the other two. Sam could read the same thoughts behind Helen's eyes. Were they going to survive this without screwing up the trip for Harry and Rita? If only their mutual chemistry wasn't so totally…opposite!

It was almost funny. If this had been a movie plot, thought Sam, it'd be obvious to even the most naive of viewers that sooner or later Helen and he would wind up in each other's pants.

And here's the difference between movies and real life.

He looked away; at Rita, who was laughing at Harry's eagerness. Sam decided that two weeks with Rita would be nice. Maybe they would even work out their future—one way or the other.

Friday.

Suzie and Meg were locked up in the hangar. Dale had assigned a rotating shift of guards over the place. Jackie's favorite dog–house had been temporarily relocated to beside the hangar's front door. The chain holding her was *long*. She thoroughly explored the area within the confines of her reach, then settled back in front of her hut and, alert as was her way, pretended that she was asleep and not really interested in what was going around her at all.

Sam shook Dale's hand and opened his mouth to thank him. The rancher's expression made him shut it again.

"Don't even *think* it!" Dale warned him.

Sam chuckled. "I won't."

"Good! Now go and have yourself a vacation. And don't forget what I told you about your girlfriend."

Aquadiënna

Mirlun bowed, but his face was troubled. "Thus, Diënna, you may destroy yourself. And then…what are we to do?"

"I will not fail," she promised him, "for now I see clearly again: and I see that the time is soon. The opening will be very near—and I must call them, for they, too, will be close."

Mirlun raised his eyes to the ethereal shape floating above the waters, unearthly in its loveliness.

"But they know not who they are!"

"Then they must learn."

"How?"

"They must take Gladius Magnus back to their world."

"Diënna!"

"This is the way it must be. Augustus has made a pact with Plius. He has promised him a power Augustus never had. Sooner or later Plius will come and take Gladius; and there's nothing I can do—for he is stronger than I, and he can see the sword, no matter where I hide it. All he has to do is take it—and then I will begin to fade, while Plius and Augustus vanquish the hearts of my people. Everything Magnus fought for will be gone."

The luminous shape displayed an array of erratic color patterns, evidencing her agitation.

"When the portal opens I shall call them, and they shall take Gladius and keep it safe—until they have learned who they are—until they are prepared."

"But when it is gone…" he objected.

"Hush! Remember who you are and do not argue over what you do not understand. But prepare yourself, for you, too, will be needed."

"Diënna?"

"Plius's Minions are gathered to await the next opening. He, too, knows that it will be soon. He may even know where. Augustus is afraid: someone might enter to challenge his control. In this instance this fear is indeed justified—as he will know when Gladius is gone. He will try to send someone to their world to retrieve it. Therefore you, too, must hold yourself at the ready."

"You want me to…go…there? How can I? I know nothing of that world!"

The glistening outlines of the sprite rippled with a brief burst of amusement. A tinkling sound echoed across the waters. "You will be well–equipped." The merriment faded. "As will be Plius's Minions. They, too, will try to make the transition."

"But—to leave you behind! Augustus will be livid. He will influence Oldecus Pistor, who is nothing but a puppet. They will come here and do their worst. Plius will gloat and leer over the rim of his lake."

"Not yet.," Diënna told him. "Still I am strong, for the legends of Cassius and Magnus sustain me. As long as the saviors come quickly—and for that I need you!"

Mirlun bowed. "I am your servant."

"You are a servant of the people." The Diënna's tone carried a note of benign *admonition. "Above all—when I send you to far shores—remember this: that you are a servant of the people, and that without you they—and I—will perish."*

Mirlun stood in an attitude of respect. *"I am—and have always been—here to serve."*

Another ripple went through the sprite. The tinkling sound of ethereal laughter floated across the waters. But it wasn't as merry as he would have liked it. An undertone of mournful sadness tainted the sound: an ominous foreboding—and it was as if the Diënna—despite all her good spirits, that had so bewitched Magnus and his people—had lost the touch of joy that had marked her existence ever since Mirlun had come to Aquadiënna to serve. The arrival of Augustus and the other two, the murder of Oldecus Pistor's wife and son…all that combined to cast a pall over her happiness, and thus over all of Seladiënna, from the farthest north to the borders of the southern jungles.

He, Mirlun, would do whatever it took—and whatever sacrifice it might require of him—to ensure that the Diënna could be happy again.

2

The wind from the Atlantic was sharp and gusty, driving a fine mist into their faces and through every crack in their clothing. The weather had cleared all but the most determined of tourists from the viewing area at Land's End. The fine drizzle and mist shrouded the rocks below in a blanket of mysterious vagueness. The Atlantic lay somewhere behind the narrow visual horizon imposed by the mist. One assumed, Sam thought, that it was there. An existential assumption, based on informed guesswork.

But who knew that it was really there? Who could *know*?

Sam liked fog: a metaphor for life. Visibility constrained to a narrow confine.

Behind: the past, already sinking into the oblivion of inexact memory.

Ahead: the future, its shape already discernible in outline, yet beyond the veil it was unknown—and if one forged ahead too quickly, who knew what might emerge at breakneck pace, to collide with one's assumptions about what there was?

To the right and left: the confines of one's current mental horizon, limited by physical perception, the constraints of contingency, imagination or the lack thereof.

Yes, Sam liked fog, and here, at Land's End—after their sojourn through the relics of a past so deep in the fog that nobody could ever hope to know what was 'real'—the fog seemed to epitomize a fundamental truth about what he had learned in the last two weeks. How much was legend and how much wasn't? Or maybe that was the wrong question. Should it be: what was it that gave rise to such persistent legend? The assumption here, of course, that there was indeed *something*: a moot point. There were those who would argue that it needed nothing to originate legend but imagination. Another fairly tale: of heroes, villains, fair maidens, love, hate, generosity, greed, loyalty, betrayal, hope, fear, life, death, sex, peace, war, violence, forgiveness, retribution, curiosity, misunderstanding, reconciliation, ambition, surrender, cowardice, courage, and whatever else happens to strike one's fancy.

Was that all? Just a figment of someone's imagination, amplified through popular tradition? Geoffrey of Monmouth, the insignificant priest who needed a metaphor for the flock and something to suck up to his superiors: of Christian conquest and the dawning of a new age?

Or was it really Lucius Artorius castus, the Roman general, who, with his 'knights', cobbled together from indentured warriors from the far-flung reaches of a decaying empire, became a hero who drove back the invaders from the north, and then was elevated to the status of legend? Who could tell? Who dared to be definite about such a thing?

During the last few days Sam had come down on the side of 'legend based on real people'. It had the ring of plausibility. Precedents abounded. The Bible. The Koran. Gilgamesh. The Vedas.

Plausibility did, of course, not make it true. Historical truth had always been concealed in the impenetrable fog of time, erosion, decay. And that's where it would stay.

Forever.

Just like…

The thought came unbidden, and tainted Sam's romantic, almost dreamy, mind–set.

Land's End. It was here that ADLER and their European counterparts had had a meeting some fifteen years ago.

Sam had worked hard to reconstruct what had happened. A contact at the FBI had provided some interesting snippets of information, allowing Sam to piece together the shadowy details of a curious mystery.

Spring 1985.

ADLER's four premier leaders—from Texas, Minnesota, Kansas, and California—went to the UK to meet up with a European contingent of neo–Nazi bigwigs from across northern Europe to discuss the possibility for coordinating their activities on an international scale: to work toward an organization that would—in some hazy utopian future where the lower races were finally relegated to the inferior position where they belonged—provide the foundation for a world ruled by the superior races.

They thought they were being subtle about their trip, taking pains to avoid attracting the attention of the FBI or other undesirable, liberal, Zionist, nigger– and spik–infested, authorities. Their tickets were booked separately. They left from different airports on different days, flew to different destinations in Europe, hired cars, and drove to their final goal, a little town called 'Helston' in south–west Cornwall. The meeting place was not chosen at random, but was imbued with symbolic significance. All the participants had agreed that meeting in the land of King Arthur was very much within the spirit of their association. If there ever had been a good Aryan, it must surely be Arthur, who'd kicked the shits out of the southern barbarians. This at least was their interpretation of hazy historical conjecture, as it could be gleaned from the 'documents' on their various associated websites, most of which, ironically, were hosted in countries that were home to those their considered racially inferior.

A number of hotels and guest–houses in Helston and environs had rooms booked to accommodate the participants; the bookings, like everything else, arranged independently, in order to avoid attracting any attention by undesirables: in this instance Interpol or Special Branch; or whoever had them in their sights. The men brought their womenfolk: it looked more realistic. The ADLER members were presently joined by others from Germany, France, Sweden, Belgium, the Netherlands, Switzerland, and Austria.

Despite their paranoia and careful preparations, their meeting was, of course, no secret, except in their wishful thinking. Just about every word uttered by any of them was duly recorded by at least three different police organizations, who were rubbing their hands at the idiots' delusions. Meetings had been arranged on a small–scale basis only. Attendees met apparently at random, being thrown together in cafés, bars, restaurants or during their sightseeing. The whole pussy–footing around profoundly irritated the conference partners, so that in the end—after having talked themselves into the belief that they had thoroughly fooled the authorities, who surely didn't have a clue of what was going on—they decided to damn it all, and have a grand meeting after all: a picnic on the grassy area beside the car park at Land's End, watching the autumn sun set over the Atlantic—where they could see any observers from a mile off and the wind snatched up their words and blew them away before even the most sensitive of directional microphones could possibly pick them up. And if they couldn't prove anything illegal about this meeting: the truth was that without good reasons those liberal, mixed–blood bastards couldn't touch them. Not in England anyway.

One sunny afternoon a fleet of rentals converged upon the car park. The few legitimate tourists enjoying the view across the waters to mythical Lyonesse were soon put off by the bunch of intense, unsmiling creeps who appeared between them like aliens from outer space. Put off by this unsavory horde, the legitimate visitors departed in some haste. The ADLER men congregated to one side leaving the women to organize the 'picnic', which consisted mainly of bags of crisps procured from a Helston grocery shop, dainty sandwich wedges prepared at short notice by one of the local guest–houses for an exorbitant price, and lots of cans of beer—which, once emptied, were duly thrown into the crashing waves, despite an abundance of trash receptacles strategically placed around the parking area and picnic ground alike.

The party, however, was to remain incomplete, its discussions inconclusive. This was the fault of two important ADLER members, Larry Unterflug from Minnesota and Clint McDermott from California. Larry and Clint, accompanied by their wives Shareen and Darienne, never arrived. In fact nobody ever saw them or their rentals again; something which later created a great deal of grief for the remaining members of the conference in general, and for ADLER in particular. The rental agency's insurance company also could not have been pleased.

A mystery, to be sure. Maybe they got lost in the fog? Maybe hell *had* swallowed them up—though it might have been expected that it also had spat them out pretty soon after when its denizens came down with stomach trouble.

"What are you thinking?" Rita tightened her hold on his arm.

"I'm glad I came here," Sam said, half–truthfully.

"Pity about the fog," Harry said.

"I like fog," Helen told him. "It's…"

Harry chuckled. "Like life, huh?"

"Yeah."

Harry gave Sam a crooked grin. "See, you two *do* have something in common."

Yeah, right! And pigs have thirty–minute orgasms. The situation with Helen hadn't become any better during the trip. Not any worse either—which was something to cheer about. She still didn't smile at him, but she didn't snarl either. Really controlling herself. Of course, Sam had worked hard on it as well.

Harry laughed. "Come on, you two! Peace! Just for the last day! Think you can manage it?"

Sam gave Harry a shut–up–or–I'll–punch–you–out look and turned to Rita. "There's something about this place."

"Yeah. It's wet and I'm getting chilly."

"She's right," Harry said. "Wanna go? We're not going to see Lyonesse today."

"Or ever," Rita pointed out.

Sam could have stayed in this spot for hours, just having the drizzle blow around his face and stare into the misty swirls and eddies. But—apart from Helen maybe, who cast a final, strangely yearning glance at the rocks and the crashing waves below—they all wanted to go; and that was fair enough. The idea of a hot shower and an early dinner was tempting.

Of course, there was always the danger that Harry, who would probably get inebriated on their last night, would also use the occasion to make a thing of the fact was it was Sam's birthday. His fortieth to be exact. Rita knew about it—but she'd promised to respect his wishes. Understood the motives. Sam's birthday was a taboo subject: since it was also the day of Katie's murder. He could not possibly celebrate it—ever again.

An intoxicated Harry was, however, not likely to pay much attention to such sensitivities. He rarely did. Alcohol, to Harry, was a verbal diarrhetic. Whatever he thought of would probably be instantly verbalized. Sam was in no mood to have anybody toast to his welfare. Especially not a lubricated Harry—or Helen.

Sam briefly considered pleading tiredness. Maybe a migraine. He decided against it. It was their last evening together. They'd had a good time, despite the occasional bickering between him and Helen. It would be churlish to bow out now because of his tender sensibilities.

In the event it turned out not to be too painful at all. They had managed to score a table in a corner of the Helston Arms. The meal, typical stolid British fare, had been passable. The wine, such as Sam conceded to consume, was adequate. The whiskey might have been, too, but Harry would have to be the judge of that.

The room was filled with the reek of booze and smoke. Especially smoke. Cigarettes, cigars and pipes combined to produce an atmosphere more toxic than Jupiter's. Europe had a long way to go to catch up with the US in implementing policies to protect those folks who chose not to die of smoking–related diseases. Sam reckoned that he had inhaled more carcinogens during this holiday than he had in the previous decade. *Everybody* smoked, and the pitiful few that didn't accepted it. Evidently the Surgeon General's Report had never made it across the Atlantic. Neither had every other bit of research into these matters. Or maybe these people were just abysmally stupid. Maybe that's why Europe was such a dump. Lots of history, but a dump. The crap almost threatened to smother the charming aspects of the place.

Sam watched a fat, noisy man at a nearby table expel a stinking cloud of cigar smoke. Driven by an errant gust of air, occasioned by the briefly opened front door, it chose to waft in their direction like a dirty blob of blue–gray ectoplasm.

"Hold your breath," he advised Rita, who wrinkled her nose and nodded.

Harry nudged Sam in the side. "Gotta die of something, old buddy."

"Yeah, well, not of this shit," Sam told him. "I'd rather pick the manner of my death."

"Nobody picks the manner of their death," Harry declared, his voice a tad slurred, but still coherent. "Time will…"

He was going to say something else, but didn't. Instead his face turned to Sam. His eyes widened.

Shit! Here it comes.

"Sam!" Harry chuckled and poked him in the shoulder. "Sam, my man! You thought you'd get away with it, huh? Thought Harry wouldn't remember! You sly sonofabitch!" He laughed loudly. "Gotcha!"

Sam grimaced. "Let it be, Harry. Please."

Harry shook his head and reached for his whiskey glass. "No way!" He raised the glass. "Here's to you, Sam. Happy birthday. How old are you now? Forty? Fifty? Who knows, eh? Who cares? Way I see it you could be in the terminal stages of Alzheimer's and you'd still fly those damn helos. You'll *die* in one of those infernal fuckers!"

Sam glanced at Rita who regarded him compassionately, her lower lip between her teeth. From his peripheral vision he saw that Helen, who had been silent for quite a while, sat up straighter and studied him with more deliberation than she usually did. He glanced at her and found her eyes narrowed and thoughtful. She hadn't known. Well, it would have been nice if it could have stayed that way.

Harry slammed his glass against Sam's on the table, knocking it over in the process. The remainders of the Coke spilled across the table cloth. Sam reacted quickly and turned up the cloth to stop the liquid from dribbling into his lap. He stood up the glass and shook his head.

"Thanks for that," he said. "Now can we let it rest?"

Harry ignored him and waved to a waitress. "Hey!" he shouted, loud enough for heads to turn in his direction. "C'mere! A drink for my buddy Sam, the craziest fuck who ever flew a helicopter! Makes them dance like prima ballerinas on speed!"

The waitress, a full–busted freckled redhead in a long–sleeved cotton top that displayed her impressive mammaries to their full advantage, came over, dropped a cloth on the spreading blotch of Cola and mopped it up, then hovered.

Harry waved at Sam. "Get him anything he wants. It's the man's birthday, you know? Forty years and still he flies and shoots them neo–Nazi fuckers."

The waitress, clearly bemused by Harry's ramblings, glanced at Sam. Sam shook his head. "Nothing, thanks."

He nudged Harry. "Time to go bed, I think. Long day tomorrow."

"No way!"

"Yes way!" Sam declared. He winked at the waitress. "Thanks, but no thanks. Gotta go." She smiled at him just a tad longer and with a bit more warmth than she had to. A hint of a suggestion that blew away as she glanced at Rita. Regretfully she swung around and headed off in the direction of the bar.

Sam looked at Rita. She grinned crookedly. "I've got to keep an eye on you!"

"No you don't," he said.

"That's nice," she said and smiled at him. The smile should have warmed his heart and set it aflutter, bearing as it did the promise of a night of immensely satisfying sexual congress. And more. It wasn't just sex. Rita was serious about him; not just as a partner, but as the focus of genuine love. Sam felt a pang of guilt and something else—maybe sadness—when he admitted to himself that the vacation had done nothing to stimulate more profound feelings. Why could she not see that he was a lost cause? Why persist in hoping? The truth was that he just wasn't capable of the kind of deep emotional passion she deserved. Not anymore.

Life was so damn difficult; especially when it came to those you cared about. How much easier to deal with those you detested. Like Helen. With her it was clear–cut and simple. Personal chemistry screwed up beyond repair. Chalk and cheese. Fish and flesh. Whatever.

He glanced at Helen again. She was leaning over the table, saying something to Harry in a voice too low to be heard over the din in the pub. When Helen noticed Sam's attention she glanced at him and gave a curt shake of her head, then returned her attention to Harry, laid a hand on his right arm and said something Sam couldn't catch.

He looked at Rita, who shrugged, then reached across the table and patted Harry on the shoulder. "Come on. Let's get to bed. Long drive tomorrow."

"Party–pooper!" Harry accused him. "Fun–killer!"

"He's right," Helen said firmly.

Harry stared at her. "What did you say?"

Helen looked like she'd bitten on something sour. "Let's go."

Harry turned his head to consider Sam for brief, inebriated moment. "Gotta do what you gotta do."

Sam patted him on the back. "Right."

The weather outside had totally gone to the dogs. Or cats. Or whatever. The drizzle was thin but so dense that by the time they reached the Range Rover only a few steps away they were soaked.

Sam drove the few blocks to their hotel, which was a modern abomination with none of the charm of old Cornwall and all the stolid dullness and insipid decor of internationalized accommodation. Harry followed Helen's guidance without further protest. Sam and Rita left them at the door to their room.

"Sleep tight," Sam told them.

"I'm going to have some *sex*!" Harry muttered.

Sensitive, discreet Harry, Sam thought. When intoxicated, Harry's lack of tact was without compare. He almost felt sorry even for Helen, who made a point of not looking at them as she unlocked the door to their room and took Harry's arm to pull him inside. Her face was flushed and angry. Harry wasn't going to get laid, that much was certain.

Sam and Rita proceeded to their own room, a couple of doors down the hallway. When it had closed behind them Rita turned around and put her arms around Sam's neck. In the still–dark room, she was a sleek silhouette against the pale rectangle of the window. She smelled of smoke and booze from the pub, but then so did Sam, and anyway it didn't matter, because underneath she smelled of woman, and her hands and mouth were doing things that left no doubt what she wanted—and somehow he wanted it, too—if for no other reason but to yield to her desire; to make her as happy as he could—even though he was a pathetic cad who didn't even have the guts to tell this lovely creature that he didn't love her and never would.

But how could he hurt her so, when what she wanted was…this…Here and now. From him and nobody else.

And so he slid his hand under her jumper and loosened her bra and cupped her breasts—and as her tongue penetrated deeply and roamed around his mouth and she moaned softly and their breath became one, he carried her to the bed and did his best to conceal the despair he felt; the guilt; the feeling of inadequacy and his own failure.

He didn't think she noticed. Her climaxes felt real. So were his own. Both of them.

⌒⌢⌣

"Let's have sex!" Harry flopped down on the bed, where he lay on his back and groped to unzip his fly.

"Shut up!" Helen hissed.

"What's the matter?" Harry's hands stopped fumbling. He lay still, staring up at her with wide, slightly unfocused, eyes and an expression of incomprehension and hurt.

Helen turned to the bathroom. "Just...go to bed!" she snapped as she closed the door behind her. She sat down on the toilet to attend to her bodily functions and to get away from Harry.

What was it with him? What was it with *her* for that matter? Did she really want to marry this guy? After the last couple of weeks her previous impressions of who and what 'Harry' was had been...not so much 'revised' as...'adjusted'. He was a sweet guy, no doubt about it. Kind, considerate, generous, affectionate, sensitive—unless he was in *this* state, of course, when he was still kind and affectionate, but more in the manner of a randy ape than a human being.

The solution appeared obvious: get Harry to stop drinking more than he could handle. She had a feeling that the elegant simplicity of the proposition hid its flaws, the first of which was that Harry simply wouldn't do it—despite many reiterations of his love for her and how he would do 'anything' to make her happy. She had already hinted at such matters—and come up empty handed. Harry had slid away like an eel, not disputing the need, and yet somehow not actually agreeing to her implied suggestions. The signs were clear and Helen found them disturbing.

Still, she loved him.

Or did she?

The question had reared its head several times during these last two weeks. She had agonized over it many a sleepless night. Her chronic insomnia, a feature of her life for as long as she could remember, had not been helped by the thoughts roaming around in her head. Five hours of sleep on a good night. Three, sometimes less, on a bad one. The last two weeks had been an unending sequence of bad ones. As long as sex took up a significant part of the waking period that was all right, but when she had obliged Harry by lying beside him quietly, instead of getting up and doing what she would otherwise have done—reading; listening to music; watching TV; working with her laptop, maybe surfing the web for her favorite sites, both work–related and for entertainment—those nights had seemed to be never–ending. And it was going to be one of those nights.

She knew it. She just *knew* it!

Maybe the most troublesome aspect of her relationship with Harry was that passion, which had never figured all that prominently, was rapidly fading into unnoticeability. Helen frowned. Maybe 'passion' was the wrong word. Or maybe it wasn't. Damned if she knew. It had something do with being *touched*, not just on the surface but somewhere near her core—so that she actually *felt* something. Anything at all. To be brought to the point where she might actually lose this damn control she seemed to have over *everything* having to do with her emotions. Stirred, even if it was to loathing or detestation, like the kind she felt for Sam. If she could only muster a similar depth of emotion for Harry everything would be work out just fine. The drinking wouldn't matter, because it would be dealt with. It wouldn't be an effort to make an effort, but a joyous labor of love and engaged affection and sheer *interest* in another human being.

She buried her face in her hands, sick in her heart with the hopelessness of it all. Sitting on the toilet, feeling sorry for herself.

What a pathetic creature.

Was she crying? She raised her head, sniffed, and tore off a few sheets of toilet paper which she used to daub at her eyes and the runny makeup and her equally runny nose.

Later she stood in front of the mirror and just stared at herself—and couldn't even get worked up over her own pathetic misery anymore. Nothing mattered. Whatever had gone wrong had gone wrong—maybe a long time ago, when her mother left the baby at the doorstep of a Manhattan church. That was an excuse, of course, but it would have to do.

Why do you bother? With Harry? With anything?

Why take another breath? Maybe dying, maybe the last moment of her life when she knew that this was the irrevocable step...maybe *that* would stimulate a visceral response of some sort. Of course, the act of suicide was counterproductive. What if she did feel something beyond indifference? What if she started to care? What if she then died, and never had a chance to make something out of what she'd found?

She knew why she took another breath.

And another.

All of which didn't solve her immediate problems, of course.

What 'problems'? She didn't *have* any problems! Everything was...fine. Her traveling companions were...nice.

That's hardly a 'visceral response'...

Funny how life insisted on not obliging.

I do have a problem.

The last two weeks had distanced her from Harry. Familiarity had bred, if not contempt, then at least a troublesome form of indifference. The truth was that, while she'd do anything in her power not to hurt Harry's feelings, if he were gone tomorrow she might feel sad, maybe even lonely—having lost a means to satisfy her natural urges, which had always been remarkably alive, despite everything else in her sometimes feeling dead—but that was about it. It'd pass quickly enough. There'd be someone else.

I wish...

Wish *what*?

Maybe that someday, somehow, she wouldn't be able to think that about someone—even if she wanted to—but that she simply *couldn't*.

That would be nice...

Helen terminated the tête–a–tête with herself by turning away from the mirror and her image. She hesitated before opening the door. What would she say to Harry? She definitely didn't want the 'sex' he'd been offering so grandly. The mere memory of him lying there, unzipping his fly, was a grotesque obscenity. Of the things she really didn't want to do right now this ranked even below...

No way!

Her hand touched the door handle.

Sam and Rita were probably having a good time right now.

Screw them!

Helen shook her head, opened the door, stepped into the room. Harry was still lying on the bed, one hand on his crotch, near his open fly. The other arm was flopped across the bed. His eyes were closed and he was snoring fitfully.

Small mercies!

Should she move him?

Chapter 2 33

Her gaze fell on a somewhat stuffy, but possibly not too uncomfortable, cheap armchair. Helen paused, thought, then took the chair and dragged it so it stood near the window. She turned off the light and sat herself down in the chair, staring out at the night outside, where the mist and the fine drizzle swirled to errant gusts through the halos of light cast by the spare array of orange–tinged street lights—growing thicker and more impenetrable even as she watched.

⸝⸱⸜

Sam couldn't sleep. This was unusual: insomnia was not on the list of his many problems. But sometime during the early hours of the morning he'd woken up. Rita was draped over the other side of the bed, snoring softly. It wasn't that sound which had woken him though. Something else…something that didn't let him back to sleep.

Maybe a dream? He closed his eyes and tried to sink back into whatever had been there before awakening.

He seemed to remember…a *song*? Woeful. Yearning.

Sam closed his eyes and sank deeper into the memory; snuck up on it gently, to stop it from blowing away like smoke in the wind. Dreams did that. You had to sidle up on them, so they didn't even know you were there.

A mirror–like surface of water. Above it a dense, swirling fog. Faces in the fog.

One face…

The image retreated behind a veil.

An intimation of a caress; like a feather, only it touched his soul with a sad, yet almost siren–like, quality. The face of a beautiful woman, ethereal and lovely. Fading in and out of existence, created by the whorls of mist dancing across the waters.

The water itself. A lake of sorts. Maybe like Loe Pool, which they'd visited yesterday. Not a particularly spectacular place. Just a tidal pool with a boardwalk for the tourists who came here to ogle yet another 'Arthurian' site: Loe Pool being one of the candidates for the mystical place whence Excalibur had emerged and whereto it had been returned.

Sam opened his eyes.

Of course! The whole Arthurian thing was finally getting to him! Harry's endless commentary. Harry Petrowski: Encyclopedia Arthuriana. Standing there, gesticulating excitedly.

The Lady of the Lake. Loe Pool: Excalibur's final resting place.

Nice story. Boring place. About as dull as it could get; especially when one saw it surrounded by video- and digital-camera wielding tourists. But Harry was in his element. The guy was an endless well–spring of Arthurian lore. Sam wondered what Rita thought about it. Or Miss Pain–in–the–Ass. Or the rest of the tourists getting the benefit of Harry's commentary.

Rita muttered something in a dream of her own and rolled onto her back. Sam turned his head and looked at her. Her upper torso was uncovered, and the dim light from the window highlighted the round shapes of her breasts and cast into sharp contrast the dark nipples.

Sam wondered how she would react if he touched her now; kissed her nipples, or maybe roamed further down. Knowing Rita, she would probably continue sleeping. Rita slept well and soundly. Unless he persisted, of course, in which case, if precedent was anything to go by, she would eventually respond favorably.

Sam decided against waking Rita. He pulled up the blanket to cover her and got out of the bed. She muttered something in her sleep, then fell silent again. He padded to the window, peered out at the dense grayness. The rain seemed to have stopped, but the fog was so dense that the street lights were only diffuse halos of light. Sam looked up. The sky displayed the faintest hint of something other than reflected illumination. He picked up his watch from the bedside console. Almost six.

Unbidden, the image of the dream–lake returned. With it came an almost real auditory sensation of the woeful song, tinged now with a new note. A beckoning. Almost a summons. A temptation.

Come...for I will show you things...
A face of swirling eddies in gray fog.
He looked at his watch.
Six o'clock.
Plenty of time to...
What?

Harry wouldn't wake up for another couple of hours. Rita, too, would sleep on unless awakened. Neither of them were morning people. Helen...who cared?

Sam came to a decision. He scribbled a note for Rita and left it on the bedside console. He got dressed and went to the toilet, put on a water–proof parka, took the car–key, and quietly left the room. He tiptoed down the hallway and the stairs. The young guy at the reception was snoozing, but woke when Sam came past. Sam told him he was going for a walk. The youth regarded him with bleary–eyed incomprehension. Sam let himself out. He stood for a few moments, soaking up the ambience: the fog; the dreary, yet romantic, clamminess of it all; the sense of something...old...surrounding him. It was at these moments that he actually felt something that was more than a tourist's curiosity; when the minor irritants didn't matter anymore, made insignificant by a sense of *history*. Mystery maybe. Whatever it was that had prompted him to come out here and now.

He went to the Range Rover and opened the door. He hesitated. The fog was so thick, it might not be such a good idea to drive. Maybe he *should* walk.

Not enough time. Not if he wanted to go to Loe Pool for one last visit. Leave here with a sense of...what? Something else but memories of pubs and hordes of tourists.

Sam shrugged and turned the key in the lock. The engine kicked over and came to life. He reached for the gear–shift when there was a knock on the passenger side window. Sam looked and saw Helen.

She opened the door.
"What are you doing?" Her tone was civil. Barely.
Sam sighed. The best laid plans of mice and men...
"Going for a drive."
"In *this*?"
"Yeah."
She hesitated.
"Where you going?"
"Why?"
"Just asking!"

Chapter 2

"Just...down the road."

He put his foot on the brake and shifted the automatic into 'D'.

She didn't close the door. Yet.

He glanced at her again. She was wearing her green water–proof jacket and looked as if she'd been up for ages.

"Anything else?" he asked, none–too–friendly.

Her internal conflict was plainly visible. Strange she didn't hide it better. She usually did. If anything went on beneath that mask it was always kept well away from the surface. Not so this time—which in itself was strange enough.

"Mind if I come?"

"What?"

"Got a problem with that?"

"Yeah." He wasn't really going to say that, but it just came out. Bang!

She stared at him. A series of expressions flitted across her face. Astonishment. Disappointment. Anger. Detestation.

She shook her head. "Screw *you*, too!" she snapped. "Why do you have to be such a jerk!" She slammed the door and stalked off, heading away from the hotel and into the fog.

Sam sat frozen for a few moments.

Shit!

What was it with her anyway? Did she expect him to be *happy* about her inflicting herself on a private moment like that? What was she doing out here? How did she know he was out here?

Damn her!

He jammed the automatic back into 'P' and turned off the engine. He left the car and looked around. As she strode away her outline was rapidly fading into the fog. Sam muttered a soft curse and jogged after her.

"Hey! Wait!"

She ignored him and continued walking.

"Helen!"

"Damn you!" She didn't turn around.

Sam stopped and fought a brief battle with his pride. Helen merged into the fog again.

"I'm *sorry!*"

Her footfall halted. She was an indistinct shape in the halo of one of the street lamps.

"What?"

"You heard me."

A moment passed. Sam started to turn away. Let her do as she pleased. It was better that way.

She started moving. Sam waited.

She halted a couple of steps away from him. Her face was in shadow.

Sam gave her a crooked grin. "Don't make too much of it," he said. "But..." he sighed "why don't you come?"

"Wow!" she said softly. With a ring of suspicion: "What do you want?"

Sam was about to give snappy retort but bit it back. Something wasn't as it usually was, and this bothered him.

"Nothing," he said. "Just… Look—you want to come or not? Your choice."

Helen heaved a deep breath and expelled it again.

"Where were you going?"

"Loe Pool."

"Why?"

Sam shrugged. "I don't know. Just…"

She nodded thoughtfully. "You felt it, too."

"What?"

"Something. Whatever. Maybe because it's the last day…" Shrugging. "I don't know. Just *something*…"

"Maybe we don't want to go home after all," he suggested.

"Yeah. Maybe." She looked around. "Not exactly ideal driving conditions."

"We'll live. It's not that far."

"I hope you drive as well as Harry says you fly," she said and started walking in the direction of the car.

Sam followed.

They took the A394 south, then doubled back at the junction with the A3083. A short distance along was the sign, telling them to turn left to the pool. The fog was so dense here they almost missed it. The Range Rover crawled along at a snail's pace. They continued at a snail's pace along the narrow road Sam briefly turned off the headlights, hoping the incipient daylight might make things easier to see. It didn't and he turned the lights on again.

"I've never seen anything like it," Helen remarked.

Sam glanced at her. She didn't appear overly perturbed or tense. Just curious.

"What did Harry mean when he said we had something in common?" she wondered.

"The fog–thing, I suppose."

"Yeah…"

She fell silent again. Sam caught himself thinking that, as she was now, she wasn't such an irritant at all.

"Why'd you get up so early?"

She shrugged. "Couldn't sleep."

"I bet Harry hasn't got that problem," he noted.

"He doesn't."

Something in her tone made him look at her. She was staring straight ahead, her face tense. There was something else, too, but Sam couldn't figure what.

The Range Rover bumped over something rough on the road. Sam jerked his attention back to steering. It wasn't just 'something' rough! Sam braked and brought the Range Rover to a halt and placed the automatic into 'P'.

"What is it?" Helen wanted to know.

"Don't know." He opened the door and saw that the car stood, not on the paved surface of a road, but on a muddy rutted track.

"What…"

"What's the matter?"

Chapter 2   37

"I have no idea," he confessed. "Seems we—" he grimaced "—lost our road…"

How do you 'lose' a piece of road? It was foggy but not *that* bad!

Sam closed the door again. "Shall we turn back?"

"Might be an idea."

Sam started a multi–point turn.

"Look!" Helen exclaimed.

Sam braked. Ahead of them the fog was thinning rapidly, revealing before them a heavily forested area. They were on a track of sorts, leading into a gloomy opening at the base of the trees.

"Where are we?"

Sam opened the door again and looked behind them. A wall of dense fog, starting maybe thirty yards behind the car, blocked out the view in the direction whence they'd come. On the opposite side stretched a forest he couldn't recall having seen yesterday. The trees were huge, looming shapes emerging from the thinning fog. Pines? Some kind of cypress? In Cornwall?

And…

"You notice something?" he asked Helen.

She tore her gaze away from their surroundings.

"I notice a lot of things," she snapped. Her expression softened a trifle. "I'm sorry. There was no need for that."

He decided to let it go. "It's *warm!*"

"You're right."

"That's why the fog is thinning."

"That's…weird…"

"Yeah."

They ought to go back. Turn around and retrace their route. It should be less than a hundred yards back to the main road. They had been driving going very slowly.

Sam looked up. The tops of the trees remained swathed in a dense mist, waiting for the sun to come up and burn it away. It would be a while yet.

"The fields aren't tilled," Helen said suddenly.

He looked. She was right. The whole thing was getting spooky.

"What now?" she said.

She glanced at him sideways in askance. He wondered what she was thinking; or why he should care. She had wanted to come. Every action had consequences. In this instance…

"How lost could we possibly get?" he said. "It's maybe a mile to the Pool. We'll get back in time no matter where we go."

She made a dubious sound. "I was just thinking," she said. "What if this isn't the way to the pool?"

"It was earlier today!"

"Maybe. But this isn't how I remember it."

Again, she was right. Still, the facts belied theory. They were here. Where else could they be going but toward the Loe?

"I am curious though," she confessed. "We've got a four–wheel drive, right? Haven't really used it during the entire trip."

This, too, was true.

Their eyes met. He thought, incongruously and somewhat surprisingly, that, no matter how much of a pain she was, he'd rather have *her* here than anybody else; including Rita and/or Harry. This came as a bit of a shock. But he got the impression that she was no sissy. He wondered how she'd function at the controls of a helo. Women on the whole made for mediocre helicopter pilots. Something about not being able to empathize with the machine. Of course, a lot of males had the same problem. And if they did, helicopters would sooner or later scare the shits out of them, and then it was all over. Lost nerves. Back to fixed–wings and thinking in linear fight paths and flap–angles.

"What's the matter?" she asked.

"Nothing." He engaged the four–wheel drive and put the automatic into 'D'. "Shall we?"

"By all means." She actually seemed to be looking forward to this.

Good! A little bit of adventure before returning to daily chores.

The Range Rover bumped over the rutted track, slipping and sliding on the moist muck. Helen glanced sideways at Sam, making sure he didn't notice she was doing it. His face was a mask of concentration and attention. As he drove his eyes weren't just in the road, but everywhere else as well. Especially on the approaching forest, now looming maybe a couple of hundred yards before them; like a fortress, the tree–line sharply demarcated, with no thinning out or transition. The track led into a gaping dark hole, left there by the trees, which curved around it like the arches of a gothic cathedral. The Range Rover's lights pierced the darkness inside, found yet more fog, obscuring what lay inside.

A frisson ran down her spine. Maybe this wasn't such a good idea after all. Not that she had any reason to think so, but what she *felt* was another matter. She turned her head to say something to Sam—then stopped herself. She wouldn't give him the satisfaction of seeing her spooked. He'd probably laugh at her. Maybe not to her face, but still…

"Are you all right?"

Damn! He'd noticed after all. Even sounded solicitous. It was probably a trap. She wasn't going to fall into it. If he thought…

The car stopped about a hundred yards before the edge of the forest.

"What's the matter?" she asked.

Sam opened the door and looked back the way they'd come.

"What are you doing?"

"Look back there!" He pointed.

She did and saw a blank expanse of fog—maybe twenty, thirty yards behind them.

"Is it moving?"

Sam nodded. "It's just as far behind us now as it was back there." He stared at his hands resting on the steering wheel. He looked up at the cathedral entrance, then at Helen. His eyes were wide and thoughtful.

"I'm going to try something," he said.

He put the gearbox in reverse and started to back up the car.

"What are you doing?" she wanted to know.

"Experimenting," he said curtly.

"With *what*?"

"The fog."

The Range Rover approached the boundary of fog, which hung there like a massive wall of fluffy cotton wool. Sam stopped the car almost precisely at the point where they would have entered it. He put the automatic into 'P', opened the door and jumped out.

"Where are you going?" she shouted. She leaned over to the driver's side to see what he was doing. He had picked up a short stick from the ground and was pushing it into the soft soil beside the trail. Satisfied with his work he straightened and looked at her.

"All right, let's go."

"Are you going to explain this?"

He climbed into the car and she retreated to her seat.

"It's just a marker," he told her. "See, when we were back there and started moving toward the forest, the dense stuff was about maybe twenty yards behind us. It still was when we got to the forest. We backed up and it didn't move back."

"Huh?" Was he serious? "Of course it didn't. What do you think? It's not *following* us! Don't be ridiculous!"

Harry had said that Sam was a bit odd sometimes, but he'd never hinted that the guy was a weirdo. A pain in the ass, yes—but she'd always thought of him as basically... well, 'together'. And now *this*!

Sam nodded. "Yeah. I thought so, too." He pointed at the wall of fog behind the car. "Then why, given that it moved along at about our speed—say ten miles per hour or something like that—did it suddenly stop just as we stopped? Of course, it didn't back away either."

"You're nuts."

Sam grimaced. "Maybe. But shall I make a prediction? Something totally ridiculous? And what if it comes true?"

"Like what?"

"Like if we start moving now it's going to start moving as well. Not right now, but once we're about twenty to thirty yards away from it. That's why I put the stick in the ground. It's a marker. Once the fog swallows it we know it's started moving again."

"What are you saying?" She didn't know what was worse: that he should talk about this preposterous hypothesis as calmly as he did—or that she should actually even think of it as anything but errant nonsense. Fact was that she didn't. The whole thing was...wrong.

What have we gotten into?

"You're not taking this seriously, right?"

Sam shrugged. "I saw a fog–bank like this once. Harry saw it, too. The whole crew did."

"What? Where?"

"Caribbean."

The matter–of–fact way in which he said it scared her more than anything.

"Let's do this," he said and started driving. "Keep an eye on that stick. Tell me when it disappears."

Wordlessly she turned around and looked out through the wide rear window to where the stick stood out clearly against the wall of fog.

And then it was gone!

She made an involuntary exclamation. Sam braked hard. He opened the door again and looked back.

"Thirty yards sound about right?"

"Shit."

Sam looked at her, his face serious.

"Shall we try this again?"

She took a deep breath. "No."

Sam nodded. "Quite. I think there's no need, is there?"

Something like a tight band was wrapped around her chest, and got tighter with every breath she took.

"You all right?" he asked; and this time she didn't care if he might be enjoying himself at her expense. Now she just needed to know she wasn't going insane.

"I remember what it was like," Sam said softly. "Approaching that thing. It just…sat there; something like a mile across and maybe half a mile high. Right there in the middle of the ocean, in the middle of the clearest day you can imagine. We were flying patrol, searching for a dope–runner boat we knew was there somewhere. And then there was this…thing. We pulled closer and flew around it. Harry and Tom, our navigator, said it gave them the creeps just looking at it. Karl, the gunner, looked spooked, too.

"I knew what they meant. This thing…"

Sam shrugged. "We reported it in. They told us to have a closer look. We were maybe a hundred yards away…and it just…vanished."

"Vanished?"

"Just like that. From one moment to another it was gone."

"Shit."

"That's how I feel about this." He pointed at the wall of fog behind them. "Except this isn't going to go *poof*."

To think that less than an hour ago I was feeling sorry for myself for leading such a boring life!

"What are you saying, Sam? Just what exactly are you *saying*?"

Don't get hysterical!

But she sounded like she was. Her voice: becoming high pitched, loud. She forced herself to calm down.

"We could turn around and drive into this," he suggested. "Somewhere behind there is the road and the hotel and…whatever."

"You think?"

"Well, I would hope so."

She looked at the forest and the gaping hole swallowing the track.

"Or we could allow ourselves to be…herded…"

" 'Herded'?"

"What else do you want to call it? Looks like it to *me*!"

"This is nuts!"

Sam took a deep breath. She suddenly realized that his relatively calm demeanor was not entirely genuine. At some level he was just as freaked out as she. The thought provided an odd kind of comfort. It brought them to a similar level. Two human beings suddenly transported from their normal lives into the Twilight Zone.

Sam was looking at her intently. She realized something else then: that he needed her support as much as she needed his. By some stupid freak chance she had ended up been thrown together with a guy she disliked more than anybody, and they had come to *rely* on each other.

Thank you, fate, for being such an ass!

"What do you want to do?" he asked her.

"What do *you* want to do?"

"The truth?"

"That would be nice."

"I want to see where this is going."

She nodded. What else? Despite the spookiness of it all, she *was* kind of curious. Maybe there was even some anticipatory excitement. Indeed—and was this a case of watch what you ask for? when last night she'd wished for something to…touch…her—something visceral…

Well, here it was: served up on a platter. Ask and you shall receive.

"Think we're still in Kansas?"

Sam shrugged. "I don't know."

They stared at each other for another couple of breaths. Then Sam pulled the seat–belt over his shoulder and clicked the buckle into place. "Shall we go?"

"Let's."

The forest closed around them. The headlights picked out parallel rows of massive trunks flanking the slightly curved track which, underneath the shielding canopy, was comparatively smooth, level, and dry, littered with the shedded needles of years. The Range Rover followed the gentle bend of the track, until they saw a brightness that was more than reflecting fog. Sam turned off the headlights.

"The light at the end of the tunnel," he said.

"Or the train."

It turned out he was right. They emerged into yet more gray fog, but this was comparatively thin, and the advance of daylight was unmistakable. The track once more turned muddy and slippery. Behind loomed the wall of the forest.

"Shall we go on?" he asked.

"Might as well."

The track wound this way and that through an area of sparse shrubbery, ferns, tufts of tussock. Every now and then the looming shapes of larger trees, contorted and twisted, some of them no more than hints, barely seen in the mist. And more ferns, their fronds rearing taller than the Range Rover, dripping with moisture.

"It *is* warm here," she said and wriggled out of her jacket.

And then the track came to an end. Just like that. At the edge of a lake, to be precise.

Loe Pool?

What else was there? Despite the differences Sam knew this was the place. The water line was higher than they remembered. The edge of the Pool was level with the land, dotted with clumps of tussock and more fern. No board–walk in sight. No car–park.

Sam turned off the engine. They undid their seat–belts and got out of the car. Sam came around to Helen's side and together they looked across the waters, which disappeared in swirls of fog that were growing brighter even as they watched. The light played strange tricks with the eddies and whorls, giving them a life of their own as if...

A jolt went through Sam. Memories of dreams...

A tinkling sound, somewhere across the water. It grew in strength until it seemed to fill the air around them. Yearning and beckoning, all at the same time. Just like he'd remembered...

A far–off splash. A flash on the water, a whirling sparkling...thing...rising from the calm surface through the gray strands of the mist. Rising higher in a graceful arc, and into the rays of the sun where it became invisible for a moment, then continued on its trajectory and, with a last display of flashes and sparks, disappeared in the fog to their right. A few moments later—from somewhere in the distance, but not too far off—a sharp sound, as of something metallic striking stone.

The tinkling ceased. A silence fell, so complete that for a few moments they didn't even dare to breathe, for fear of disturbing its perfection.

Finally Helen let out her pent–up breath.

"What was that?" she whispered.

"You're right," he said.

"What?"

"This isn't Kansas."

He took off his jacket and threw it into the car. "Pity I haven't got my camera. Nobody's going to believe this."

Again they looked at each other. They knew what the other was thinking.

If we get a chance to tell anybody.

"Are you all right?" he asked her.

"Are *you*?"

"I don't know." He pointed in the general direction of that last clanging sound. "While we're here..."

She glanced at the car. "Should we..."

Sam shook his head. "We need it here."

"What for?"

"So we know where the track starts. We need the car as a marker."

"That's not going to do us much good if we wander off on foot and can't find the *car* again! How about using a stick again?"

"Too easy to miss."

Sam chuckled. "Technology," he said, went around to the driver's side and took out the key with the security remote. He held it up for her to see. He pointed it and depressed a button. A couple of sharp beeps.

"What kind of a range has this thing got?" she wanted to know.

"Enough—I think."

They headed off along the lakeshore, in the general direction of the brief noise, which, Sam thought, sounded like maybe a falling metal object had hit a boulder. Behind them the mist had swallowed up the car. Sam turned around and operated the remote. A beep echoed across to them.

"Satisfied?" he asked her.

"Sort of."

They continued for maybe another hundred yards. It was hard to tell. Their horizon had less than half that radius.

Then they stopped dead.

"What the…"

His notion of a metal object striking a rock had been more than accurate. Except that he hadn't anticipated the object to be a sword—and even less that it should be impaled into a man–high boulder like the proverbial sword–in–the–stone. On the other hand, so he told himself, there was an insane logic to it all. Given the context it would have been stupid to expect anything else. More reasonable, maybe—but stupid anyway. Moving further into the Twilight Zone.

"Shit!" She grabbed his arm.

"Yeah…" He really didn't have anything more profound to contribute.

A moment passed. Helen let go of Sam's sleeve. They approached the object with cautious steps; as if it was going to jump out of the rock at any moment.

It didn't.

They stopped before the boulder and started up at the sword sticking out of it. Close up now Sam saw that the blade was shiny, untarnished by rust or scratches. The hilt was large enough to be gripped by one hand. It looked…Roman. A legionnaire's weapon maybe.

Without needing to communicate the issue they started looking for a way up the rock. On the other side they found a number of rough steps hewn into the stone.

They looked at each other. Sam motioned. "After you." Helen gave him a wry look, shrugged, and preceded him to the top.

The tip of the sword was one with the rock. It was hard to tell its length, but Sam guessed there was maybe another foot of steel. The blade was thinner than he had expected. Legionnaire swords were somewhat broader and stubbier. Still, it probably wasn't too heavy to wield with one hand.

"I don't want to say it," Helen said softly, "but I guess *somebody* has to."

"Say what?"

"That this is insane." She looked at him, like she was searching for something. "Sam, what are we doing here? You and I? And this…thing?" She shook her head. "It doesn't make any *sense*!"

He gave her a crooked grin. "Why not?"

"Are you saying it *does*?"

Did it? Not in any sense he could figure out easily. Still…

"We're here. Both of us. Unless we're dreaming this…"

"Which we are not."

"N–no."

"You're not sure?"

He dug in his pockets and came out with a crinkled piece of paper, which he unfolded. It was a register receipt from last night at the pub. He read out the name of the pub and the details of his purchases. Twice.

"What are you doing?"

"We're not dreaming," he declared. "At least I'm not. Which leads me to suspect you're not either."

"And you know this how?"

"Ever tried to read something in a dream and have it come out the same twice?" He shook his head. "Can't be done. But I did it just now. So I'm not dreaming." He pointed at the sword. "Meaning that this is really here—as are you and I."

She grimaced. "Has anybody ever told you you're a real pain in the ass?"

He chuckled. "You have. Repeatedly."

"Well, you are! Do you know how…infuriating it is to have someone like you around?"

"What did I do?"

"You think you have all the answers!"

Sam laughed. He couldn't help it. "I don't…"

"Sshh!" She raised a restraining hand.

Sam stopped laughing. "What?"

"Hear that?" She cocked her head to one side, her gaze far away as she listened.

A rumble of sorts, growing almost imperceptibly louder. Heading this way—whatever it was.

He looked at the sword and reached for the hilt. His hand closed around it and he jerked. The blade bent but the sword didn't budge. He felt Helen's eyes on him and let go of the hilt. "I guess I'm not Arthur," he noted wryly.

She looked at it thoughtfully, grasped the hilt and pulled—only to be foiled like he had been.

The rumbling had taken on a subtly different tone. Over the continuous—and growing—noise he could now distinguish a number of syncopated beats. The sound was vaguely familiar. Like…

"Horses!"

"Heading this way," she completed.

"I think maybe we should leave."

"Let's."

Both cast a last look at the sword. Sam felt an odd kind of…regret…at something not done that should have been done. They hesitated; looked at each other.

"There's a third possibility," he said.

"What are you talking about?"

"You failed. I failed. But this thing…it was put here for *us*! I know it! How? I just *do*!" He pointed. "So, it's got to be the third possibility. You hold it, too!"

"What?"

"*Do* it!"

She glared at him, but reached out and grasped the hilt. His right hand closed over hers.

The sword came out of the rock like it was soft butter.

They stood there, their hands on the hilt, staring at it.

"*Now* we leave."

"Take the damn thing!" She let go of the hilt. Sam lifted the sword. It was lighter than he had thought it would be.

They didn't bother with the steps, but jumped from the rock onto the soft ground and started running. The ominous sound behind them grew. The sword slowed Sam down, but he held on to it. Somewhere, something told him that this is why they were here: to take this thing, and to take it away from those who made the sound.

How he knew didn't matter.

He knew.

Chapter 2

He fumbled for the car key and pushed it into Helen's hand. She pointed the remote and kept on pressing the button, aiming it here and there, trying to elicit a response. Then, from ahead, came the beep of the Range Rover.

"*You* drive!" she shouted and handed him the key as they ran.

He held out the sword, and she took it. They reached the car. Sam opened the door and fumbled to get the key into the ignition. On his left, Helen clambered into the car and maneuvered the sword onto the back seats. She settled in her seat, looked up.

"Shit!"

Sam glanced up. The fog spewed forth a column of about a dozen riders. Tall figures, covered in a black armor of sorts, their heads shrouded in equally black visored helmets. Not like knights: more like a cross between Roman cavalry and Samurai. Their huge black chargers bore down on the car.

The engine kicked over and roared into life. The charge slowed and came to a halt. The horses veered aside, closed into a circle around the Range Rover. The dark riders drew swords from scabbards. Sam jammed the automatic into 'D', floored the gas pedal, and turned the wheel to the right until it locked. The Range Rover jerked and jumped. The wheels kicked up a barrage of soil and stones. Sam righted the wheel and kept his foot on the accelerator. The Range Rover leapt forward like a living thing and gained the track.

A crash. The sound of breaking glass. Helen screamed. In the mirror Sam saw a long sword probing around in the rear. The back window had been shattered to smithereens. More blows rained down on the roof and the sides. More sound of shattering glass.

Don't let them figure out about the tires!

He kept his foot flat on the floor. The Range Rover lurched and heaved, threatening to get out of his control. Sam eased the foot off the gas and focused on the track.

Stay on the track!

The Range Rover handled superbly given the circumstances. But the chargers were naturally better equipped to handle the terrain. From his peripheral vision Sam saw them gaining.

We're going to die!

No—damnit! Not here, and not now. Not when he was responsible for Helen as well. He was *not* going to fail again.

The sword!

Without taking his eyes off the track he shouted at her.

"Take the sword!"

"What?!"

"Take it! *Use* it!"

"I can't!"

"You want to *die*?!"

Damn him! What did he expect her to do. Take that damn sword and wave it around or something? The way they were being jolted about she'd probably injure herself!

Another blow on the roof. And another. She looked up and saw it buckling. Another rear window smashed. The Range Rover's engine howled in protest. The hooves of the huge horses pounded the ground beside them.

"Do it!" he shouted at her.

Fuck you, Sam!

The rider who'd pulled level with her raised his weapon. She stared at the impenetrable mask and flinched aside as he brought it down. The weapon cut into the roof right above her head and stuck there. He wrenched it out and lifted his arm again. The Range Rover lurched to the left, impacted on the horse. The animal screamed as it was thrown aside: an almost human sound. The rider, eerily silent in his efforts, attempted to control it. He slammed into the trunk of a small tree and was thrown off. Helen craned her neck to see him get up off the ground—only to be run down by his companions, who redoubled their efforts and soon pulled alongside.

Helen reached around with her right hand, found the hilt of the sword as it bounced about on the back seat. Her hand closed around it. She pulled it around the seat, got it wedged, fumbled as the car bounced about and another blow landed somewhere on the roof, managed to get the weapon free and finally had it in the front, holding it as far away from her as she could, stuck at an awkward angle, the tip on the floor before her.

"The window!" she shouted. By some miracle the passenger side window was still intact. Sam did something. The electric window rolled down. A rider raced up alongside and raised his weapon. Helen, not thinking but just *doing*, pulled the sword up, managed to push it out the window, poking its jerking tip at the rider. He saw it coming and tried to jerk aside. Too late. The blade sliced into his abdomen like a hot knife into butter. He roared: the first sound she'd heard out of their pursuers—an unearthly howl that ended a moment later as he toppled off his horse and the body bounced along the ground before disappearing from her sight.

Helen, stunned by what she had done, almost let go of the sword—but *something* made her hold on, pull it back and into the safety of the car. Her victim's blood dripped off the gleaming blade.

She heard Sam shout something. She tore her gaze away from the blade, turned around—to see that they'd come to the forest. The Range Rover swerved onto the dry segment of track, the wheels caught hold, the car accelerated forward. She looked around. The riders charged into the tunnel opening, filling it with their presence, relentless and lethal.

The fog in the tunnel had almost disappeared. The Range Rover bolted through the passage, it's headlights picking out thick, striated trunks from the stygian gloom. Then they were at the other side—plunging straight into the wall of fog.

Helen heard someone scream; realized it was she; bit down on the other screams that were just waiting to come as they careened blindly through the impenetrable grayness.

And then it was all over. Another jolt. The car swerved and skidded. Bright sunlight shone down from a cloudless sky. Before them the gray strip of…a *road?*

Where are we?

The car clambered up the embankment, it's wheels spinning, gripping, missing, gripping again. Then they were on the asphalt. The front wheels gripped tightly. The car jumped forward. Sam controlled the resultant skid and jerked the car onto the road. Another swerve and he had it under complete control.

Then he braked.

"What are you doing?!"

Sam gave a curt shake of his head and looked back through the wrecked rear of the car. She followed his gaze; saw a thick wall of fog. As she watched it dissolved.

And then she heard thundering hooves. Out of the vanishing fog charged the riders. They noticed the car and started in their direction.

"They don't give up, do they!" Sam hissed. The engine howled as Range Rover pulled away, showering their pursuers with a hail of churned-up gravel. The riders veered aside, then pulled up and stared after the receding car.

Helen heaved a sigh of relief and leaned back in her seat—then noticed that she was still holding the bloody sword in a tight grip. She glanced at Sam whose attention was focused on the road, carefully maneuvered the weapon onto the back seat and dropped it there. She leaned back in her seat and wiped her hands on her jumper.

Sam slowed down again and presently pulled off the road into farm track which led through a small copse of trees. When they had gone far enough to be out of sight of the road he stopped and turned off the engine.

The silence was deafening.

They looked at each other, breathing heavily, the adrenaline rush slowly ebbing away, leaving them fatigued and limp.

Helen's eyes, Sam noticed, were wide—the pupils dilated, staring fixedly at his face, but quite possibly seeing nothing. He knew the signs. He reached out. She jerked back. Sam shook his head and continued the motion, touching his hand to her cheek. Again she jerked, but he left it there. The worst thing about shell-shock was the sheer *distance* of other human beings: a distance that could best be bridged by the simple expedient of touching someone.

The touch worked. Her eyes lost their unfocused mien. She blinked. Her facial muscles relaxed. He leaned over and put his arms around her.

"It's all right," he said softly.

Still she was stiff and unyielding, but he held on and presently she seemed to relax—and then she dug her face into his shoulder and started sobbing.

When it was done and the spasms stopped he let her go. She straightened, sniffed, and wiped her eyes.

"I'm fine."

"Sure?"

"Sure."

She swallowed, leaned back, closed her eyes, took a couple of deep breaths. She opened her eyes again and looked at him.

"I just killed someone," she said tonelessly. "With…this…" She looked at the backseat…and made a small exclamation.

Sam turned around and tried to see what had alarmed her.

The back seat was…*empty*.

Sam corrected himself. Not empty. There were the bloodstains. There was also a small rolled up piece of light sepia paper.

"What," she was breathing hard, "is going *on*?"

He reached for her in alarm. This could push her over the edge. Hell, it might just push him right after her! He eyed the roll paper. What the hell…

No time! It didn't matter. Not now. Helen first!

She had started hyperventilating. Sam, against her resistance, pulled her close and buried her face against him. She fought him, but he didn't yield and kept her face close to him where the air she inhaled was low in oxygen, much of it being her own recycled breath.

After a while her struggles subsided and she slumped against him. Her breathing calmed down, her arms went around him and tightened. A distant portion of his mind—that not engaged with feverishly trying to figure out where that damn sword had gone! noticed that at this moment he didn't feel any of the resentment against her that had been a constant presence whenever she'd been around. Indeed, despite the circumstances, it was actually *nice*...

Sam jerked himself out of the thought. Helen must have sensed the swing in mood. She stiffened and tried to pull back. He loosened his arm around her and she pulled back, twisting to get away from him. For a moment their faces were only inches from each other.

In that position they froze.

Her eyes widened, her mouth dropped open.

"Oh, my," she whispered; tried to pull away.

"Please don't," he said.

"Sam, I..."

"Don't," he repeated—and she stopped trying.

Shit—it was like that crappy movie plot after all...

The constant bickering and fights. The sniping and insults. Contrived by both of them to keep at a distance...

Now, with preternatural clarity, he recalled the fist time he'd seen her—when Harry had introduced them. He remembered it better than he remembered almost anything in his life—Katie's smile excepted. That smile was etched into his memory with deep indelible lines. As was the first time he'd met Helen, when they stared at each other across the table, instant attraction turning into instant antagonism to keep the other from getting too close to even *think* about the unthinkable.

For Harry was his friend—and her boyfriend. Some things you just didn't do: not in Sam's world anyway. In particular you didn't muscle in on your buddy's woman. It seemed that in her universe of values certain constraints applied as well. And so they had turned it all into an extended charade of mutual loathing.

"No more lies," she whispered.

"No more lies," he agreed.

Her eyes clouded over. "What am I going to...what are *we*..."

He pulled her to him again, felt her breath against his cheek. "Not now."

She put her arms around him and they just held onto each other. Sinking into each other's presence, still too surprised and just stunned by the whole thing to do anything else.

Finally, reluctantly, they separated. As if on a signal both looked at the blood–stained back seat. Sam reached out and picked up the rolled–up piece of paper. He held it up and examined it. It was made of thick, stiff parchment, set into the cylindrical shape. It unrolled into a sheet about US Letter size. He held it up for them to see. When Helen caught sight of the drawing she gasped. It was the representation of a sword: just like the one they *thought* they'd had in their possession only a short while ago.

"I'm going to say it," she declared.

"Feel free."

"It's impossible."

"According to the precepts of accepted rationality: Yes, it is."

"But there's blood."

"There's that, too."

"So..."

"So, how about we just assume, for the sake of argument that it's *not* impossible. That it happened. All of it."

She looked toward the road. "Meaning these things could be coming after us," she said darkly.

Two cars passed along the road, heading in opposite directions.

"I don't think so," he said. If these creatures—he couldn't get himself to think of them as 'people'—were out there, they had other problems but to follow them.

As, he reminded himself, did they.

"We're in deep shit."

She gave him a tentative wry grin. As she looked at him now it was subtly different from...before. The guardedness had gone. In its place was...what?

Above all, she felt relief from the terrible pressure, as the lie imploded on itself. A whole year of it: lying to herself; Harry; the world; Sam. She saw it all now.

Stupid. Stupid. Stupid!

A whole year wasted. Accepting a proposal from a man she had no intention of ever marrying. Knowing that it was so even as she did.

She wanted to cry and she wanted to laugh. Because the tightness, the suffocating weight of living with this pathetic, unnecessary, pointless *lie*—it was all gone. Just like that.

"I don't care if we're in deep shit," she declared. She just couldn't help it. The laughter bubbled forth despite all attempts to hold it in. She took Sam's surprised face in her hands and kissed him. She'd been wanting to do that for *so* long.

Sam's response, after a brief hesitation, was unequivocal, gratifying, and uninhibited; two pieces to a puzzle locking together in a perfect fit.

Her body responded to the kiss with a breathtaking, stunning completeness. She found herself uttering sounds she'd never allowed herself to make and had no control over at all. Her tongue had a life of its own, roaming his mouth, as far inside him as she could—to be one, to just...be. A delicious shiver shook her as his hands slipped under her sweatshirt and touched her there, moved up, pushed up her bra, teased her nipples, cupped her breasts and squeezed them gently, then slid down her back.

Breathing into his mouth, more sounds that couldn't be hers. Her hands with a life of their own, under his shirt with the buttons somehow torn off by someone, sometime, fumbling with the buckle of his belt, jerking to get it loose, finding the button and the zip, finding him. His own inarticulate groans, mouth against mouth, breathing each other, forgetting who and what and where, pushing and pulling, twisting and clambering over the damn gear–lever—her jeans down to her ankles, as she sat herself sideways onto his lap. Completion, long in coming; finally here. She looked into his face, saw a passion matching her own, bent to kiss him, and as she did and he moved inside her he touched her and she spasmed and felt herself rocked with a sudden near-painful climax. He made a little sound against her mouth. She felt him inside her, climaxed again, screamed maybe, pressed her mouth against his, their lips one, teeth crunching together, tongues sliding over and around each other in a delicious moist embrace.

Their mouths detached—reluctantly; came together again for another caress. Still he was inside her, touching her here and there as she moved, eliciting involuntary little shudders.

She broke the kiss to look at him.

"Wow!" He grinned weakly, oozing contentment. She'd never seen him that way.

Never seen myself that way either!

The constant guardedness and control. All gone. Just like that.

Was this what it took?

This?

His hands moved up her back. Another little shudder went through her. She swallowed and took a deep breath. Her lips were sore—but it was a precious pain: a testimony to abandonment; forgetting who and what you were, and just being one with another—something she'd always thought possible but had never...

She looked into his eyes, saw them crinkle at the corners as he endured her inspection. She kissed him again; softly this time; passion mellowing into a sweet tenderness. She took couple of breaths to calm herself; smiled against his lips. "Oh my!"

"Indeed."

"We're in trouble."

"Big trouble." He didn't sound as if it bothered him.

Still, the words conspired to jolt her awareness back to their current situation. They had just made passionate love in the wreck of a car—after having undergone a series of quite impossible experiences, being chased by a bunch of freaks on giant horses, one of whom she had...

He must have seen it in her face and looked at her with concern.

She gave a tiny shake of her head. "I'm fine."

'Impossible experiences'? What was 'impossible'? After what they'd just done—how could she even conceive of 'impossibility'?

She looked at Sam and thought that she wanted to stay like this forever. Or maybe just a tad more comfortably. Like in a bed, lying on top of him; or the other way around. Warm and cozy and wet, and smelling of love and sweat and inhaling the cloud of pheromones swirling around them like a halo, and his breath, and feeling him inside her like this.

But the battered car around them was real and they'd have to face Harry and Rita. A *lot* of explaining to be done! A lot of guilt–feelings that should be there, but weren't.

Why not?

Why not, indeed...

The answer came, and it was so simple that it shocked her: because this was as it had to be. Because it was *right*, and because what had gone before had been wrong. The pretense of the last year! The dumb–ass questions last night in the bathroom.

The wrong questions. Now, after having been given the answer, she finally understood that.

And Sam? How did *he* see all this? What was *his* understanding? Could she expect him to...

She could.
She did.
He did.
They did.
It was as simple as that.
"I'm glad," he said softly.
"So am I."

He grinned crookedly. "We'd better..." The grin broadened. She bent down and nibbled on his ear. "We'd better," she agreed.

The act of separating and getting their clothes back into some sort of order gave rise to giggles and chuckles from both.

"Next time we'll use a bed!" she said firmly, as he helped her pull up her panties and jeans, and she squirmed and twisted to help him with it. The exercise, despite its humorous aspects, also carried an odd familiarity; a paradoxical mix of having known each other for a long time, intimately acquainted with the other's most private affairs—and the exultant giddiness of a couple of terminally horny teenagers who'd just discovered each other's existence.

"Next time—" He paused and they looked at each other, both thinking the same thing. If only the 'next time' could be now. Or in the next hotel they came across. Just the two of them, today and tomorrow and always. Catching up with the last year—with their whole damn lives! All the time they'd wasted not being with each other.

Following an impulse too strong to control she grabbed him and kissed him again; found herself getting lost once more, and feeling him losing it, too. But a truck roared past on the road and honked at something, and it reminded them of reality and the problems of the world.

A little while later they stood beside the car and considered its impossible appearance.

"We have to come up with a story," Sam declared. "Something credible, yet explaining...this." He paused. "And the blood on the back seat," he added.

You know I don't care? I just want to...

With an effort she controlled herself.

Sam looked at the sky. "Have you noticed?"

"What?"

"The sun!" He glanced at his watch. "It says nine twenty–eight. But look at the sun! Closer to noon, I'd say."

"Shit!"

"Yeah."

"Where are we anyway?"

Sam pointed. In the distance some low buildings and a tower. "The airfield," Sam said. "It's in the north, maybe north–east— so over there must be the A3083. Helston's a few miles north–west. Something like that. I wasn't really paying attention to where I was going."

Helen let out an sudden breath.

"They'll be worried!"

"I'd say so."

"What are we going to *tell* them?"
"And the police."
"The police?"
"How far you think we're going to get in this car without being pulled up? Once we drive into Helston *everybody's* going to look at us!"
"Shit!"
"We need a story. A good one."
"Like what?"

Sam had been right. Everybody stared. They pulled up at the hotel, to have people stopping dead in their tracks; locals and tourists; shop-keepers emerging from their places across the road.

Sam and Helen got out. Harry and Rita came running out of the hotel. Harry saw the Range Rover and stopped like he'd run into a wall. Rita ran over to Sam and threw her arms around his neck.

"Where have you *been*? We were so *worried*!"

Helen caught Sam's glance across Rita's shoulder. She made an effort to keep her face studiously neutral and turned to Harry who stepped slowly forward, his eyes still on the battered Range Rover. He shook his head in disbelief and enfolded her in a hug.

"What happened? Are you all right?"

"I'm fine." She detached herself. "It's been...an adventure."

"Where did you *go*?"

She shrugged, noticing that Sam and Rita had joined them. Sam gave the growing crowd around them a nasty look. "Do you mind?" he said loudly, glaring at them. He won the brief staring match. The people dispersed with reluctance, but disperse they did.

Sam turned to Harry. "We'd better call the cops," he said. "There are some *very* nasty people out there."

Two members of the local constabulary arrived ten minutes later. Over a belated breakfast Sam and Helen related their contrived tale to the policemen and Harry and Rita alike. No mention of rutted tracks through strange forests or a sword that mysteriously became a drawing on a piece of parchment. That was something they hadn't even worked out for themselves. Maybe they never would. It certainly was not for public consumption!

The story had metamorphosed into a blend of fact and fiction. Getting lost in the fog—God only knew where! was true. Driving around, trying to figure out where they were: half true. Being attacked by a bunch of lunatics on bikes, wielding swords: sort-of true, except for the bikes. Helen had been dubious about sticking to swords but he told her that the forensics guys would figure it out anyway. Sticks wouldn't suffice. Neither would axes. Swords it was. And then there was the mud on the car, requiring additions to the story, about being forced off the road and nearly getting stuck, and...

Still, such details didn't present half as many explanatory problems as the couple of hours or so that had gone missing.

"We've got to explain the extra time," he'd told her.

"Why should we have to explain anything?"

"Because there's blood. Which means *somebody* got hurt. All of which triggers a whole lot of procedures that otherwise would not have been used. They're going to question us: together and separately. If our stories match too closely they'll get suspicious and ask more questions. If they don't match enough they'll do the same. Believe me, I know this shit. There are criteria and check–boxes. Get the wrong box checked and this could be real trouble. So we've got to get it right!"

He'd been right there, too. Detectives appeared. The Range Rover was loaded onto a truck and carted off to a destination unknown. They were subjected to separate sessions of endless questions, some of which sounded innocent, but, as Sam had forewarned her, "They're like Mormons; politicians; insurance peddlers…take your pick. Every question, every statement has one and only one purpose: to get information out of you—and preferably to catch you contradicting yourself."

She'd never been subjected to such an interrogation, but that changed now. Being on her guard and after Sam's careful coaching made it easier and, in the final analysis, helped her to get out of it quicker. As he'd told her: "They're not *really* out to arrest us; they just want to be satisfied that they know what happened—and ultimately they can't do a damn thing anyway, because there are no bodies and no victims but us".

As for the other issue:

Female constable: "You *stayed* there? For over an hour? I find that hard to believe. You must have wanted to get away, to somewhere you'd be safe."

Helen: "Sam and I, we have our issues, but one thing's for sure: after how he handled the asshole who came into the car and tried to rape me…I had no doubt that I was as safe with Sam as I could possibly be. I didn't like to stay put, that's true. But I also believed Sam. He said we should hide from them. He was right."

What did it in the end, she thought, was that Sam wasn't just anybody. Once Harry had briefed the cops on the history of Sam Donovan they became considerably friendlier. He had, after all, been a cop of sorts. Someone who had worked in 'law enforcement', even if it had been in the air over the high seas. And he was famous. Once the association had been made between Sam and *Eagles in the Storm* the issue was basically settled.

She told Sam as much when, later that day, they sat around a table in the pub and talked out the events of the day. He wasn't so sure.

"Of course that's it!" Harry asserted. "Otherwise they would have grilled you for hours!"

Sam shrugged and grimaced. "So, the flight's re–booked for tomorrow?"

"Tomorrow it is," Harry affirmed.

Helen glanced at Sam; thinking what she was thinking.

Do it now?

She'd tried; earlier, after she'd had her shower and Harry wanted to make love. Not 'have sex', like on the previous night when he lay there like a beached manatee, but using the politically correct terminology. He was glad to have her back; no doubt about it. Pathetically so.

But could she possibly make love to him? Or maybe just a mercy–fuck…

Could she? After this morning? Just *thinking* about it made her go warm and *very* randy—and so she tried very hard not to. Even Harry, kind and caring, but basically incapable of even guessing at her thoughts or any but her most openly displayed feelings, would notice *this*. Men usually did. Maybe it was the pheromone thing; maybe a hundred other clues, too subtle to define, but adding up to a giant signal that she was as horny as hell. Which she was—but she wanted *Sam* in that shower, not Harry.

So she tried not to think about him and invented a reasonable-sounding though wholly fictitious excuse, having to do with stress and female hormones and how she just couldn't, and would he please understand. She felt like a piece of shit when he told her that it was all right, and that she should just take her time. He hugged her briefly—long and close enough for her to feel his arousal—but then let her get on with the shower she'd wanted since they came back, but had had no chance to take with all the police interrogation.

She locked herself in the bathroom—the same one she'd sat in last night; and how far away was that and the woman who'd stared at herself in the mirror wondering whether suicide might just give her a buzz.

A 'buzz'? Ha! More like a beehive's worth of buzzes! Weirdos chasing them and making love to Sam and…

She put a firm brake to her thoughts and continued toweling herself down. She just couldn't tell Harry. Not now. He'd tried so hard to make this vacation work. It was true that it had been mainly for his own benefit, but he'd organized literally everything and made it a smooth run for all. To ruin it on the last day would be cruel. She'd tell him after they got back. Maybe ease him into it by shelving the marriage idea; then slowly broach the Sam-thing. It was sneaky, maybe even cowardly, but she really, really didn't want to hurt his feelings.

You're going to do that no matter what!

And Sam would lose a friend. Harry would never forgive him. Her and Sam hadn't had a chance to talk about it before they arrived back at the hotel. But they both knew it anyway.

What a mess! If she'd handled things differently a year ago…

If, if, if…

If only there were a painless way of doing this. For Rita, too. Rita was a nice girl. She didn't deserve to be hurt like that. Sam said that he'd do his best to make it easy, but he knew and she knew that there was no 'easy'. They'd tried it once, and look what had happened

Helen looked across the table at Sam. He noticed her regard. His mouth twitched into a wry grimace.

Here we are, playing games again.

"How're we going to get back to London?" Sam asked Harry.

"We should get a rental later today. AVIS said they'll deliver it by tonight."

"They're actually renting us another car? After what we did to their last one?" Helen asked.

Harry chuckled. "Yep." He looked around the table. "So, we have the rest of today. What do we do?"

"Nothing," Sam said firmly. "I think we've done enough for today. Let's go for a walk and just lie low."

Rita turned to Helen. "I suppose…with these lunatics roaming around the countryside…"

Helen looked up. Someone approached their table: one of the policemen from this morning. Constable Higgins; a lean individual in his thirties, with the rugged countenance of a man who spent a lot of time exposed to the elements. Definitely no office slouch. He looked from Helen to Sam and back again.

"Won't you sit down?" Harry offered.

Constable Higgins shook his head. "Mr. Donovan, Miss McCormick. Could I ask you a couple more questions?"

Sam shrugged. "Sure."

"Those men—the ones who attacked you—you reported that they rode motorcycles. Big ones you said. But you weren't sure of the manufacturer."

"That's correct."

"Not horses?"

Sam narrowed his eyes. "Why?"

The constable looked at Sam for a few moments, his expression thoughtful. "I think I will sit down, if you don't mind." He got himself a chair from a neighboring table.

"The thing is this," he said. "Your story—it's pretty wild. You probably know that yourself." He glanced sideways at Helen. She looked over to Sam whose face was carefully disinterested.

"And?" he prompted.

Constable Higgins sighed. "Hypothetically—and I mean purely hypothetically—if someone was to undergo such an...experience...someone such as yourself," nodding at Sam, "who is well versed in police procedures and what is..." he cleared his throat "required for the sake of credibility..."

Sam interrupted him. "Why don't you say what's on your mind?"

The policeman righted himself. "I'm asking you, Mr. Donovan—Ms. McCormick—if your attackers were really on bikes...or if they maybe rode very large black horses."

Sam gave him his crooked grin. "And what makes you ask that?"

Constable Higgins fixed Sam with a level stare. "The fact that a farmer reported finding eleven very large black, fully saddled horses of an unknown breed grazing beside the A3083 near his property. Being a good citizen he immediately called the police. Beside the horses the attending officers found a number of...helmets, made of a hard black leather with facial protection masks."

"Really?" Sam's face was still neutral. "Did they find swords?"

"No."

"I see." Sam glanced at Helen, doubt and a silent question in his eyes. He looked at Constable Higgins again. "You are correct."

Higgins nodded, unsurprised. "I thought so. Is there anything else you might wish to communicate at this point?" He looked from Sam to Helen and back again.

Sam chuckled. "Your report has been entered on a computer? Well, you might wish to substitute all occurrences of 'black leather' to 'black armor', and 'balaclava' to 'full–face black hard–leather helmet'."

"I see."

"You are," Sam amplified, "looking for a group of large individuals. Six foot plus. Arms like small tree–trunks. They don't talk much—if what we experienced is anything to go by. But they're extremely unfriendly. And I suppose they still have their swords."

Higgins considered Sam from narrowed eyes. "Yet you wounded one of them? Without being injured yourself."

"What can I say?" Sam grinned. "I'm good. Besides, you saw the car. Why do you think we hid until we were sure they were gone?"

"Hmm." Constable Higgins stared at Sam for a few moments. "Thank you for the clarification. I should like to point out that it would probably have been better of you'd told us the truth to begin with." He stood. "Though I have sympathy for your caution. The details stretch credulity. Without this additional evidence…" He paused, considered them thoughtfully. "I hope you enjoy the last day of your holiday. We may have to get in touch with you in the US. I believe we have your contact details." He turned to leave. "Good day to you." With this he departed.

Harry looked across the table at Helen. "Horses? Armor? Helmets?"

"We didn't want to complicate the issue," Sam said.

"You could have told *us*!" Harry protested. "We…"

"We were about to," Helen interjected. It was a lie, but it would have to do.

"Why didn't you want the police to know?" Rita asked Sam.

"Higgins had it pretty much figured out," Sam laughed.

"Sam's right," Harry said. "Interrogation 101: the criminal's edition. Rule one: don't strain plausibility." He signaled to the waitress. "I need a drink. We all need a drink. Even you, Sam."

Sam placed a hand on his half–empty glass of Coke. "No thanks."

So, he thought, they left the horses behind. And their head–gear.

Which meant what?

"Shit!" Sam pushed back his chair and got up.

"What? Where are you going?"

"I have to talk to the cop."

Sam ran out of the pub. Constable Higgins was about to drive off. Sam waved him down and opened the passenger door.

"If they left their horses behind—what does that suggest?"

Higgins shrugged. "That they knew they'd be conspicuous. I suppose they were worried about you notifying us."

Sam shook his head. "That doesn't make sense."

"Why would you say that?"

"Because…" How could he put it without incriminating himself?

"How did they get away? You think they had a vehicle stashed nearby?"

"Why not?"

Sam shook his head. "Think about it. A bunch of lunatics who like to play the evil riders from the Black Lagoon, and terrorize innocent people…and they just leave their gear behind at the side of the road? In the middle of nowhere? When they could have hidden them at least?"

"What do you suggest?"

"That they flagged down a vehicle. Maybe more than one. Maybe a truck. A *bus* for all I know. I also suspect that the driver or drivers and/or the passengers of said vehicle of vehicles are not very happy people right now—*if* they are still alive that is!"

Higgins gave him a sharp look. "A lot to deduce from scant evidence. Mr. Donovan."

"Maybe," Sam agreed, "but I've confronted them. They are very nasty people. I don't know what they want or why they did what they did"—this was only a partial truth—

Chapter 2   57

"but I think you should find them. Soon."

"You may be right." Higgins put the car into gear. "I'll do what I can to convince the powers that be."

Sam gave him a wry, humorless grin. "I don't envy you."

He stepped back and closed the door, watched the police car drive off. The sick feeling in his gut, which had manifested first when Higgins had told him about the horses and the armor, wasn't going away.

He looked up and down the street.

Did he really expect some lumbering giant to skulk in a dark corner?

He touched his jacket, felt the shape of the rolled parchment in the inside pocket. He didn't understand what was going on. But there *had* been a sword. Helen *had* used it to skewer one of their attackers. And now there was no sword, but a piece of paper with the *drawing* of a sword. Whatever interpretation he chose to place on this configuration of circumstances, these were *facts*. To deny them would be simply stupid. So what if they didn't fit into his neat system of reality? Neither did eleven horses and suits of armor lying beside the road.

Given that all of this was true, what else might be possible? Was it really so stupid to expect one or all of the riders to lurk somewhere waiting to pounce on him? Or Helen maybe!

Please, not Helen!

Guiltily he reminded himself that there were also Rita and Harry. But maybe they were safe! After all, they had not pulled a—magical? sword from a lump of rock. Arthurian legend, only not quite. It had taken the two of them to make it happen. What did it mean? Would any two individuals have been sufficient? Did they have to be male and female? Or was it Sam Donovan and Helen McCormick? How could he know the rules which applied to this situation? That it was Helen and himself suggested itself, if for no other reason but that the sword had been flung from the water *as they looked on*. An broad hint if there ever was one.

And what about the riders? Their pursuit had been single–minded, conducted in an eerie silence—if one didn't count the scream of the one Helen had killed. No challenge or demands to halt had been issued. Not that they would necessarily have understood them, but the tone would probably have given it away. No, the only sound had been from the dying rider, and that was like a cry of rage; of an unearthly anger at having *failed*.

They wanted the sword.

He glanced at the parchment in his hand.

An object and its image.

Where was this leading? Sam shook his head and dismissed the thought. Immediacies pressed upon him. If, as he had suggested, the riders had hijacked a car or cars—if they were looking for the sword, or the parchment in his jacket pocket—if they had any way of knowing where it was: a rough sense maybe, something that drew them, like they had been drawn to the rock where Sam and Helen had found it...

Assumptions; maybe unfounded. But taken together they contrived to make Sam very uneasy indeed. He returned to the pub and sat down. "How soon can we have the car?" he asked Harry. "Is there anything you can do to get it as soon as possible?"

Harry looked at him puzzled. "I can try. Why?"

"Because," Sam looked around the table and saw that he had their full attention, "we have to leave here. Now."

"The plane's leaving tomorrow night!" Harry pointed out.

Sam shook his head. "I don't care. If we have to drive through the night we'll drive through the night. But we have to leave."

"Gonna tell us why?"

Yeah, how was he going to say it? Package it up for Harry's and Rita's consumption. He didn't need to tell Helen. The expression in her face told him that she knew.

"Because," he said slowly, "those freaks are looking for," he nodded at Helen, "us."

"Huh?"

"Trust me."

"You're crazy. How would they know where you are?"

"We were heading back here," Sam pointed out. That was a lie, but it would have to do. "They can guess. If they're trying to prevent us from identifying them they'd start searching here. If I were them I know *I* would."

Harry stared at Sam for a breath or two. "You're serious."

"Very."

Harry got up. "I'll call AVIS." To Helen, "Start packing. If Sam's right…" He gave Sam a strange look. "You're really spooked. I haven't seen you like that since…" He frowned, shook his head, and headed for the bar and spoke to the waiter.

Helen and Rita got up and prepared to leave.

"Wait," Sam told them. "You're not going out there by yourself."

Rita eyed him curiously. "You're starting to scare me!"

"I'm sorry," he said softly.

Rita turned to Helen. "Whatever happened out there, it must have been terrifying."

"It was," Helen agreed. She turned away from Rita and caught Sam's eye.

Not all of it.

Things unsaid…

Later, in their room, as they were packing, Harry suddenly stopped what he was doing and looked at her with a curious expression.

"You haven't fought."

"What?"

"You and Sam. You haven't been bitching at each other. Not once."

Now would be the time.

But what she said was, "Sam and I, we…" She shrugged. "I guess you could say we've made our peace."

"After all this time? Fancy that."

"He saved our lives," she said. "if it had been anybody else…"

Harry raised an eyebrow. "Ha! Sam's the big hero *again*? What about your fiancée?"

Now!

She smiled at Harry. "You would have done the same."

No, you wouldn't. Harry wasn't a hero. Neither could he move her the way Sam could and had from the instant they laid eyes on each other.

Say nothing. You'll only make it worse.

"Thank you," he said, just a trifle acerbic, and returned his attention to closing a badly–packed suitcase. His packing.

"Sam's always been the hero," he said suddenly.

She looked up, found him staring out the window.

"Even when he was being an unreasonable asshole, he always ended up the hero. The first time the Guard decorated him for courage under fire. The second time they threw him out, but Hollywood made a movie about him. No matter how he screws up, he just can't lose. Lucky shit."

She regarded him with astonishment. He'd never talked like that about Sam. Never a hint that there was this…envy?

"What are you looking at me like that for?" he wanted to know.

She shrugged. "I'm just surprised, that's all. I thought you and Sam were friends."

"We are. I just call a spade a spade. Don't get me wrong! Sam's a great guy—" why did that sound like a rehearsed line? "—but his heroics are a bit too suicidal for me. Pointless, too. Those three scumbags from the gulf: they should've been left there to drown. Instead they're back out on the street. Tony Ricci was never even charged with anything. Went straight back to his loving drug–pusher daddy."

"You said he straightened out."

"Maybe he did. Maybe not. With a father like that how could you end up as anything else but a scumbag? Kid never had a chance. One day he's gonna kill someone. Or maybe someone kills him." Harry snorted. "It would have been more humane and cost–effective, to let him drown. But, no, Sam had to be a fucking hero."

"But you all got out!"

"Listen to you! You're defending *Sam*? You of all people? You hate the guy!" He shook his head. "At least you did! See what I mean? The man doesn't know *how* to land on his head and crack his skull. Like a damn cat."

"He lost his daughter—and his wife."

Harry grimaced and sighed. "So the score isn't perfect. Tough for Sam." He made an apologetic gesture. "Look, I *like* Sam! He's my best friend. My only friend maybe. He's certainly the only one I know who's never once asked me for a favor. He gave me orders when he was perfectly entitled to do so, but he's never actually taken something from me. Always makes sure the scales are even. Even on this holiday. Notice how he makes sure that he pays his way? Gas, food, drinks, whatever. You'd catch him dead before you'll find him bumming favors off you. When we were at high–school together—we used to smoke then." He grinned at her astonished face. "Yes, Sam used to smoke! Hard to imagine, huh? But he did. A pack a day. Then one day he stopped—God only knows why. Without side–effects! He's got what they call a non–addictive personality. Something about brain chemistry.

"Anyway, about cigarettes. We all used to bum them off each other. You know the way it goes. Sneaking them in breaks and on the way home. Well, I'd swear Sam kept a mental ledger of the smokes he bummed off others. I bet you he never took one that he didn't return the next day at the latest. And he's still like that! People think it's generosity. I think it's obsessive-compulsive. Some kind of weird guilt-stuff. I blame it on his father. Apparently he was like that, too."

That's what you think of your best friend?

Helen wondered what she should say—whether she should say anything at all. Telling

Harry about being terminally in love—*Love? Is that what this is?* with his obsessive-compulsive buddy really didn't seem like the thing to do at this moment. Not only would Harry be hurt: he would be devastated. He wouldn't just be 'angry' at Sam: he'd *hate* him.

The realization—triggered by Harry's soliloquy about his friend's shortcomings—that she was indeed in love with Sam, hit her like a bomb. It shouldn't have, of course. After this morning...

But that could have been just pheromones and crazy biochemistry. That she should be 'in love' was a different notion altogether. Love implied a whole lot of things that didn't necessarily come with good sex. Like caring and attachment and trust and....

Like either of us is particularly 'trustworthy' right now! Look what we're doing to our friends.

But things weren't that simple. This thing was...

She'd never known what it meant: 'bigger than both of us'—but now she thought she did.

We could have chosen not to.

Really?

We chose not to for a whole year. Look where that got us in the end!

It had been more than just sex, hadn't it?

How did she know?

How *could* she know?

Having to play this stupid game with their friends, not being able to talk to each other freely...it made it so damn hard!

She wanted to tell Harry here and now—have it over and done with. But she knew she couldn't. Whichever way you turned this thing it was a mess. How do you tell someone you're engaged to that you've just found your soul mate, but that it was somebody else, thank you very much?

How did Sam feel about all this? If what Harry said was true, Sam must be feeling like a piece of shit.

So did she.

A3803

From his hiding place behind a bush Mirlun watched the boundary on the other side of the road. He had seen them drive into it in their strange vehicle. Now he waited for them to return—for there was no point in him being here if they did not. He didn't want to be stranded in this world for almost two whole moons for absolutely no purpose.

Without them…

He pulled his thin cloak closer around himself. The Diënna had not told him how frigid this world was. Or maybe she didn't know: the kind of detail that escaped even someone like her, being, as it was, too insignificant, and thus getting lost among the things that mattered.

He considered the road. Another detail. He wondered about its paving. What kind of substance was this? It looked like a mix of pitch and fine sand, spread over tiny stones; though how it had been rolled as flat as it was…

'Rolled'! Of course. They must gave giant rollers here, to make it even like this.

His thoughts were interrupted when another of this world's strange vehicles came along the road at a dizzying speed. Like all the others he had seen this one was small, apparently self-propelled (like the Diënna had said they would be), enclosed its occupants in a shiny shell (this one was red) with glassed windows. Mirlun discerned a single individual, looking forward intently, completely ignoring the strange bank of fog that lay on the side of the road—despite the sun rising into a bright blue sky. The vehicle passed, it's tiny fat black wheels singing on the paved road. Mirlun sunk back behind his bush. A strange world indeed. The world of Augustus, who knew things that Plius craved to know.

Another vehicle came rushing along the road, traveling in a direction opposite to the last one. This one was huge, making a terrifying noise as it approached at a breakneck speed and roared past him, leaving him holding onto his bush not to be blown over by the gust of errant air currents it left in the wake of its passage.

A transport of sorts? This world's version of a covered wagon? In Seladiënna such wagons were drawn by teams of horses and took many days to traverse the full width of the empire. This thing might do the same in a few days.

Another noise. Mirlun crouched. From the boundary burst a shape.

They!

The vehicle had been battered; its windows smashed; its clear, sharp lines destroyed with the marks of violence. The vehicle roared, struggled up the slope to the road, gained the flat surface and stopped. An opportune moment! Mirlun made as if to rise.

The thunder of hooves reached his ears. No!

They noticed it, too. The vehicle roared again, lurched forward, skidded, stabilized, and accelerated away, out of his reach. From the boundary burst forth the cavalcade of Plius's Minions. They made as if to charge after the departing vehicle. Then, a bellow from one. The group halted, the horses stood in eerie stillness. Mirlun ducked deeper. If they found him…

From the leader came hoarse commands. The riders dismounted, made moves to chase the horses back into the boundary.

Too late! The boundary, with the swiftness of smoke sucked into a back–draft, simply vanished.

The riders stood, apparently undecided. More commands from the leader. They moved closer to the road and looked up and down its length. As if on a signal, they discarded their helmets, revealing crude visages with dead, black eyes. They flung the headgear into the shrubbery behind them and stood alongside the road.

Waiting.

Mirlun held his breath. The worst of his fears—the worst of Diënna's fears—had come true: Plius's Minions had gained this world. Not just one, but eleven of them. It meant that a lot of people would die. So might they, in the end, but until the last of them was exterminated whoever was left would go after Gladius Magnus with grim, unwavering determination.

The Diënna had expected one or two of them to be dispatched to find the sword—if they managed to take it back! But eleven? This was grim news indeed.

Along the road came another vehicle. A big one. Different to the 'covered wagon' type he'd seen before. This one was like a large box with a continuous row of large windows through which peered a number of faces. Men, women, even a child.

The vehicle slowed: the road was blocked by the figures of the riders.

Mirlun wanted to get up and shout at them to continue. Plough through the phalanx and leave this place behind at best speed. But he didn't, for he knew that all he could do now was to be a witness to horror.

He averted his eyes and tried to close his ears to the sounds from the road as the vehicle stopped and the riders boarded it. The screams of the people inside. Intimations of deeds too terrible to even contemplate.

Of course, they would let some live. For a short while at least—while the riders absorbed their lives and what these people knew. The gift of Plius to his Minions—and when they returned—if they returned—their knowledge would be his, as he took it from them the same way they had taken it from the people they slew.

Another, small, vehicle came racing along the road. Two riders stepped into its path. A screeching sound as the vehicle came to a halt. The occupants, a woman and a...girl—*please don't let it be another child!* had time for just a brief moment of uncomprehending terror before their screams were choked off. Mirlun crouched behind his bush, shaking, not with the chill but with his complete helplessness and abasement.

Presently both vehicles started moving off. They were controlled by Minions and the deft sureness with which they moved off indicated to Mirlun that the Minions had absorbed important fragments of knowledge their victims and were capable of using it competently and without hesitation.

The vehicles disappeared into the distance, heading in the opposite direction to where the Saviors had gone. As yet, it appeared, the Minions had not picked up their trace. Merlin closed his eyes and tried to feel around for Gladius Magnus. He sensed the slightest emanation from a different direction. In this world, like the Diënna had said— and like always, she was right—his senses were dulled and would require sharpening. The Minions would suffer from a similar handicap. But, like him, they would learn— and they would find the sword and those who held it in trust.

He had to get to them first!

Resolutely Mirlun rose and stepped out of his hiding place. He looked around. The

Minions' mounts grazed quietly among the shrub on the opposite side of the road. Mirlun looked along the road and steeled himself for what he had to do. For he, too, needed to know about this world—what to do, how to behave, how to move around, what was the correct conduct and what was not. He, like the Minions, needed to tap the minds of those who lived here. But, unlike them, he did not need to kill. The Diënna's gift was a gentler one; in as stark a contrast to the Minions' as the Diënna was to Plius.

Mirlun looked up. A faint sound. In the distance appeared a tiny dot, growing fast.

3

They left Helston in the evening and drove through the night. The replacement rental was a UK-made Ford, a far cry from the high-class Range Rover. Harry took the first shift. Helen occupied the passenger seat. Sam and Rita shared the back. Rita made herself comfortable against Sam and dozed off. Car engines were magic with Rita. Always had been, apparently. Never the slightest problem in car or plane. The noises of engines sent her to sleep without fail. All of which was fine with Sam. He didn't want to answer any more questions or talk about this to anyone but Helen.

Alone.

Driving back to London now also relieved him having to deal with other complications. As long as they were *doing* things he wouldn't have to face up to Rita in a…sexual… situation. The truth was that he had never been unfaithful to anyone in his life. Keeping it simple: when it came to relationships that's the way he preferred it. Things were much more tidy that way. People didn't get hurt. Not because he had screwed up anyway. It sounded like he was playing it safe, and some might even call it 'dull', but he preferred it to the more 'interesting' alternatives.

The present situation served to demonstrate the virtues of his approach. Subterfuge and deception had entered the very moment he'd let go and admitted his sin: self-deception. Screwing with his own mind. Denying what was obvious because he'd wanted to avoid messing things up.

Life is what happens while you're making other plans.

John Lennon. Maybe.

Life indeed. In the shape of Helen, to be specific, who sat in the front seat beside Harry, carefully avoiding any expression of interest. Sam wondered what was going on in her mind. The sneaking around, the pretending, was already becoming tiresome.

"If these characters are coming after you two," Harry pontificated from behind the wheel, "how far you think they'll go? Is chasing us out of Cornwall enough, you think?"

"Don't know," Sam said. "I hope so."

How far will they come?

"Sometimes I think it wasn't real," Helen said softly.

"It was," he assured her.

She turned her head and looked at him. "Everything?"

"*Everything*," he said.

In the reflected lights from the oncoming cars he saw a tiny smile around her mouth.

"What a bunch of freaks," Harry muttered.

"Let's hope they leave us alone now," Sam said. He smiled at Helen. "I know it may not seem quite as real now," he told her. "It often is that way when things calm down. But I remember everything just as vividly as you do. Whatever happened back there—it's not going to go away just because everything else seems to have returned to normality."

"I don't think I'll ever be the same again," she said.

"Neither will I," Sam agreed.

This was as far as he dared go. Helen knew it, too. She turned back to look out the windscreen. Sam studied her profile and noted that she kept on smiling.

They stopped in Weston Super–Mare and found an Italian Restaurant where they had dinner. Sam offered to drive the rest of the way to London and Harry accepted. He ordered a reasonably expensive red wine, which they—with the exception of Sam—consumed, together with antipasto, a fairly authentic looking dish of lasagna, followed by coffee with a delicious concoction of fried banana and ice cream.

Rita presently declared herself to be too full to do anything but go straight back to sleep.

Harry voiced similar inclinations. "If you don't mind, I'm going to be out of it for the rest of the night."

He peered at Sam from slightly inebriated eyes. The whiskey on top of the wine had pushed him into the not–quite–here category again.

"Why don't you both sleep in the back?" Sam suggested. "Helen can keep me awake." He looked at her. "Unless you're going to drop off on me as well."

"I'll manage," she said crisply. A bit of the old Helen poking through, though Sam suspected it was for Harry's and Rita's benefit. As she bent to open the door of the car she grinned. Now he was sure of it.

They didn't say much until Harry's snores from one side of the backseat confirmed that he was a goner. Rita had dozed off even quicker and lay ensconced in her corner of the back seat. Helen leaned over and inspected the sleepers. Satisfied with what she saw she turned to Sam and, somewhat tentatively, placed a hand on his left leg.

"Did you really mean it?"

She wasn't talking about the freaks.

"Every word."

She still needed assurance. Someone, thought Sam, had done something to her—and whoever it was, he was going to find out one day and get his hands on the asshole's throat. He regretted every nasty remark he'd ever made to her.

"Good." She let out a small, pent–up breath.

"I don't do this kind of thing with every day…or with every girl I meet."

"Good."

He took his left hand off the wheel and covered hers. "Trust me."

He had to keep an eye on the road. The M5 was still busy and killing himself and everybody else in the car by being an asshole wasn't on Sam's agenda. But from his peripheral vision he had an intimation of her face, turned in his direction, studying him.

He allowed himself to smile.

"I know it's hard."

"You have no idea."

"But I do," he said gently. "And right now—doing what I'm doing to…—well I'm not sure how I have the gall to ask you to trust me—but asking I am."

"I don't know if I can."

"Then it's not going to work."

"Maybe we'll just have to work to...oh, I don't know. Building this?"

Maybe. Under normal circumstances that was probably the way to go. But this wasn't 'normal'. He and Helen had had a relationship for a whole year. They just hadn't known it.

There could be no half-measures with a thing like this. You went the whole hog or you didn't go at all. It was like the thing Harry never understood: about how you don't wimp out of what you've signed up for with open eyes and a clear mind. The word was 'commitment', and Sam believed in it. Not to everything. Very few things in fact. The ones that mattered. Certainly not to everybody—in his case not even Rita, who really had deserved better. But he'd never lied to her, and he'd done his best to be clear about his reservations. Whether she understood him was a different matter. People hear what they want to hear. There was no way you could change that.

But with Helen...

"No," he said. "We start at the top. That's the only way. The 'work' is to make sure we stay there—and all it takes for that is..." He glanced at her, then back at the road. "You know what it takes."

She was silent for a long time. The Ford cruised along in the middle east-bound lane, surrounded by a slowly thinning stream of vehicles who gradually peeled off at the exits along the way. Helen's hand underneath his and resting on his leg transmitted the warmth of her body into his. She hadn't taken it away: a good sign.

He felt her hand move, turn palm-up, take hold of his. Fingers intertwined.

Helen, after another furtive inspection of the back seat, leaned over to Sam and brought her mouth close to his ear.

"Do you have any idea of what I'm going to do to you the next time we're alone?" The way she said it—together with the memory of this morning—was enough to trigger whole bunch of remarkably uncontrollable physical responses.

She moved so he could see her face without taking his eyes off the road. The tip of her tongue was held suggestively between her teeth in a slightly parted mouth.

He gave her a stern look. "Don't," he mouthed silently.

She grinned and leaned back in her seat, leaving her hand where it was, her fingers locked with his, as the car sped on, heading east.

They checked into the Heathrow Hilton—or whatever it was called—in the early hours of the morning. Harry had slept off much of the drink, while Rita remained slightly woozy.

"Don't wake me," she muttered. "Just get me into bed."

Sam was happy to oblige. The check-in was painless enough. Harry had done a good job. He signed for the rooms, which he'd booked on his AMEX and everybody trundled off to their rooms, Harry with a possessive arm hooked under Helen's, who looked uncomfortable and edgy, but did her best to play along. Sam didn't envy her what she would have to undergo once the door had closed behind them. Harry was on his second wind for the night and might desire to be entertained. Helen would have to deal with this on her own. But deal with it she would, and, come the next day, Harry would not be a happy man. He mightn't sulk, but Sam knew what Harry was like disappointed. A 'no' was always a rejection, no matter *how* much of a good face Harry put on it. Over the many years they'd known each other Sam had learned to read all the signs.

Poor Harry.

Poor Rita, for that matter. He resolved to clear the decks at the first opportunity after getting back home. He hadn't lied to her before today. She deserved better.

Rita plonked onto the bed and went out like a light. She was like that. Interrupted sleep didn't seem to bother her, blessed as she was with a benign cerebral chemistry.

Sam stood at the window, looking out from the tenth–floor room over the lights of the endless metropolis that was London. He hated cities with a passion. Their endless spread made him claustrophobic. To his right lay Heathrow. A brightly illuminated 747 touched down on the end of runway. Its nose dropped, bounced more than it should have, dropped again. The plane disappeared from view.

The lights in the hotel–room had been extinguished, but near the window it almost bright enough to read. The whole thing reminded Sam of the cityscapes in *Blade Runner*. Not quite there yet, but nor far to go either. Far too close. There were cities that came even closer, like Taipei.

His mind veered off into the events of the morning. This, his first truly quiet moment, brought him new perspectives on the subject. He had no answers; no solutions—but somewhere in his mind connections had been made, impossibilities discarded, implausibilities analyzed and sifted, consequences weighed. Facts had been tentatively classified and filed away for future reference and consideration.

Facts like the sheer *existence* of the roll of parchment, still in the inner pocket of his denim jacket. It was a given—as was his memory, and Helen's!, that it once had been something quite different. Unless they labored under a shared delusion the reality of the…change? metamorphosis? transmutation?…could not be denied.

The riders were equally real. The only question was where they were and what were their intentions. They labored under certain constraints which would prevent them from readily following Sam and Helen out of the confines of their immediate environment. Certainly the Atlantic would place a definite barrier into their path—even if they did have the motivation to follow them this far, or the ability to figure out where their quarries had gone. This world was an alien place for them—just like whatever lay beyond the fog and the strange forest had been for himself and Helen.

One could presume that they were safe here, and would be even more so once they stepped onto that plane tomorrow. Until then he would keep his eyes open and ask Helen to do the same. Paranoia sometimes saved lives.

Once back home he would address himself to the parchment and what it represented or *was*. Somehow it and the sword were one and the same thing. Sam didn't know how, but it had to be this way.

But why would the sword now be a drawing on a piece of paper? When had it happened? What process had initiated the transformation? What were the requirements for the process to be reversed? There were rules. There had to be. The whole affair, crazy as it was, still hung together with a weird kind of logic. Once one accepted a series of basic axioms everything else would follow.

The thing between Helen and himself—that, too, was somehow connected with it all. The series of events which had led to them realizing what they should have known for a long time had an inexorable kind of compulsion about it. Starting with him waking up

Chapter 3 69

and not being able to get back to sleep. The weird dream before that, the urge to visit Loe Pool, Helen wanting to come with him, their brief altercation, what happened after that: it all hung together like a chain, each link essential for the sequence to complete.

Sam pondered the likely shape of the future.

The people.

Rita: hurt very badly.

Please, let her find someone who's good to her!

Harry: never forgiving him. This was a certainty. Helen was like Harry's prize. A validation of his existence. Harry needed validations, and the knowledge that someone actually wanted to marry him was a big thing with him.

I'm going to lose my oldest friend.

And was he going to do anything about it?

Sam turned from the window and went over to the chair, where hung his jacket. He extracted the roll of parchment and took it back to the window.

How did it work? Did he have to say something? Recite a magical incantation? And then what?

I'm swallowing this, hook, line, and sinker!

What else could he do? Any other way lay madness.

This way madness lies, too!

But it was madness of a different kind. You just had to hide it from those who would prefer to disagree—possibly for excellent reasons of their own. But the madness of denying simple and undeniable *facts*, that he could not abide.

Ha! I've been 'abiding' the denial of the truth for long enough!

No more.

⚜

"Aren't you coming to bed?"

Helen sat in a chair at the window, staring out. She turned her head. How long was it going to take Harry to go to sleep?

"I won't be able to sleep."

"You really should see a doctor about this."

"You know I have. Apart from pills they don't seem to have any answers."

He was an indistinct shape as he levered himself up on one arm.

"Come to bed," he said gently.

She sighed. "Please..."

She could see him lie back again.

"I know you don't want to hear this," he said carefully, "but maybe you should at least consider..."

"Counseling?" she completed.

"Sudden violence like this: it can be very traumatic."

"I'm fine."

"Trust me: you need to talk to *someone* about it."

"Maybe Sam..." It was the wrong thing to say, but it had just come out.

From Harry there was a moment's pregnant silence.

"Sam?" he said derisively. "You think Sam's qualified to counsel anybody on anything?"

He can't even counsel himself! That guy's got enough demons for a squadron."

"He was *there*!" she just couldn't help saying.

Silence again.

"Sam's not going to be any help. He hasn't even dealt with Katie's death yet."

"I'd hardly blame him for *that*!" she retorted.

"He's been trying to kill himself ever since," Harry said mercilessly.

Really? Was that what made him inspire Hollywood to make a movie about his life? Heroism disguising suicidal urges?

"Hardly the guy to go to for fixing up the inside of your own head."

Poor Harry! You have no idea...

She said nothing.

"You never told me," Harry said, "why you went out on that crazy jaunt in the fog anyway. With Sam of all people!"

"I couldn't sleep. I looked out the window and saw him walk to the car." She paused.

"And?" Harry prompted.

"I was thinking of going for a walk myself. So I just…well, you know—people just *do* things."

"You almost got killed!"

"That wasn't Sam's fault!" she snapped.

"I didn't say it was," he retorted.

"If it wasn't for him I wouldn't be here!"

"If it wasn't for him you wouldn't have gone on this crazy trip in the fog. This is *so* typical of Sam. What was he doing? What was he thinking? Why did he want to drive down to The Loe? Of all the people in the world, why Sam? He put on a good show, but I *know* he wasn't really interested in this trip. He did it for Rita's sake—because she wanted to get him away from his helos and his obsession with ADLER and everything." Harry snorted. "This morning—that was just a typical dumb–ass–Sam–Donovan–spur–of–the–moment–thing. Like…" He fell silent.

"Like what?" she challenged him.

"Like…always. Never mind the consequences. "

She saw him turn away from her. She didn't know what to say; what to do. In truth she was getting to the point—had been working her way up to it for the last couple of weeks; only now, with the Sam–thing it was all coming to a head—that she didn't even feel all that sorry for Harry anymore. Especially when he got stuck into Sam. The guy was his *friend*! Not that she had any particular experience with all the things friendship entailed, but being 'friends' to her always seemed to imply a kind of loyalty. Like the thing with Sam who had turned their instant attraction into instant detestation: for the sake of Harry and nobody else. At the time there wasn't even a Rita.

That was loyalty: don't screw your friends. Don't run them down. Certainly don't harbor the kinds of grudges Harry seemed to carry around with him. What was going to happen when he finally found out about *this*?

Don't screw your friends…

Look what we're doing here!

The silence grew oppressive. Helen got up. "I'm going for a walk."

"Whatever." He didn't turn around or say anything else. Which was just as well. The

Chapter 3

less said the better.

She took the entry card and left the room; stood in the hallway, undecided what to do. She just knew she had to get out of the room with Harry in it. The whole thing was getting claustrophobic.

Is this what it's like having an affair? Sneaking around and feeling guiltier with every breath you take?

We've got to end this! It's like a soap opera…

Indeed!

There's only one reason I'm out here.

She went down the hallway and around a corner; stopped outside Sam and Rita's room. She hesitated for a moment then, very gently, knocked. Once.

How long should she wait? If he didn't come to the door, should she knock again? What excuse would she contrive of it wasn't Sam? How could she…

The issues were laid to rest by Sam's appearance. He was fully dressed. When he saw her, he tucked the entry card in his hand into his pocket and stepped outside, closing the door behind him with exaggerated care. The lock snicked shut. Sam turned around, took Helen's hand in his and, without a word, tugged her toward the elevators. The hallways were empty. The elevator took a while in coming. Sam looked up and down the hallway, took Helen in his arms and started to kiss her.

The elevator–bell rung; the door slid open They separated with difficulty and stepped into the elevator.

"Where shall we go?"

"Nowhere far I'm afraid," he said.

The elevator accelerated downward. She put her hands behind his head and pulled him down to her and kissed him again; putting *everything* into it: her being; her total *wanting* him; the promise of love and more; a plea for reciprocation. His response was unequivocal and utterly satisfying.

The elevator came to a halt. The door opened. They jerked apart, peered out guiltily and, seeing there wasn't anybody watching, heaved a sigh of relief, then headed for the reception. She grinned when Sam moved to walk slightly behind her.

"Mr. Donovan, I believe you're being shy!"

"Sue me."

"Walk closer."

"That would make it worse. I'm trying to calm down."

She chuckled throatily.

The concierge on duty pointed them at an all–night bar and cafe on the lobby level. They went in there, found it empty. They looked around and found a table in the back, in a nook surrounded by trellis with real ivy climbers woven through the framework. They sat down together on the short bench behind the table. A somewhat tired–looking waitress appeared and took their order: orange juices for both of them.

When the waitress was gone Helen leaned over and kissed Sam again; somewhat more sedately this time. At least that's what she had promised herself she'd do. But that chemistry thing—or whatever it was, and why not call it 'love'? betrayed them yet again, and it took significant self–control to remember where they were.

"We've got to stop this." Sam was breathing heavily.

"Yeah," she said weakly. "Your hand…"

"Oops."

But he left it there. She didn't care. She *liked* it where it was, and wished it'd go a bit further where it had been heading—and if anybody looked closely enough to see what it was doing, let them be scandalised! They pushed even closer together and sat in silence for a moment, wanting nothing much else at this very instant. She leaned her head into the crook of his neck and slipped her hand into his shirt and, where it couldn't be seen, under his waistband. Then she just rested there listening to him breathing, feeling a gentle rhythmic current of air play over her hair.

That's how Harry found them.

Sam had closed his eyes for what had seemed like just a few moments. He was so content it was almost indecent. His desire for her was strong, but there were constraints on what they could do at this moment and just sitting here would have to suffice. His left arm was around her waist, his hand under her sweatshirt and her bra, cupping a breast.

Nobody should have noticed. Nobody should have looked closely enough at the couple sitting in the dim light of their trellis–ringed alcove. But Harry was looking and he came close enough to see just whose hand was where and what it all meant.

Sam opened his eyes and saw him standing there, an expression on his face such as Sam had never seen before. Strangely enough, the first things that came to Sam's mind was that he was glad it was over. The second was that he was witnessing the moment where he lost his oldest friend. The third was a guilty realization that for the sake of the woman in his arms he would gladly lose every friend he had, conquer worlds, break every precept of conduct he might have held sacred. For there were more important things than rules: even those that were self–imposed.

The moment of eye–contact between the accuser and the accused drew on. As yet Helen did not know. Still she lay against him, relaxed and content. Sam moved his left hand. She murmured something, pushed closer against him.

Then she sensed it. Sam felt her tense. Her head turned. Another hesitation. Her head lifted off him.

"Harry," she whispered. But she did not pull away from Sam. She didn't wriggle to make him take his hand from underneath her bra; nor did she remove her own from him.

"Bitch." Harry's voice was a hoarse whisper. "You fucking bitch."

His eyes wandered to Sam's face again. "How could you do this to me?"

He swallowed hard, took another deep breath, spun around, and stalked out of the bar.

Helen sunk back against Sam, releasing a pent–up breath.

Sam stared after Harry's retreating back. He felt physically sick—not so much because of what had just happened, but…

"I know what he's going to do."

Helen lifted her head and nodded. "You'd better go now, before he…"

"Will you be all right?"

"I'll be here. Just…do what you have to."

They disengaged the various intimately connected parts of their anatomies.

Chapter 3   73

"I'll be back soon," he promised.

"I know. Just go."

He hurried after Harry.

The elevator lobby was empty. Damn! Sam touched a pad which lit up. One of the four doors slid open. Sam lunged inside and touched the pad for the tenth floor.

He stepped out of the elevator through half–opening doors and ran along the hallway, turning a corner just in time to see Harry's figure disappear into his and Rita's room. The door shut as he reached it. He pulled out his entry card, swiped it through the reader and stepped inside.

Harry was standing in front of Rita, saying something. At Sam's entrance he fell silent and turned his head.

"Get out," Sam said tonelessly.

Harry ignored him and turned back to Rita. "You know what this guys has *done* to you? You know what a kind of…"

"Shut up, Harry," Rita said, softly but distinctly.

"You don't know what…"

"Just leave."

"I was…"

"*Get out!*"

Harry cringed like a dog expecting to be whipped. It was, Sam thought, a pathetic sight.

Harry opened his mouth again.

Rita turned to Sam. "Throw him out if you want to," she said coolly.

Harry looked from one to the other. His face twisted into a sneer of disdain.

"You…"

Sam to a step in Harry's direction. Harry stormed past him, slamming the door behind him.

Sam and Rita stood in silence, looking at each other. Her expression was kind–of sad. Resigned maybe.

Sam took a couple of steps and stood in front of her.

"Time for the truth," he said tonelessly. "And guilt. And shame."

Rita shook her head slightly. "So," she said, "Harry was the last to find out."

The import of her words failed to sink in for a heartbeat or two.

"You *knew*?"

The sadness in her glorious eyes was heartbreaking. Her mouth twisted into a wry grin. "How could I not?"

"When…"

She chuckled softly. "Sam, Sam…" Shaking her head. "You are a good guy, and, as men go, you're amazingly sensitive. But you're also *very* dense sometimes." She laid her hands on his shoulders and considered him thoughtfully. "Though women's intuition wasn't really necessary. Besides, Helen didn't figure it out either." She grimaced. "It was this morning, wasn't it? After whatever happened to you two out there."

Sam nodded.

"I thought so. When you came back, the tension between the two of you, it was stronger than ever—but it was all…inverted. Before, when you two came physically close, it was always like something was pushing you apart; like equal poles of a magnet.

This morning," she sighed, "you could get far enough apart to stop yourselves from being pulled *together*."

She pulled him closer and kissed him lightly on the lips. When she drew back he saw that she was crying.

"I'm…"

"I know. You're stupid!" She smiled through tears. "When two people have such antagonism for each other as you and Helen did—it's usually for one of two reasons. Either you're in direct competition for something or somebody. In this case that would have been Harry, and I knew that you had no disposition whatsoever to 'compete' for anything having to do with Harry—who, by the way, and let me say this to you now that I can, is a total loser. You know it. He knows it. And he hates you for it."

"Harry…"

"Is a loser. Period. Certainly not someone to compete for. Which leaves only the second main reason for the antagonism between you and Helen: sublimated attraction." She grimaced. "Listen to me! Always the psychologist."

"But if you knew, why did you tolerate it?"

A wry grin. "I guess I hoped it'd change. Maybe I also lied to myself a bit. But one of the reasons why I wanted to go on this vacation was that I knew it'd probably sort things out. Two weeks together like this: something would give way."

"Rita, I'm so sorry."

She leaned against him and he hugged her. "I know you are," she said, her voice muffled. "So am I. But I know you didn't know until today." She pulled back. "There's never a right moment for something like this."

They separated.

"You screw up, Sam," she said. "Like everybody does. You may try to avoid it, but life will get you there somehow." She ran her hand through his thinning hair. "But you're good man—and I *don't* feel betrayed. I just wish it had been different. But I had a good time. You were always very sweet, and I liked that."

"You deserve better than this."

She grimaced. "I do! But my life isn't over yet." Her hands dropped away. "And now you better go and make sure that Harry doesn't do something really 'Harry'."

"Rita…"

"I see you later." She grinned crookedly. "We still share rooms and we're gonna catch a plane together, right?"

"Right. Well, see you soon."

He felt her regard on his back as he went to the door and let himself out.

In the bar he found Harry standing in front of the table, staring down at Helen, who said something Sam couldn't hear.

Harry's reply was loud and heated and laced with crude invective. He leaned forward and placed his hands on the table.

Helen's eyes turned in Sam's direction. Harry straightened and spun around.

"For the record," Sam said softly. "This was not…planned."

Harry shook his head. "Fuck you, Sam. How could you do this? How could you *do* this? You and that…*bitch*."

He stalked away.

Chapter 3

Sam sat down beside Helen.

"How was it?"

She screwed up her face. "Draining." She touched his face. "How's Rita?"

"Rita? Rita's a terribly nice person."

"She knew, huh?"

"Yeah. How did you figure *that* out?"

"Women know women. I didn't know *what* Rita knew, but I knew she knew something I didn't. Now it all becomes clear."

"She did her best to let me off the hook easily. I didn't *want* to be let off, but she did it anyway."

"Harry wasn't so gracious."

"I didn't expect him to."

She tucked her arm under his. "What do we do now? We can hardly just go back to our rooms and pretend nothing happened."

Sam looked at his watch. "We've got almost five hours." He got up. "Come on."

They went to the reception. The concierge didn't raise an eyebrow when Sam asked if they had a spare room for the night.

"Only a suite."

"Which is gonna cost me a mint, right?"

The concierge quoted a price. Helen gasped.

"We'll take it," Sam said.

"Sam!"

He grinned at her. "The much–vaunted Sam Donovan impulsiveness," he told her.

The concierge allowed himself the faintest of smiles. "Under the circumstances, I think I can take responsibility for a special rate."

"Do what you can," Sam said firmly. "Just get us the room."

A few minutes later they were in the elevator, on their way up to the top floor.

"Let's just wait," he whispered into her ears. "I'm sure they have cams in here."

She drew in a sharp breath. "Earlier…"

"Yeah, well, who cares."

Sam operated the card lock to the 'suite'. Helen stepped inside. Sam touched a panel to the left of the door. The lights came on.

"Wow!"

"Five hours," Sam said and closed the door.

She turned around. He dropped the card key on the floor and went to her. He didn't see what was around them, and neither did he care.

They didn't make it to the bed.

Sometime later…

"We said," she panted, "we were going to do this on a bed."

"We said a lot of things."

"I think we should go to the bed now."

"I can't walk."

"I guess it's hard, with your pants around your ankles like that."

"Very. Especially with you straddling me."

"I guess I just have to get down."

"Regretfully, yes."

"I better do it now."

"Take your time."

"You sure?"

"Absolutely."

"You're not tired?"

"Maybe. How would *I* know?"

"Where were you all my life?" she said against his mouth.

"Where were *you*?"

He felt her lips twist into a smile. "For the first thirty–odd years of your life: unavailable."

"You seem available enough now."

"Oh, yes!"

Helston

The trace of Gladius Magnus was becoming easier to detect. He hoped that it was just he who sensed it growing stronger; that it was his sensibilities adjusting to this world—that Plius's Minions, brutes that they were, would not adapt so easily. He was Diënna's creature, and thus influenced by her personality and her being. The Minions had only Plius. Their senses were brutish, though ultimately they would prove just as effective as his, making up for the delicacy of his perception with the ruthlessness of their exploitation of human souls. Among them they would sense the track of the sword just as he did, though maybe for them it was not the almost luminous trail engraved upon the very fabric of space.

Still, hurry he must. Eventually the trace and his sensitivity would fade and he would be left without a guide to their whereabouts. Urgency tugged at him. He must steel himself to do what he had to. Though he would not actually harm his victims they would still suffer from temporary disorientation and loss of memory; like the woman, who had picked him up at the roadside, taken him in her strange vehicle—which, he now knew from her mind, was called a 'car'—to the little town where the trace of the sword became ever stronger, winding through the streets, until it entered the local equivalent of a hostelry, emerged again, to trace along another road into directions unknown...

This woman, who had taken him, and had provided him with the language and the first inklings of his current context: she now sat in her 'car', dazed and confused and unaware of where and who she was. Someone, no doubt, would find her and help her. Or so he hoped.

The task. Focus on the task!

He forced himself to ignore the ignobility of having become a thief who had robbed an innocent woman of what might be her only few coins—and the strange paper 'money' they used in this world! He didn't think so: anybody who owned a vehicle like her must surely belong to the wealthier members of this society.

More information! He needed it so badly. His mind was reeling with what he had already absorbed. Yet he needed more. Much more.

The hostelry—known here as a 'hotel': his next stop. Inside would be people who knew more about the man and the woman who had Magnus' sword. He would find out whence they had come—Diënna had said that it was from far away! and whither they had gone. Then he would follow—and hope that he was quicker than the Minions, whose presence he sensed, distant as yet, but still too close for comfort. Their emanations, already enhanced by their absorption of the minds of those they had murdered, grew more pronounced every moment. Soon they would be here, and by then he'd better be gone.

Information and transport.

And clothes.

The Diënna had equipped him with clothes that appeared not too outlandish in the current context. They had been tailored by a man in Ystian, according to the Diënna's instructions; who had scoured her memories for what she knew about the garments worn by Laurentius Augustus and his now–dead companion when they first came to Seladiënna years ago.

His current clothes, Mirlun reflected, *would do for a time; but he needed to blend in, be unobtrusive, a nobody, a shadow following his quarries to wherever they went. Whatever helped with these goals, it must be pursued.*

So: the 'hotel' first; garments maybe next; then transport to wherever he needed to go.

Mirlun straightened and crossed the road to the hotel, taking care to use his newly acquired knowledge to avoid the traffic of 'cars' and 'lorries'—sometimes called 'trucks'—on the busy afternoon street.

4

The bed had not been slept in, but a lot of activities had taken place atop its luxurious linen during the last few hours. The two participants in said activities now rested on the enormous emperor–sized bed, their limbs entangled, faces touching, sharing their breath, gloriously sweaty and exhausted.

Sam hadn't said so, but Helen knew that they shared this; that this was an experience almost as novel as a first kiss. Never in her adult life had she allowed herself such abandoned, frank, and unconditional passion. She wanted to cry but didn't. And then she couldn't help it and she did—and Sam held her and made soothing noises, and him just being there suddenly made it all right. All the fuckups of her life—starting from week one and right through to the Harry-thing—they all had, quite without her trying, led her to this point; and if that's what it took to get here—even if had been twenty-eight years of…whatever—then so be it. This was a place where people dreamed of going and most never got to. She had. She was here. Sam was here. They were here. If she died right now it would, after all, be without a damn regret in the world.

She wasn't going to tell him she loved him. Everybody said that, and you got the feeling that nobody knew what it meant, and that they said it just because it was the kind of thing you said. But then he said it first, and when he did—and it wasn't in the heat of passion, but during one of their brief periods of rest—she told him that she finally understood what it meant, and that she did love him—and then they forgot all about talking again until sheer exhaustion finally got the better of them.

She laughed softly. "We're going to be sore."

"I don't think so," he whispered. A hand slid down her back. She wriggled closer to him—as if that were possible. He was right: lubrication had not been an issue. They'd lost a lot of body–fluids last night.

Through a tiny slit in the still–drawn curtains a bright shaft of sunlight shone right into her face. She pushed her head against Sam's chest. It was so good being able to do this: just cuddle up against someone and know that it was all right, no matter what. She hadn't had a lot of 'someones' to cuddle up against. Her adoptive parents hadn't been the touchy–feely type. Good people they'd been, but when she looked for warmth she usually found benevolence, and when she just wanted someone to listen, she invariably ended up getting advice.

For a while she'd believed the notion that she was an island; that ultimately that's the way things were—and maybe it was the way they should be—and that isolation was a natural state: not just for her, but everyone. The thought had its attractions. Every success was one's own. Every fight won on her own didn't require credit to be given to anyone else. The same went for failures. Learn from them and do better next time. 'Realize' yourself. Find the 'true' you. None of this co–dependency crap. Even those closest to you were really just 'partners'. Co–workers in the opus of life. Companions on the way from the cradle to the grave. Close companions maybe. Lovers even. Separated nonetheless.

She'd subscribed to a version of this philosophy because it was consistent with her experience of what could be. She'd watched herself and the world and found that humankind was not a continent but a scattered group of islands. Cooperative, dependent for survival, but ultimately separate.

Yesterday she learned that she had been wrong. Sometimes a whole was more than the sum of its parts. Completion was not found alone. The two people on the bed were self–sustained individuals; no question of that. But, until yesterday, they had not been complete.

She pushed closer to Sam, felt him respond with an air of someone who may have had the same thoughts. She reached up and put her free arm around his neck.

"You and me both," she whispered.

"You and me both," he confirmed.

"I don't want this to end."

"It won't. Not if I have anything to do with it."

She pulled back and looked into his face. "You've got a lot to do with it."

"I know."

"Wanna take a shower?"

"A real one, or another one like last time?"

"A real one. I think we need to get serious about getting up—cleaned up, too."

"I rather like you smelling like this." He kissed her. "And tasting like this, too."

"Other people might take offense."

"Screw other people."

"Getting bored with me already?"

"Hardly."

"Then carry me into the shower."

"I'm not too sure I can. Not after last night."

"Try."

He did. She had to help him, but somehow they managed to get into the bathroom. They also managed to have an ordinary shower—with extraordinarily diligent mutual cleaning maybe, but cleaning it was.

Sam knocked on the door to his and Rita's room. A few moments passed, then she appeared. She was dressed for travel.

"You got a key, haven't you!"

Sam shrugged. "I didn't want to intrude. I don't have the right. Not anymore."

Rita gave him a wry, somewhat wistful smile, and shrugged. "Come in, for heaven's sake." She peered across his shoulder as he did. "Where's Helen? I thought…"

"She's gone to Harry's room."

Rita closed the door. "Shouldn't you be there? Just in case?"

"She wanted to do this on her own."

Rita pulled a dubious face, but said nothing. She turned away.

A knock on the door. Sam went to open it. In the door stood Helen, looking worried.

"He's gone."

"What?"

"Harry's gone?"

Behind him Sam felt Rita approach. "Did he leave a note?" she asked.

Sam stepped back to let Helen come in. She closed the door behind her. "His gear is gone. His bag is gone. He left my stuff, my passport and cards." She looked at Sam. "Where, do you think, he is?"

Where indeed? Sam tried to put himself into Harry's position. He found that he couldn't.

Helen had turned to Rita, trying to find something to say to cover the awkwardness of the situation. "Rita, I…" She sighed and shook her head. "I don't know what to say."

Rita did something amazing: she embraced Helen.

"Don't think I'm not pissed off," she said softly. "But some things are out of your hands. All our hands. This was one of them. Harry and I never had a chance."

She let go of Helen and stood back, grinning crookedly. "It would be easier if both of you were perfidious assholes, whom I could hate with all my heart." She shrugged and pulled a face. "Why couldn't you just?"

Another moment's silence. "Want to come down and have breakfast?" Sam asked Rita.

She shook her head. "Been there, done that." She eyed them curiously. "Where were you anyway?"

Before he could say anything she shook her head. "I don't want to know. I'll see you in the lobby. An hour?"

"We'll check in our bags," Sam agreed. "Then we have the rest of the day."

12

17 DEAD IN CORNWALL
HORROR BUS MASSACRE

The headline leapt out at Sam as he picked up the paper from the stand at the reception. There'd been one lying beside the door to their room, but he had ignored that one, just as he had the one outside Rita's room.

Ignorance no more.

"What is it?" Helen peered at the paper. "Omigod!"

Sam took her arm and pulled her away from there, out of the bolus of people waiting to check out. Standing behind a column they read the article under the headline. When Sam reached the part where it said 'stabbed with unknown weapons, possibly machetes or swords', he stopped.

"It's them," Helen whispered.

Sam felt as if he couldn't breathe. They had brought these…things…here. Now seventeen people—maybe more by now! were dead. A bus full of men, women, children! in the wrong place at the wrong time.

A major contingent of heavily–armed police units were on their way to western Cornwall. The article made no mention of eleven horses or a previous attack on two tourists in a Range Rover. Somehow the police had either managed to keep that from the reporters, or come to an agreement to keep it under wraps for the time being.

"We did this," Helen whispered.

"No," he said firmly.
"We took the sword."
The sword…
Still inside his denim jacket.
Something was in his pocket.
He looked at his watch. Nine–thirty, just about.
Had Harry read the paper? It was safe to assume that he had.
"That sword was given to us," he said. He gave Helen the newspaper and pulled the roll of parchment out of his jacket." She jerked back from it was if it were a live snake.
"This," Sam said, "is what we have. It may be what we pulled out of that boulder—or it may not. It may just be a roll of parchment."
She regarded it suspiciously. "Whatever it is," she declared, "we took it, and they came after us because we did. I know it."
"I agree. But…" He took her arm. "Let's find a table. I need something to eat. You've worn me out."
He'd said the right thing. An impish grin flashed across her face. She stood closer. "Dear Sir," she said lowly, "are you're truly blaming me? May I remind you that is was you who contrived to find the room—and the bed! and that you carried me there despite the pants around your ankles?"
She grew somber again. "You're right. I'm starved, too."
They found a table in a large restaurant adjacent to the lobby, which also offered a buffet breakfast. They availed themselves to the buffet and ordered black coffee for the both of them. By an unspoken agreement they didn't return the conversation to the subject foremost on their minds until their plates were empty.
"Fairy logic," Sam said then.
"Huh?"
"Fairy logic. The rules prevailing in fairy–tales and fantasy literature. Not necessarily the rules we're used to, but once you accept the premises there is a logic here nonetheless."
"You're serious!"
Sam pointed at the newspaper. "This is as serious as it'll get."
"And what does 'fairy–logic' tell you?"
"You agree that we were given this thing?"
She shrugged. "I guess."
"What's the next question?"
" 'Why'?"
"Exactly."
"I have no idea. Why us? Why now? Why at all?"
"Why us?" he said. "Maybe because whoever gave it to us knows something about us we don't know."
"Or maybe it was a mistake."
"There's that."
"How can it be anything else?"
"I don't know—but let's assume for the sake of the argument that it wasn't."
She pondered the issue for a moment or two.

Chapter 4

"Someone decided that we should have it."

Sam nodded. "You're getting into the spirit of this!"

"Wait till I get going!"

"A scary thought."

She nudged him under the table. "Hey, mister! Just because I slept with you…"

"You haven't yet."

"I will."

"Ha!"

"Someone either wants us to keep it safe, or to do something with it."

"My thoughts exactly."

"Do what?"

"Or for whom?" he asked.

Helen pulled a face. "The way I see it, probably for somebody else's benefit."

"Precisely."

"For which the sword is essential."

"Sounds reasonable."

"And these…things…"

"…either want it back because they need to use it for something…"

"…leaving us with the dirty work of pulling it out of the rock…"

"…because it had to be us?"

"Maybe."

"Or could be they want it back because they don't want us to do with it whatever we're supposed to do."

"That's if we're supposed to do anything."

"Naturally." She grimaced. " 'Fairy–logic' is giving me a headache."

"Shall we finish this train of thought?"

"Hmmff. So they're after this thing—whatever it is—and we have it and so they're after us."

"An unpleasant thought."

"How could they possibly find us?"

"How did they know we were where we were in the first place? If they can know that, why not this?"

"Now I'm scared!"

"Yeah." Sam picked up the parchment and held it between the index fingers and thumbs of both hands.

"It's hiding," Helen said suddenly.

"Who?"

"Not 'who'! 'What'! The sword. By your 'fairy–logic', it's simply hiding itself from view." She reached out. "Can I have it?"

He gave it to her. She unrolled it and examined the drawing. She let it go and it snapped back into its rolled–up shape. Helen stared at it—then at Sam. She held up the roll.

"That's about the size of the grip, isn't it?"

"Just about."

"What if…" She hesitated and looked around. "Can we go somewhere private? I don't want to try this in public. Besides, I think we may need some more space than we have here."

"What're you up to?"

"Remember your 'third possibility'?"

"Sure."

"How about the room? What time's checkout?"

"Ten–thirty." He looked at his watch. "We have half an hour."

"Let's go."

"You are a genius and I love you."

She pushed open the door. "I love you, too. Madly."

They stepped inside the spacious room and Sam closed the door. Helen walked to the middle of the room and held up the roll of parchment in one hand.

"Hold it vertically," Sam told her. "Until we know which end is which."

"Shit!" She unrolled the parchment, inspected the drawing, let it snap into a roll again.

"It's pointing counter–clock wise."

"Here we go." Sam reached out and gripped the other half.

The effect was instant and stunning. The sudden weight jerked their hands down. The tip of the sword hit the carpet. It stood there, held up by them, its blade gleaming brightly.

They stared.

"You are a genius!"

"I have my uses," she said modestly.

"You're amazing."

"You're biased."

"Sue me."

"Let's try to reverse the process."

He let go.

Nothing happened.

"Now you let go as well."

Helen placed the grip on the floor, let go, and stood back.

For a few moments nothing happened.

They waited.

Still nothing.

"I hope this is reversible," Sam muttered. "Otherwise we're in deep shit."

At that instant the sword…vanished. In its place lay the roll of parchment.

"Fairy–logic?" Helen asked.

"We'll have to explore this," Sam said. "It needs both of us to make it appear. If either of us keeps a hold of it, it stays 'appeared'. When we both let it go it disappears again—after a while."

"Why are we not more…"

"…just totally freaked out by this whole thing?" he completed.

"Something like that."

"Hmmm."

"I think we should try this again."

"I think so, too."

After repeating the procedure several times—with some exploratory variations—they thought that they had figured out some of the sword's 'fairy-logic'. The blade always appeared in the same relationship to the rolled parchment. It required both of them to bring it into existence. The average delay between it being released and reverting to its 'parchment state' was just over one minute, give or take a few seconds.

"I'd hate to think what would have happened if we'd pointed this thing the wrong way when we made it appear," Helen muttered.

"Maybe we should mark it," Sam said and looked around. He found a ball-point pen in the drawer of a bedside unit, together with stationery. But when he tried to draw on the parchment the pen refused to work. Sam scribbled on the writing pad in the drawer and then tried again.

"It doesn't like being marked," Helen said critically. She unrolled the parchment and studied the drawing; ran her fingers over the precise black lines.

Sam looked at his watch. "Time to check out. Rita will be down there soon."

Helen gave him the parchment. "You hold on to it. I'd feel spooky having it close to me all the time."

As they left the room Helen stopped and pointed. "You remember what happened right there last night?"

"How could I forget?" he said, slipped his hands around her back and pulled her to him.

"Think we have the time?"

"I wish, but…"

"Then we'd better go," she panted.

"Regretfully, yes."

"Let's go and get our bags."

Arm in arm they left the room.

Rita was waiting in the lobby, looking somewhat forlorn and making Sam feel like the piece of shit he was. Helen must have noticed it, too, for she went up to Rita, put her bag down, and hugged her. Rita looked surprised but also better for the experience. If these two were men, thought Sam, and he were a woman, who had just changed the focus of her affections, as it were, those guys certainly wouldn't be doing any hugging—unless it was to see who could crush whose rib cage into a pulp.

Not that he was complaining. This was much preferable; though he could imagine that—not in this instance, where the gesture was genuine—women, too, had their ways. You couldn't see what the hands around your back were doing. Holding a sharp knife maybe.

Sam grinned.

"What're you smiling at?" Helen wanted to know.

Sam shrugged. "Nothing." He looked at Rita. "Have you checked out yet?"

"Yep."

"The room was on me!"

"I think I can handle it," she said firmly. Sam knew the tone and refrained from objecting.

He handed over his credit card and paid the still-exorbitant fee for the 'suite'—while

Helen kept Rita's attention engaged otherwise.

When Sam was done he went back to where they stood.

"Shall we go?"

They took a cab to Heathrow and checked in their bags at the United counter. Sam enquired about Harry with the check–in clerk, who advised him that Mr. Petrowksi was no longer booked on this flight. Helen saw her look at them queerly, as if wondering what had happened so that they didn't know what their friend had done. The woman's glance flicked to Sam again, and from him to Helen and Rita. Helen grinned inwardly. She wasn't thinking that. Surely not.

Helen glanced sideways at Rita whose face was carefully impassive. Wondering the same thing, no doubt.

Check–in done they decided that there wasn't much to do around here. A cab ride into London looked more attractive.

Rita was somewhat hesitant, and Helen thought she knew why.

"We're just three friends," she told her.

Rita looked from Helen to Sam and back again, thinking it over.

"Please," Sam said softly.

Rita gave them a wry grin. "We're a strange threesome," she said. She shrugged. "I'd rather spend the time with you two than alone."

"Good." Sam hugged her. From close up he looked into her face for a moment, then kissed her on the cheek. The gentleness of the gesture, which was an apology, a plea, and a gesture of affection, all wrapped into one, revealed to Helen another facet of Sam Donovan's character. She decided that she liked it.

The cab dropped them in Piccadilly Circus. They found themselves a cafe with grotesquely inflated prices and just sat down, watching the traffic and people flow past their window table.

Normality, thought Helen. It all had been stood on its head within the space of just a day or so. It was difficult to believe that only yesterday morning she and Sam, still fighting like cats and dogs, had gone out for a drive that would change their lives forever.

The three walked around the city, over the Tower Bridge, and along the Thames. They had contemplated an art gallery or a museum, but there was no time for that. The day was sunny, and so it didn't matter. London was putting on its best face for them.

The sun was slanting down toward the west when they took a cab back to Heathrow and headed straight for the international departure lounge. Sam was the last to pass through the metal detectors. A plangent alarm rang out. A couple of security guards converged on him and ran their hand scanners over his body. The alarms went off when they passed over his left side. Helen held her breath. It seemed like the sword's concealment wasn't perfect.

Sam extracted the roll of parchment and handed it to the guard, who ran his scanner over it. Again the alarm went off. Sam unrolled the parchment and the guards looked at it. He explained something to them; what it was she couldn't hear: she wasn't allowed to come close enough. Still, whatever it was he told them did the trick. One guard even broke his stiff style and smiled at something Sam had said. The parchment was returned to Sam and he came over to join them.

"What was that all about?" Rita asked curiously. "What triggered the alarm?"

Sam shrugged negligently. "A drawing I picked up." He showed it to her.

"Where did you get this?"

Sam sighed and considered her for a moment. "You don't want to know."

"I don't?"

"Trust me."

Her eyes narrowed. "This doesn't have anything to do with," she gestured, "all of this?"

"It does."

"Would you lie to me if I pushed it?"

"Definitely."

Rita's face closed up. She turned and walked away. Sam looked at Helen and grimaced. Together they followed Rita along the endless walkways. By the time they'd arrived in the gate area, Rita seemed to have dismissed the matter from her mind. They sat down in a cafe and chatted about inconsequentialities. Above a set of tables nearby hung a large TV screen, relaying the current BBC schedule. Several people sat around it in arm–chairs.

Their attention was diverted away from their conversation when the news reader uttered the words "bus horror massacre". Apparently the police had pulled out all stops on this one. The perpetrators had been located and surrounded by armed police and special units. A telephoto shot of the confrontation highlighted the reality behind the reporters narrative. The scene was one of chaos. Events proceeded with dizzying suddenness. A bunch of figures clad in black emerged from a house and charged the cordon of police, waving swords, apparently oblivious of the complete uselessness of such weapons. They were met with a hail of gunfire, which slowed them down, ultimately killed them, but not before several had reached the cordon and—and here the clip was censored—started hacking into the offenders. Two of the policemen had been beheaded, another three died of the wounds they received from what the reporter called "drug–crazed freaks".

Helen heard a gasp from Rita. "Oh my God! Were those the guys who came after you?"

Helen nodded mutely and concentrated on the TV.

"How did you manage to get away?" Rita whispered.

Helen glanced at her. "Sam did the driving," she said.

Sam turned his head. "Nine."

"What?"

The reporter said "nine".

"Shit! That means there's…"

"…two more out there," Sam completed.

"Are you sure about 'nine'?" She prayed that he wasn't, but he nodded.

"They'll get them soon enough," Sam said. "They are like fish out of water. They couldn't function here any more than we could…"

He stopped himself. Helen remembered Rita, who was regarding them with wide, puzzled eyes.

"There's stuff here you have told anybody, isn't there?"

Sam sighed. "Yes—and we're not going to either."

"Why?"

"Because we don't want to end up in a lunatic asylum."

"Sam? What happened to you?" Rita whispered.

Sam's face was oddly tender. "Please don't ask."

Rita leaned back and looked from one to the other. Finally she nodded. "It must've been something," she said to Sam, "if it freaked you out like this."

"It was spooky," Sam admitted, but would say no more. He was right. Despite everything, despite the evidence mounting up—now existing in the form of nine dead bodies that would surely give the forensics people more than just fleeting headaches—this was not something she wanted to talk about either.

Mercifully, Rita dropped the subject. The news returned to other items—some not really any less disturbing; just further removed. For the participants in the dramas depicted no doubt just as traumatic.

Departure time approached, and presently they were herded onto the plane. When the 747 finally charged down the runway Helen found that she was breathing somehow more freely—and when it took to the air she thought that maybe, just maybe, she shouldn't worry about the two remaining freaks, as yet on the loose somewhere among the misty hills and moors of the West Country.

Helston

He heard that the astunos—'police' to use the local term—had killed nine of the Minions, but the thought afforded little comfort. The remaining two were still at large. Quite sufficient to accomplish their task. The others had sacrificed themselves for their mission. Attention would have been diverted for long enough to help the remaining two to get away.

They stood out with their size, of course. As such they would have to be much more careful than he, who was ordinary in so many ways. Still, they did not have his inhibitions. They would extract whatever knowledge they required from whoever happened to be close. Between them, they probably already knew more than he—despite their otherwise inferior intelligence and somewhat sluggish disposition.

But did they know that the two Bearers had discovered Gladius' ability to hide? He had felt the power surges accompanying its metamorphoses. It implied that the Bearers were of a curious and intelligent disposition. This would make it easier for him when he finally confronted them with the truth.

A nagging element of doubt occupied his thoughts; for he sensed that Gladius was distancing itself from him at a great rate. From his relentless investigations so far he concluded that they had boarded an 'airplane'—a vehicle capable of flight! and were heading home, across the ocean. So far away! How would he ever find them? The land on the other side of the water was as immense. How could he possibly...

This was a strange and frightening world. So much colder than Seladiënna! The people had different concerns and worries. History had proceeded very differently here—not necessarily for the better. Though there was no Plius, there was also no Diënna—and how could a world without someone like the Diënna possibly be a world worth living in? So cold, so stark, so grim. More orderly, regulated. The strange vehicles on the roadways and streets: propelled by mechanisms he only dimly understood. Those whose minds he had melded with knew little of such technicalities.

The smells in particular occasioned not inconsiderable discomfort. The inside of his nose was irritated by the acrid fumes, his head ached from the noises, his mind was awhirl with the pace of life. In the larger cities—the larger ones so huge that his mind at first refused to accept it—everything would be magnified several times over. If he wanted to enter these places—and enter he must if he was to follow the Bearers to where they lived—he had to prepare himself for the worst. He needed more information! As reluctant as he was, more people would have to suffer unconsciousness and, albeit transitory, discomfort, in order to help him proceed.

Above all now, he was hungry. He scanned his acquired memories and found the place he was looking for. He looked around him but as yet he was not prepared to find his way through this little town.

A man passed by him, moving with swift strides.

"Excuse me." The words came hard and clumsy, but they sounded right. Thus might speak a man foreign to this place.

The passerby halted and turned around. He was a middle–aged individual with thinning hair, a pair of tired, red eyes, and, like so many others, he wore garments whose colorlessness was almost oppressive. In Seladiënna color was a given—excepting

Plius's Minions, who eschewed color in favor of their black armor. The new elite troops serving Laurentius Augustus also wore this grim garb, which make Mirlun shudder each time he laid eyes on them. The darkness radiated from them and slowly seeped into the hearts and minds of Seladiënna, and one day maybe even the Diënna might find herself at a loss to fight this inexorable trend.

Mirlun straightened. Two moons less two days. That's all the time he had to find the Bearers, persuade them to his side, and bring them back to the intersection. Doubts and vacillation must be suppressed: the goal was all that mattered. On this he must focus, no matter how tired or frightened or confused he might be.

He took a breath and smiled at the man before him. His lips and tongue labored with the strange intonations of this unfamiliar language, as he carefully enunciated his request for directions to the tavern of his choice.

5

Coming home.

It wasn't as Sam had anticipated it two weeks ago. A return of sorts, to familiar faces, places, and activities. Yet everything was different. It didn't even look the same. The cause for this, Sam realized with a small shock, lay within himself. *He* was different: not Dale or the hangar or his house, of his clients, or even the helos, which stood silent and waiting in their hangar, poised to leap into the air at his touch yet again.

A touch of melancholy adhered to it all. He came home to a definite close on his past. Harry was gone from his life. Rita, after a final hug at the airport, had said goodbye with an air of finality.

As for the rest…

Sam took Helen to the hangar the day they arrived back. She had never been here; had avoided it like the plague, like she had avoided everything having to do with Sam. Now she had become a part of his life and so he introduced her to the objects of his passion—though they had, he realized, been suddenly displaced from the top rung. Which probably meant that he wasn't quite as dysfunctional as he used to be.

"What are you smiling at?" Helen wanted to know as he pushed open the hangar door under the watchful eyes of Jackie, who had been temporarily left here on her own, with Dale needing all his hands for a roundup that day. Jackie and Sam knew each other well. Despite not being a dog–person, Sam had even developed an affection for the animal. Maybe Jackie sensed it, because she seemed at ease with him. Now she stood a couple of steps behind him, watching alertly as he opened up the building she'd been guarding for the last two weeks.

Sam turned to Helen and kissed her. "Because you're here," he said simply. He took her hand and made an expansive gesture at the hangar. "My babies."

"Wow!" Helen stared. People always did. The sight of a couple of almost identical helicopters, lined up precisely, like he always did, inside the hangar—where they looked much bigger than they did out in the open—that always got them.

"I say it again: Wow!"

He tugged her into the hangar. "Want to go for a ride?"

"Try and stop me."

His face hurt with the grin. He was so content he just couldn't help it.

"Help me push Suzie out."

" 'Suzie'?"

"This one here. The other one's 'Meg'."

"Girls?"

"Unstable girls."

"Huh?"

"It's a long story. All about donuts, really."

"Now you've got to tell me."

"Well, it's like this…" As they pushed Suzie out into the open, he did.

She laughed. "And what if a girl's doing it? The metaphor kinda breaks down."

"I could suggest some tweaks."

"You have a dirty mind."

"That's far enough!" he called.

They stopped pushing. Sam went around the helo and pivoted the auxiliary wheels out of the way, so that the skids made contact with the concrete. As he straightened he looked right into Jackie's watchful gaze. The animal had backed off to a respectful distance as the strange–looking object had come crawling out of the hangar, and now stood there in a position of readiness, eyeing Suzie with attentive suspicion.

Sam hunkered down and held out a hand. "C'mere."

Carefully, circumspectly, Jackie sidled closer. Sam patted her and did something he knew she liked behind her ears. The dog relaxed a trifle. Sam patted her again. "Good girl. Thanks for looking after my babies." Jackie wagged her tail, less tense, but still alert.

Sam stood up. "Pre–flight," he said to Helen, "and then we're off."

It came to him, sometime after the circuit around the hangar, as Suzie was flying over the expanse of Sam's ranch, that he had been an idiot. The notion appeared as he noticed the *absence* of certain familiar thoughts that always accompanied him when he was in the air: especially the one about ending it all with a last *bang* against some hill–face. In hindsight that was so abysmally dumb that it didn't even bear thinking about. Of course, a couple of weeks ago it hadn't seemed dumb, but perfectly sensible. He liked to think of that epoch as 'B.H.': 'Before Helen'. Amazing really what it took to make a guy see sense.

Helen was suitably impressed by the ride. She didn't say a word, but he could see that she just drank it all in and how the magic just zapped her into submission. When he had sat Suzie down on the landing area outside his house she looked positively disappointed.

"What do you think?"

The rotors were spinning down.

She shook her head. "Where've you been all my life?"

"You asked me that before."

"I'm asking you again."

"For the last year, right in front of your nose."

She looked at him sideways. "Do you know just how totally horny this has made me?"

"No—but if you say so…"

"I do." She pulled of her earphones and reached for him, pulled off his and dropped them between the seats.

"I think we'll skip the post–flight," he said, his voice sounding strange.

"Whatever that is," she agreed, "I think we should."

"Yeah."

It was amazing that they made it into the house. Well, not quite 'into'. Out of the sun. Just.

She looked beautiful against the clear blue sky as she straddled him. The New Mexico sun, poking around a corner of the house, imbued her hair with a halo of bright gold, and cast the contours of her body into sharp relief with clearly drawn shadows and highlights.

She looked down on him. "And now, Sam Donovan, you can fly me back and we'll do it again at the other end."

He reached up and pulled her face down to him. "Payment for services was never this gratifying."

"Just wait until I get you to teach me."

"Are you sure?"

"Try to stop me!"

Stop her? Who would even *think* of stopping her?

The following three weeks were amongst the happiest in Sam's life. He was doing things he loved doing: flying; teaching a new, eager, and remarkably apt, student; and just getting to know Helen. Every hour not engaged with activities that required them to be apart they spent together. Though she didn't move in with him 'officially', his house had become 'their' house, and was referred to as such.

During the second week they had their first 'fight'. Not that it was a novelty: they had, after all, fought many times. But this one was the first 'A.H.' fight, and as such notable. As was to be expected it was over a piece of trivia—and more designed to get rid of steam than anything else. It flared suddenly—as their previous fights had—and died just as quickly. They made up in a most satisfactory manner that occupied the entire night, and promised each other that, no matter how hard they fought and over what, they'd keep it *clean*.

Helen, never having been in a 'long–term' relationship wanted to know more about the boundary between 'clean' and 'dirty'.

"Did you and Frances…"

"Yes. I suspect it happens in most marriages. That doesn't mean it *has* to happen, but it does. People forget who it is they're married to—you know, the person they were in love with, the one they were never going to get tired of, the one they swore to honor and blahblahblah…" He sighed. The memories were not pleasant. Behind them, he knew, lurked the reason why Frances, in the end, had walked out on him: why she had chosen to blame him for Katie's death and the subsequent death of their relationship.

He pulled Helen closer and wondered if *they* would avoid getting to the point where you looked at your lover and suddenly saw not the lover, but a 'partner'—which was a giant step backwards as far as Sam saw it. The fact that the word had entered the vernacular, at least among those past their mid twenties, as a trendy, politically–correct, and ineffably pretentious gender–neutral substitute for 'husband' or 'wife'—or even 'lover', 'boyfriend', or 'girlfriend'—was surely symptomatic of more than just the vagaries of linguistic usage. In some ways 'partner' was *more* than 'lover' or 'girlfriend', and certainly not as loaded with semantic baggage as 'wife'—but on the other hand it detracted from whatever had started it all; made it into a tacit admission that even a relationship such as he and Helen had right now was ultimately a socio–biological thing, and that these amazing and giddy feelings they had for each other were just a ruse to initiate some serious pair–bonding.

He'd been there and seen it happening. Participated—against his will, but still as a matter of choice: because the alternatives were too grim—and because Katie needed a family and because Frances deserved his commitment.

True enough, just as it was true that kids might well hold marriages together, and that the re-focusing of a relationship on the new arrival was a biologically sensible thing. The problem was that somewhere along the line the romance was usually lost, to be replaced by more 'mature' considerations in which 'partnership' substituted for 'romance' and 'sensibility' for upwellings of feelings that didn't make sense and didn't need it either.

But why accept substitution, just because it seemed like the thing to do? because most people did it automatically, like pre-programmed robots—which, if one accepted the socio-biological paradigm, was *exactly* what they were.

But here and now, at this instant, Sam was conscious of another truth. He didn't quite know how to label it—if label it he must—but it went beyond biology and pheromones and pair-bonding and evolution and socio-biology. It had something to do with that profound joy and happiness he felt just because Helen was *there*. Something he'd never known before: with Frances or anyone else. It was vast like the spaces between the stars; and scary like he'd felt when floating in the ocean during a survival exercise, when he'd suddenly been aware of all that unfathomable depth below him. It overwhelmed him with it irresistible and undeniable presence; left him breathless and dizzy—and sometimes, like now, it made him almost want to cry.

"You all right?" She raised her head to look at him. "I didn't mean to bitch like that."

He laughed. "I'm fine." He took a deep breath and stroked her back. "And I didn't mean to be a pain-in-the-ass." He ran his hands lower and rested them on her buttocks. " 'Clean'," he said, "is when fighting basically is just about letting off steam. Like today, when you just weren't 'getting' it, and you were pissed-off, and someone close had to get it. And I was pissed that you didn't get it either, because I think it's all so damn easy, but it isn't, and I know that and I shouldn't have been pissed. But we all have our 'down' times when we get nothing right, and then you get to scream at each other over a piece of trivial shit like we did."

He kissed her. "And you've got to make up," he said. "Always. Without emotional blackmail, without conditions, or crap like 'if you do that again'. That's 'clean'. 'Dirty' is when the fight's for power over the other; when one's trying to get an emotional advantage; when one sulks to 'get even'; when there *any* desire to 'get even' for anything at all. Harboring grudges. Stuff like that. That's 'dirty'." He smiled. "You've got to trust. Always."

She was very serious. "We won't fail."

"That's the plan."

"It's more than a plan, Sam."

"I know."

"I mean it! I'm staking my life on this. 'Tomorrow' *means* something now." She hesitated. "We *are* talking about our future, aren't we?"

"We are. To be honest, I haven't thought about the future much, except in terms of…" How could he say this? *Should* he? What would she think of him?

Honesty…

She was waiting.

"Except in terms of just when I was going to run Suzie or Meg and me into a hillside and have it all over and done with."

Somehow she didn't seem surprised. "And now you're not." It wasn't a question.

"Now I know how dumb that was," he said. "Or maybe how clever I was *not* to do it." His gaze roamed her face, from her eyes down to her lips.

She smiled and brought her face so close to his that the tips of their noses touched.

"I think you were *very* clever," she whispered.

Of course, there was the matter of the sword and what happened in Cornwall. The news–value of the affair had waned as was the wont of these things. The remaining two killers had apparently not yet been caught, though Sam was in no doubt that the police were still searching frantically. He wondered how they had managed to hide so effectively. They knew nothing of this world: this much could be deduced from the stupid way in which they had confronted the cops. So, what did the remaining two know that the rest hadn't? And where were they?

Sam and Helen were no wiser about the 'why' of the whole affair either. The sword in its 'disguise' was always with them. It wasn't the kind of thing you risked leaving lying around where someone might steal it. Whatever its purpose, it was important: this much they knew. It had been given to them, if for no other reason maybe than to be held in trust for some unknown future purpose.

It couldn't really be anything which involved *them*, of course! There wasn't anything they could possibly use the damn thing for—except to slice'n'dice big men dressed in black armor. All of which didn't sound like much of a use, and their possession of the thing assumed an air of pointlessness. Maybe, thought Sam, they should just bury it somewhere safe, and let it be done with. Maybe they would do just that soon.

The Harry–thing was a no–thing. It was unfinished business, but that's where it stayed. Harry was back in town—this much Sam had established by calling his office—but he also made no effort to get in touch. Which, Sam reflected, was probably the best thing. After what had happened what *could* he possibly do to make up to Harry?

ADLER, however, raised their ugly heads, just over two weeks after Sam's return. The debacle with their first emissary—now in the hospital wing of the county jail awaiting trial—had stalled them for a period, but not for good. While they hadn't dared to approach Sam's house yet, they finally targeted his mailbox, which was near the road, about a hundred yards from the house, and to which during the dark of one night, someone nailed a sign with a crudely painted black swastika, on which perched a scrawny eagle from whose talons dripped blood.

The legend underneath the artwork proclaimed:

**THE DAY OF RETAILIATION IS NEAR YOU
YOU ZIONIST SCHWEIN**

Spelling was not their forte. Nor was their sense of style.

Helen was not amused.

"What if they get more daring?"

She was right, of course. This was just the beginning. They would get bolder as time went on.

What were they likely to do next? Try the hangar again? Go for him personally? Or—and here his blood ran cold—go for Helen? For they would know that she lived with him. They would draw the inevitable conclusions. If they could not get at him directly, Helen was the obvious target of choice. Terrorist logic.

Despite this he tried to ease her apprehension.

"Bullshit!" she stormed. "Honesty—remember?" She was devastatingly beautiful when she was angry like that.

He sighed. Why did she have to be right?

"I'll have to do *something* about them," he admitted.

"We."

"What?"

"*We*. You and me, both."

"This is…"

"Not just your fight anymore," she snapped.

He raised a placating hand. "You're right!"

"Of course I am," she declared, calming down already. "Got any idea what to do?"

"It depends on how nasty they want to get."

"Frank Ricci?" She'd told him some time ago that she knew.

"I don't want to do that."

"What if they don't leave us with any choice."

"Ricci is a drug–dealer."

"So?"

Good question…

He took Helen into work and elicited a promise that she was going to wait for him to pick her up. Then he returned home, flew Suzie back to the hangar, and spent the next couple of hours on the web, fishing around for ADLER related stuff.

He was in the middle of tracking down another possible web–link to European neo–Nazis, when he suddenly looked up and saw a man standing in the door to his office cubicle. He had appeared without a sound and was looking at Sam with a fixed and penetrating stare. His age was difficult to guess. Appearances indicated mid–forties, but there was something about the eyes that suggested much more. The face was gaunt and tired, thin–lipped, with a sharp nose. He wore a pair of denims and short–sleeved shirt from which protruded a pair of thin, sinewy arms.

"What can I do for you?" Sam asked.

The man considered him for another moment, then spoke with deliberation.

"You are Sam Donovan."

Quite without volition Sam's hand crept under his desk to the Beretta sitting in a holster attached to the underside.

"I am," he agreed. "Who are you?"

"I am Mirlun," his visitor declared. "I have come across the ocean to find you."

The name rang a bell, but whatever it meant remained elusive.

'Come across the ocean?' Who talked like *that*? But Sam's hand withdrew from the

Chapter 5	97

gun. Whoever this guy was, he wasn't ADLER. With a swarthy complexion like that? No way!

Sam got up and indicated a chair.

"Please."

The man nodded and sat down without taking his eyes of Sam.

"And what did you come to see me for?" Sam asked.

"To ask for your help."

"Help? With what?"

"The Diënna needs you."

"Pardon?"

"They are almost here. You will need help. The sword alone will not be enough."

Sam stopped breathing.

"*What* did you say?" he asked sharply.

"I know that you know how to make it change," the man calling himself 'Mirlun' said.

'Mirlun'?

'Merlin'?

Merlin!

No way!

Yet he sat down again and considered his visitor from a new perspective. 'Mirlun' tolerated the inspection with equanimity.

"Tell you what," Sam finally told him. "There's someone else…"

Mirlun nodded unsurprised. "She, too, is needed."

"Ah, yes." Sam cleared his throat. He reached for the cordless phone. "If you'll excuse me for a few moments…"

He took the phone outside the hangar and dialed Helen's number.

"You wouldn't believe who just showed up at my doorstep."

"Who? Harry?"

"No way. Someone much more interesting."

"You gonna tell me?"

"Merlin."

"Huh?"

"You heard me."

"You said 'Merlin'."

"I did."

Silence at the other end.

"He knew about the sword," Sam amplified.

"What??"

"Exactly. Look, can you get away from there?"

"I can try."

"Good. Get me someone who can clear me for using the helipad, will you?"

"Wow! The red carpet."

"I was thinking more of speed and safety."

"You're a darling, you know that?"

"I love you, too. Now, for the helipad…"

He finally managed to get hold of the right personage. The matter was remarkably simple. A credit card number to charge the fee, a booking, the rest was up to him to clear with the appropriate authorities controlling the airspace over the city. Sam filed an emergency flight–plan, after some hum–ing and ha–ing managed to receive approval, and presently guided Mirlun to Suzie.

His visitor eyed the helo fascinated attention.

"This…object…it *flies*?"

"It's a helicopter," Sam said.

Mirlun narrowed his eyes and froze in a pose of deep thought. It lasted a few seconds, then his eyes focused on Sam again. "I understand. And you are a…pilot."

"Exactly. A helicopter pilot."

"Interesting."

"We are going to pick up Helen now."

"Helen…the woman!"

"She's 'the woman' alright," Sam grinned. He shook his head. This thing was becoming seriously weird again. He'd kind of hoped that the whole affair with the sword might just go away if they left it for long enough.

Surprise, surprise—you didn't really expect that to work?

Not really…

Sam shrugged and proceeded to install Mirlun in the helo, then climbed in himself and started up the engine. He used his cell phone to tell Helen to expect him in no more than twenty minutes. Probably less. She promised she'd be there.

When Suzie lifted off the ground Mirlun turned white as a sheet. Within a couple of minutes or so, after nothing terrible seemed to have happened, he relaxed visibly. Sam admitted to himself that he admired the guy. If he was from…over there…he must be a bewildered man indeed. That he managed to find Sam and had come here all the way from *Cornwall* was astounding beyond compare. Whatever this fellow knew or could do, he was a man to be reckoned with. The quiet demeanor could not gloss over the fact that he had done things Sam probably wouldn't have been able to. Just to think of it: the sheer volume of—to him *new*—information required to do this; the *money*; the tenacity; the relentlessness. He'd even gotten himself a *passport*!

He eyed his passenger with increased respect. Now, about five minutes into the flight, Mirlun was already fully adapted to the new situation. He watched the terrain passing underneath with keen interest—and as the city came into view and the center with its tall buildings reared below them he merely nodded as if all of this confirmed something he'd already known.

Sam cleared the last leg of his flight path and presently set Suzie down on the helipad atop the building housing among its tenants the advertising agency Helen worked for. Near the access stairs, holding onto a handrail, stood Helen, waving at them. Sam glanced sideways and saw Mirlun smile. Contentment; like that of a man seeing that he had finally reached a goal he'd worked toward for a long, long time.

Suzie sat down. Helen came running and let herself into the back seat, strapped herself in, fitted the earphones over her head, and finally took the time to take a good, long look at Mirlun. He smiled politely and bowed his head. "I am Mirlun, and I am honored to finally meet you."

Helen glanced at Sam and smiled. "A man of discernment and manners," she chuckled, and extended her hand, which Mirlun took and held for a moment, as if in contemplation. He smiled again, almost beatifically.

"Now I have hope."

Sam shook his head. "Let's find somewhere quiet to talk."

He sought clearance for takeoff, received it, and presently they were on their way to Sam's house, where, so he hoped, everything would be explained.

Everything.

Probably not. But *some*thing would be nice.

6

Mirlun's tale prompted Sam to retrieve his copy of Gibbon's *Decline and Fall of the Roman Empire* from the bookshelf and to have a good look at it. The first thing he realized was that he should have done it before. He would have found an explanation for the odd sense of familiarity he'd felt when he saw the armor of those Mirlun called 'Plius's Minions'. *Lerica Segmentata*, the segmented suit of armor worn by Roman soldiers for centuries. A somewhat modified version, to be sure, but the origins were unmistakable.

Piecing together what Mirlun related to them, and comparing it to what he could get from the *Decline and Fall*, there emerged a strange story of…what? Parallel worlds? Worlds lost in time? World split off from the one they knew? Who could tell?

Somewhere, beyond occasional strange veils of fog, there lay another Earth. It actually *existed*; not just as the stuff of fantasy, but somehow, inexplicably, it was *there*. Or maybe not so inexplicably—but explanations would have to wait; right now more immediate concerns pressed on them.

Earth 2. Not very imaginative; certainly used before; but useful nonetheless. *E2*. As opposed to *E1*, which they currently inhabited.

"There were animals?"

"Not those they knew from their home," Mirlun said. "There had been, it seemed, no domestication. The people the Legion found lived as primitives. Dirty, eking out a meager living from the land. Hunting in the forests and on the hills. As we once might have lived."

'The Legion'…
How it all began.

During Hadrian's last years, the emperor dying of a diseased heart, his brain preoccupied with paranoid schemes to keep his imagined enemies at bay, he gave an absent-minded order to send a legion from the then-Londinium to quell a minor rebellion in that region of the British Isle now known as Cornwall. Had he been in his right mind, he would have realized that a legion was overkill and that a couple of heavily armed cohorts could have done the same job. But Hadrian was not a well man and his judgment was lacking. So, a legion, under its commander-in-chief, the *Legatus Augusti Legionis*, Gaius Flavius, and led by their *Praefectus Castorum*, a certain General Marcus Antonius Cassius, set off to crush the pathetic rebellion in the west.

The four-thousand-odd strong legion presently arrived at what Sam concluded must have been the location of today's city of Plymouth—said to be the center of the uprising. Approaching it from the north, proceeding down the Tamar valley, they encountered a bank of a strange dense fog. Scouts were sent ahead. They returned, reporting that it appeared safe to proceed. The auxiliaries were sent ahead to attract the enemy's attention, if such there was to be. Nothing happened. The legion proceeded. The fog grew thicker, then vanished with unnatural abruptness. Marcus Antonius Cassius noted that just under half his legion, the rear portion, had literally disappeared from the face of the earth. His half of the soldiers found themselves in a place that looked like Cornwall—if one ignored the heat, which was more like what one expected from the shores of the Mediterranean. They encountered no rebels, though the scouts claimed to have found tracks that suggesting that there might have been not too long ago. Cassius sent dispatch riders back to Londinium, only to have them return soon after with the astonishing news that they couldn't find their way back.

Over two thousand Roman legionnaires, auxiliaries, and support personnel found themselves stranded in *E2* with no idea of where they where, what had happened, or what to do next. It was a testimony to their general's spirit and flexibility of mind that these men survived. Indeed, they provided the most important injection of human stock into what must have been a world where evolution had simply neglected to invent man. Still, an extensive and methodical searching of the countryside revealed the existence of several villages and small towns with people who, after the language barriers had been overcome, had the strangest story to tell. No stranger than the legion's though. They, too, had been stranded, usually as individuals, over the years. By some incredible good fortune some of them had survived and formed tiny communities which had begun to grow very slowly.

Cassius was a rational man, under no illusion about their predicament. He dismissed his commander-in-chief's suggestions that they had somehow died and gone to the fields of Elysium, and hypothesized instead that they had simply been transported to another world, significantly different from their own. All things considered an incredible feat of mental agility—and one that happened to be perfectly accurate.

Over the years that followed Cassius and his men effectively took over the whole of Cornwall. He had an firm grasp of population dynamics. He also had the ruthlessness required to draft the few existing women into becoming breeding machines, to produce as many children as possible with as many different men as could be arranged. Cassius, a homosexual who was impotent with women, sired no children himself. But he selected one of his captains—a certain Lucius Artorius Magnus, who was a prodigious breeder, and sired more children that he had any right to—as his successor. It was a inspired choice. When Cassius died Magnus took over the leadership of the army—which still operated under Roman law, and whose rare defectors were dealt with summarily and decisively—and the reins of power in general.

On this basis was founded the empire which almost two thousand years later encompassed the British Isles—which were no isles in *E2*, but connected to the bulk of the continent—and all of central Europe, reaching even across the Alps and as far south as was sensible. Nobody really wanted to live in the jungles of the south, though expeditions found occasional pockets of humanity, brought there by what their inhabitants usually considered grim misfortune. But the rulers of the empire had no interest in these pathetic remnants. They maintained their grip on their subjects, which were plentiful, distributed over a number of flowering cities and possessed of a blooming culture. The empire was called 'Seladiënna', which derives from the phrase 'Selina Donna', or 'Selina, the Lady'.

Sam procured a physical map of the British Isles and Europe which he'd bought for their recent trip and spread it out before Mirlun. Their visitor nodded and drew outlines with his finger.

"Here," Sam gave him a pencil.

Mirlun drew outlines over the continents. About some he was firm, less certain about others. Still, it appeared that almost two millennia of culture had resulted in a fairly accurate mapping of coast lines and other geographical features.

Looking at Mirlun's drawing, Sam reflected that other things but evolution had diverged: geological features, sea levels, climate.

And what about diseases? If people got caught in these transit areas—which seemed to spring up at random all over the place—and went across to *E2* (or maybe came *back*? did that happen? *had* it happened?) they would have taken diseases with them and exposed the inhabitants in the other world. The history of colonization was replete with populations wiped out by epidemics that were harmless to those who brought them: colds, influenza, measles. How much worse would it be in a world that knew no human habitation? Unless, of course, such outbreaks partially accounted for the sparse population of humans the Legion found when it made the transit. If new arrivals brought disease, population growth could be severely retarded. At the same time the populace would build up resistance. The germs carried by subsequent arrivals might not prove quite as devastating as those of their predecessors.

Sam filed away these considerations for future reference.

The capital bore the name of the empire: 'Seladiënna'. It was located roughly where on *E1* lay the city of Torquay, in south–west England.

"What year is it now—in Seladiënna?" It was the first time Sam had spoken the name aloud. It flowed off his tongue with ease.

"One thousand eight hundred and eighty four," Mirlun replied. Sam could see that it took some effort to translate his system of numerals into theirs.

Sam looked at Helen. According to his calculations the year of the legion's 'transition' must have been have been around 117 A.D.

She nodded. "Time flows at the same rate in both worlds," she said. She'd worked it out quicker than he had. He'd noticed that before: she could do things with numbers he needed a calculator for. Should have been a mathematician maybe. Indeed, Helen had a lot of talents. Her photographs and her paintings, a couple of which now hung in the lounge, were compositions possessed of an incredible vitality and impact. The agency must love her—but the truth was that she was wasted there.

In the empire, Marcus Antonius Cassius and Lucius Artorius Magnus were revered as divine beings. Magnus in particular attracted the people's imagination when, some years after the death of Cassius, he made the mistake of actually falling in love with a certain Selina, one of the women he was bedding for the ostensible purpose of procreation. As legend has it, she died in childbirth; though the child, a girl he named Lucia, lived. Magnus was so distressed at his lover's death that he was about to take his own life—but then a water sprite…

Here Sam interrupted the flow of Mirlun's tale.

"Water sprite?"

Mirlun nodded.

"That's like...what? A nymph? A dryad?"

Mirlun's face assumed an air of concentration. Sam guessed that he was searching through his recently acquired 'memories'.

"I don't know what those are," the Seladiënnan admitted.

"Incorporeal life forms," Sam supplied. "Said to be attached to bodies of water, trees, whatever."

Mirlun nodded. "Water sprites are like that. Their bodies are ethereal, though they have certain powers which exceed those of mortal men." Mirlun frowned. "So it is true..."

"What?"

"There are no sprites in this world. I have attempted to sense their emanations—but there's...nothing..."

"That sounds about right," Sam said wryly.

'Water sprites'...

Next thing, Mirlun was going to start with the Lady of the Lake!

The water sprite caught the still–roaming spirit—essence, soul, bio-plasm, whatever—of Selina, and thus effectively *became* her. This was the origin of the bond between Magnus and the one who was known to be as 'La Diënna'—translating into 'The Lady'—after whom an empire would be named. Unfortunately, the sprite, like all of their kind, was bound to a body of water whence she originated: Loe Pool—or, to be more precise, it's counterpart in *E2*, which was about twice the size of the one they knew.

Since the Selina–sprite was incorporeal, Artorius Magnus' relationship with her lacked a certain physical component—though it was said that the ecstasy of their spiritual communion was even more satisfying than their previous, more physical, encounters. When Artorius finally died, it is said that he did go to the fields of Elysium, but alone, for the sprite could not follow. This was the ultimate tragedy of Artorius Magnus. But he left his sword—*Gladius Magnus*—in her care, thereby imbuing her with a part of himself, guaranteeing her persistence of form and purpose even after his death. The sword was to be guarded for all time, only to be given on a temporary basis to those who might be needed to save the world he had helped to found; those worthy enough to wield it. For such a time, he predicted, would come. It always did.

Maybe, thought Sam, people *did* make the reverse transition. It all sounded a lot like the stuff of Arthurian legend. Lady of the Lake. 'Artorius' Magnus. 'Mirlun'.

Maybe a distorted form of this story, was carried back to *E1* by one or more dazed and confused individuals who had made a reverse transit, and gave rise to some of these legends. Even the 'round table' was in there: Magnus was in the habit of extensive and frequent consultations with his chief officers, during which he used a circular table to emphasize the equal value of the counsel of those assembled. As for the Holy Grail: the Christians had probably done their thing—as they always had.

It all made a crazy kind of sense.

The Seladiënnan Empire spread and filled with people. Where once there had been a few thousand, there now were millions. The continuing trickle of people from *E1* into *E2* contributed to keeping the legend of their origins alive. Stranded travelers from *E1* were welcomed as ambassadors from their original home. The stories they brought with them of *E1* —meaning, for a long time, *E1*–Europe! were eagerly awaited and widely circulated. Almost all of them ended up being brought to *Aquadiënna* (Loe Pool), where the Diënna tried to probe their souls. This was done at her own insistence. For there was a puzzle here: why could she not 'read' the newcomers like she read every *E2* 'native'? Why could she not even 'see' them or what they would bring?

The Diënna's preoccupations were not vapid. As a melange of sprite and human, she was possessed of an intentionality that transcended mere mortal lives. She was also clairvoyant and therefore labored under the grim foreknowledge that *Gladius Magnus* would have to be retrieved from its watery hideaway one day, to fend off an unknown threat to everything Seladiënna was. The nature of that threat however remained elusive, even to her. What the sword could possibly accomplish to avert the threat was even more obscure. Only one thing was certain: if she failed it would destroy her and the foundations of what made her world different and—despite all human folly— good. Seladiënna was not Elysium—nothing *could* be! but it was a better world than her lover had known: something terribly precious and infinitely worth preserving.

The sprite who was also a woman knew that one day a man would stand at the edge of *Aquadiënna*—gaping at something he or she simply did not comprehend—who would threaten everything Cassius and her beloved Magnus had built. Salvation from this threat would be found with two others—a man and a woman—whom she must find and bring here.

At this point Mirlun paused and regarded them significantly.
Sam shook his head. "Us? Hardly."
He glanced at Helen, who looked as puzzled as he did.
"There must be a mistake," she said.
"The Diënna does not make mistakes," Mirlun said emphatically.
"Why would she think it's *us*"'" Helen wanted to know.
"Why? Not even the Diënna knows. But she *sees*. And she has seen that your arrival, your actions, your very presence, *will* save her world from Plius." He shrugged. "There is no 'reason'. There is only the knowledge that certain events will precipitate others. The absence of such events will have different consequences. This is what the Diënna sees, what she knows—and this is why she needs *you*!"

The Diënna watched and waited. Over 1800 years had passed since she had lost Magnus. From across the ocean she sensed tremors of many new arrivals.

Sam interpolated: *E1's version of the North American continent suffered a wave of transition events, which on occasion involved significant numbers of people, some of them quite possibly in the machines of their times. Maybe even war–planes and ships. Most of them would have found themselves on a wild continent, climatically radically different to their own; maybe populated by a sparse population of descendants of transited North–American natives and no organized civilization in sight. The continent would have absorbed them without much of a trace. Whatever culture they brought with them, most of it would have washed away like a tear in rain.*

It sounded plausible enough. The twentieth century had seen many strange disappearances, some of them now a firm part of established folklore and urban legend.

In *E2*–Europe, Seladiënna had reached another peak of cultural development, teetering again—as it had done several times over recent centuries—on the brink of a gentle, but inexorable slope of decline. The scales of the seemingly eternal power struggle between the *Senatus* (a popular council consisting of 634 elected members, serving sometimes as a governing body, sometimes as a council and legislature) and the *Praetor* (the figurehead—his powers alternating over time between nominal and near-absolute), had swung back in the direction of *Praetor*ial rule, with the *Senatus* relegated to running the imperial bureaucracy and making sure that the *Praetor's* decrees were realized. Republican feeling was at a low ebb. The people seemed happy to exist under the benevolent tyranny of one Oldecus Pistor, who had been in office for several decades and, given the longevity of Seladiënnans—the average age at death for a Seladiënnan was about 115 years, the maximum life span being about 160 years—would probably remain there for another few more. The *Praetor* became 'emperor' again.

Then, in 1985 A.D. 1868 in Seladiënna—Diënna's dire premonitions were finally realized.

Three strangers from *E1* had arrived, together with a peculiar vehicle from the other world: two men and a woman, the mate of one of them. The other's mate had died of injuries sustained during the passage. The Diënna's clairvoyance told her that at least one of these people was the one she had to fear. Since her clairvoyance seldom worked with newcomers from the other world, this must surely be significant! Maybe, she wondered, all three should be killed outright. That way she could be sure to have eliminated the threat.

But then she remembered the other part of her visions, and she knew that killing them would simply not work: the one in question would live, no matter what she did. Such was the nature of her confidence in what she saw. She may or may not have been mistaken in this, but she was convinced of her rightness, and so she let them live.

Fifteen years later Oldecus Pistor, though still *Praetor* by title and emperor in fact, was like soft putty in the persuasive hands of his two chief counselors: the men who had arrived at her pool that day. The *Senatus* had been reduced to a bunch of public service functionaries. The legions were being equipped with new shiny black uniforms that struck terror into anybody watching them exercise. A new spirit was afoot; a cloud of darkness lay across the empire. Expansion was in the air, though it was difficult to conceive where *to*. There never had been enemies to conquer: the land lay open, awaiting settlement; the worst enemies had been natural contingencies and the internal strife inevitable in human society: even this one. An empire was always in danger of fragmenting. Hence the continued existence of an army.

Oldecus Pistor's counselors seemed to favor expansion to the west, across the ocean. A strange goal if there ever was one.

The Diënna had the soul of Selina, a gentle woman, who saw in her beloved Magnus the traits of a man of peace; no matter what he did; and she believed that he wanted peace if at all possible. Her attendants, sequestered in a small temple beside *Aquadiënna*, brought disturbing reports of strange new goings–on; of summary law, of the construction of an arena at the outskirts of Seladiënna, where criminals were to be made to provide spectacles for the populace. She remembered what Magnus had told her about old Rome—and the implications of what she heard terrified her.

Then came the news of the death of Oldecus Pistor's wife and son. The Diënna had 'seen' that something terrible was going to happen, but specificity had eluded her. Now she knew. Here was the terror of her visions: the man who had recently adopted the name 'Laurentius Augustus', and who was now heading the destruction of her world. She was certain of it when he contrived to have the two who'd come with him executed on charges of treason. She summoned her chief attendant, who had given up his true name to assume the titular appellation 'Mirlun'. She explained what had to be done and done soon—for the time of crisis was fast approaching, and Plius was growing stronger by the day.

'Plius'?

Even Mirlun paled under his swarthy complexion when the name was mentioned.

Marcus Antonius Cassius and Lucius Artorius Magnus had been no peaceniks, but they also had no taste for war. As professional soldiers they understood that war kills people—and as things stood now they needed as many people as they could possibly get. So they tried to discourage martial activity among all but those selected to be soldiers. Their descendants—encouraged by the sprite with Selina's gentle soul—inherited that ideal, and Seladiënna, though an expanding entity, did so without too much fighting. After all, there weren't a lot of people to conquer. Expansion was the conquest of the land, not the indigenous inhabitants. At the time of the arrival of the man who would become Laurentius Augustus, only about 2000 men were at arms, though these represented a definite elite. In many ways they were more as a homage to Cassius and Magnus than a necessity. Civil policing was done by the *astunos*, a police–force independent of the army.

Even before Laurentius' arrival there had been those who opposed what they perceived as the thinning of the Roman martial spirit. They formed a clique whose name, *Plius Filii*, translated into *The Sons of Plius*, held secret meetings in dark nooks or behind carefully closed doors or windows, practiced peculiar rituals involving incantations to newly–invented or resurrected deities, and festered and brooded for centuries. Their first leader, one Maldecus Orosius, died of a mysterious disease, which seemed to eat him from the outside in as his skin grew purple and yellow blotches that festered into bleeding pustules, until he screamed with the pain and cursed everybody in and out of sight for inflicting this upon him. When he finally died— under the sword of his lieutenants who decided that they couldn't stand his presence any longer—his spirit, just like that of Selina, was captured by an eager entity who effectively became Maldecus. This spirit, too, was associated with a body of water near the northern edge of what corresponds to *El*'s Cornwall, *Lacus Draconis*, so–called because of its curious outline, which, when viewed from a jutting cliff on it's eastern shore, suggested to imaginative viewers the head of a dragon.

Soon, the lieutenants who had assassinated their obnoxious, fatally diseased, leader felt themselves irresistibly drawn to this place. One by one they were horribly killed and disfigured by what lurked in the lake. The only one left alive, one Gaius Darius Petulatus, who had refused to join in on the murder of Maldecus (though he hadn't seen fit to prevent it either—which however seemed not to unduly offend the incorporeal Maldecus), was to become the first follower and *sacer* of *Plius*, as the new entity chose to call itself.

There soon grew a cult, which eventually counted among its followers up to five percent of Seladiënnans. This was a minority, but a significant one, because those attracted to the cult inevitably were made up of individuals whose discontentment, boredom, or inclination toward criminal mischief more than made up for their lack of numbers. Plius became a powerful presence that even the Diënna had to reckon with. He was kept in check, but only with difficulty.

The situation was unstable, and when Laurentius appeared on the scene that stability collapsed. He increased the number of soldiers to almost 4000 and had them assume certain civil functions, outranking the astunologia. Laurentius also embraced Plius and his Minions, and soon became their leader—as much as he was soon *de facto* leading the empire, helped along by Plius' exertions on his behalf. However—so Mirlun interpolated—Laurentius also knew full-well that Plius needed him just as much as it was the other way around. They therefore made a pact: Plius' assistance for the eventual goal of the adoration by most, if not all Seladiënnans. This is what he wanted: adoration and control. It was all a sprite could ever want; the highest goal it could aspire to. Adoration, worship, veneration was a validation of the sprite's existence. The Diënna was not exempt from such motivations, but hers were more benign. Plius' were at best parasitical, at worst destructive.

Plius, being a sprite and therefore basically immortal—barring certain unpleasant, but unlikely, contingencies; the same that might annihilate the Diënna—appeared happy to take the long-term view. He wanted to dispose of the Diënna as expeditiously as possible. But Laurentius knew that terror alone would not persuade Seladiënnans into changing their allegiances. Unless he could actually *destroy* the Diënna, other measures had to be considered. Laurentius took the first steps toward instigating the necessary changes.

Sam sighed. "Let me guess. A dash of terror; an appeal to the basest possible motives and appetites of the lowest common denominator component of the populace; suppression of those actively opposed; making sure that those who speak out are silenced—murdered or 'disappeared' if necessary; clandestine eradication of the opponent's power base; lowering the general level of education, without being too obvious about it; control of the media; provide ample distractions to satisfy the people's appetites for the lurid and the sick. "

"It is much as you say," Mirlun agreed.

"The tactic is well known," Sam said. "History is a never-ending litany of its application. Later I'll show you how they do it in this country today."

Laurentius' next goal, the Diënna knew, was to get hold of *Gladius Magnus*. As long as it existed and the Diënna had it under her spectral wings, people would look to *her* as the mouthpiece of their beloved Lucius Artorius Magnus. This was apparently immutable: the power of the legends of Magnus and Cassius, and the stubborn belief that the Diënna had some sort of monopoly on their wisdom and left–over moral code. The removal of the physical symbol of that association was vital for the furthering of Laurentius' and Plius' plans. Plius wanted the sword even more than Laurentius. It would instantly transfer powers that had never been his, and at the time deprive the Diënna of one of the foundations of her existence.

"And this is why she needs you."

"She is mistaken."

"She sees the possible futures. I, who carry her with me, can do the same. It helped me find you. This and the trail left behind by *Gladius Magnus*."

"You carry her with you?" Helen echoed. "How?"

"The Diënna is a creature of *Aquadiënna*, just like Plius is one of *Laco Draconis*. The waters are their substance. We, her servants, drink the water, and so it becomes the water in our bodies, and thus the Diënna is with us, and so she sees what I see—just like the Minions carry Plius and he sees everything."

"She knows what you know?" Helen asked.

"Everything."

"But you do not know what she knows?"

"I am not the Diënna—thought I sometimes sense her wishes, and her urgency, which drives me on."

"By that logic," Sam pointed out, "as time passes and you replace the water from the Pool with normal water, the connection must grow weaker."

"It does. Already I feel it fade. By the time I reach the intersection I will be alone."

"The intersection?"

"The place where we may make the transition. It will appear..." he picked up the map and ran his fingers over it, until he came to a place somewhere in northern Spain. "Somewhere here," he said.

"That seems a big...vague," Helen remarked.

Mirlun nodded. "When I am close to the location, at the time of the intersection, I will be able to sense it. That much of the Diënna should be left to me."

"How do you know even approximately where it will be?"

"The Diënna knows. But she only knows the place in *my* world—and I have no notion of what it is like here; or even exactly where." He leaned back and closed his eyes, sat quietly for the space of a few breaths.

He opened his eyes again. "*Amici*, I am fatigued. Please allow me to rest."

Helen got up hastily. "Of course. You poor man! We never thought..."

Mirlun waved her apology aside. "Do not! I thank you for your patience."

"It is you who was patient!"

He shook his head and somberly considered them both. "My world needs you. This is a fact. I will do whatever is necessary to make you understand that. Your patience is what matters—for it is *I* who is petitioning *you*."

They showed Mirlun to the guest–room. He regarded the bed with longing.

"Rest now," Sam told him. "Tomorrow we will talk some more."

"Thank you."

Sam and Helen turned away.

Sam stopped as if he'd run into a wall. A persistent subconscious nagging, with him since Mirlun had told them…something…whatever it was he couldn't remember…now it had finally stimulated a critical thought.

"Wait!"

Mirlun turned around.

" 'Laurentius Augustus'?"

Mirlun nodded. "This is what he calls himself."

"They came about fifteen years ago? Sometime in the early spring?"

Mirlun's eyes fixed on Sam's face. "This is correct."

"Laurentius…do you remember his real name? The one he gave when he came there? Was it maybe 'Lawrence'—or 'Larry'?"

"You *know* this man?" Mirlun stood frozen with shock.

"His companion," Sam continued, "the male: his name was 'Clint'?"

"I believe it was," Mirlun whispered.

Sam took a deep breath.

"I don't believe it. I don't fucking believe it!"

"What is it?" Helen grabbed his arm. "Who *are* these people? How do you know them?"

Sam looked at her. "Larry Unterflug. Wife: Shareen. Clint McDermott. Wife: Darienne." He glanced at Mirlun. "The surviving woman: she was called 'Darienne'."

Mirlun nodded mutely.

"Sam!" Helen's grasp on his arm tightened. He put his arms around her and hugged her tightly. He almost couldn't bring himself to say it. Even just *thinking* about it was nearly too much.

"In 1985," he said, his voice sounding strange to him, thick as it was with loathing and foreboding, "Larry Unterflug, Clint McDermott, of ADLER fame, and their wives disappeared in Cornwall. They were never seen again—and the world was a better place for it."

A sharp intake of breath told him that she understood. Over her shoulder he looked at Mirlun.

"It appears that some things just don't go away so easy."

He turned to Mirlun. "It appears that there *is* a connection here after all."

7

One of the many things Sam liked about Helen—*really* liked! was that she had an extremely high PCI, or 'Personal–Contact–Index'. It was Sam's half–jocose attempt to quantify something most people would have considered unquantifiable. Human interactions defied quantifications. This was especially true for individual ones. Larger numbers might behave in more statistically significant ways, but Sam realized that what he'd done was probably scientifically ludicrous. Yet, he could not help but wonder…

Sam had invented the notion of 'PCI' one night when he and Frances lay in bed, a few months after Katie's death, and neither of them could sleep, but they weren't talking either, and things were going downhill fast. Her PCI was zero by then. Negative maybe.

That night Sam had looked at the women he'd had relationships with—pre– and post–Frances—in terms of their PCIs. As might be expected, PCIs tended to be highest during coital nights. PCI computation on such nights started after post–coital activities had ceased, no more activity was forthcoming or intended, and everybody basically just wanted to go to sleep. On non–coital occasions PCI timing started after the last 'good–night', or whatever other ritual preceded the decision to forthwith cease wake–time activities like talking and to go to sleep. The formula to compute it was simple: divide the time spent in any–but–accidental physical contact during a sleep–period by the total length of the sleep period. The result was a number between zero and one. One was best. It meant you maintained some sort of physical contact throughout. Zero was terminally grim. You might as well sleep in separate beds. Or get divorced. Which Frances had.

PCI tended to peak in the early stages of a relationship. After that it was all down–hill, with varying degrees of decline. Frances' and his had been stable at something like 0.1 after their initial courtship—possibly less on non–coital nights—then declined further to an average of maybe 0.01 before Katie's death. This he had computed in hindsight, but he was quite confident that his estimates weren't too far off the mark. Rita's score after a couple of months had dropped to 0.2, and on their last night in Helston it was maybe 0.1—and given that that night had been definitely 'coital', that was pretty miserable.

Bed manufacturers made a mint out of partners' low PCI.

Avoid Roll–Together!

How much science had gone into making beds roll–together–proof? What a waste of effort! What a damning reflection on the nature of human relationships! No doubt *some* people's sleep activities were severely deleterious to their bed–partner's welfare, but in order to make an industry out of avoiding 'roll–together' the thing had to have epidemic proportions. A plague of I–want–to–sleep–with–you–but–not–too–close. Sam, on the other hand, was a high–PCI kind of guy. Close to one. He didn't mind being woken by a lover's sleepy–time antics. The closer together they were the better. Arms and legs entangled, on top of each other, tucked in here and there, back–to–back—it didn't matter. Even on stinking hot nights when he lay there sweating, hoping for relief from the relentless swelter—even then…

It wasn't a terribly macho thing to do, and he wasn't really the touchy–feely kind; but there was something fundamentally, profoundly intimate and fulfilling about not just sharing a bed with someone, but also sharing some area of skin.

Being a high–PCI individual in a world of low–PCI people was stressful. It meant holding back something very important and intimate—after the first few months' high of passion and pair–bonding activities anyway. Something missing, leaving a nagging, unfulfilled void somewhere. Nothing truly terrible, but it wasn't pleasant. Sometimes he'd wondered if maybe he was pathologically abnormal. Maybe this was a fetish of some kind. An aberration from a 'healthy' behavior pattern. Something akin to co–dependency. Unresolved traumas from his deprived early–childhood days coming out as this need for night–time physical contact.

Until Helen.

He'd been apprehensive and gun–shy about that aspect of their being together. Trying to figure out where she fit in. Worried about what would happen when the PCI timer kicked in.

He needn't have worried. Helen's PCI was way up there with his own.

Why? Maybe she suffered from the same traumas. Maybe she was just not as chronically–low–PCI as the rest of the human race. Who knew? Who cared? Her presence was a release from a subtle but oppressive tension that had been with him for as long as he could remember. She liked being close, sleepy–time or not. On a couple of occasions he'd noticed that, after having become 'detached' during their sleep movements, she'd muttered something incoherent and wriggled close to him again. Like you pulled your pillow into position. Pushing herself until she fit nice and snugly against him. In the morning she had remembered nothing of these episodes. When he'd talked to her about it she had become very serious.

"I guess I just *like* being close to you. I don't know how it could be any different."

He'd talked about it then. About Frances and being married, and how a lot of things sort–of went downhill, especially when Katie was on the way and after that. Mother instincts taking over and supplanting lover's instincts. Playing the 'parent' role. The whole damn pair–bonding stuff. Losing something of the really important things along the way.

"We can do better than that," Helen told him.

"It's not going to be easy."

"Let's not stop trying. I think when you stop trying, that's when it…just goes…"

It was good having her here; like always, but right now especially so. Problematic, too, because what had looked like a foregone decision—telling Mirlun that he was wrong and would he please find someone else—wasn't. Not after he found out that Larry Unterflug, who happened to have been the uncle of one of the freaks who murdered Katie and her class–mates, was the second most powerful man in an empire that spanned Europe—and about to do his ADLER–inspired worst.

She raised her head and looked into his face. "What makes you think I'm going to let you go by yourself?"

Chapter 7

"Huh?" He hadn't even said anything—yet.

"Were you going to ask me?"

"I just assumed..."

She narrowed her eyes in half-mock disapproval. "Assumed, huh? What did you say about assumptions?"

"But..."

"My life? My job? That sort of thing?"

"Yeah."

"What about you? You have a life, too. What about Suzie and Meg? This house?"

"I'll miss Suzie and Meg."

"You'll miss more than I do."

"You know this is likely to be a one-way trip."

"Maybe."

"No 'maybe'."

"The Diënna seems to know when those intersections appear."

"She may not want to tell us once we're there."

"We could work it out ourselves."

"Huh?"

"What if they're not random? What if there's a system? These people just haven't figured it out because they don't have the mind-set." She grinned. "I did some stats at college—before I decided that I didn't want to do it anymore. But I was good at it!"

"No shit?"

"None whatsoever."

"How would you go about working this out?"

She pursed her lips. "We don't have to tell the Diënna what we want. We just try to wheedle the information out of her—about as many past events as possible. Where and when. Give me a computer and with enough data..."

"Meaning we'd have to *take* a computer. A laptop I suppose. And batteries. And a charger—solar power probably." He stopped talking and looked at her. "Do you realize what we're doing?"

She kissed him lightly. "We're planning to leave this world." She chuckled. "Literally."

"It could be dangerous. Amend that: it *will* be dangerous."

"So's life here—with your lunatic friends stalking you."

"Shit!" He'd almost forgotten. ADLER freaks: infesting not just this world but another as well, like some plague from hell. Sam felt soiled just thinking about them.

"So," she whispered, "are we going to do it?"

"I'm glad you're with me in this."

"You and me both, remember?"

"We'll have a shit-load of preparation to do."

"I'm going to quit my job tomorrow."

"Sure?"

" 'We have a shit-load of preparation to do'—and I'm quoting."

He took a deep breath. Helen laid her head on his chest and it rose and fell with his breathing.

"Want to make love?" she said softly.

'Make love'. Funny expression that. It had meant a lot of different things over the period of its usage: from mere courting to sex.

But, yes, that's exactly what he wanted to do. Make love to Helen—with her, inside her, above and beneath her. Just as long as she was there.

"That would be nice," he said.

She chuckled. "Took you a while to figure that out!"

His left hand slid from her shoulder to her breasts. She raised herself on her arms so he could cup them both; made a sound of pleasure and contentment as she straddled him. Her hair hung down beside his head. She lowered her face and kissed him.

"Contraceptives," she murmured, her lips curling into a smile against his.

"Lots," he agreed.

They told Mirlun in the morning. Helen watched the man's face.

Relief!

"A world will be in your debt."

"Yeah, right," Sam said gruffly. He held up a hand. "There is a saying: never count your chickens before they are hatched. I think we should proceed accordingly."

"The Diënna..." Mirlun began.

Sam cut him short. "The Diënna knows what she knows. We know what we know."

Mirlun inclined his head. "I am at your service."

"Exactly much time do we have?" Helen asked.

"Thirty-four days until the intersection appears."

"Less than five weeks," Sam said. "Take away one for getting there, and that leaves us with four. Not a lot of time to learn your language, sell the house and the helos, and whatever else may come up." He looked at Helen and pulled a face. She smiled back, though she did feel a certain twinge of apprehension. Sam was right: it wasn't a lot of time.

"I have to go and talk to my boss," she said. "I owe him that much."

"I'll take you," Sam said. "How much time do you need with him?"

"You're going to *wait*?"

He grinned at her. "If they let me hog the helipad."

"Let me make a call." She went off and called her office. She asked for Jeff, was told by Nara that he was in a meeting.

"Until when?"

"Eleven. Maybe longer."

"Tell him I'll see him at eleven sharp."

"What?" Nara's voice conveyed her disbelief.

"Eleven sharp. If he's not there I'll leave without talking to him."

" 'Leave'?"

" 'Leave'. So make sure he gets the message, huh?"

She hung up. Maybe she shouldn't have said anything about leaving. In a few minutes the whole office would know; Nara would see to that.

Helen returned to the room. Sam was making coffee—a novelty for Mirlun, who got quite excited over it. They sat down around a table. Sam placed a writing pad in front of him and they started some serious planning.

"What do we need to take?" Sam said. "Let's just write down everything we can think of that's relevant. Then we whittle it down to what we *can* take."

Several categories suggested themselves:
1) Medical
2) Weapons
3) Tools
4) Clothing
5) Miscellaneous

Sam tore out five pages, spread them out and started filling them in.

Medical:
>First Aid kit
>Antibiotics
>Antiseptics
>Antihistamines
>Surgical instruments

Helen added 'contraceptives'. Mirlun's forehead crinkled in thought. He seemed to go into a brief trance, from which he emerged blushing.
Sam grinned. "What do you do in your world when you don't wish to procreate?"
Mirlun wasn't comfortable with the subject; this much was certain.
"I am not in a position to tell. The 'Mirlun' does not consort with women. The only ones he knows are the Diënna's attendants—and they are…" He squirmed.
"Unavailable?" Helen suggested gently.
"The 'Mirlun' does not consort with Diënna's attendants."
"Don't evade the question," Sam said firmly. "We need every bit of information we can get, and we expect that you'll provide it; whether you like it or not."
Mirlun sighed. "It shall be as you say." He paused. "There are methods for preventing conception."
"Such as?"
"Abstinence."
"I doubt that's very popular. What else?" Sam pushed mercilessly.
"Some couples practice certain…methods…which make conception less likely. Timing is often a factor…"
"…and not a good one," Helen supplied.
Mirlun shrugged. "Others avoid…" Under his swarthy skin the blush was almost a fire.
We're being cruel to the poor man.
"…contact between genitalia?" Sam asked. "They do it with their hands and their mouths? Is that it?"
Their visitor was beyond speech. Sexual practices apparently weren't really talked about in Seladiënna either.
Mirlun nodded, but said nothing.
Sam chuckled. "Maybe we can introduce some new methods to your people."
Mirlun remained incapable of speech.

Weapons:
> Handguns
> Rifles
> Knives
> Ammunition

"I don't know how to fire a gun," Helen pointed out.

"By the time we leave you will be. You'll also know a few other things about how to level the odds a bit. The only thing I'm worried about is how we're going to get this stuff into *Spain*. We can't exactly take it with us on the plane!"

"What do you want to take?"

Sam ruminated for a moment. "Three handguns. One for you, one for me, and one to spare. All the same type, so we can cannibalize one for spares if we need to, and we need only one type of ammo. 9mm Berettas I think. Rifles, in case we need long–distance weapons. No scopes. Scopes break too easily. As much ammo as we can carry."

He made another entry: 'Shotgun—sawn–off.'

Tools:
> Folding spade
> Binoculars
> Flashlights
> Swiss Army knives

"Batteries," Helen reminded Sam. He duly wrote it down.

"A spade?" she wondered.

"There's always a need to dig," he chuckled. "Trust me, it's going to be the most useful thing we take."

Clothing:
> Protective gear (Kevlar)
> Hiking boots
> High–quality socks

"It's hot there, yes?" Sam asked Mirlun. "If it's hot in England it's going to be tropical in Spain. And it's going to be summer at that."

"It will be very hot. The plains of northern Iber are parched and deadly. The jungles of the coast are humid and infested with vicious life."

Helen added 'animal venom remedies' to the 'Medical' list.

"Anybody live there?"

"There's one city. Lenos. It is outside the empire—full of outcasts."

"Outcasts? From what?"

"The empire."

"What have they done?"

"Sometimes nothing; sometimes much. Many choose Lenos in preference over Seladiënna. Life in Lenos is…different." He paused. "Laurentius has declared that

Chapter 7

he would like to see Lenos annihilated. If he does this, it may be the only virtuous accomplishment of his life."

Sam nodded thoughtfully and glanced at Helen.

Sounds like an interesting place.

"So," Sam concluded, "it's hot to warm. Meaning we won't need thick clothing. Rain and wind protection. Maybe a couple of thermals. Light stuff, which is good."

"Kevlar?" Helen pointed at the entry.

"Lightweight, protective. I know a guy who makes custom Kevlar clothing, jackets, pants, whatever. Of course it's prohibited to import them into the European Community—except as sports–gear, say for fencers—but the way Jack does them they'll never know." He thought for a moment. "A couple of flak–jackets might be good, too. Preferably camouflage colored. Or maybe black...Why not?" His eyes widened. "Helmets! Swords!" He wrote them down.

"Only soldiers wear helmets," Mirlun said, "though certain itinerant..." he was searching for a word.

"Mercenaries?" Sam suggested.

"What are 'mercenaries'?"

"Men—sometimes women—skilled in martial pursuits who lend their weapons and skills to those requiring them; for an appropriate fee, of course."

Mirlun nodded. "Mercenaries. They are hired by land owners to hunt down those who often steal their livestock. Some operate as scouts for the legions; others do less savory work. Society unfortunately is not perfect. The astunos keep order, but underneath corruption always festers."

Sam nodded. "Surprise, surprise!" He glanced at Helen. "We will have to travel some distance. It seems to me that assuming the disguise of mercenaries has distinct advantages."

"I know nothing about fighting!" she objected.

Sam grinned. "You will by the time we leave!" To Mirlun he said: "Mercenaries usually are avoided. Am I right in this?"

"From my limited experience: yes."

Sam. "Good. Then we need swords—and I'll have to find someone to give us some very fast and very intensive training." He paused. "*Gladius Magnus* will remain concealed once we re–enter Seladiënna?"

Mirlun nodded. "Until you make it appear. Then it will retain its true form."

"We can't 'un–appear' it again? Like it does here?"

"Seladiënna is its home."

Miscellaneous:
    Hand–held communication devices
    Digital camera
    Batteries for all equipment
    Battery charger
    Backpacks
    Tent
    Canteen
    Currency

"A laptop is too big and fragile," Sam declared. "It won't last."

"I need something that'll run a stats package!" Helen pointed out.

"A laptop's too fragile. We need something smaller. A QTel maybe. It's small and light and the batteries last forever. You can hide it and put in a padded box so it can be knocked around."

"*And* run the stats packages?" she retorted.

"You don't need a stats package," Sam said. "All you need is some software that takes in a sequence of space–time coordinates and predicts the next member."

" 'All'?" she echoed.

"Yeah. We'll contract someone to write one for you. Shouldn't be too hard."

She didn't exactly like the idea, but she could see Sam's point. A laptop, plus batteries, plus recharger: that was a lot to carry around.

"I'll see what I can do. Maybe…" She was almost going to say 'Harry could help', but stopped herself. Sam knew anyway and gave her a crooked grin. She shrugged. "I'll try."

"Good. Next item. Digital camera? What for?"

"To record stuff. If we ever manage to get back we might want it. A few high capacity memory sticks should do the job."

Sam turned to Mirlun. "Money. What do you guys use for money? A civilization like that won't function on barter alone. There've got to be taxes, a unified currency of sorts."

"Dinars," Mirlun said, "copper, bronze, silver, and gold." He extracted several coins of varying size and material from a pocket and laid them on the table. They picked them up and inspected them.

"A gold dinar is worth twelve silvers," Mirlun said. "A silver is worth twelve bronze, who are each worth twelve copper ones. A silver dinar is a fair price for a good horse under most circumstances."

Sam inspected the coins. "We'll have to get someone to do some forgeries."

Helen looked at her watch. "Shit, I've got to go!"

Sam got up. "Your air–taxi's ready and waiting. Clearances already procured."

"When did you do *that*?"

"While you were having your shower."

She looked at him and felt strange and warm all over. "You are a useful man, Sam Donovan."

He grinned at her. "We aim to please." To Mirlun he said, "make yourself at home. We should be back soon."

Mirlun opened his mouth as if to say something, but then shut it again. Maybe he guessed that they needed to talk alone, and that this was their excuse for doing so.

He inclined his head. "I await your return."

Suzie lifted off and headed off toward Albuquerque. "You're not going get this kind of service where we're going," Sam said dryly as he righted Suzie. He requested a flight path clearance and corrected his course before glancing at her again.

"All a bit unreal, isn't it?"

"Four weeks seems rather short to organize all this," she admitted, because it was. "And how you expect me to learn wielding a *sword*…"

Sam laughed. She loved it when he laughed like that. It gave him a boyish air that was absolutely charming. Not that he needed it. He had her hook, line, and sinker. This was just a bonus.

"I know a guy…" he began.

"You know a *lot* of people," she broke in. "For an antisocial fellow like yourself that's pretty amazing."

"I did a job for the SCA once. Jack's their master–at–arms. He does fight choreography for movies and stuff like that. He's also into iaijitsu and other disciplines. Wields a very lethal sword."

" 'SCA'?"

"Society for Creative Anachronisms. They like to dress up in medieval garb, re–enact scenes from the period when knights were valorous and damsels chaste, and every now and then go at it with real swords."

"They fight?"

"Mock fight."

"Strange people."

Sam laughed. "Not as strange as you and me—and that wiry fellow from 'Seladiënna'."

She fell silent. He was right, of course. She was losing sight of just how totally *weird* all this was.

"Four weeks to learn sword–fighting, a language, even their writing!, shooting, and what else? *Four weeks?*"

"We'll make a schedule," he promised.

Yeah, like that was going to help!

"It'll help," Sam said.

She glanced at him. He couldn't have! But then, she sometimes knew damn well what he was thinking, too.

"Four weeks," she muttered.

He patted her leg with his free hand and left it there for a few moments. The warmth of his palm seeped through the fabric of her trousers and with it came something soothing her anxiety. Somewhat anyway.

"I don't know how I'm going to feel acting the Amazon mercenary," she said. "Silly, probably. Like I was drafted into some stupid movie."

"Yeah." He sounded thoughtful.

"Are you worried at all?" She knew *she* was!

"I'm concerned. About you mainly. I don't want anything to happen to you."

"How do you think I feel? I have this image of you wading into the thick of it all at the first opportunity!"

"That's just Harry talking." He chuckled. "I'm really quite a careful guy."

"Please be careful for me."

"That's my intention. I'm not going there to commit suicide. I just want to terminate Larry Unterflug's delusions of imperial grandeur. The man's a disease that's got to be eradicated."

"Just don't get yourself eradicated in the process," she said darkly. The very thought opened a dismal void inside her. Their cause was noble, and she had a sense that this was very much what she wanted to do as well. It gave life a dimension of meaning that went far beyond anything she had ever known. But all that paled into insignificance before what she had with Sam. If she lost Sam in the process...

She glanced at him sideways. He noted her regard and winked at her before focusing on flying Suzie again.

Would Sam get carried away with this quest of his? Was he the kind of guy who needed that kind of external validation of his existence, giving it purpose and meaning by wading in and saving everybody else, and maybe killing himself in the process?

"I'm not."

Her head snapped around. He wore his crooked grin.

"I'm not going to kill myself—and I'm going to make sure you're not going to be harmed. There's nothing more important than that."

"How did you know what I was thinking?"

He chuckled. "You're a woman. You're in love. You don't want to lose me. Harry's told you a lot of shit about me walking into trouble and doing the thinking later. What else could you think?"

He shook his head. Suzie made a beeline for the helipad, which was about a mile ahead.

"I'm not like that," he said. "I know I can't fix the world and rid it of its evil–doers. But I can try to do *something* to halt the spread of this...infection. Maybe it won't work, maybe it will. But I know, and you know, that we've got to try this."

"And after that?" she wondered. "Another quest?"

Sam grinned. Under his deft touch the helo circled the helipad, faced into the wind, and began to set down on the target cross.

"After that I'd like you to stop using contraceptives for a while."

Wow!

Suzie touched down, settled on her skids. The persistent whine of the rotors—audible, albeit muffled, despite the noise–filtering earphones—climbed down the scale.

She started at him. "Sam, I..."

"If that's what you want, of course," he said. "*Only* if that's what you really, really want, too."

"I do."

"Good."

The rotor noise was dying down. Sam took off his earphones and gestured for her to do the same.

"Something else." He seemed hesitant. Embarrassed even. Shy.

She didn't know how, but suddenly she *knew*.

'Wow' again!

She leaned over and kissed him.

"I would like *that*, too."

"Are you sure you know what you're agreeing to?" His eyes were dancing in his head.

"Are you sure you know what you're proposing?"

"I'm *proposing*. Period."

"And I accept."

"Registry office?"

"Sounds good to me. How long does it take to get a marriage license?"

"Too long."
He looked happy. She kissed him again. "I better go and see Jeff."
"I'll be here."

Sam watched Helen disappear down the access stairs. He hadn't actually *planned* to propose like this—or propose at all! but suddenly it seemed just right; and it was what he wanted. A formality maybe—but they'd go to Seladiënna as husband and wife, as lovers, as brethren–in–arms. No half–measures. No provisos. No hedgings.

Helen disappeared from view. Sam pulled the cellphone from his jacket and searched its directory for Jack's listing. He found it and dialed. Ten minutes later he had pinned Jack down to a firm schedule for the next four weeks. Three hours a day. He was, as Jack pointed out, very lucky. It happened to be a slack time between engagements. Fate, thought Sam, was dove–tailing things nicely.

Do I really believe in that shit?
Did I believe in parallel worlds a few weeks ago?

This whole affair was fairy–logic in action. Only an idiot could ignore the uncanny synchronicities at work here.

Jack prodded for more details about what lay behind Sam's sudden urge to make himself and his girl–friend into sword–fighting experts.

"You're not involved in some really weird shit, are you?"
"What's 'weird shit'?"
"Well, the SCA is strange but they're not weird. But there are some folks who like to go the whole hog. Invitation–only tournaments with real blood–letting. Maybe deaths."
"You're kidding."
"No. It's the next level up from illegal boxing. These guys are like gladiators—except they do it by choice. Get paid a shit–load of money, too."
"And they get hurt."
"Yeah. Badly. The things are usually organized by rich bastards with money dangling out of their assholes like piles. They can even afford their own doctors and private clinics—so nothing ever gets out when some cut–up would–be gladiator's brought in with his chest carved open or his arm missing."

With weird crap like that big freaks on black horses almost make sense...

After making the call to Jack Sam sat for a while, staring at the phone. Then, with a sigh, he looked for another number, found it and dialed.

"Hello?"
"Can I talk to Frank?"
"Who are you? How'd you get this number?"
"Tell Frank it's Sam Donovan."
"Sam who?"
"Donovan."
"What do you want?"
"None of your business."

There was silence on the other end. Sam thought he heard faint voices, muffled maybe by a hand over the mouthpiece.

"Sam—my *man*!" That was Frank all right.

"How's it going? Business good?"

"Brisk. Moderately profitable." A laugh. "Hey, Sam, good to hear from you. I thought you'd *never* call!"

"How's Tony?"

"At *college*! Would you believe it. My little Tony at college? If mama had lived to see it…"

Sam bit back a comment. Frank was such a stereotype, it was almost funny.

"Is he doing well?"

"Yeah. Great! He'll love to hear you finally called."

"Tell him I said hello. And keep him on the straight and narrow."

"Are you kidding me? Of course he's going straight. A kid of mine at college—who would have thought."

"What's he studying."

"Law."

"Ah."

"No!" Frank said firmly.

"You sure?"

"I'm gonna make fuckin' sure."

"That's good, Frank. Really good."

"Yeah." A pause. "So, this ain't a social call, right?"

"No."

"Come to cash in some chips?"

"Yeah. I think I need to."

"Don't want to talk about it over the phone, eh? Industrial espionage and all that stuff."

"Quite."

"Wanna meet? I'd love to talk to ya. Catch up on old times."

Sam chuckled. "We have no 'old times', Frank—and what there may be you don't want to talk about."

"Yeah, well…wanna meet anyway?"

"Sure, but I'll have a hard time getting away from here."

"Where are you now?"

"As if you didn't know."

A rasping laugh at the other end. "OK, OK. I come and see you."

"That's a long way."

"Anything for Sam Donovan. I owe you big. Hopping on a plane isn't gonna make a dent in *that*."

Sam came to a decision. "As soon as you can?"

"Is it a disposal job?"

"No."

"You're still not ready to trash some eagles?"

"I'm off to hunt some. Need some assistance though."

"Shit! Really? Look, lemme get back to you. I've got some business here. Maybe in a coupla days, huh?"

"Sounds good to me."

"Yeah! Be great to see ya." He laughed. "Especially now that you're not in the 'service' anymore." Another cackle.

"See you, Frank."

"Yeah, you, too. Watch them eagles. The fuckers'll shit on you before you know it."

Sam chuckled. "Shit I can handle. It's the claws I'm worried about."

" 'Claws'? Leave it to me. We'll clip 'em soon enough."

"Bye, Frank."

"See ya."

Sam broke the connection and stared across the rooftops of metropolitan Albuquerque. He'd sworn to himself that he wasn't going to do this. Frank Ricci wasn't a nice man. Sam had lost count of the number of guys in the employ of the likes of Frank he'd helped to put away while with the coast guard.

But Frank Ricci was also a father, and a proud one at that. And Tony was the apple of his eye—and Tony was alive only because of Sam. There was enough of old Sicilian ethics left in Frank to make that into a major issue. Frank would wipe ADLER of the face of the Earth if Sam asked him to—and with the information Sam had accumulated over the years: names, addresses, hangouts, training camps...

Frank would enjoy setting his dogs onto ADLER—and make a profit besides. 'Waste not': one of Frank's favorite phrases. The weapons in ADLER's training camps alone would save Frank's organization a shit–load of money and trouble.

Sleeping with the devil...

A grateful devil, but that didn't change anything. It just meant that Sam had a credit balance.

Helen emerged from the access stairs. Her appearance worked an instant miracle on his soul, preoccupied as it was with gloomy considerations of the ethics of what he was doing. She sprinted to the helo and plonked herself in the seat.

"Quick and painful," she said.

"You all right?"

She pulled a face. "Let's just get out of here."

"He didn't like it, eh?"

"I suppose I should feel flattered. But he tried to pull the guilt–trip thing, and that always gets me pissed off. I have enough guilt as it is. Don't need some bastard trying to add his bit."

Sam touched her face. "No guilt," he agreed.

Helen smiled at him and pushed her face against his palm. She reached for the earphones. "Let's go."

On the way back he told her about his call to Frank Ricci.

"What do you want with *him*?" she asked.

"He's going to get us the illegal stuff and have it ready and waiting for us in Spain. We pick it up and disappear."

"Sounds good."

"Of course Frank still wants me to tell him to go after ADLER."

"Which you're not."

He sighed. "It's tempting, but no."

Not yet.

8

Sam spied a blue Ford sedan on the road, about a mile from his place. It was parked beside a straggly copse of mesquite bushes and it didn't belong to anybody in the neighborhood. Sam brought Suzie down and circled the car, hovered low to look inside, and decided that it was vacant.

"What's the matter?"

"I don't know. People don't generally stop here; not unless they've broken down."

They circled the Ford once more; then Sam took the helo up, heading toward the house, which was on the other side of a low, rocky hill. It was then that he saw them, creeping through a narrow arroyo, eroded out of the hill–face by uncounted years of contraction and expansion and sudden, usually brief, floods gushing down the slopes. From this distance it was hard to tell much about them, except that they were wearing sandy–to–khaki colored clothing that should have hidden them, if only they hadn't tried to find some cover as the helo appeared in their sky.

Once spied they couldn't be missed. Sam pointed. Helen suppressed a gasp. She knew as well as he just exactly who was sneaking up on Sam's house. Big guys, who probably at one time had worn black armor.

Sam thought quickly. There was no time to land and prepare. At a run they could be over the hill and down on the gently sloping other side quicker than he could set down and get Helen and himself into cover. Calling the cops was out as well. They'd never make it—and inside the house was Mirlun, who didn't seem like an match for these two freaks.

"They've adapted well," he grated. He glanced at Helen. What he was going to do?

She saw his look. "Don't mind me," she said.

He hesitated for another moment. "Hold on to something. Tight!"

The two Minions were still in the arroyo, thinking, not without justification, that they were out of reach of the helicopter.

Yeah, right!

Suzie banked sharply and swooped down onto the arroyo.

Helen gasped, and not just because of the maneuver. "They're *shooting* at us!"

So they were! With handguns. At this distance? With a lot of shit luck maybe…

Shit luck happens!

Sam banked sharply, weaved Suzie back and forth as he swooped, and came to a halt with a gut–wrenching turn right above his quarries. He couldn't see them, but he knew that the downdraft from the rotors would be creating a minor hell in that narrow confine. Dust and rocks, tiny and bigger would be zipping about like an cross–fire in a war. Even a Minion should be spooked by the noise and the pandemonium.

He was right. Underneath the two figures had clambered out of the arroyo and were running toward the ridge, slipping and sliding on the loose rocks, with the skids hovering just a few yards above and behind them. Then, as if on a command, they suddenly stopped and turned, raised their pistols—both semi–autos—and fired.

Too close! A second webbing appeared beside the one the ADLER freak had put into the canopy. Sam jerked Suzie sideways and, as they adjusted their aim, swooped back down.

Another webbing appeared.

Good! They were doing the logical thing: aiming and aiming well—at the obvious target: the cabin and its occupants. Which was stupid. The plexiglass was armored. The rotors were a much more potentially lethal target.

They were also extremely lethal weapons...

Suzie bore down on them. They separated. One ran for the ridge, the other in the opposite direction, back down the slope.

Good thinking boys!

Sam made an executive decision. One of the Minions cleared the ridge and disappeared behind it. Sam pulled up Suzie and saw him running down the slope toward the house.

"Close your eyes," he said grimly. "This is going to be very ugly."

"What..."

Suzie cleared the ride and plummeted down following the slope. The running figure weaved forth and back as it ran, aiming the gun behind him as he did. Sam saw it buck as he fired, but you generally don't hit things when firing handguns while running.

Suzie caught up with the Minion.

"Hold on!" Sam shouted. Suzie flared and slowed, tilted forward again following the running man at pace. Sam's hand on the controls tightened. For a moment he hesitated. Then he thought of a bunch of riders chasing a Range Rover with the blows of swords raining down. He bit his teeth together. Suzie was immediately behind the man. She tilted forward steeply, the tips of the rotors almost touching the ground. She lurched forward, the rotors lifted slightly, their circle intersected in time and space with the Minion's head, the high–speed buzz–saw send a red spray into the air as the head disintegrated. Helen stifled as gasp as Suzie pulled up and out of the way, came around and circled the headless corpse on the ground, lying in a pool of blood, then swooped back over the ridge and in the direction of the road—where the car was starting to pull away in a cloud of whirled–up dust and stones.

"Hold on again," Sam grated.

Suzie swooped, a predatory insect descending for the kill.

"*Really* hold on," Sam warned her.

The helo pulled over the car and dropped with sickening suddenness. There was a sharp jerk as the skids hit the windscreen. Sam jerked Suzie back up and back to inspect the effect of his action. The windscreen had shattered, the roof had a sharp dent.

"Once more," Sam warned her. Suzie accelerated ahead of the car, turned in mid flight and descended at the onrushing vehicle. In the last moment, when Sam could actually *see* the Minion's face, a stolid determined mask of mindless purpose, the guy lost his nerve and jerked the steering wheel aside.

Sam pulled Suzie up and into a turn to see the car careen off the dirt road and plough down the embankment through some mesquite bushes, only to come crashing to a halt against a hip–high boulder.

Sam banked and set the helo down with a wrenching jerk.

"You know how to fly these things!" he said to Helen, who looked at him from wide eyes. "Do it! Get it out of the way."

"What are you doing?"

"Finish it," he grated and reached under his seat for the Beretta—not the one the cops still had but the one he'd bought the day after the ADLER freak had tried to torch his hangar.

She called something after him but he didn't hear it. He ran toward the crashed car, the Beretta in a two-handed grip out in front of him, aimed at the car and its occupant.

From the car: a movement. The minion, shaking his head, still half-dazed, kicked open the door and tumbled out. Behind him Sam heard Suzie's rotors change pitch.

The minion straightened, shook his head again, looked in Sam's direction. Sam stopped dead, aimed, squeezed off a round. The shot sounded thin in the open arid air.

He missed. Surprise. At least a hundred feet. He wasn't *that* good a shot. He started running again. The minion bent down, came up with a gun of his own. He aimed and fired. It kicked in his hand. And again.

Asshole! It's a gun, not a magic wand!

Sam stopped, froze, fired. Missed. He forced himself to stay put and brought the gun back into line, fired again, this time hitting *something*. The minion tumbled, the gun fell from his hand. Shoulder hit maybe. A roar of anger bellowed across to Sam. The minion hesitated, then started running—*toward* Sam.

Sam fired again. Another hit, but it seemed to make precious little difference. Thirty feet maybe. The minion bellowed something in an unknown language: a guttural, unearthly curse. Sam saw his face. Black eyes; bared teeth, all rage and fury. He fired again, hit the minion in the chest, with negligible effect.

Twenty feet. Almost point-black range. Sam fired again, barely waited until the sights were in line, and fired again. The bullets left gaping holes in the Minion's chest, jerked him back, only to have him come with a fierce, relentless inertia. Now he was almost upon him. Sam aimed at the head and pulled the trigger. The Starfire round caved in the face: a gaping hole appeared where the nose had been. The roar became a distorted gurgle, but the body, incomprehensibly, continued to move. One hand lifted to reach for Sam—who fired again—and again—and again, squeezing them off as fast as he could. With each impact the head disintegrated more; the body jerked, though the limbs kept moving seemingly of their own accord, as if animated by some fiendish puppeteer. The hand reached for him. Sam threw himself aside. His right shoulder hit the rough ground. A pain shot through his arm, but he absorbed the impact and rolled over and back onto his feet. The gun was still in his hand. He aimed again—and held his fire, for the body with the shattered head continued on in a straight line for another two steps, then stumbled and collapsed, to lie inert as dark blood pumped from the jagged opening in the head onto the dusty ground.

Behind him Sam heard the whine of Suzie's rotors. He looked around to find her hovering maybe twenty yards above and behind him. He raised a tired hand and waved. Helen sat Suzie down on the ground a safe distance behind him, whirling dust and debris into his face. The pitch of the rotors changed as they spun down and Helen came running toward him through the dust and threw her arms around him and said his name again and again as she buried her head in the crook of his neck so she didn't have to look at the ghastly corpse on the ground.

"You're going to call the cops?" Helen wanted to know.

Sam set Suzie down on the landing area behind the house.

"I don't think so."

"But..."

He looked at her significantly. She grimaced but shut up. She knew as he knew that this was a bad idea. Still...

"What about the bodies?"

"We bury them."

"The car?"

That was a more difficult issue. They couldn't just leave it there. It was probably a rental and sooner or later it would be missed. Besides, it wouldn't be too long before one of Sam's neighbors drove past that spot and saw the car. The cops would become involved and sooner or later Sam would have a lot of explaining to do.

"Shit!" The one way out wasn't what he'd had in mind. Still, his hand had been forced.

He pulled out his cellphone and found the number, dialed and waited.

"Gimme Frank. Now. Tell him it's Sam Donovan again."

"Frank's busy."

"If you don't let me speak to Frank *now* I'm going to make sure you won't be *able* to pick up this phone again. Ever!"

A pause. Then...

"Sam?"

"I need your help. On the instant."

"Name it." Frank was all business. No chit–chat. He must've heard something in Sam's voice as well.

"I need someone who will come to my place immediately, ask no fucking questions, and take away a car that's never to be seen again. Plus whatever's in it."

A pause on the other end of the line. "I'll get you back in a few minutes. You calling from a cellphone, yes?"

"Yep."

"Don't use it again. You gotta be freaked out! What happened to the old paranoid Sam Donovan?" A siccant chuckle. "Gimme another number."

Sam did. "Be there," Frank said and hung up.

Helen eyed Sam with wide eyes. Sam gave her a crooked grin. "Never say never. I had no idea that was ever going to apply to me."

He put an arm around her shoulder. "Are you all right?"

She shook her head. "No."

"Sorry.."

He hugged her to him as they went into the house.

"Mirlun!"

The Seladiënnan emerged into view. "They came." It was not a statement.

"They did."

"You killed them."

"I did."

"I knew you would."

"That's comforting," Sam said testily. "Now, if you don't mind, we have a lot to do—most of which has to do with the disposal of all evidence of what just happened—and

I need to focus on that. So just stay out of my way, because if you don't I'm going to get very unpleasant."

Mirlun considered him for a moment then nodded and disappeared in the direction of the guest–room.

Sam turned to Helen. "I'll be back in a moment." Then he went into the bathroom where he hung his head over the toilet bowl and emptied the contents of his stomach.

When he came out again he didn't feel any better, but at least his stomach was empty. Helen however still looked white as a sheet. He hugged her and held her for a while. She said nothing, but then, sometime after, he felt her shake and he knew that she was going to be all right. Not immediately—because she was a human being and she had just witnessed some truly violent deaths; gruesome beyond anything she'd ever imagined in her worst nightmares; sudden, unannounced, mercilessly clear. Worse than what had happened in Cornwall, where her life had been at stake and she'd had little or not control over events. This here had been different: more deliberate; calculated even.

Sam wished she could have been spared; but, given what they were setting out to do, maybe it was for the best. A harsh way of looking at things, but that didn't make it any less valid.

The phone rang. Sam let Helen go and picked it up.

"He's on his way."

Sam didn't ask how just exactly *who* was 'on his way' knew where he lived. It was a given that Frank would know.

"I'll meet him at the main road," Sam said to Frank.

"I'll see you later this week."

"Thank you, Frank."

"Don't mention it."

Another neighbor, Gert Thighe, drove past as the tow truck operator winched the Ford—with its contents, discreetly wrapped in some old tarps—onto the back of a large flatbed truck. Gert stopped and stuck his head out the window.

"Shit—what happened?"

"Someone came to visit me," Sam told him. "He kinda lost control."

"He all right?"

"All went well."

Never lie if the truth will do.

Gert shook his head and waved. "City slickers," he said disdainfully. Gert considered himself a 'local', despite the fact that he'd only been out here about ten years, which meant everybody else around here would *not* have considered him as such, but Gert chose to ignore this detail. He grinned at Sam, winking to indicate that he considered Sam one such as well, but maybe not totally in the 'stupid' league with the rest of them. Presently he drove off, leaving Sam to heave a big sigh of relief.

The towie finished his job, tipped his cap at Sam and, without a word, drove off in a cloud of dust. Sam returned to the house to find Helen standing at the back door, staring at Suzie.

He came up behind her and put his arms around her. She pushed herself into the embrace and leaned her head against his cheek.

"I'm sorry you had to see this," he said softly.

She sighed. "So am I."

She turned around to face him. Her eyes sought his. "I'm all right," she said. "Really—I am. I'm just glad *we're* alive."

She craned her neck and looked at Suzie, standing silent and inert on the landing pad, the canopy marked by the bullets.

"You said she was a living thing that only needed a brain. I never understood it—until…" A grimace. "You think that's what we are, too? Our bodies? Animated by some…thing—a spirit, a soul, some weird ectoplasmic ghost? pulling the strings to make us live and dance?"

"Puppets don't *feel*," he said. "They just *do*."

"My, you *are* a philosopher."

"Just enough to get by."

"I think this body needs to 'feel' something," she said.

He knew what she meant. Something other than death. Something that put death to shame.

"Come on," he said and took her hand. "We'll talk to you later!" he called to Mirlun, pulled Helen into the bedroom (not that she needed to be pulled), and closed the door. She was soft and warm and alive, and though the memories of the day were still strong and terrible, there was, in her touch and scent and taste and the sounds of her abandon, a redemption and a promise that gave everything sense and meaning and hope.

Evening came. Already another day had passed. One less day to prepare. They had dinner and started with their first language lesson. Initially Sam found it as difficult to concentrate as Helen but somehow they made it through that hurdle.

The language, as far as he could see, was basically Latin, which was to be expected. It was, however, different from the scholarly 'dead' Latin of his school days. As a living language it had undergone changes, adaptations, metamorphoses; though eighteen hundred years had left less of a mark than one might have expected. The same applied to the writing. While recognizably Roman, it had lost some of its edginess. The font had become almost cursive, gained ornate swirls and flourishes, and acquired un–Roman idiosyncrasies. How and when, Mirlun did not seem to know.

It didn't matter. The language was as it was, and they had to learn it. They went to bed exhausted, but with a sense that with this, at least, a beginning had been made.

"What a day," Helen said to him when they were alone again.

"And we haven't even really started yet."

"Don't say that!"

"Fine. I won't."

Her face was close to his, her eyes dark pools, framed by her pale skin, highlighted by the wan light from the moonlit desert filtering through the thin net–curtains.

"There's going to be more of this, isn't there?"

"Probably worse."

"Sometimes I think," she said softly, "that I've stepped into a dream—and it's all wonderful and nightmarish at the same time. What I really want of course is all the 'wonderful' and none of the 'nightmare'. But I'm not going to get that, am I?"

Chapter 8

"Not at the moment."

"Ever?"

"Maybe can chip away on the 'nightmare' stuff."

"Doesn't mean we can't have some of the 'wonderful' though, huh?"

"I think we should take what we can."

"You know what I want to do—right now?" The arm that had been draped over his neck started moving; a hand slid down his back.

"Screw my brains out?"

"You're a mind–reader, too?"

Sometimes Sam wondered just how the world looked from Mirlun's perspective. It must have been a strange place—and his reaction might well be representative of how they would in turn react when they finally were confronted with Seladiënna. Of course, Mirlun had some advantages. His ability—like that of the now–defunct Minions—to tap people's brains for just about everything they knew…that was plain scary. The notion that they were going to enter a world where there were more like him—and some even more powerful, and few of them of benign disposition—that was scary, too.

Still, Mirlun also was faced with frightening perspectives. The level of technology of *E1*'s third millennium fascinated him, and it took a lot of convincing that very little magic was involved. Seladiënna, it appeared, with the lack of a need to actually conquer other people, had persisted at a level of technology remarkably constant since the Roman days.

On the other hand, so Sam reminded himself, maybe that wasn't so surprising at all. After all, even in *E1*—particularly in Europe—the major technological advances had been made in the last two to three hundred years—and the biggest ones of those in the last fifty. Technology, apart from selected areas such as war–craft, some chemistry, and maybe precision engineering, had been remarkably stagnant, if not necessarily static. Things that had been known in previous times had been forgotten—often as results of barbarians overrunning established civilizations and destroying everything in their path—only to be re–learned much later. Others had never been known because of the lack of the technological and scientific prerequisites. The apparent lack of development in Seladiënna's technology was not entirely inexplicable.

Some curious failures stood out. For example, gunpowder had remained unknown—despite the occasional transit–events, which must surely have brought *someone* across who knew about it, and maybe even how to make it. Still, when asked about, it Mirlun professed ignorance—and he simply did not comprehend the principles behind the operation of fire–arms. Cross–bows were more to his taste: weapons of such type were known (had indeed been in rudimentary use with the armies of Rome), though conventional bows were the long–distance weapons of choice for a variety of reasons.

The Seladiënnans also had made little progress in the medical field. They had for example no concept of sepsis or its epidemiology—or of the system behind the transmission of diseases. Their notions were about as fuzzy and misguided as those prevalent during the middle ages. Plagues had ravaged the empire on several occasions.

However, it seemed that Larry Unterflug had done at least something useful. Modern ideas about germs and diseases had begun to spread, originating, Sam presumed, from

Larry and Clint, who, though dense as neutron–stars, must have had *some* idea about such matters. Only a complete moron would not have absorbed at least a smidgen of scientific knowledge.

As a result, surgeons now used alcohol to disinfect and sterilize wounds and instruments. Nobody believed the story about invisible germs of course! It had been modified slightly to become a tale of conflicting spirits—those of the infection and those resident in the alcohol. According to the new folklore the latter oddly enough were pretty much the same spirits that made a man go funny in the head if he imbibed too much liquor. It seemed that they had two faces, benevolent and mischievous.

Mirlun listened with polite interest and barely–concealed disbelief to Sam's explanations of modern biology. He expressed his reservations, convinced that scientific explanations were merely a curious set of misconceptions about the truth. After some futile attempts at convincing him otherwise Sam and Helen left it alone.

More than by science and technology, however, Mirlun was fascinated by world cultures and the current modes of behavior in the societies he'd witnessed. The size of the cities staggered him, the lifestyles were an endless source of wonder. Seladiënna, it appeared—with some notable exceptions, such as the outlaw city of Lenos—was a fairly uniform empire. After all, it had been formed by a single group of people, even though that group itself had contained a number of diverse ethnic sub–groups—especially among the auxiliaries. These had, however, mostly merged, and thus effectively become one.

Mirlun admitted that the centuries of expansion had wrought changes.

"The citizens of Minotar are different from those of Seladiënna, who in turn are different from those of Novalonda. This much is true. But they all worship the Diënna, and that makes us all one."

A cult based around a water–sprite that had endured for the best part of two millennia.

Curious—but no more curious than cults centered around local prophets and visionaries which had developed into world–dominating religions in *E1*.

Mirlun provided answers to just about anything Sam and Helen cared to ask. Occasionally he professed ignorance, but this was a rare event. On other occasions he blushed with embarrassment; especially in the early stages of his stay, and then usually when sexually related matters came up. The questions about women's underwear almost left him speechless for a while, though in the end he proved himself to be more knowledgeable than one might have expected from a man committed to a life of chastity—in body and, as the Diënna apparently insisted, also in mind.

Yes, women wore underwear. Bras even—or something very close. Indeed, the bikini seemed to have been 'in' for just about always, with only minute variations upon the theme. The first reason was simple: climate. The second, thought Sam, was equally simple: the lack of the Christian influence and its associated sexual repression, and the associated tendency to conceal sexually stimulating aspects of the body. The 'Christiani', as Mirlun pointed out, were a minor cult—started by the paltry few who'd been with the Legion—who'd hung on despite all evidence to the contrary. This evidence, according to Mirlun, was the existence of the Diënna; which clearly belied the whole Christian premise. A bunch of them had retreated to a minor town in the northern alps and there practiced whatever was left of their curious rites. In the rest of the empire they simply didn't exist.

Likewise, Islam never even had had a chance of being born. Which was just as well. Sam had little time for the repressive proclivities that religion either. Though it provided cultural contrast and diversity—which was inherently desirable—he found it abhorrent. Fanatics, no matter what their creed, were unpleasant people; and to have whole nations of them was truly scary.

The gods of the Roman pantheon—also eclipsed over the centuries by the Diënna and other, lesser water-bound sprites and entities—and occasionally a major one, like Plius, whose name meant 'Javelin'—had always been male chauvinist pigs, but at least they had never engendered the psychotic hang-ups and schizoid morality of medieval (and some contemporary variants of) Christians or Muslims. Being a woman in Seladiënna meant to be subjugated to some degree to the male, but far less than had been the case in old Rome or subsequent ages in *E1*. Female mercenaries did indeed exist! Even the *Senatus* had in its ranks a small complement of women. Females also commonly controlled the household purse-strings. Their influence varied from region to region, but it was the general pattern. The striking of women by their husbands was considered a criminal offense. Domestic disputes involving violence were usually settled by a kind of court set up to deal with minor crimes, and composed of elected representatives of the local community. Major offenses were referred to *Arbitrares Imperii*, who were assigned to the provinces by the authority of the emperor himself.

Endless things to learn. Plus the language of course. Four hours a day in intensive study. Slowly they were getting the hang of it.

"Should've paid attention in my Latin classes," Sam told Helen.

"Yeah, and you should have known *this* was going to happen, too!" Helen laughed, grabbed hold of his T-shirt and tumbled him onto the bed.

Time passed in a blur. Days merged into days. Weeks came and went with frightening indifference to their requirements. Helen knew what it meant to 'be busy'. She had worked in a high-pressure environment, with constant deadlines, panic-stations, and never enough time to finish what had to be done.

But this here was different: breathlessly so. Getting up before first light to two hours' of language lessons and Sam's endless questioning of Mirlun for more details about Seladiënna—a procedure mirrored at the end of each day. The last thing before they dropped into bed and each other's arms—usually too tired even to do anything but exchange a kiss and fall asleep, but always close together, limbs entangled, bodies fitted together. On two occasions they did, however, half-awake sometime in the middle of the night—and there was a touch and a sleepy kiss, and the tiredness gave way to a sudden rush of passion that was half dream, but not any less real.

For several hours each day they saw Sam's buddy Jack, the swordsman; two, sometimes three, hours of intensely focused sword-play. In the end Sam had opted for an Asian style of weapon and training. Jack, who had 'connections', had managed to procure a couple of modern replica *katanas* with blades almost as good as anything Japanese weapon smiths had been able to produce. They trained with bokkens, wooden swords, for hours on end—then took the real swords to cutting arm-thick green bamboo and bundles of wet straw.

Helen's arms ached, her back ached, her legs ached. Jack recommended a good masseur who managed to alleviate the worst of the symptoms on a daily basis. But then Sam took her to the hangar and she had to fire the damn Beretta until her hands and arm hurt again, and she could really have used another massage. On alternate days they also spent two hours in the dojo of another guy Sam 'knew', learning the basics of Karate: just enough to get by. Sam's acquaintances enquired about the nature of the urgency that had prompted him to draft them into these high–intensity training sessions at such short notice, but his vague replies must have left them in no doubt that the subject was to be avoided. Tactfully they did, and instead focused on getting the job done.

Then there were visits to the dentist to have old fillings replaced and any dubious areas attended to. A suspicious wisdom tooth was extracted from Helen's mouth, leaving her tongue probing for the newly created void. They had other doctors' appointments for complete physical checkups on both of them, and for her especially. Sam was right: the last thing they wanted was not to be able to get back and be stuck in some backward medical voodoo–land with a child on the way and her having unexpected complications, like that her pelvis was too narrow to accommodate the passage of a baby's head, or genetic defects that she had never bothered to investigate.

She came out of this with a clean bill of health; and that provided some comfort among the relentless schedules of the week.

Other issues were just as pressing. The marriage license had come through. They set a date: the coming Friday; between sword and shooting lessons.

"What about the wedding night?" Helen wanted to know.

Sam laughed, picked her up, and whirled her around once before setting her down again and kissing her in a most satisfactory fashion. "The night will be ours—and ours alone."

"That would be nice. Maybe we can skip the exercise for the day and exercise something else."

"You want a wedding *day*."

"That would be nice."

Sam also had a meeting with Frank Ricci: where, she didn't know and didn't *want* to either. She felt even less good about this than Sam did, but given the circumstances there seemed little way out. When Sam returned he told her that the gear he'd requested would be waiting for them.

"The debt now is paid?" she said.

"I would have thought so," Sam muttered. "Frank won't have any of it. 'You ask me to ditch a coupla bodies and get you a coupla guns? That's fucking *nothing*!' he says and laughs at me. Then he slaps me on the shoulder. 'Sam, that kid's my *life*. The only fucking thing I've ever done *right*.'" Sam shrugged. "Sicilians are a strange bunch. I don't know if they're just insane or if this blood–debt thing is some sign of terminal morality."

Frank Ricci, it seemed wasn't out of Sam's life yet. Maybe he never would be. But it also appeared that the guy was benevolently inclined. Sam did have some odd friends.

Friends.

Which brought matters back to Harry. Now there was a friend that hadn't quite worked out. Not least because of her.

Did we screw up badly here?

Sometimes she wondered. The only alternative to what they'd done would have been if, at the time of their first meeting, they'd followed some primordial instinct—not too much different really from what they'd done a year later—and jumped each other there and then. That wouldn't have gone down well either, and probably have had the same result. Agonizing over what should have been was rather unproductive, actually. The *only* alternative that would have kept the friendship between Harry and Sam was the complete suppression of her and Sam's force–of–nature like attraction. She knew now that that wouldn't have worked. Even if she'd been so stupid as to marry Harry: sooner or later she and Sam would have ended up in each other's beds—or wherever.

What a tangled web...

It was like something out of Harry's medieval fantasies, with Harry himself as the cuckolded Arthur and her and Sam as Guinevere and Lancelot, respectively. Surely, she thought, the irony could not have escaped even Harry, if and when he thought about it—as surely he must; though 'brooding' would be more like it. Harry would brood and stew and be very, very angry and hurt.

Rightly so!

The Harry–issue raised its head one day into the second week, two days before they were going to get married. She was attending to the matter of vacating her apartment. She stood by as two burly men, supervised by a wiry individual who answered to the name of 'Jimbo'—and who had introduced himself as such—were in the final stages of moving out her affairs, to have it all transported to Sam's house, where it would hardly have time to gather dust before it went—together with Sam's stuff—into a free corner of one of Dale Ashburn's barns, which Dale had generously offered to Sam. They didn't feel like just selling, giving it away, or just dumping it as yet; an indication maybe that neither was as yet prepared to concede that they might never see this world again.

Harry appeared as the movers were just about done. He'd come in quietly and must have stood there watching for a while until she finally spied him.

Helen froze when she saw him.

"That was quick," he said. "You've hardly known the guy and already you're moving in with him. You wouldn't do it with *me*."

"Harry, stop it!"

"Why?"

"Is that what you came for?"

"I came because I heard you quit your job, and I wanted to know what was going on. Now I come here and I find you're moving as well."

She saw no harm in telling him. "I'm leaving the country."

"Huh? Where you going?"

"Europe."

"What?! With Sam I suppose?"

She nodded.

"What for?"

"To...live."

Harry shook his head, totally puzzled.

"I don't understand. Sam can't stand Europe."

She said nothing. The silence grew heavy. The moving men came and carried out some more boxes. Harry looked after them, then at Helen again.

"Why Sam? What happened? You used to *hate* each other!"

He still doesn't get it!

She sighed. "Harry, we never hated each other. It's just that…well, Sam was being a loyal friend—and I was being a faithful girlfriend."

Harry said nothing, walked to the window and looked out at the men loading up the van.

"You never loved me, did you?"

"It wasn't like…"

He whipped around. "Don't lie to me!" he snapped.

"It wasn't like that," she said. "I thought I loved you."

"But you didn't."

"That's just the way it is."

"But you love Sam."

"I do."

Harry grimaced. "What the f…" He stopped as the men came in again. Harry waited with a stony face until they were gone with another couple of boxes each.

"Tell me," he said then. "What is it with Sam? Why do people…take to him like this? He's such a…he has no…future…no life…no…drive…Yet he's the fucking hero! No matter what he does, somehow he's always the fucking hero! Now he even takes my girl…"

"I was never your 'girl'," she said quietly.

"You were—until Sam came on the scene."

"Sam was 'on the scene' almost from the start."

He regarded her with that hurt–doggy look of his. "I suppose you're going to marry him, too."

"Friday."

He exhaled sharply and shook his head. "You bitch," he said softly. "You fucking bitch."

He turned and left without another word.

Sam wasn't impressed with Harry's performance. At the same time he also didn't appear overly surprised. "I knew Harry had 'issues'. I didn't realize that they were with me. Always thought that was just normal envy. He wasn't happy when I made couple of million bucks from *Eagles in the Storm*, but I didn't think it went that deep."

"I'm sorry you lost your friend."

He made a curious, very Sam–like, gesture, expressing fatalistic acceptance of the inevitable. "So am I. But I don't regret what we did."

Neither did she.

They got married on Friday afternoon, at the registry office, with Dale and his wife as witnesses. They exchanged a brief passionate kiss and took the witnesses out to an early dinner. Maddie Ashburn—a striking woman in her fifties who somehow had avoided the twin scourges of photo- and climate–aging of her face and looked like a mature thirty–something—lamented their imminent departure. Dale dropped a minor bomb–shell by offering to buy Sam's house and property, which, he said, would be a great retirement place, and anyway Sam's asking price made it into an excellent investment

Chapter 8

no matter what.

The deal was made there and then. Since Sam had never signed an exclusive agreement with any realtor and thus didn't need to pay commission, the outcome was as good as it could be.

"And if you come back," said Dale, "and you…"

Sam shook his head. "Thanks Dale, but that's extremely unlikely."

"At least you didn't say impossible," Dale rumbled.

"I gave that up a while go," Sam told him.

Everybody laughed.

"What about your helicopters?" Dale wanted to know.

"Meg is sold. I'm holding onto Suzie for as long as I can. I've two interested parties who're willing to let me use it till the last moment—for an appropriate reduction in price."

"How much do you want for her?"

"From you?" Sam took two-thirds off the price he'd asked of the others.

"I'll take her," Dale said.

"You don't fly helicopters!"

"I've always wanted to learn."

Maddie nudged her husband. "No, you're not."

Dale grinned. "Ignore the interruption. You gonna sell me Suzie?"

"Dale, I…"

"If I don't I get someone in to help me use her for rounding up. Now that you're gone…"

Sam eyed Maddie, who winked at him.

"All right," he said to Dale.

'Good." Dale reached across the table and they shook on it. "You're gonna stop flying helicopters completely? I don't think you'll last for long!"

Sam laughed. "Where we are going there won't be much use for it."

"What *are* you going to do—in *Spain* of all places for chrissake!"

"Learn Spanish?"

"You're going to be back here before you know it."

Helen felt Maddie's eyes on her. She shook her head ever so gently. "I don't think so."

Dale squinted at Sam. "I…look, don't take this the wrong way, but I…"

"Go on," Sam laughed. "I won't jump at you."

"It's just kinda insulting, that's all—and I should know you better. But," and here he shrugged and glanced at Helen, "I thought maybe with you two so serious about each other and all and maybe you're even wanting to start a family…" He stopped.

Helen guessed what he was getting at. "You think we're running from ADLER!" she said. "You think Sam's doing this because he wants to protect me!"

"It would be a sensible thing to do," Maddie said softly. "Maybe not strutting-manly—but damn sensible if you ask me. Especially if…"

"It's not that," Sam told them. "We're just…starting a new life…from scratch."

Dale guffawed. "Sounds like a pretty hairy proposition to me!" He grinned. "Your oddly secretive visitor wouldn't have anything to do with all this?"

Helen glanced at Sam who made a wry face and laughed. "I was wondering when you'd latch onto that!"

"He does, doesn't he?" Dale said eagerly.

Helen saw Sam bite back a grin. "You might say he came here to employ us."

"*Both* of you?"

"Yeah. Seems like we each bring some required skills to the job."

Helen had to stop herself from laughing. Watching Sam tell the truth without telling it was a treat.

"You're not going to tell me more, are you?" Dale complained.

"It's very hush–hush—that being a condition of the employment. I *can* tell you is that it's a kind of security job."

"Big organization?"

"Hmm, yes."

Dale shook his head and picked up his wine–glass. "I still think you're mad to leave—but mad or not, we wish you all the best." He grinned at Sam. "I sure hope it's gonna be good for the both of you." The four clinked glasses. "To the future," Maddie said.

"To the future," they all agreed.

They skipped the language lessons when they got home and told Mirlun that it was customary for newlyweds to spent the time after the event in activities that might be described as 'recreational'. Mirlun stated, quite accurately, that they had indulged in such recreation since the day he'd set foot in their house.

"Indeed," he said dryly—in English, and quite unlike the shy and easily–blushing prude who had come to them a few weeks ago—"you exhibit an unusual enthusiasm for this 'recreation'. I have no real standards for comparison, of course. The Diënna is the center of our lives and all her servants are needs chaste. She will no doubt be…interested…to observe your…" he groped for the appropriate description, "close connection." His tone didn't reveal whether he expected his Diënna to be pleased about this or if he thought she might disapprove of such un–chaste carry–ons.

Sam took Helen's hand. "Be that as it may," he said firmly, "the house is yours for the rest of the night."

"Where are you going?" Mirlun was perplexed. "Your privacy will not be violated by *me*!"

Helen laughed. "On an extremely brief honeymoon," she told the Seladiënnan. "It is another custom, and since this is probably the last breathing space we get, we're going to use it!"

The bed in the hotel was huge and they made good use of it. The walls, hopefully, were reasonably thick. If not, it certainly would have made for interesting listening.

Not that they cared.

9

Sunday.

Five days to go until departure. It still wasn't sinking in. The mind could only deal with so many things at once. With everything that was going on, even ADLER had receded into the background; especially since there wasn't any sign of activity from that quarter. Sam did his best to keep his eyes open. But it was difficult to focus. Too many things to attend to. Little things that added up to a flood. The software for Helen's QTel; finding a medical book that was small enough to take with them, yet extensive enough to cover not only the basics of what one needed to know about anatomy and physiology, but also about diseases and their diagnosis and treatment; the fabrication of the custom Kevlar clothing and items such as reasonably authentic looking, artificially aged gear one might expect of itinerant mercenaries: armor (a modified flak–jacket) and a kilt of leather strips, which had remained virtually unchanged for the last two millennia, if for no other reason but that in the prevailing heat it was the most useful of alternatives, and custom–made footwear according to Mirlun's descriptions; sun–block (which wasn't going to last for long, but they had to start somewhere); growing a beard (barbers, Mirlun had assured him, were a service to be avoided—good for gossip, but dangerous to one's health); a custom–made crush–proof case for the QTel (the protective housing was machined from Teflon and was guaranteed waterproof to 50 feet); forged coinage.

More items were added to the lists: compass; sun–glasses; more books, about stuff that you never really thought about, because it was provided by the framework of civilization—basic technology, minerals, how–to–make–or–find–X (where 'X' stood for everything from gunpowder to copper to bread), drugs, what–have–you.

How to take this information? Books were heavy and clumsy. They did, however have the advantage of not requiring high–tech devices to access.

In the end they opted for a new very expensive kind of solid state data storage, something along the lines of memory sticks, that came with a reader which plugged into the QTel. They transferred several CDs' worth of medical and other info into these devices.

Most of the moneys left over after everything was paid for were converted into gold–certificates, which, together with a DVD containing Sam's entire database about ADLER, he deposited in a safe–deposit box which required a user–code and two passwords, but no other form of identification, to access. The net value of what went into that box was almost half a million dollars. A much smaller amount went as advance payments into their credit–card accounts. By the time they left this world—literally! they would do so with a credit balance.

On Sunday evening Frank Ricci called. Helen picked up the phone, listened, and wordlessly handed it to Sam.

"Find a secure phone," Frank told him without a preamble, "and call me at my usual number."

Sam was quiet for a moment. 'Secure phone?' He didn't like the sound of that.

"Will do," he said and hung up.
"What is it?" Helen asked.
He told them.
"Is he saying the phone's bugged? By whom?"
"I have no idea."
"How?"
He held up the cordless receiver. "It doesn't take much."
"How're you going to call him?"
"Let's go for a drive."
They found a card–operated pay–phone in a gas station on the main road into the city. While Helen and Mirlun waited in the car Sam dialed Frank's number.
"What's going on, Frank?"
"You tell me!" Ricci retorted. "Whatever it is you're doing, *somebody's* interested!"
"What do you mean: 'interested'?"
"Enough to set a P.I. onto you."
"Shit!"
Who?
He paused. "Frank, how would *you* know anyway?"
"Because I know things, that's how."
"You got a tail on me?"
"Two actually."
"Why?"
"Because guys who need disposal services generally are in *some* kind of trouble."
"I can handle it."
"Yeah, I know, but…well, just in case…"
"In case what?"
"In case…whatever…Look, Sam, you know what Tony would do to me if he knew you're in trouble and he knew I knew and I'd done nothin' to help you and something happened to you? You know what he would *do* to me?"
Sam sighed.
"Besides," Frank told him, "it wasn't just those ADLER fuckers after you."
"What do you know about ADLER?"
A siccant chuckle at the other end. "Notice how they're leaving you alone?"
"You didn't!"
"Think of it as guardian angels in action."
"What did you do?"
"I didn't do nothing. Somebody else did though." Frank chuckled. "Nothing you'd disapprove of. Just enough to scare them off."
So *that* was it! ADLER hadn't forgotten about him at all. They just had some troubles of their own. Frank Ricci kind of troubles.
'Guardian angels'?
Mobster guardian angels.
It was almost funny.
"Who's the P.I. work for?"
"Don't know. Yet. Wanna know?"
"How long's he been there?"

"About a week."

"Who?"

"Ex–cop. Ex–crooked–cop, to be precise. I hate the fuckers!"

"Got a name?"

"Dan Bronowski."

"How long till you can tell me who he works for?"

"That's what I was gonna talk to you about. I know you're an ethical kinda guy and all that and you'd be pissed off if we…well…Anyway, we *could* find out in a coupla hours. Max!"

"No!"

"Didn't think so. Well, we tried his office but the info ain't there. Paranoid motherfucker."

Sam digested the implications of 'we tried his office'. The Frank Ricci thing was definitely getting out of hand.

No good deed goes unpunished.

"By the way, the stuff in Spain's waiting for you. As arranged and where arranged."

"Good."

"Have you got those packages ready for pickup?" Frank's oblique reference was to the two *katana* replicas, which they would never get into Spain legally—and so Frank's contacts were taking care of that as well.

"Yep." Fed–Ex'ed to a neutral contact address.

"Good. They'll be there, too."

"Thanks, Frank."

"Don't mention it. Hope you not gonna get dead on me with whatever it is you're gonna do. Tony'll be pissed off if you do."

"I'll try."

"Yeah, well, work on it. Anything else I can do for you?"

Sam laughed. "Frank, I think you've done enough."

"Watch the ex–crooked–cop motherfucker P.I.!"

"I will. Hey, can you get me a picture of the guy? Just so I know his face when I see it."

"Sure. I'll have someone take a shot at him."

"*Of* him!"

"I was having you on!"

"Yeah."

"And, by the way, congratulations!"

"Huh?"

"Getting hitched. Couldn't happen to a nicer guy. I hope she gives you many hot sweaty nights and sucks your brains out through your dick. Whatever you got left of them." He cackled at his own joke.

"Bye Frank."

"Watch your back!"

"I have no idea." Helen shook her head.

"Your work? Afraid you might like to jump agencies and give away their trade secrets?"

"Nah. Everybody does. Why should they hire a private investigator?"

"What," Mirlun wanted to know, "is a 'private investigator'?"

"A mercenary of sorts," Sam explained. "Hired to obtain information about a person's or organization's activities."

"A curious profession. There is a lot of demand for the services of such people?"

"They make a living."

"I wonder how a person like that feels," Helen commented. "Making it your business to invade people's privacy."

"Sometimes it is a necessary evil," Mirlun said.

"That's the usual excuse," Sam agreed.

"ADLER?" Helen wondered. "Maybe they…"

Sam chuckled. "I doubt it." He told them about his 'guardian angels'.

"You have strange friends," Mirlun said.

"You're telling *me*!"

The matter of the P.I. remained vaguely sinister, though Sam could see no reason why it should change their scheduling. At best, whoever paid the guy would end up puzzled about their bizarre activities. Shooting, sword–fighting, karate, jujitsu, the commission of strange custom–made garments and QTel software, purchases of sundry items of consumer electronics, having some odd–ball coins stamped. Something to give the P.I.'s employer something to wonder about—but surely nothing to give away the game. The truth was so bizarre that nobody would even consider it.

One hoped…

When they got to Spain, of course, they'd have to be more careful. There they would have something real to hide. Like guns! Sam wondered if the P.I. would follow—or maybe someone else take over at that end. Another level of complications they could have done without.

On the following day, in the city, Sam and Helen returned to their rental car; having sold their own a week before. As Sam turned down the sun visor, an envelope fell into his lap. It contained a shot of a man, sitting in a car. It probably had been taken with a digital camera and wasn't all that high–quality, but Sam knew that when he saw this guy he'd recognize him—unless he used some bizarre disguise, of course.

"Compliments of your guardian angels?" Helen commented.

"Good service, huh?"

The week passed. Friday arrived. What was done was done. Unfinished business would remain thus.

Dale and Maddie Ashburn saw them off at the airport. Dale enfolded Sam in a bear–hug. "Watch your back," he said. Sam remembered that Frank Ricci had said the same thing. Maybe he should make it a point to listen to the advice.

Mirlun wasn't with them. He would take a different plane, though they'd end up in New York on the same flight to Madrid. An unnecessary bit of complication maybe, but they'd arranged for it anyway.

Presently their plane took off. A few hours of peace. Just by themselves with nobody to bother them. It was possible, of course, that the P.I. was on the plane, but Sam had looked carefully and he didn't think so.

In the event they didn't talk much. This was a period of respite; a time to hold hands and just sit back and be together. Easier said than done, given the circumstances, but they tried—and, in a manner, succeeded.

In New York they met up with Mirlun who seemed glad to see them. Maybe, thought Sam, he'd wondered, just a bit, if they'd bow out of the enterprise after all.

The plane for Madrid left two hours later.

10

Madrid was a madhouse. It started at customs, where most of the Kevlar clothing passed inspection without as much as a raised eyebrow, though some of the other stuff, which must have looked like costumes for a masquerade, occasioned mildly curious queries. The fake Seladiënnan coins underwent more scrutiny, but Sam's explanations eventually satisfied the inspectors. They knew nothing of a medieval festival to be held in Santiago de Compostela, but neither did they question it.

Mirlun's fake passport—procured by him on his own when he first arrived in *El* from a forger in London—held up under inspection. The bar–code must have been genuine. Sam reminded himself yet again not to take Mirlun for granted. Here was an individual of exceptional resources and tenacity. The word 'dangerous' came to mind. Sam dismissed it: Mirlun had given them no reason to think of him as anything but a friend. Still, Mirlun was who he was. He had an agenda which appeared to coincide with theirs; but his loyalty ultimately lay with his 'Diënna', and this must be considered in all their interactions.

They had booked a rental car, a Spanish *Seat* 4WD 'Aventurista': the Spanish equivalent of the Range Rover; with a diesel engine, at Sam's request. It wasn't as luxurious as its British counterpart, but spacious enough for three people and their gear. Good road clearance. Maybe good enough for some real rough terrain. The rental agency might or might not see the car again. Ever. Just as well they didn't know that.

They left Madrid in a hurry, sometime in the early hours of the morning, after they'd finally gotten through the airport procedures. After a few hours' drive, under a blue sky, they arrived in Valladolid, where they found a hotel that accepted guests early in the day. They rented two rooms and retired. Sam and Helen flopped across their bed. Helen just managed to take off her blouse and bra, opened the buttons on his shirt and tugged it out of his pants, then crawled on top of him and promptly went to sleep, her breathing soft and even just beside his right ear. His arms closed around her, slipped down her back and into her jeans. Thus secured they remained there as he, too, went to sleep.

They stayed in Valladolid that night and took advantage of the stay to imbibe the atmosphere of Spain. It reminded Sam of Mexico, where he'd spent several years of his youth. It meant that he spoke Spanish with reasonable fluency: something that had come in useful during their language lessons.

They left the next morning and drove to Santander, arriving there in the late afternoon. The drive had convinced Sam that his fear of being followed was probably groundless. If they had a tail he was *good*. And in a foreign country at that.

They had booked themselves into the *Hotel Altamar*, a fifteen–storey establishment only a few blocks from the waterfront, with sweeping views of the Bay of Biscaye and a spacious balcony from which to enjoy it. Sam, despite Helen's protestations, left her with Mirlun and went off to find a public phone, from which he called the number Frank Ricci had given him.

A man answered in Spanish. Sam identified himself by the required code name.

The two conducted a brief, scripted conversation, which established to both parties that everybody was indeed who they should be. They arranged for a meeting on the following day, and Sam returned to the hotel.

"Looks like it's all going according to plan. We'll pick up the stuff tomorrow and drive to Ribadesella." He looked at Mirlun. "You still sense that all this will happen as the Diënna predicted?"

"It is close," Mirlun confirmed.

They went out and found themselves a nice restaurant, dined on Spanish cuisine, and presently retired to their respective rooms. The night was mild, the breeze from the sea carried only the faintest hint of a chill. They stood on the balcony and looked out over the lights of Santiago, and breathed in the scents of a city as they knew it. The stink of petrol and diesel mixed with the salty tang of ocean and maritime decay products and the melange of cooking smells from thousands of dwellings and establishments.

"I think it's slowly sinking in," Helen said softly.

He knew what she meant.

Three days...

"We can still pull out."

"No, we can't."

"Nothing's stopping us. Until we make the transit—until then we have a choice."

"Mirlun would not be pleased if we changed our minds."

"Mirlun doesn't choose for us."

"But something chose us!"

"That may be so. But until Wednesday we are free to decide if we accept the nomination."

She smiled. "We're going, and you know it. It's scary and I've got a pit in my stomach—but we're going."

She was right and she knew that he knew it.

They left the door to the balcony open, went to bed, and made love with an odd tenderness, slowly and deliberately, and never taking their eyes off each other's faces. Finally she cried out softly above him, arched her back and called his name, clamped down on him so tightly that it almost hurt; and then his own climax shook him and he poured himself into her and the spasms went on and on and didn't seem to want to end.

Afterwards they lay there, content, still locked together, their cheeks touching, their heads turned to the balcony where the lights of Santander glittered in the night and a pale moon cast a shimmer across the endless ocean.

They didn't talk.

There was no need.

The man's name: who knew? Jesús, Ramón, Pedro, Vicente, whatever. It didn't matter. They pulled up beside his van in a small alley in the harbor quarters of the city. Nothing was said. Two soft travel bags were transferred from the van to the back of the Aventurista. The man tipped a finger to his grimy cap, climbed into the van, and departed.

They left Santander on the most expeditious route and presently found themselves on the coast road west, heading for a small town called Ribadesella, where they intended to stay for the night. Somewhere near here the intersection would appear.

The 'somewhere' is what had Sam worried. Mirlun still wasn't sure.

What, Sam wondered, if the point lay over the ocean? There would be no way they could get to it in time. Everything depended on it being in an accessible place and on land.

The Asturian countryside reminded him of California. The same rugged coastline, with beaches of varying sizes nestling in bays surrounded by steep cliffs, or sprawling out just alongside the road, inviting people to come and interrupt their journeys for a while. Few did. The traffic was almost city–like. People were on their way to *somewhere*. No time for smelling the roses or getting some sand between their toes.

Just like us.

As they approached Ribadesella, Mirlun exhibited increasing excitement.

"It is close," he declared, his eyes wide, his voice animated.

"You actually *feel* something?" Helen asked him.

Mirlun nodded. "It is drawing me."

"Can you sense a direction?"

"Not quite—just a little."

"Where?"

Mirlun hesitated, then pointed. Sam heaved a sigh of relief. It looked like they wouldn't have to swim!

They reached Ribadesella, a charming little city straddling a river. It would be nice to spend a night here.

"We must go on," Mirlun declared. "That way." He pointed.

Sam looked at Helen. She shrugged. "We might as well."

Goodbye, Ribadesella…

Not yet. Sam stopped at a store selling camping equipment and purchased a small single–ring propane camping stove with a spare cylinder, cooking utensils, a plastic ten–gallon water– and a metal ten–gallon gas–container. At a big *tienda* nearby he bought *chorizos* and salami, canned beans, several sticks of bread, ground coffee, tea–bags, long–life milk, cookies, honey. On the way out of town they halted at a gas station to fill up the tank, check the oil, and fill the water and spare–diesel containers. Then they continued west, following the coast road, which wound through the verdant Asturian countryside. Small towns came and went. Most of these still exhibited traces of the charm they must have once possessed, though their character had been altered drastically by the addition of the unimaginative, functional block architecture of the newer dwellings, erected there after prosperity hit Spain in the latter half of the twentieth century.

The day progressed. They stopped for a snack at a roadside restaurant in a town called Caravia, then drove on. Presently the road approached the water and swooped into a shallow valley. On their right, the expanse of the ocean exhibited a profusion of whitecaps under the northerly winds.

"This is the place," Mirlun declared with certainty.

Sam slowed the car and pulled over to the side of the road to allow the traffic behind them to pass. A car and a truck roared past them down the hill.

"Here?" Sam asked.

"Close."

Sam scanned the countryside ahead. The shallow slightly undulating depression was dotted with the houses of *veraneantes*, summer–visitors from other parts of Spain, possibly as far as Madrid. Just ahead of them a small collection of buildings lay clustered around a bridge crossing a small stream. Beyond that, behind eucalyptus groves and coastal vegetation, the signs of a small township on the seaward side of the road.

"Maybe we can find a place to stay there," Helen suggested.

They drove another mile or so and came to a turn–off. A sign read *La Isla*. The Island. They turned down the narrow road and presently found themselves in the town—a village, really. Beside the arc of a beach flanking a bay, maybe a mile across, in the midst of which lay a rocky island, topped with a mat of green. To their right a promenade, lined on the seaward side with a row of massive ancient eucalyptus trees. A few buildings from older days, their stonework showing. Everywhere else evidence of the main income of the villagers. What once might have been a place of fishermen and farmers had become a tourist resort. Nothing on the scale of the monstrosities of southern Spain, but enough to obliterate much of what surely once have been a truly idyllic place. Sam remembered similar places from his sojourns in Mexico. The beach was loosely flecked with tourists. It wasn't quite the season yet. In summer you wouldn't be able to move here.

They drove to the central plaza of the town and finally located a pension with several spare rooms. They booked two and paid for three nights in advance. Euros were not required. They accepted just about every credit card going—with an electronic card reader hooked up to the phone. Signs of the times.

As discreetly as they could they unloaded Frank Ricci's stuff from the back of the car, carted in into their room, and inspected the goods. Frank had delivered as requested—and better. The flak–jackets; the swords; two stainless–steel 9mm Berettas with extra high–capacity magazines and a spare for each gun; two compact modified–for–9mm Glock 17s with spare mags. All guns had been modified to accept screw–on silencers, two of which had been supplied: a special, rather expensive type, not quite as effective as the use–and–discard versions with compacting steel wool, but with a complicated system of baffles to absorb some of the surplus blast. The package also contained 1000 rounds of 9mm ammunition; holsters for the guns; a bore–cleaner brush and a bottle of gun–oil; two carbon–steel commando knives with cutting edges that would do for razors; assorted antibiotics and medical supplies; three camouflage–patterned military backpacks; super–compact sleeping bags, probably military commando issue; Kevlar abdominal guards that doubled as back supports and protectors of important areas right down to the crotch; four containers of mace; six hand–grenades; two canteens; army dried food rations; vitamins; water–sterilization tabs; more bits and pieces essential for survival.

Helen and Mirlun eyed the equipment spread out over the bed.

"We're not traveling light," Sam told them, "but we can discard what's too much once we're there."

"Looks like you're expecting to go to war," Helen muttered darkly.

Sam chuckled. "I didn't request flame–throwers, machine guns, or grenade launchers. Not even a rifle." He turned serious. "Let's hope we'll never use any of this shit. But chances are we will. If Larry Unterflug is involved…"

They spent several hours getting their packs ready for immediate departure. The

Chapter 10

Seladiënnan 'costumes' they put into the pack Mirlun was to carry, together with some of the ammunition and victuals. They'd go in their 'earthly' garments. There'd be plenty of time to change before having to dress up for the occasion. The way Sam had it worked out from his maps and the ones Mirlun had drawn, they would enter the Seladiënna universe a good fifty miles from the nearest human habitation: Lenos. Fifty miles through what was quite possibly jungle. With some luck, and if they were able to take the car across, they might drive a part of the way. The further the better.

When the packing was done they sequestered their gear in the Aventurista and made sure it was well-locked. This one had an alarm system—also at Sam's request—and one would hope that whatever larcenous elements lurked in this comparatively idyllic place, would be smart enough to keep their hands off it. Besides, the vehicle was in plain view of just about everybody—and this was still the place where people knew who was who. The elderly men with their berets, standing around in a group near the whitewashed wall of a local *tienda* that also doubled as a bar and restaurant, were a good-enough deterrent. They wouldn't miss a thing. They had little else to do but chew the fat and watch for anything interesting that might eventuate around them. Gossip, Sam reflected, was not just a female pastime.

They went into the *tienda* and found themselves a table. They had a meal of garlicky meat fried in olive oil with roasted potatoes, preceded by large salads, and followed by caramelly flans, coffee, and a cognac. The wine served was cheap and tart and went well with the food. Sam and his companions drank sparingly. Alertness was the watchword, and though this might be their last meal in this world—*any meal* now could well be their last here! they knew that moderation was essential.

This close to their transition, Sam's attention was not entirely on their food.

"It *must* have happened! It wouldn't make any sense if it hadn't. Even if we assume that out worlds are 'lined up', if you will. There's obviously a *lot* of land area in your world that lines up with ocean in ours. So, what happens when an opening appears there? You'd expect a major natural disaster—for the duration of the event anyway. Salt-water pouring in! Maybe some boats or ships with it! Or what about different elevations? I mean, you can't assume that erosion worked exactly the same on both sides; not over millions of years. There've got to be points where anybody making the transit would either run into a solid wall or fall off a cliff! And who says the openings have to be at sea level? What if they happen high up or deep down?"

Mirlun shook his head. "We have no records of such events."

"They could have happened somewhere else," Helen pointed out. "Maybe just not where anybody noticed. Maybe…" She made an odd little gesture.

"What's the matter?" Sam asked.

"Why?"

"What are you thinking?"

"Just wondering."

"About what?"

"If we forgot anything."

"We probably did."

"Ziploc bags!"

"For what?"

"Ziploc bags are *always* useful."

"Let's get some then."

"We'll need something to wrap our documents in."

"Not that they'll be much good to us."

"Unless we think of getting back one day."

"That is an unlikely contingency," Mirlun injected. "Openings are extremely rare. Their location and timing is difficult to predict."

"The Diënna seems to be quite apt at it," Sam said dryly.

Mirlun's face assumed an oddly stubborn expression. "It is extremely rare. Even the Diënna cannot always tell." Which, to Sam at least, was not necessarily a sequitur, but Mirlun seemed to see it that way.

Sam and Helen exchanged a glance; too quick for Mirlun to notice.

"Then how come she predicted this one so accurately?" Helen asked the Seladiënnan.

"She knows some things," the Seladiënnan replied evasively.

"She may know more than she tells you," Sam suggested.

"The Diënna will tell us what is necessary to know ."

Sam eyed Mirlun sharply.

"The Diënna," Helen said, "may have to become more flexible."

"Quite so," Sam agreed. "We will not labor in an ambience of partial ignorance. That way lies disaster."

"The Diënna..." Mirlun started.

"Toilet–paper!" Helen interrupted. "We forgot toilet–paper!"

Sam grinned at Mirlun, who looked as if he really didn't feel like talking about this at all.

"Good point," Sam said. "How *do* you clean up after...business?"

"Practices vary," Mirlun said crisply.

"We're eager to hear more," Helen said.

Mirlun cringed. "The wealthier members of our society—those who are conscious of the requirements of corporal cleanliness—their lavatories contain certain facilities." He stopped. Helen and Sam looked askance. Mirlun grimaced. "Beside the device for... discharging wastes, there is another, which uses water, usually at some pressure from a hand–operated pump, which..."

"Bidets?" Helen exclaimed. "Wow! That's very...civil."

"We are a civilized people," Mirlun declared stiffly.

"Nobody disputes that," Sam said. "What about the practices of the common folk?"

"Most dwellings have ablution chambers. Maybe no bidets, but the practice of rinsing with water...afterwards...it is common enough."

"And in public 'ablution chambers'?"

Mirlun shrugged. "It depends on the establishment. A copper dinar will avail the use of a facility with water for cleaning purposes. Two coppers grant entry into one with a rudimentary 'bidet'."

Sam and Helen looked at each other. It would be interesting indeed to look at this aspect of Seladiënnan everyday existence.

The degree of a civilization may be measured by the cleanliness of its toilets.

And a lot of other things, too, of course—and maybe the technology of personal waste disposal wasn't as important as those. But a civilization based on the notion that

Chapter 10 151

humans were different from animals—part of that difference being certain elements of hygiene—invariably sanitized the methods by which people performed their most basic and profane of bodily functions. Those with the economic means usually made first use of these. The real question was how much the practices had filtered through to the 'ordinary' folk, since that partially reflected on how *they* saw themselves—or were seen by those providing such facilities.

Or on the economies involved.

If people were willing to *pay* for the use of ablution facilities that left them clean after the process, this implied a certain pride in that cleanliness, and therefore reflected on the very nature of the culture and society.

"I'm taking toilet-paper," Helen declared. "As much as I can."

Sam shrugged. "It's a consumable light, and bio-degradable. Pad out the empty spaces in our packs all you like."

"Then we better get it now!"

Sam laughed.

They paid—by credit card! didn't anybody just do 'cash only' anymore? and found another *tienda* which sold toilet paper. The middle-aged overweight woman behind the counter eyed them curiously, but said nothing, when they bought two dozen toilet rolls and several packs of differently-sized Ziploc bags, or the Spanish equivalent.. God only knew what she must have been thinking!

Helen somehow managed to squeeze all the rolls into their packs. "We could get more," she said hopefully. "There's space."

Sam flopped back on the bed and laughed. "The look on her face...I don't know if I could face it again."

Mirlun excused himself and went to his own room. Helen lay on her belly beside Sam, her face close to his.

"You scared?" she asked softly.

"Apprehensive."

"I hasn't sunk in yet."

"Probably won't until we're there."

"Still sure you want to go?"

" 'Sure'? Not really."

"Then..."

A knock on the door.

"I'll get it," Sam levered himself off the bed and went to the door. Helen rolled around to look after him. She liked to look at him—his economical walk, the way his butt moved, his face, his eyes, mouth...

Sam opened the door. Helen froze with shock.

In the door stood Harry.

"Harry?" Sam's voice expressed disbelief. "What are you doing here?"

Harry looked over Sam's shoulder and saw her on the bed. Still fully dressed and just as well.

"Can I come in?"

Sam hesitated for a moment, then stepped aside. Harry came into the room and Sam closed the door. Harry gave the room a deliberate scan, hesitated when it came to rest on the three backpacks in the corner, the swords tucked in behind them. Helen pushed herself into an upright position, unsure of what she felt, or how maybe she *should* feel. Self–conscious, certainly. Embarrassed, no. Puzzled, definitely.

Harry's gaze returned to Helen. Sam had stood a small distance behind him.

Harry nodded softly, as if to himself.

"Harry!" Sam's voice had a hard edge.

Harry turned to look at Sam.

"What am I doing here?" he said slowly. "I'm looking for answers."

"So am I," Sam grated. "Beginning with how you found us here."

Harry grinned mirthlessly. "A P.I. and some hi–tech gadgetry."

Helen saw Sam's eyes widen, then narrow in thought. "*You* hired Bronowski?"

"You knew?" Harry's turn to be surprised. But then he shrugged. "You're pretty careless."

"Bronowski followed us to Spain?"

"No. I did. But he has contacts in Spain. He found out you hired a car. His buddies here waited for you and put a tracer on it." He grinned, profoundly pleased with himself. "Remember the guy at the rental compound gate? Charged us a thousand Euros for the favor. Greedy bastard."

Helen remembered. When they left the rental compound the gate man had actually taken their rental papers and walked around the whole vehicle.

"I actually arrived in Madrid a day before you. All I had to do was follow the tracer."

How much had Harry seen?

"You went to a lot of trouble," she said.

Harry gave her a crooked grin. "I want answers. I want to know why you did all that stupid shit before you left. Bukido, shooting, stats–software, custom Kevlar gear, and strange costumes. And what did you get the other day in Santander? What was in those bags?" His eyes bored into Sam's. "And what the fuck happened in Cornwall?"

He went to a chair and dropped himself into it. "You two think I'm *stupid*?"

Sam went to the bed and sat himself down beside Helen. Despite his relaxed mien she sensed the tension. The way he moved, the way he sat, it was like a predator waiting to leap. Harry might be under the illusion that he was in some sort of control over the situation here, but he had no idea. Sam was in no disposition to play games.

"No," Sam said.

"All right then—time for the truth."

"You're going to have a hard time believing the truth."

"I'll risk it."

Sam studied his former friend for a few moments.

"The short version," Sam said, "is this. That morning in Helston we got lost in the fog. It turned out that at the other side of the fog, if you will, there was…another world. We found a sword stuck in a stone and pulled it out. A bunch of freaks on horses tried to kill us and followed us back into our own world—but ran into some problems with the cops and didn't make it. A guy calling himself 'Mirlun' arrived at my house some weeks afterwards and recruited us to do some world–saving for him. You know, kick–ass some bad guys—including, it seems, one Larry August Unterflug, formerly of ADLER, who is over there now and calls himself Laurentius Augustus."

Chapter 10

He paused and looked at Harry, whose face seemed carved of stone. Impossible to tell what he was thinking.

Harry had set the P.I. onto them? She still had trouble digesting it.

Harry? What was going on in his mind? Was it just insane jealousy? Envy? Of Sam? That had never been quite as clearly expressed as in that last exchange at her apartment. It was obviously more than just an occasional itch. Harry, she began to understand, carried a serious grudge.

For what? Was there some deep dark secret between him and Sam: something buried under layers and layers of taboo?

She glanced sideways at Sam, for a moment wondered if maybe she knew as little about him as she obviously had known about Harry—despite going with him for a whole year. Was there something similarly dysfunctional about Sam? How could she know?

And then she *knew* that whatever there was—*because there's muck in all of us*—it was nothing like that at all. Couldn't be. As she sat there and took in the silence between the three of them—that silence that seemed to go on and on, with Harry's stare fixed on Sam, and Sam getting somewhat impatient with it—she felt the warmth of Sam's proximity like it was a physical thing. Which it probably was, but it was also more than that. It was like it wrapped itself around her and flowed through her, and she knew that she *knew* Sam; like she'd never known anybody: maybe not even herself. And that was quite wonderful, and it made her feel whole.

Without being conscious of it she leaned closer to Sam and touched his shoulder. He turned to look at her, the faintest of smiles on his face, the moment one of a soft, furtive, yet exquisite kind of intimacy.

Sam turned back to Harry.

"So," he said, "that's that in a nutshell."

Harry shook his head. "Why?"

"Why what?"

"Why *you*?"

Sam shrugged. "We were there. It just happened." He leaned his elbows on his knees and looked at Harry. "You actually believe this, do you?"

Harry made an odd little gesture. "Why not? It's too crazy to be made up. It's also impossible, of course. But it explains what you've done over the last few weeks." He made a face as if he'd bitten on something sour. "Still doesn't explain though why it had to be *you*!" He spat out the last part of the sentence. A glance at Helen. "And you…"

"I'm sorry, Harry," she said gently.

"Sorry my ass!" he snapped. "Besides I don't *want* you to be fucking sorry! I can do without your pity and your contempt."

He stood. "This is a one-way trip, isn't it?" he asked Sam, who nodded.

Harry indicated the backpacks. "What's in there?"

"Survival stuff."

"You're taking guns, aren't you? That's what you picked up in Santander. Guns and ammo. Couldn't have brought it into the country." He narrowed his eyes. "Frank? So you finally got to cash in some chips, huh?" His eyes widened just a trifle. "Did you say 'Larry Unterflug'?"

Sam nodded.

"What's *he* doing there?"

"Seems like he got stranded. From what we've been told he's now basically in charge of an empire."

Harry chuckled softly and unpleasantly. "ADLER again, huh? This time a fucking *big* eagle! I don't think you'll make it, Sam! You sure you want to get *her* killed to get even with ADLER? Add to the tally of people you couldn't protect?"

Sam stood. "Get out, Harry." Something in his voice almost scared her.

Harry went to the door. "Don't bother." He stopped with his hand on the handle, looking at Helen. "One day," he said, softly but venomously, "you'll realize just what kind of a loser you've picked. He looks such a fucking hero—hey, now they even want him to save a *world*!—but just wait and see. One day…"

He left without another word.

"Bastard," Sam whispered as the door closed behind him.

She tucked an arm under his and hugged him to her, feeling the stiffness of every muscle in his body.

"What did he mean?" she said softly.

Sam closed his eyes and took a few even breaths. "He may not be wrong."

"Sam?"

"Three people died because of what I did," he said emptily. "Three who would have been alive had I done what I should have."

The silence spread. She just held onto him, waiting for it to come out—for it would.

"They all depended on me. They all died because I was doing a job when I should have been there for them."

"Katie. Who else?"

"Five years before that," he said hoarsely. "My mum and dad. They came to visit me. I was supposed to pick them up at the airport. I was late. I had extended my patrol schedule that day to follow a distress signal that turned out to be a hoax by some sicko with nothing else to do but to waste coast–guard time and resources. They thought I wouldn't come, so they took a cab. A truck ploughed into them on the highway. They put the bits and pieces they could pry off the car–wreck into a single casket."

He was silent for a few moments. "Harry's right, you know. In his own twisted way he's quite right." He looked at her with a tortured expression. "Let's stay here. Let's not do this. It's crazy. I have this…feeling. I mean, screw Larry Unterflug! Screw the Diënna! This thing is *dangerous*. It could get you killed. And I don't want you killed. I don't want a single hair of yours harmed. I want to have a family with you and just have a *life*, and maybe do the right damn thing for a change. And I don't want to fuck up again. I really don't want to fuck up again…"

You won't, she wanted to say, and she meant it. Because he wouldn't. Because he *hadn't*. Not then. Not ever. It was just bad luck! How could he not see that?

Because those were people he loved.

"It wasn't your fault—you know that!" It sounded inane, even to her own ears.

" 'Fault' is not the issue," he said softly. "But the facts are what they are: through my actions, however indirectly, I have caused the deaths of those dearest to me. In both instances I was distracted with attending to others but those I should have attended to. I don't want this to happen again. My gripe with ADLER just isn't worth it."

"Look at me." She stood where he *had* to look at her and gripped his shoulders.

Chapter 10

"This isn't about you and ADLER," she said. "It's about a whole *world*! And—remember! I was 'recruited', too!" She peered at him. "Get it? It's not just your decision. I have a word in this, too."

He smiled ruefully. "Touché."

"I think we should do this," she declared. "I think those people really, really need us."

"I'm not sure that's a good enough reason to go." He sighed. "I know this sounds selfish, and maybe it is, but not a lot of people are given a second chance at doing something right. I've been given a *third*! How many people get that?"

"I love you, too," she whispered. And it was so. The mere notion that, by some terrible misfortune, he might suddenly not be there anymore…that was almost more than she could bear—and the idea of *her* not being there anymore to receive that love: that was just as terrifying. It wasn't just death. Death she could probably handle. If life wasn't that great who cared if you lived or died. But to have something to lose…

His mouth twitched in an incipient smile. "I know. I'm kind of wondering if that's not more important than all the world–saving we could ever do."

"Maybe we can have both."

He sighed. "You haven't read the books, huh?"

"What books?"

"The ones that tell you it can't be done."

"Oh, those. Read them all. But what if they're wrong?"

"Big 'if'…"

"You're not going to screw up."

"You're extremely prejudiced, you know that?"

"I know *you*."

It shut him up. Which was just as well, because she was *not* all that sure, and if he'd argued longer she might not have stood her ground.

Please, don't let me screw up!

"I wonder what Harry's going to do now?" he said.

"Go home?"

"He set a P.I. onto us. He bugged our car. He followed us here. We told him some unbelievable stuff. And you think he's just going to go off back home? Seems to me like you don't know Harry."

"What do *you* think he's going to do?"

"Not just go home: that's for sure."

"What else can he do?"

"Try to stop us."

"Why?"

"Because he can," Sam said wryly.

"I thought…"

"He'd be glad to be rid of me—given the circumstances. And you, too."

"Something like that."

"Harry isn't like that."

"Why should he stop us?"

"Spite? Envy? Because it's what we want to do?"

"How could he? What's he going to do?"

Sam chuckled without a trace of humor. "He knows we've got guns. And those swords! All highly illegal around here. All he has to do is go to the police and drop a hint. Maybe he's doing it right now."

"Shit!"

"Which means we'd better..."

A rap on the door interrupted him. Helen's heart missed a beat.

"Damn!" Sam hissed and jumped up. He looked at the packs in the corner. "Who is it?" he called.

"Mirlun."

Helen exhaled a sigh of relief and hastily opened the door.

"We must leave," Mirlun declared without preamble.

"No shit?" Sam said.

"It is here."

"How very convenient," Sam said dryly.

Helen gave him a quick look, saw the relief in his face.

See? We're meant to go! Not even Harry can stop us.

Sam gave her tiny grin. "Don't even *think* it."

"Thoughts are free."

"Yeah, right." Sam took a look around the room; a bit regretfully she thought. Maybe, like her, he'd hoped for another night with just the two of them alone.

"Let's go then." He handed them their packs and took the two canteens into the bathroom. She heard water running as he filled them. She grabbed her jacket and put on her sneakers. By the time he came out again, she and Mirlun were standing at the door waiting to leave. Sam picked up his own bag and they made their way downstairs. The receptionist eyed them curiously.

"*Volverémos mañana*," Sam told her as they went out the door.

They heaved their packs into the Aventurista. Sam shined a light around the underside of the car and finally came up with a small device which he dropped on the ground and crushed.

"Let's go."

They got into the car and drove off, down the narrow streets, through the plaza and out of the village.

"Where to?" Sam asked Mirlun, who pointed west.

They came to the main road and turned right.

"It is close," Mirlun declared.

"Is it...open?" Helen asked.

"It is coming into being." Mirlun sat with the attentive mien of a dog following a scent in the air.

From ahead came a car. As it passed them they saw that it had 'POLICIA' stenciled on the doors.

"Harry didn't waste any time," Sam muttered. His eyes were on the rear–vision mirror. Presently he heaved a sigh of relief.

"Where is it?" he asked Mirlun.

Mirlun pointed to their right, toward the water.

"Tell me it's not in the ocean!" Sam muttered.

Then Helen saw it: an indistinct nebulosity, faintly illuminated by the lights of La Isla behind them and a couple of *veraneante* houses beside the road.

"There!" She pointed.

From Mirlun came a brief utterance.

Relief. Anticipation.

Sam slowed down. No side-tracks were evident. Sam pulled over and engaged the four-wheel drive. The Aventurista climbed down the roadside and lurched through a narrow ditch, to gain the field beyond. Sam gunned the engine. The vehicle bumped over the dry furrowed field. Ahead the lights picked out a spreading wall of impenetrable mist.

Sam glanced at Helen.

"Last chance to bow out," he said.

"I know." She put a hand on his leg and squeezed.

He smiled and concentrated on driving. The fog closed around them, the car-lights found only a milky haze. Sam slowed down to a crawl, but kept going. Helen rolled down the window; a clammy moist odor invaded the cabin, together with a chill…

…that presently turned into something else. An errant gust of sweltering air blew in, carrying with it a strange fetor, like of rotting vegetation, maybe animal exudations, and another, sweeter scent as of…flowers…

Sam wound down his window as well. The draft brought with it more heavy, humid air and the fecund smells of rich vegetation.

The fog thinned, the car lights cast bright cones of light into the night. Sam braked the car to a halt as a wall of trees and undergrowth came into view.

They stopped a short distance away from it. Sam reversed, turned the car around so that the lights pointed back the way they'd come. The wall of fog was dense, but even as they watched it drifted sideways and out of the range of the headlights and off into the darkness.

Sam turned off the lights and the engine.

Silence and darkness fell.

Above them, the stars became visible one by one—and then by the hundreds, until it was a blazing carpet of light above their heads. They got out of the car and stared up at them—and as they did, behind them the sounds of the jungle slowly started up again and the denizens of that murky world resumed their briefly interrupted lives.

11

Laurentius Augustus, who was counselor to Oldecus Pistor, Emperor of Seladiënna by the grace of the Diënna, didn't like to be reminded of the old days. In fact, he didn't even want to remember his original name, which once upon a time had been Lawrence (a.k.a. 'Larry') August (a.k.a. 'Augie', and he *hated* that one!) Unterflug. A far cry from 'Laurentius Augustus', which sounded much more weighty, and which had associated with it a position of power that gave him the greatest permanent hard–on ever.

But the girl he was screwing, and who was heaving on top of him with an enthusiasm so fake that even Larry couldn't help but notice, somehow reminded him of his mother; and that definitely killed the hard–on and the whole fun of it. His mother had been born Carlotta Marie Nielsen, who duly turned into Carlie Unterflug, and had been known prior to her marriage—and for some time after—as 'Curly Carlie', for reasons never revealed to Larry. Not that he desired revelation. The possibilities were too disgusting even for his imagination.

Carlie Unterflug had also been an alcoholic chain–smoker, who died of some horribly disgusting disease, coughing out her lungs in bloody bits and pieces over a period of about five years. When she had finally expired—a pale, limp rag of bones and skin reposing on a hospital bed—his father, Otto, had taken Larry and his sister Eva home and explained to them that it had been the Jews who killed their mother, and that he was definitely going to do something to get even with those fuckers.

Larry, a dull boy in his early teens, hadn't asked his father what the Jews had done to kill his mother: he took it for granted that dad knew. Dad always knew, because he had read books and shit. Besides, it had all been proven by Adolf Hitler's scientists, only that the Global Zionist Conspiracy had suppressed the research, and made it look like Hitler was the bad guy, when it reality he had been the last bulwark of civilization against the Zionist Tide. Now that he was gone, little guys like Otto Unterflug had to take up the good fight and make sure that the Zionists and their cronies—who were easily recognizable by virtue of their swarthy or even darker skin coloration, slitted eyes, funny accents, or screwy names—didn't finish off what the Jews had tried to accomplish throughout history, and indeed were still working on, as evidenced by the conspiracy of the cigarette manufacturers who made a huge wad of money—all of it used to line their own pockets and help the Zionist cause—out of killing people like Larry's mother. Otto had seen the evidence: clandestinely copied documents smuggled out of Germany before the Allies had bombed the shits out of the research facilities— the Allies of course being in the service of the Zionists, who needed to make sure that nobody knew of their dirty secrets.

And now Larry's mum was dead because of them and Otto was finally going to take up arms. So they sold their home in Detroit and moved to Kansas where Otto knew other people who also knew the truth. They lived in a tiny village you couldn't find on any map, because it was on a farm owned by Hank Sherman, another one of those folks who 'knew'. They formed the core of an organization called *Aryan Defense League for European Races*, or A.D.L.E.R., which was German for 'eagle' and so was a very significant symbol for all of them. It was emblazoned on the chests of the brown uniforms the leaders wore and displayed prominently over the entrance gate to Hank Sherman's farm.

The years passed. Otto worked on the farm and trained with his comrades. Larry joined the youth–corps, a bunch of five boys of ages ranging from thirteen to seventeen, who were duly trained to continue the good fight when their turn finally came. Larry took to the training like a fish to water. He loved shooting and martial arts and all that stuff you needed to kick the shits out of any fucker who pissed in your face, especially if he was a Zionist or one of their co–conspirators.

Sadly, Eva, Larry's sister, was less enthusiastic about joining the girl's brigade. Two years older than Larry she was a hoity–toity little bitch who thought she knew better than her father or her sibling. Repeated punishment for her insolence from Otto and Larry (Larry was half a foot taller than Eva, and about twice as heavy, so she didn't have much of a chance when he set his mind to slapping her around) made little difference. Eva was stubborn and eventually, at the age of twenty-two, fled the farm in the middle of the night, evading the guards who should have stopped her. She also used the Colt .45 semi–auto she'd stolen from Otto, to shoot and kill another ADLER member, who saw her ambling along the road during her flight, and stopped and tried to take her back.

After her escape, Eva went to California, to take up with a cop of all people, and a black one at that. She must have told him what the folks at the form were doing, because not much later the Feds started taking interest in the operation, and there was even a raid. Fortunately all the illegal weapons were well hidden. The Feds left again, none the wiser for the exercise and with no arrests to show for their trouble.

ADLER began to spread, and Larry was on the forefront of the movement. His enthusiasm and unflagging devotion to the cause rocketed him into organizational stardom, eclipsing his dad, who seemed to resent it and became surly and uncommunicative, rather than exhibiting justified pride in his prodigal son. Larry was assigned to a group in Texas and proceeded with vigor to expand ADLER's region of influence. In 1985 the Texas chapter had over a hundred active members, who trained in various camps for the day that must surely come when the pinko Zionist swine aided by the UN were going to take over the world, and then all that stood between them and total subjugation of humanity and assumption of power by the forces of evil were the loyal troops of the eagle.

Then came that 1985 meeting in the land of King Arthur. If there ever had been a good Aryan, it was Arthur, who'd kicked the shits out of the southern barbarians, who had probably come all the way from the south of Europe and were therefore very likely tainted by Zionist genes. Meeting in Arthur's land seemed fitting and symbolic, and never mind the costs of getting everybody there.

Larry often wondered how everybody had reacted when he and Clint didn't show up at the Land's End picnic. Because they hadn't shown up. Because that's when it happened.

Larry, Clint, and their wives, Shareen and Darienne, left their hotel to drive to the meeting. On the way they encountered a dense bank of fog and, before Larry could stop

Chapter 11

the car, instead of driving along an inadequate Cornish road they suddenly ploughed into a field and came to a crashing halt among the furrows. Since they didn't wear seat belts—which was a matter of principle, laws in this regard being part of the coffee–colored conspiracy to deny civil rights to all pure–bred folks—the deceleration threw them forward in their seats. Shareen went through the windscreen and died on the spot. Larry braced himself against the steering wheel and suffered only minor damage. Darienne and Clint fared better. Both were bruised but otherwise unhurt. Hardly had they recovered from the shock, that the fog suddenly cleared, and they found themselves in a place as humid and warm as Florida in spring, and with not a road in sight.

Larry, after a perfunctory inspection of his wife—whom he mourned only minimally, what with her having recently turned into a nagging bitch whose racial antecedents he'd begun to seriously question—addressed himself to the issue of their whereabouts. Being much more mentally agile than Clint, Larry soon grasped what had happened, especially when they were confronted by a group of peasants in weird clothes, who spoke gibberish and looked at them like they came from another world!

Which was exactly what had happened.

Clint and Darienne took somewhat longer to get used to the outrageous idea of being stranded in a 'parallel world'—didn't they read sci–fi, for fuck's sake?—but come around they did. In due course, the three of them were arrayed at the edge of a lagoon called *Aquadiënna* by the natives, to face an apparition rising from the water.

The Lady of the Lake if ever there was one.

"Fucking Arthur," Larry muttered. "Where's fucking Arthur?"

Larry resolved there and then that he would make the most of the opportunities offered to a man from his day and age in this cesspool of primitive culture. Fifteen years later Oldecus Pistor, though still *Praetor* by title, was soft putty in the persuasive hands of his chief counselors: Larry and Clint from the U.S. of A. The *Senatus* had been reduced to a bunch of public service functionaries. The legions were being equipped with new shiny black uniforms that terrorized the shits out of anybody watching them exercise. A new spirit was afoot. Expansion was in the air, though neither Larry nor Clint had any idea of where to. Maybe, they thought, across the Atlantic. Columbus had done it and why not see what one could find in this world? But you had to expand! This was the essence of history. Expand or be screwed.

Clint didn't see it that way, of course. Clint was becoming a pain–in–the–ass for a number of reasons. One of them might have been that Darienne, seeing which way the wind was blowing, was doing the best she could to be on the winning team; which included coming onto Larry like a lioness in heat, indicating her availability and willingness to do just about anything required to get what she wanted. Larry tried her out for a few weeks, but finally decided that blow–jobs from the big–titted women and pubescent girls from around Oldie Pissie's palace were much more enjoyable and inflicted with less consequences than Darienne's. They were racially tainted, of course, but so what? Pussy was pussy and who cared about rest? The whores around the place were something else and especially enthusiastic around the guys from the other world. One had to watch what they brought in, of course — but at least there was no shit like AIDS, and the local remedies for minor problems like the clap were amazingly effective. Considering what a bunch of primitives they were otherwise—if one neglected their architecture, which was absolutely amazing! their medicine was great. Not very good at surgery, but their herbalists were something else.

   Larry's disdain for Darienne meant that when he put a word in Oldie's ear and they hauled Clint's ass out of bed one morning, they took Darienne as well, and executed them both without further ado. Which left Larry in control here, because Oldie was a spineless piece of shit, who preferred having his brains sucked out through his dick by little girls and boys alike, and really whimpered not one bit when, through the gentle offices of Larry some years earlier, his own wife and daughter had died of unknown causes.

   Larry in control! A nice thought. Except there was the fucking Diënna and the equally fucking Plius—which meant 'javelin' in a civilized language called 'English', which nobody around here seemed to want to know about. Meaning that Larry had to learn this stilted shit they spoke around here. Made you think you were in some giant college class where every fucker spoke nothing but Latin. Larry Unterflug having to learn *Latin*, for chrissake! It was enough to make you puke. And stuck in this racially tainted setup at that! Nine out of ten people had skins that were a dead giveaway for racial inferiority. Italians mostly, and the blood of the few pure folks in the legion when it had been stranded here had long been diluted with the inferior lines of the rest. There'd been talk of a small village somewhere in the northern reaches of what he thought of as 'Denmark', though according to local maps it was nothing like it. Hell, the whole world was nothing like he knew! I–fucking–talians ruling England and Germany and everything. What a pathetic setup!

   His ruminations across the desolate landscape of his memories took the heat out of Larry's ardor and his erection with it. The girl was getting panicky. And so she should! What kind of a stupid whore would let her client go limp like that? She smiled, but it was her lips only. Her eyes reflected her sense of failure. She lifted her hips off his dysfunctional organ and went to work on him with her mouth instead.

   Larry lay back, feeling nothing much. Even his automatic reflexes betrayed him. For now he was thinking of Plius, Seladiënna's nemesis, and, if the truth be admitted, quite a contributor to his own rise to power. Though he would have preferred to think it was all his own doing, he had to admit that Plius' assistance had clinched the deal in the end. The disposal of Oldie's advisors and the insertion of Larry in their place was not something he could have done on his own; despite his position, which Larry thought of as 'consultant', assassinations and disappearances had been quite out of his league. The old–boys network here had been quite powerful, and extremely off–putting to interlopers. Well, the old–boys network was in tatters once Plius's Minions and some of his less visible agents had done their work.

   All of that meaning that Larry *owed* the motherfucking water–phantom, sprite, whatever you wanted to call it, a great deal—and Plius had every intention of making sure that Larry stuck to the bargain they'd made all those years ago.

   Not that 'owing' necessarily meant a whole deal to Larry, but Plius had ways of enforcing deals: this much had been demonstrated on other unfortunates. Larry considered himself intelligent enough to take a hint when it dropped on you with all the subtlety of an rhino turd. One day he was going to dispose of Plius—he had no idea how, but he would: there just *had* to be a way! but until then he was, at least superficially, going to cooperate. And if that meant braving the Diënna, so be it. Rather her than the sprite.

Chapter 11

The whore was a total loss!

Larry—Laurentius Augustus—pushed her off him and kicked her off the bed.

"Useless cunt," he snapped—in Latin. He thought it sounded quite good at that; he'd obviously underestimated his talent for languages—though, of course, he'd rather have spoken English than this gibberish any day.

He sat up, pulled down his light tunic to conceal his pathetically shriveled manhood, and shouted a command. At the entrance appeared two of his *Praeti*, suitably dressed in their shiny black uniforms.

"Take her away!"

The girl looked around in panic and scrambled to grab her skimpy bits of clothing off the floor. The guards came up beside her and dragged her away. Larry caught the eye of one and made a significant gesture with his right hand, snapping together the tips of thumb and index finger. The guard's face remained unmoved, except maybe for the twitch of an eyebrow. He gave faintest of acknowledging nods. Larry looked after them until they'd disappeared around a corner. She would be taken downstairs to the *Praeti*'s quarters where everybody would have their fun. Then they'd kill her and dump the body somewhere in the harbor quarter at night. It was politic not to make it too obvious that she'd died at the hands of her last customer, of whose identity her colleagues might or might not be cognizant. But she had to die. Couldn't leave the cunt alive to tell everybody that Laurentius Augustus couldn't get it up. Never mind that it was her own fucking fault: she was a professional and a high–class one at that. What kind of bitches did they train these days? Was there some training at all—or was it just natural talent and practice? If so, it certainly had left something to be desired in this one!

Maybe he should leave the pros alone. Maybe doing it Oldie's way was better. Kids smelled better anyway. Still, there was something faintly unsavory about screwing a teen. It was like fucking your daughter—and Larry had been brought up a moral man, though not a Christian one, what with Christianity being Zionist and all that shit. But the gods of Valhalla had their own code of ethics and fucking teens wasn't in the deal. Only degenerates like Oldie and his cronies went in for that kind of shit. Of course, in extreme cases it might be necessary—like to preserve racial purity when that was the only way—but just for *fun*, that really went beyond what you might call 'moral'. And you had to be moral. If you weren't, what else was there? Might as well put a bullet in your brain—or a knife in your heart, as was more appropriate here, what with these goofies not even knowing about gunpowder. They'd had centuries and they were still using bows and swords and javelins and stuff. Mind you, he'd seen some nifty engineering. Concealable bows that worked like crossbows, only they were tiny, had whooping strong springs and shot arrows barely bigger than bullets that killed you just as dead. Of course they were single shot, and just about as effective as old front–loaders.

A kingdom for an Uzi! Or a Glock!

He could revolutionize warfare in this place. Hell, with an Uzi he, Larry, would be a match for a couple of cohorts no sweat! Pity he didn't really know how to make gunpowder. They never taught him that at the base. And then there was the whole problem of engineering guns, of course.

Should've learned gunsmithing!

Yeah, well, too late. The goose was cooked. He'd had to make do with swords and bows. All considered, it wasn't too bad, the way it had come out.

Except for Plius and the Diënna—and the other snag: Plius' insistence that trouble was on the way in the shape of more folks from what Larry thought of as the 'home-world'. Never mind *how* Plius knew. He knew. And he had already been right—because the Diënna had given away the sword; the troublemakers had already been and gone. Only now they were about to return...

But he had a good idea where and when, and though it was somewhat outside the realm of Seladiënnan influence, they were expected and wouldn't get very far. He couldn't really send legionnaires to Iber; not without knowing precisely where his putative adversaries had to be. But he could make sure that its only port, Lenos, that hive of crime and sin, was riddled with spies and mercenaries, hired to dispose of the nuisances with alacrity, and to return the sword into his and Plius' care.

Shouldn't be a problem finding them. They'd stick out like sore thumbs with bandages.

He wondered who they were.

12

"It would be prudent not to venture outside during the darkness," Mirlun had advised; so this is what they did. The wisdom of this course of action revealed itself soon enough when, after he discerned a shadow moving across the star–lit field, Sam turned on the headlights, only to reveal the suddenly frozen–in–shock figure of a feline with the blotches of a panther, but the size of a tiger. The animal crouched in the glare for a few instances; snarled defiantly, baring a set of impressive teeth; then slunk out of the beams and into the darkness. Sam told Helen he wished he'd added a .357 Magnum to his arsenal. No puny Beretta slug would kill this baby in time—if it came to the crunch. A magazine–full might, but only of you managed to squeeze off enough rounds before it got you.

On the other hand, the razor-sharp *katanas* were another matter. They'd slice through anything organic with equal ease. Even practicing with them was fraught with danger. They'd cut themselves in all sorts of places more than once during Jack's drills.

"How far across the empire do you find these pussycats?" he asked Mirlun, using the English word 'pussycat' inserted into his Seladiënnan phrase.

"They inhabit the southern reaches only."

"Just as well."

"Your weapons…"

"A hand grenade perhaps." There was another, highly unsporting, way, thought Helen, to deal with a large cat. "We'll stay in the car," she interjected practically. No way she was going to go out there.

Sam was agreeable. "And we stay put. Might as well make ourselves as comfortable as possible."

With Mirlun looking away discreetly—and probably dying with embarrassment—she divested herself of surplus items of clothing which had suddenly become too warm and too tight. No way she was going to spend a whole night with a bra digging into her and jeans weren't made for sleeping in. In fact they mightn't even be so good for daytime use either.

Just as well we remembered the sewing kit.

In the morning, while Sam tried to find a way to head the Aventurista toward the putative 'Lenos', she would convert them into shorts. Meanwhile…

Mirlun, trying to get as far away as possible from whatever he might see that he shouldn't—the man was more of a prude than the average monk!—made a space for himself between their packs in the rear loading area, while she and Sam clambered onto the backseat and snuggled up there. Sam retrieved their guns from the packs and placed them on the floor of the car, within easy reach.

"Just in case," he told her.

It might have worried her, but it didn't. Besides, wearing only a T–shirt and panties and with Sam having stripped down himself to the bare essentials, that being a pair of briefs, it was quite impossible not to get aroused; despite Mirlun's disapproving presence on the other side of the back seat. Not that he said anything, but you could almost *feel* how totally scandalized he was about it all.

The night was hot and humid. There was a thin film of sweat on their bodies and lying beside each other didn't really work on the backseat either. She slid on top of him—as she knew he liked it, and so did she—and slipped her T–shirt over her head. She stifled her giggle by pressing her mouth against his—but even so Mirlun must surely have heard.

Sod him!

Something about the heat, the humidity, the slick film of perspiration between them, that made their skins slide against each other at the slightest movement. Something deliciously naughty about having to be so totally quiet about doing what they did. Even kissing. You couldn't just let go. Every sigh, even the softest involuntary sounds of passion, the scrape of fabric against skin, the snap of elastic—everything was suddenly amplified into noisy punctuations of silence. The task of discreetly slipping down her panties and shifting her position so she could receive him; of just keeping *quiet*. He draped the T–shirt over her as a token–gesture of modesty; and she smiled and shifted her hips, shook with an uncontrollable, delicious little shiver, climaxed before she even knew it was coming. Pressed against him and drank his breath and gave her own to him.

Their climax subsided. She lifted her head and looked down into his face. "I love you," he whispered into her ear.

They stayed that way for a long time, though in due course they must have fallen asleep. But there was something about the heat and the humidity, or maybe their position, or the whole damn crazy situation…

To be like that forever.

Except that, eventually…

"I've got to pee," she whispered in his ear. The prospect was not enchanting, but neither were the alternatives. She raised her head to look out the window, saw the first intimations of a pink dawn. How long had they slept?

Reluctantly they released their intimate connection, contrived to get her T–shirt on again and her panties back into position.

"Might as well get up," Sam said lowly.

She kissed him. "I like being with you, Mr. Donovan," she said softly.

"And I with you, Mrs. Donovan."

"Just as well. We're married you know."

Mirlun remained silent, presumably holding his hands over his ears to avoid even *hearing* what went on, as she peered out through the window, but saw nothing that should have alarmed her.

They opened the door and peered out. Deep grass, thick with dew from the night.

"Shoes," whispered Sam.

She looked at him.

"You don't know what's crawling around in there," he noted.

The thought gave her pause.

Sam grinned. "Just make some noise before you…crouch."

"I need toilet paper."

Feeling faintly ridiculous in T–shirt, panties and sneakers, she finally stood outside the car as Sam opened the rear gate and retrieved a roll of toilet paper from one of the packs. They snuck away to a safe distance—'safe' from Mirlun's ears, and maybe eyes that was. Sam stood watch while she relieved herself.

My first pee in the new world.

It was kind of funny, despite the strangeness of it all.

She stood watch while Sam followed her example. With bodily functions taken care of, they took the time to look around themselves. The glow of dawn had brown brighter and they saw that they were on the gentle slope of a long incline, occupied mostly by a dense forest, as yet lying in mysterious darkness, but surrounded by a less dense periphery of thin bush that should allow a comparatively easy passage to the car.

Sam said as much, and Helen had to admit that she was relieved. The car would have to be ditched soon enough. Either that or it might just get stuck somewhere, and they'd have to take it from there. They slipped their arms around each other as they walked back to the car, where Mirlun had now risen and stood, facing discreetly away from them. As the sound of their approach he turned, almost averted his eyes again when he saw their half–dressed state.

"It occurs to me," Sam said lowly, "that this guy doesn't *need* Christianity, or Islam, or whatever shit there is. He's got enough sexual hang-ups for a whole regiment of assorted priests."

Helen was inclined to agree. Maybe the lesson was that religion in itself was not a prerequisite for sexual dysfunctionality, but merely a ready–made fertile breeding ground. If it wasn't religion it was going to be something else. The cult of the Diënna may or may not have qualified as 'religious'. Whatever it was, it brought with it, at least for her immediate 'attendants', a requirement of unnatural chastity.

'Unnatural'?

Definitely. Sexuality was a basic component of human existence; the need to find sexual release almost as fundamental as the need to eat, drink, or dispose of bodily wastes. If it wasn't with the assistance of someone else, auto–eroticism was still preferable to nothing at all. Oddly enough, that was even *more* of a taboo that licentious sex.

Why? Who knew? Maybe the notion that one could find this kind of basic gratification of a fundamental human *need* without taking recourse to the sanctification of its implementation by society's regulating mechanisms—like law, morality, and/or religion—and without any real possibility of it actually being controlled…maybe that was the most abhorrent thing of all to those who wanted—or needed! that control.

Control, control, control.

Control even of that most intimate of activities, or the most intimate of relationships. Not 'even': 'especially'. For here resided a profound kind of anarchy, a powerful and disruptive of emotional energy, potentially threatening everything that was *not* a part of the relationship.

Helen smiled to herself. She and Sam *had* gotten married! Not exactly an act of defiance of social conventions. However, she knew why he had proposed and why she had accepted. Not that either had been conscious of it, but they both knew it anyway. It was an affirmation, more than anything else. No hedging of bets, no holding back, no second thoughts. They were *it*—and that was that. Marriage had just been a gesture of that affirmation; a confirmation of the irrevocable fact of their togetherness; making it to themselves, to Harry, to Rita, to the whole damn world! Even to Mirlun, who lived in a mind-set where marriage for anything but a 'social' purpose was essentially meaningless. From his propoundings on Seladiënnan morality it was amply clear that little had changed since the days when the Legion had made the transit. Social change had been *much* slower than it had been in their world. In many ways they were walking into a society considerably more oppressive than their own. Homosexuality might be more accepted—this much they had been able to ascertain from Mirlun, who seemed to have less of a problem with this than her and Sam's unconcealed, and from Mirlun's point-of-view disturbingly open, sexual and emotional chemistry. This wasn't the kind of thing the man could handle. It certainly wasn't approved of in Seladiënnan society—though, and here their companion had injected a distinct note of scorn, in places like Lenos and other hives of illegality and social deviance public sexuality was much more rampant.

Interesting...

Helen smiled and tightened her right arm around Sam as they approached the car. Mirlun continued to avert his face. Just as well. They might have looked just a tad ridiculous, walking along like that, Sam with the Beretta in his right hand and she with a roll of toilet paper in her left.

Welcome to the new world.

"Last packet of coffee," Sam said darkly.

"Damn!"

"You can say that again!"

She chuckled and, since Mirlun wasn't looking slipped her hand into the back of his briefs.

"Stop that!"

She pinched him.

"Bad girl!"

They stopped at the car. "We might as well get going," Sam suggested.

Mirlun excused himself and withdrew to a safe distance and behind a bush to attend to his necessities.

"The poor man," Helen said to Sam. "We were *bad*."

He looked at her and if it hadn't been for the situation and Mirlun she would have jumped him right there and then.

"Don't even think about it," he said warningly, but his eyes were laughing and there was a catch in his voice. She allowed her eyes to wander slowly, provocatively down to his crotch. It really wouldn't take any effort whatsoever.

"I can think about it all I want."

"I'm going to put on some pants."

"As if that was going to make a difference."

Mirlun emerged from behind his bush. Sam, with a wink, turned away and leaned into the car to retrieve their discarded garments. She didn't mind watching.

Mirlun did his prudish best, pretending they weren't there as they put on their pants. Helen procured scissors and told Sam what she wanted him to do with her jeans. He trimmed them while she was wearing them, then had her do the same to his. It was the only sensible thing. They had a spare pair in their packs. Not that they were likely to wear them so soon.

She decided to forego sewing them up. The tattered look was probably better under the circumstances. They might have to discard them completely for the sake of looking authentic. Mirlun disagreed. Similar kinds of garments had as of recent become fashionable; possibly as a result of Laurentius' influence, who had also introduced new trends into the art of shoe–making, as well as something approximating mini–skirts. As a result, so it seemed, a strange blend of Roman and latter–20th–century fashion had come into existence. Mirlun, not unexpectedly, disapproved of the exhibition of excessive amounts of female leg. He pointed out, very primly, that such new customs might prove disruptive to established patterns of social behavior.

And what about the widespread use of the bikini? Here was a garment that exposed a *lot* of flesh! But then she recalled that Mirlun had expressed certain reservations about that custom as well.

Anyway Helen thought, it was likely that other 'established patterns' were likely to be upset in the near future. If she had to spend the rest of her life in this world she was going to do her damn best to shape it to her liking.

Sam used the compass and a map of Spain, with Mirlun's superimposed Seladiënnan coast lines, to gauge the approximate direction of their travel. Now that the sun was up, and with the day clear, though already hot and humid, they could see the ocean in the distance. Despite a careful scan with binoculars from their elevated position however they found no sign of human habitation; even less a city. Which meant nothing but that they just couldn't see it. It might well be there, but hidden by yonder elevation or simply lost in the mist. Fifty miles was an estimate. It could be seventy. Maybe a hundred. One hoped it wasn't, but who could tell?

The Aventurista lumbered off across the grass, skirting the edge of the forest, winding its way through the sparse bush down the gentle incline. Diesel fumes poured into the clean air. The noise of the engine disrupted the susurration of the wind, the chirping of cicadas, the songs of the birds; the track of the tires evidence of the passage of something extremely alien to this world.

The day wore on. They stopped an hour later, hungry now. The bread was dry but edible. The coffee, with a dash of the UHT milk, was delicious, especially since it was their last pack. The cookies were excruciatingly delicious. Only sex was better. Sex and chocolate—but Sam had refused to bring that.

"It'll melt."

Indeed it would have. So what? They could have poured it over the cookies. Silly man!

Silly her, too. She should have thought of that *then*!

If that's the worst of our problems, who cares!

They drove on, winding their way around patches of dense, jungle–like forest, weaving through the lowlands. By now they were at about sea–level and orientation was difficult. No knowing what lay ahead. Lenos could be around the next hillock, or it could be days away.

Sometime in the afternoon the sky clouded with abrupt suddenness. An hour later a torrential down–pour stopped them in their tracks. It lasted for maybe half an hour. Helen told Mirlun to look away if he couldn't handle it, dragged Sam out of the car and into the luke–warm sluicing rain, stripped down, and pulled the clothes off him as well. They used her T-shirt to rub each other down, then rinsed it and, standing in their underwear in the streaming rain, wrung everything out. Not that it did any good, and so they put it on again, soggy as it was.

Sam, the water dripping off his face and body, eyed her chest. "You'd win."

"Huh?"

"The 'Wet T–shirt' contest. *Any* 'Wet T–shirt' contest."

"You think so? I didn't think they were *that* big."

"Size isn't everything."

"You're a charmer." She kissed him and it was very sexy indeed. The warm rain; the squishy grassy ground underneath their feet. A pity they weren't alone. "Now put on those shorts," she panted before she got too carried away.

Barely sociable in their wet gear, they returned to the car. Mirlun radiated disapproval and fastidiously kept his eyes averted from Helen's top. The seats were soaked with the wetness of their clothes, but who cared?

Presently the sky cleared again. The Aventurista plodded on across soaked soil, with Sam driving very carefully to avoid getting it stuck beyond a hope of extraction.

They stopped again as the sun slanted toward the horizon. By now their soaked clothes were dry again. They located a patch of rocky soil near the shallow spur of an elevation, just qualifying as an extended hill. Vegetation had not taken here, and what had, probably had to battle against being washed away in what she suspected were daily torrents of rain, at least during some parts of the year. As they drove around the spur they discovered a gentle slope on the other side. The 4WD labored its way up the incline and finally came to a halt on a piece of level rock near a boulder which prevented further progress. Helen and Mirlun disembarked and helped guide Sam to turn the car around, so it was facing downhill.

Their position here provided just enough elevation to afford a view across the patches of forest between them and the coast. Not that they could see very far: the humidity was high and the air was heavy with mist.

Their evening meal was pleasant. Despite the evidence of watchfulness—provided by the sight of the gun in the holster clipped to Sam's belt, as well as the feel of her own against her hip—there was a relaxed air about it all. Sam had carefully scouted their immediate environment and appeared satisfied with what he found.

"What were you looking for?"

"Unpleasant surprises."

"Like?"

"Like I don't know. Caves with large cats maybe."

"I thought you liked cats."

"Not that size."

He hunkered down beside her and adjusted the *chorizos* above the fire. Their garlicy smell wafted across the camp. Her mouth started watering.

"Last of this and last of that," she said thoughtfully.

Sam put an arm around her waist and squeezed. She leaned against him, thinking that as long as some things didn't change it was all right.

Night fell. The smell of *chorizos* was replaced by that of coffee. Sam's theory here was that they had to finish it off before getting to Lenos, so they might as well enjoy it while it lasted.

Night also brought a pleasant surprise. Lower temperatures meant a drop in the humidity and clearer air. Above the trees they now saw the lights on the horizon.

"Lenos," Mirlun stated with certainty.

"Well navigated, Mr. Donovan," Helen told Sam.

"Why, thank you Mrs. Donovan. If only everything else were that easy."

"I'm sure you'll make it appear that way."

They left Mirlun to do the dishes and stoke the fire higher, while they retreated behind a ledge to sit against the rock beside each other. Sam looked around carefully and finally placed his Beretta on the ground near him.

"Just in case," he said. "Maybe you should do the same."

"You're beginning to spook me."

He nodded. "Be spooked! We're in sight of civilization; and if we're to believe Mirlun, an unpleasant example of it. We're also still far enough in the wilderness to attract the attentions of any large pussycat that happens to stroll around nearby. Two good reasons to become excessively paranoid."

She did as he'd asked her to and then leaned against him. His left arm went around her shoulder. "So, oh prospective conqueror of the evil Laurentius—what's the plan?"

"Plan?"

"There is a plan!"

"Sort of. It all depends."

"Hmm. But the intention is always the same."

"There's only one: remove Larry Unterflug from any position where he can do some real damage. Just exactly *how* we're gonna do it...I have no idea. Whatever happens, we'll have to do the best we can."

"He's not going to just *go*."

"Probably not."

"Meaning..."

He hugged her. "Yes," he said softly.

They sat in silence. Helen liked silence with Sam around. She never had before. Not with her female friends—such as there had been—not with Harry, with whom silence had always been a heavy thing, just waiting to be broken with some inane, pointless remark. It wasn't like it was with anybody else. It just *was*. Unhurried. No pressure. No effort. Just...being. If it was broken, it was OK. If it wasn't, it was OK. In a way it was like talk without words, a sharing that went beyond what she could define. Time to be, think, enjoy, relax, just feel him right there beside her.

It was all so wonderfully weird, this thing between them. Sam, the one guy who used to get her just so totally *tense* every time his name was even mentioned. As it turned out, the first person in her whole damn life with whom she could actually *relax*.

As if he'd known what was going on in her head, Sam chuckled softly.

"What are you thinking?" She turned to him.

"The sword," he told her. "I suppose it would be nice if we could just wade in there, wave it around, declare Larry to be persona–non–grata and that'd be that."

"It isn't going to happen, is it?"

"Hardly."

"Then what good is it to us?"

"I have no idea. It has a symbolic value, I guess. But beyond that..."

"Let's just be careful."

"Definitely."

They sat in togetherness and silence for another while. From far away came a howling, as if of wolves.

Wolves? Europe had long been occupied by them, and why not here? As if to confirm their existence the first call was answered by another, and another, and presently there was a burst of chorus all around the camp–site.

Helen tucked herself closer to Sam. "Do you think we'll be happy here? After it is…done?"

"As long as you're with me."

The man knew how to say the right things. More importantly, she believed—no! *knew*—that he actually meant them.

How lucky can you get?

A warm breeze wafted across from the ocean, somewhere just beyond the blob of light marking Lenos, halfway to the horizon, which was a darker line against the carpet of stars merging into the water. The wind carried the by–now–familiar odors of the rain–forests and the fire just around the corner.

Helen felt a curious mix of happiness of melancholy. Maybe it was finally sinking in that they had indeed left their world behind—and with it everything that was familiar. This is how the colonists to the Americas must have felt: knowing that they could never return; looking ahead to circumstances beyond their current scope and possibly beyond their understanding.

She felt a bit like that. Of course, she and Sam were prepared: as much as they could be. And yet, how could anybody be prepared for *this*? Without being conscious of it, she tucked herself closer to him; felt enveloped by the cocoon of his presence and the comfort she derived from it—and he derived from being with her. It was good being like this. Though, of course, she could do with just a little more…

"Come on." His arm around her shoulder loosened.

"What is it?"

"Let's get away just a little further."

"Can you really read my mind?"

He kissed her. "Don't know. Probably just pheromones."

"I like to think of it as two minds as one."

"Whatever."

"What about the pussycats?"

"I don't think they'll be out yet."

"You make this up as you go along, don't you?" she chuckled.

"No."

"Not that I care."

They got up and tucked the guns into their holsters.

"Tarzan and Jane," she laughed. "Masters of the jungle."

"Let's show them our mettle."

They retreated out of the light of the fire, to where a few straggly shrubs clung to the rocky ground.

"Far enough," Sam said.

"Ground's a bit hard."

"Who said anything about the ground? Have you forgotten the grand suite?"

Chapter 12

"Mr. Donovan! I don't know *what* to say!" She pulled the T-shirt over her head and dropped it on the ground. The stars provided just enough light to see his face. She looked down at herself and back up at him. He grinned. She tugged on his shirt and jerked it up, pulled it off...

And Sam froze.

"Did you hear that?" he whispered.

From the camp another outcry.

Mirlun.

"Shit!" Sam hissed.

Sam drew the Beretta. Its stainless steel finish reflected the dim light from the stars.

"Come on," he hissed. "Quietly!"

She scrambled to pull up her panties and jeans. The belt with the heavy gun came up awkwardly. Sam stood with alert attention as she grabbed their T-shirts from the ground. Hurrying back toward the camp, she pulled hers over her head.

From the direction of the camp she now heard the voices of several men.

They stopped behind the rocky ledge. Sam motioned Helen. She ducked behind him as he peered out cautiously. He raised his left hand, four fingers extended. He pointed at the gun in her hand. "Can you fire that?" he whispered. "At a human being?"

Can I?

She remembered the horror of the chase by the riders, the hunt for the two Minions in Sam's helicopter.

This is different.

No point lying about it. The facts were brutally clear. If these four men were of an unpleasant disposition they would die. This was a horrible truth. There was no other way. They would die with bullets in their bodies, and one or more of these might well be fired by her.

Can I do this?

Their lives were at stake. This was as brutally real as it could get. The constraints of their civilization might still be upon them, but that same civilization was far behind.

She nodded mutely.

Sam eyed her and she saw that the knowledge of her turmoil hurt him deeply, but that he, too, knew that matters had taken on their own momentum.

A moment ago we were about to make love.

"You stay here," Sam whispered. "Cover me."

She nodded. Sam, holding the gun behind his back, stepped out of the protection of the ledge.

The sound of his appearance halted the discussion between the men standing in a circle around Mirlun, who was backed-up against the car, surrounded by the four, looking very uncomfortable. So far, it seemed, he had not been hurt. Maybe knocked around a bit, but nothing serious.

Sam took in the men; their appearance; their clothing. All were dressed similarly; short kilts made of hanging strips of thick leather, held together by a strings affixed to each strip with a rivet; the torsos covered with short-sleeved leather jerkins and not much else. At their sides hung scabbards, now empty, the swords in their hands, pointed at the ground or at Mirlun.

At the noise of Sam's appearance the men turned around. Swords pointed in his direction. Sam felt a dismal pit in his abdomen. That they would have to die was a terrible certainty. Their faces, illuminated by the flickering fire, betrayed their dispositions as clearly as if they had declared themselves in a long speech. Mercenaries. Robbers. Maybe worse. If they didn't die, Sam and his companions would. This was a certainty.

Wounding? Out here, miles from nowhere, a wound was a virtual death sentence.

One of the men, his sword pointing at Sam, stepped forward around the fire.

Sam, fighting a gagging reflex, brought the gun from behind his back. The man halted. His companions, perhaps understanding at some primal level of their being that the man facing them represented a very real danger, stepped away from the car and into a circle around Sam.

No time.

If at all possible he had to keep Helen out of this. If he hesitated much longer this would become impossible.

He raised the Beretta.

"Halt!"

The man before him twisted his face into a sneer and advanced another step.

Sam aimed at the center of the chest, fought down his revulsion, and pulled the trigger. The shot rang across the campsite. The man stopped in mid-motion, a curiously uncomprehending expression on his face. Then his knees gave way and crumpled to the ground beside the fire.

With shouts of anger his companions leapt forward at Sam. He took aim at the closet of them and shot him in the head, brought the Beretta down from the recoil, into line with the next man and shot him, too. The fourth man, finally realizing that death was staring him in the face, turned and ran.

"Halt!" Sam shouted again.

The man continued running.

Sam fought a brief internal battle, then lowered the gun, aimed at the legs, pulled the trigger. The man gave a hoarse shout and fell forward on his face, where he lay, twisting around to hold his injured leg and muttering curses, interwoven with expressions of pain.

Sam motioned to Mirlun. "Take care of his wounds. I will get you the medi–kit in a minute."

"Kill him!" Mirlun said curtly. "Why did you not kill him?"

Sam, who had already turned away to Helen who had stepped from behind the ledge, pivoted and faced the Seladiënnan. "What did you say?"

"Kill him. He would have done the same to us."

"That's hardly a reason!" Sam snapped.

"You killed the others."

"They were attacking me."

"He would have, too."

"But he didn't. He ran away."

"Because he feared for his life."

"And rightly so!"

"Why do you let him live?"

Sam took a deep breath. What was it with Mirlun? This blood–thirst was a new thing.

"Why should I not?"

"Because he is *prehensi*!"

Sam glanced at Sam who had come to stand close beside him, avoiding looking at the three corpses.

"*Prehensi*?" Sam repeated. The word was new to him. "What is a *prehensi*?"

Mirlun groped for words, fell into English. "A…seizer. Of men. Of women. Children."

"'Seizer?'"

"Maybe he means 'taker'," Helen said.

"'Taker'?" Sam asked Mirlun. "Of what?"

Then he understood.

"A *slave* taker?" He gaped at Mirlun. "Seladiënna has *slaves*? You never told us this!"

"It is not significant."

"We'll be the judges of that," Sam grated. He pointed at the corpses. "If you don't want to attend to him, get these out of our sight."

Mirlun stared at Sam defiantly, but Sam didn't budge, and presently Mirlun dropped his gaze.

"Get the kit," Sam told Helen and, holstering the gun, went to the injured man, who regarded him from wide eyes.

Sam hunkered down beside him. The man jerked away from him.

"Let me see your leg," Sam grated in his clumsy 'neo–Latin', as he thought of the language.

The man raised his hands in supplication. Sam bent down and inspected the wound. The guy was lucky; the bullet had gone straight through his calf–muscle, missed major blood vessels, and if it had knicked bone it certainly hadn't shattered it.

"You are fortunate," Sam said carefully.

"You are one ones," the *prehensi* declared, making it a statement of fact.

Sam wasn't sure he'd heard right.

He turned his head and called for Mirlun, who hesitated at first, but then approached with laggard steps.

Sam turned to the *prehensi*. "Say this again," he commanded.

The man looked at him from narrowed eyes.

"Speak!" Mirlun grated.

"You are the ones that are to come," the man said. "Laurentius Augustus wants you."

Mirlun said something, too fast for Sam to understand completely. It sounded like a demand for clarification, followed by a threat.

The injured man replied in an equally rapid staccato, making him barely intelligible. The words 'Laurentius Augustus' figured prominently on several occasions.

Helen approached with the medi–kit and hunkered down to inspect the wound. The *prehensi* regarded her with astonishment as she brought forth a sponge and gauze and began ministering to him.

He muttered something incomprehensible.

A sharp remark from Mirlun, its vernacular making it equally incomprehensible, silenced him.

Still, Sam guessed at some of the meaning.

"They're waiting for us." he said in English.

Mirlun nodded.

"These men," Sam asked, "they were out here to look for us?"

"No," Mirlun said curtly. "They were looking for a group of slaves who escaped from Lenos some days ago. They killed their guards and fled into the wilderness. The *prehensi* sought them in this area, which is a favorite with runaways. The forests here provide a ready source of victuals."

"What was he saying about us?"

"Laurentius Augustus has many men in Lenos—looking for us," Mirlun said.

"Meaning he knows we're arriving in this area of the county, and that he's expecting us to pass through Lenos." He glanced at Mirlun. "How would he know this?"

"Plius."

From his peripheral vision Sam saw the injured man jerk.

"Hold still!" Helen said sharply in English. Her tone carried the message clearly enough. The man lay back and again studied her with a curious regard. He understood they weren't going to kill him and it took the edge off his fear. Sam wondered what to do with him.

"This will do." Helen finished the bandaging, closed the medi–kit, and stood up. She smiled at Sam went to the car. Sam considered the injured *prehensi* and the corpses arrayed around the fire.

Already there's a use for our spade: burying corpses.

He said as much. Mirlun promptly objected. "The animals will dig them up. The gesture is meaningless and wastes time."

Helen seconded Mirlun's position.

"They're people," Sam pointed out.

Helen took his hand and led him away, out of earshot of the other two.

"I feel exactly the same," she said. "But they're *dead*. Their bodies will either rot in the ground and be eaten by maggots or they'll stay on the surface and the cats and whatever scavengers there are will get them. Is there really any difference?"

He looked at her and he realized that she was having a hard time being so damn sensible—but she was nonetheless because she was even more worried about what the killing had done to *him*. He put his arms around her and they hugged each other.

"I'm sorry," he said into her hair.

Against his chest he felt her shake her head.

Sex and death. It was almost a platitude to say that they were close kin. The Janus face of life.

Sex and death. By the agency of those two, evolution had eventually brought forth mankind in general, and Helen and himself in particular.

Sex and death.

It sounded grim—but the truth was that ultimately their antecedents didn't matter. This he understood as they stood there, because her closeness and what it meant for him—for both of them—somehow gave it a meaning that transcended all of the grimy details of evolution and history. If this is what had to happen to make this moment real, then so be it. He'd take the moment. Screw the past.

There was plenty of dry wood: kindling and bigger chunks of long–dead trees and shrub. With the *prehensi* looking on in dim comprehension and against Mirlun's protest, which Sam cut off with a sharp remark, they labored to pull it all together at a spot not far from their present camp fire, heaping it all into a big pile.

Sam drove the car some way off down the hill, to a safe distance from the pyre. With Mirlun's help he heaved the corpses onto the pile—though not without divesting them of their purses first. Real dinars: mostly copper and bronze; a collection of silvers. More wood was heaped onto the pile, covering the corpses. When they were done Sam instructed Mirlun in the use of the Beretta and told him to stand watch for the next few hours. Then he and Helen washed their hands with water from their supply. It was a gesture both symbolic and hygienic.

"Shoot at anything that moves," he told the Seladiënnan. "Including," he pointed at the *prehensi*, "him. Before you do however, maybe you can wheedle some more information out of him. It will serve to keep you awake."

Mirlun's face twisted into a grimace of distaste. That he should actually talk to the *prehensi* yet again...

"*You* were a slave once," Helen said suddenly.

Of course!

Mirlun's expression confirmed her assertion.

"How did the Diënna choose you?"

"Why did she choose a slave?" Mirlun shook his head. "The Diënna does as she does. She chose me."

"Whatever," Sam said curtly. "We need to know everything we can know from this man. You have several hours to find out."

"What will we do with him?"

"We're not going to kill him, if that's what you were wondering."

Mirlun looked disappointed. Maybe he had hoped Helen's act of charity was done purely for keeping the *prehensi* alive for just lone enough to ask some serious questions. Sam glanced at Helen and made a wry face. He went over to the captive, who sat leaning against a tree, watching the goings–on around him with attention, and hunkered down before him.

"What is your name?"

He man hesitated. "Plenus."

"Plenus." Sam was struggling with his new language, searching for words, finding maybe the right ones, and substituting guesses for others. "I am a tired. I am angry. I have just killed three men. I have not killed you because you did not attack me. I will not kill you unless you give me a reason to do so." He considered Plenus' coarse, brutish face for a moment or two before continuing. "Do you think this is weakness?"

"I think I would have killed you," Plenus said frankly. "I think you allowed me to live for inquisition."

Sam allowed himself a thin smile.

"You will live after the...inquisition. If you threaten me or my companions, you will die. If you do not threaten us you will live. This I swear."

Surprise replaced the cynical mien of Plenus' face.

"Why does Laurentius wants us?" Sam asked.

Plenus hesitated. Then he uttered a quick staccato sentence, of which Sam caught only fragments.

He turned to Mirlun. "What did he say?"

"That Laurentius offers twelve gold dinars for a head and a hand of each of us," Mirlun said in English.

"Really?" Sam muttered. "That's a lot of cash, right?"

"Laurentius has also promised a number of other rewards, including a supply of" —Mirlun hesitated fastidiously—"whores...of any sex to the bearer of our head or heads; plus a position of significance in the *Praetori*."

"That's even more incentive. Job security. Status." Sam glanced at Plenus again. "You have your life," he said. "That is of more value than twelve gold pieces, or a dozen whores, or anything Laurentius can offer. I have therefore rewarded you with more than he ever could. Do you not agree with this?"

The *prehensi* regarded Sam with a quizzical expression.

"Why do you honor your enemies?" he asked.

Sam wasn't sure he had understood the question correctly.

"Honor?"

"He wants to know why you burn them," Mirlun said in English.

"It is an honor?" Helen asked.

Sam and Helen exchanged a glance. Here lay the explanation for Mirlun's earlier protest. To burn the *prehensi* corpses: that was even more offensive to Mirlun's sensibilities than allowing Plenus to live.

Sam addressed the *prehensi*. "They were men." He groped for words, but could not find 'misguided' in what he thought of as his 'Neo–Latin' vocabulary. "Foolish men," he substituted. "They are dead now. I do not want to leave them to *scawagi*."

From behind a sharp inhalation from Mirlun. Sam concluded that exactly this was done to those one wished to *dis*honor: leave their corpses to be eaten by maggots or other scavengers. Those you honored you burned. Burning was a ritual, an effort. Not something you did for low–life like these guys.

Mirlun had a lot to learn. There would be times when Sam didn't have the luxury of being able to bury his dead foes. But here he had a choice, and here we chose to do as he did. It was the least he could do for three men he had effectively murdered—for they'd never had a chance. The factor of self–defense mitigated his guilt somewhat, but the truth was as it was. He would have to live with it; and he could. But the gesture had to be made.

Sam stood and took Helen's hand. "We are going to try and get some sleep," he said to Mirlun. "You can rest tomorrow. Tonight watch over this pyre and keep the fire going. Tomorrow before we leave we will set it alight."

He turned to Plenus. "Do not attempt to escape."

The man nodded. "I am not a fool."

In the car they lay down on the back seat. The fire cast a flickering glow across the inside of the roof. They lay there, just holding onto each other.

"You know," she said , "our love–making probably saved our lives."

He hadn't looked at it that way, but, yes, she was right. Had they remained by the fire they would probably have been surprised and unable to defend themselves effectively. Chance had contrived to prevent this from happening.

"That proves it," he said. "Love is good for you."

"Did you need proof?"

"No."

And somehow death, though just a few paces distant, was further away than it had ever been.

13

Morning.

After setting the pyre ablaze, they departed. Plenus was left behind. He would have to make his own way back. Helen examined the wound, pronounced herself satisfied with the result, and put the dressing back on.

"When you return to Lenos," she told the *prehensi*, "wash it with…" She looked at Mirlun. "Strong liquor."

"*Schnasi*," Mirlun supplied.

"*Schnasi*," Helen told Plenus. "It will keep the wound clean. It will hurt, too."

Plenus regarded her with that quizzical expression he always had when she was close. Sam thought it a mix of astonishment, fear and desire.

The slave–taker nodded mutely.

The pyre burned hotly as they left. Mirlun, having quizzed Plenus about the best way to Lenos, indicated the eastern edge of the rain–forest ahead. "That way. We skirt the forest and head for the basin yonder."

Sam thought it might be about twenty miles to the town. They'd have to ditch the car long before that. It would be a long walk at the end of the day.

"Did the *prehensi* tell you more about the prize on our heads?" Sam asked Mirlun.

"It seems that the whole city is on the lookout for us."

"Maybe we should avoid Lenos altogether."

"It is a long way into Seladiënna," Mirlun said darkly. "From Lenos we can catch a ship to the capital. It will avoid much overland travel and many dangers. It will also save much time."

Sam thought about it. "You may have to go in there ahead of us. We need more… authentic…clothes. Hats to conceal our faces. Find us some travel–packs such as itinerant mercenaries might use. Maybe even horses."

Mirlun nodded his agreement. "What are you going to do in the meantime?"

"We'll find a place to hide and wait for you there."

Mirlun clearly wasn't enthused about the idea, but Helen supported Sam's suggestions. "It looks to me like we won't have a chance without it."

Mirlun fell silent and spent the rest of the next few hours deep in thought. They didn't try to disturb him. He was a man of resources and this they had to leave to his devices.

The Aventurista bumped along for much of the morning, before they halted for a late breakfast.

When they finished Sam climbed back into the car and looked at the speedometer. "Twenty–eight kilometers. That's about…seventeen miles? With detours and all…Still, I think we're just about close enough. Let's find a place to hide this thing."

They drove on, skirting the edge of the rain–forest, until they came upon a high–lying patch of ground that was dry and mostly rocky. Sam stopped the car, got out, and looked around.

"There's nowhere 'safe' to leave the car," he told them. "Plenus will be following our tracks and he'll find it, no matter what we do. I certainly don't want that." There really was no alternative. "We're going to burn it."

"What?" Helen stared at him.

"What else can we do?" He knew how she felt. Another link to their world severed for good.

"Shit!" Helen muttered.

"Yeah."

"We'll take the coffee!" she declared.

"And the *chorizos*," he added.

They drove the car to a spot where its conflagration would not spread through dry grass or bush, readied their packs and shouldered them. Then Sam poured the remaining diesel fuel around the interior of the Aventurista, the engine compartment, over the paintwork; placed the container with the rest of the diesel into the back–seat, stood back and lit an old piece of crumpled newspaper which he threw into the window.

They walked away from the pall of smoke rising into the sky, neither of them looking back, focusing instead on getting as far away from here as possible. Someone might see the smoke and come to investigate. They'd rather not be around when they did.

The day wore on. The sun beat down from a sky flecked only with a insignificant few shreds of high cloud. The packs on their backs increased in weight and size until it seemed that they couldn't possibly go on carrying them any further. But they did. Among the small mercies: the fact that they'd brought sun–glasses. Without them it would have been even worse, it was so bright.

Lenos announced itself not by sight but smell. The wind blowing from the north carried a strange melange of scents and reeks in their direction. Then they came upon a lonely house, tucked away into the bush. It had been fabricated from rough, now–rotting, logs and appeared long–deserted. They investigated with great caution and found two human skeletons, cleaned out by time and ants. Both still wore their clothes: male and female. The man's skull had been split apart, the women's breastbone been crushed. Lives brought to a violent end.

Farmers? Just folks who thought they could come and settle out here and eke a living from the land?

Sam and Helen ensconced themselves in the hut and sent Mirlun off on his errand.

"When do you think he'll be back?" Helen wondered.

"It depends, I suppose."

"We may have to spend the night here."

"Possibly."

She shivered. Clearly the notion of spending a night with the skeletons of two murdered human beings did not enchant her—or him.

They opened their packs and took stock of what they had. If they had to re–pack, some of the items might have to be left behind. Sam hoped that Mirlun managed to organize horses and that he was intelligent enough to get them out of the city in such a way that no–one noticed.

Too many imponderables…

The day wore on. The afternoon brought a cessation of all air movement and a sweltering heat wave. They reclined languidly, out of sight of the road, resting on the ground beside a big tree at some distance from the house and its human remains. Here you could almost forget what was back there. The ground was covered in tall grass. Closer inspection revealed it to be apparently free of little critters. Sam and Helen spread out their long waterproof parkas and used them as ground–sheets. The situation was not unpleasant; a short interlude of enforced inactivity in what was almost an idyllic setting. The guns lying on the ground beside them belied the impression, but not fatally so.

"I wonder why there aren't any mosquitoes," Helen said, took another swig from her canteen, and reclined on her back again. They were just about through with the water. Rain would be most welcome and soon. In the west, the first signs of cloud towers were rearing into the sky. Just like yesterday, before an ocean had emptied on top of them.

Sam raised himself on an elbow and looked down on her. He ran the tip of a finger through the perspiration on the skin between her bare breasts, traced it down to her belly–button, completed a loop around the indentation and traced the finger back up again. Helen smiled languidly.

"Maybe evolution missed that whole branch of the insects just like it failed to produce humans," he said.

"Funny, isn't it?" she mused. "I wonder how all this works."

"You and me both," he agreed.

"You think this place once was the same as our world? Then it did what? Split off? Went away on its own?"

"Maybe," he agreed. "My knowledge of esoteric physics isn't up there with Stephen Hawking, but it makes some crazy kind of sense. Something happened, and it was different in our world to what it was here—and so we get two."

"How long ago do you think it happened?"

"I suppose we could figure it out. Approximately. No humans means what? A few hundred thousand years at least. No mosquitoes may mean millions. I think it's probably more like that."

"Yet the worlds still stay in contact somehow."

"Looks like it."

"Maybe one day we'll figure out a pattern."

"That would be good."

"We might not."

"That's fine, too. We've made our choice."

"You think it was the right choice?"

"What's 'right'?"

She smiled and took one of his hands, kissed the palm, placed it against her cheek..

"This is."

"Definitely."

She eyed him speculatively. "How long have we been together now? Eight, nine weeks?"

"Something like that."

"You think that should be long enough to stop me from wanting to jump you every time we have a few spare minutes?"

"Not in my book."

"What book's that?"

"The one that says: I want to make love to Helen every time I have a spare minute." She smiled. "I'm serious."

"So am I."

"Almost–thirty–year olds like me aren't supposed to behave like this."

"Oh? What are almost–thirty–year olds supposed to behave like?"

"I don't know. Not like terminally horny teenagers, I guess."

"Remember what it was like then?"

"I try not to."

"Not a good time, huh?"

"Is it for anybody?"

"I guess not. How was your sex life?"

"OK."

"OK?"

"Yeah."

"Were you in love with anybody?"

"No. But I had sex. Didn't everybody?"

I didn't. Not until I was twenty–one.

"I was shy," he said.

"You?"

"Very."

"Frances…"

"…was my first."

"Wow."

"It happens."

"Not a lot. Maybe to religious freaks."

"That I was not, am not, nor will I ever be."

"That's a relief." She smiled.

"But you weren't in love, were you?" he asked her. "Not then."

"I was never in love—until us."

"Snap."

"What about Frances?"

"Not like *this*." He leaned closer to her and held her unwavering gaze, knew that he had spoken nothing but the limpid truth.

Where were you all my life?

Her lips twitched into a smile; her wondrous eyes crinkled at the corners.

"Tell me again," she teased. "A girl likes to hear these things. Again. And again."

"I'm afraid," he said huskily, "that Dr. Donovan, the world–famous psychologist, is unable to give a coherent analysis at this point in time—since he is entirely bewitched."

She heaved a deep breath; her breasts rose and fell suggestively. "Then I have Dr. Donovan exactly where I want him."

"I still want to know why I'm behaving like a horny teenager," she said later, now happily exhausted. Her head lay in the crook of his right arm, her face turned to look at his. "Is Dr. Donovan, the word–famous psychologist, now in a post–coital state, capable of analyzing the situation with more clarity?"

"Who invented 'Dr. Donovan' anyway?"

"You did, pre–coitally."

"Did I?"

"Don't change the subject."

Sam chuckled. "I think you…both of us actually—and for me it's even 'later' than for you!—are catching up with something we should have had many years ago. Only we're having it now, as adults. I think love like this is wasted on teens—and I don't want to miss a single moment of any of this." He held her closer. "I also think—I *know*—that this isn't just teenage horniness transplanted into later–age. You and me: we're *it*. It's a simple as that."

He traced the outlines of her face with his index finger. She was smiling. He liked it when she smiled. He'd liked it even before their 'coming out', when they were still at each others' throats. He might not have admitted it to himself then, but it was there all the same.

She tucked herself closer to him. At that very moment the first fat drops of rain hit them. Helen squealed, then fell into uncontrollable giggles as the drops became a flood in the space of few seconds. The rain was luke–warm but compared to the sultry heat from before it was like a cool tonic. It pooled in the parkas underneath them and it was like lying in a shallow bath. Sam was about to get up, but Helen wasn't having any of it. She pulled him down again and slid on top of him, took his head between her hands and kissed him deeply. Against expectation he became aroused again; and though his reserves were temporarily too exhausted for an orgasm, he rejoiced in hers as she arched on top of him as the rain streamed off her upturned face—before she sank and buried it in the crook of his neck—and the rain continued to pour down and cleanse them of the sweat and the grime of the day.

Just before the downpour finished Sam remembered about their canteens. They turned the parkas around and held them so the rain pooled into them. Then Helen handed her sides of the fabric for Sam to grasp, thus forming the parka into a temporary bag. She held the canteens underneath and Sam poured the water from the spout formed by the hanging garment. They repeated the procedure and by the time the rain ceased had managed to fill up both canteens.

They wrung out their soggy clothes and put on what Helen thought of as 'crotch–wear'. Not that it mattered, but just in case Mirlun happened to show up suddenly—or maybe something else. Helen decided to try the custom–made Kevlar bra, fabricated to conform to Mirlun's descriptions of what women wore around here. Might as well try it out. Though topless *was* nice. The heat and the humidity, it made you feel like you didn't want to wear any damn thing at all. But, as events on the previous night had demonstrated, you never knew. If she was of a mind to jump Sam again—which she might well be—the bra would not present any obstacle.

The afternoon wore on. They rested and talked as the sun slanted down. Evening approached. Mirlun was nowhere in sight. The shadows of the trees lengthened until they merged into a solid carpet of darkness. Despite the unsettling presence of the skeletons, Sam and Helen decided to retreat into the house, which provided a defensible area.

Defensible against whom? They found out soon enough when the first wolf–calls sounded: this time unsettlingly close, the chorus seemingly all around them.

They didn't dare light a fire, not this close to possibly inimical civilization, and instead barricaded the two entrances with walls of branches and logs. Then they made themselves as comfortable as possible, propped up against their packs, their guns at the ready, alert to every sound of the night.

Helen didn't think she could possibly sleep, but somehow she did—for part of the night anyway. Then she was woken by Sam, whom she was using as a pillow. A scrabbling, scraping sound at one of the barricaded doorways. Sam shined his flashlight. Two pairs of pinpoint reflections revealed the presences behind the defensive works.

Helen sat up.

"Hold your hands over your ears," Sam told her.

She did. He squeezed off single shot in the direction of the eyes. Even through her hands it was deafening in the small confined space of the hut. The eyes disappeared. Helen took her hands from her ears.

"I can't hear anything," Sam said, rather loud, she thought. Then she realized that he'd be hearing even less than her. "Let me know if you can hear them," he told her. "At least until my senses come back."

Sometime later he told her that the ringing in his ears was finally subsiding. The flashlight revealed no more tell–tale pairs of luminous dots.

"They never heard a shot in their lives," Sam remarked. "It probably scared the shits out of them. Wolves are very intelligent, and this lot probably decided that they'd find easier, less noisy game somewhere else."

"That and the smell of man, I suppose," she added.

"That, too," he agreed.

They settled back down. Helen tucked herself to Sam and listened to him breathing. Not all of their problems, she thought, would be dealt with in a similarly expeditious manner. Wolves might be scared off by noises, but even they would ultimately get used to it. People would do so much quicker. Guns, as Sam had pointed out some time ago when they were getting ready for the trip, were not a solution. Indeed, they were dangerous. To be armed too well made you think that you were much better prepared than you really were. Kevlar vests, flak jackets, guns, even antibiotics and anti–inflammatories: these were defensive devices, protective armor, that could and probably would be breached. It was only a question of time and contingency. Survival ultimately depended not on their use, but on their use as auxiliary devices in a larger strategy of survival, which must include appropriate preparation and consideration of every even remotely potentially–dangerous situation.

Vigilance, forethought, a goodly streak of paranoia. Don't sit with your back to a door, leave your weapons where you can find them in the dark, keep your hands free—and always try to anticipate, anticipate, anticipate.

We didn't do too well last night.

And luck! Yeah, luck, too. And last night it had been luck.

Does love attract luck?

Not if you asked Romeo and Juliet, of course.

Who wants to ask them?

Chapter 13

Maybe last night was a lesson they had to take to heart. For Sam had broken just about all the precepts he'd tried to drum into her the weeks before. About the only thing you could say about what they'd done, just before hell broke loose, was that they'd most *definitely* kept their weapons where they could get at them in the dark.

The thought made her smile.

"What are you smiling at?" He must have felt it against him.

"Last night."

She felt him laugh quietly. "We're a strange pair," he said softly.

"A nicely strange pair," she corrected.

"Definitely."

The night passed without further incident. Finally, dawn filtered through the barricades and the cracks in the walls. They rose and found a place to attend to their bodily functions. Toilet paper, thought Helen, was something she'd definitely miss. Strange how little oddments like that should assume such significance.

The sun cast its first rays across the trees. The dawn chorus of birds fell silent as they went about their business. Mirlun had not put in an appearance as yet. Helen was getting worried.

"Let's give him until noon," Sam suggested. "I think a day is not unreasonable."

Maybe not, but it was wearing on her nerves. Not knowing at all...

"The man followed us from England to the US!" Sam must have guessed her thoughts. "He procured himself a fake passport, for heaven's sake. That guy is not going to be fazed easily."

He was right, of course, but...

Sam handed her a mug of coffee, stewed up on his gas stove which he'd insisted on taking, despite the weight. Black, no sugar. She liked it white, with just one, but what the heck.

"Here," he said. "Stop fretting. Enjoy your penultimate cup of Real Earth–One Coffee."

They clinked plastic cups, and she laughed despite her tension.

"What are we going to do until then?" she wondered.

He chuckled. "Isn't it funny? Here we are, on the quest to save a world, and we have no idea what to do with ourselves." He grinned at her. "We could make up for lost time to come!"

"Mr. Donovan, are you suggesting..."

"I am suggesting," he said, "that we get everything packed ready to go, and then lie down in the grass—maybe over there, where we've nicely flattened it already!—and do what we do so well."

"The day's hardly started!"

"So?"

"You're insatiable."

He shrugged. "Sue me. Must be a guy–thing."

She shook her head. "No." She smiled. "It's a Sam–and–Helen thing." She squinted into the bright sun. "You think we're weird?"

"I think we're...*right*."

"Yeah..."

The morning passed in languor, despite the uncertainties. It was amazing, she thought, what sex could do for you. Better than Valium, Prozac, St. John's Wort, chocolate, meditation, religious ritual, or anything else anybody had ever figured for the healing of the soul, put together. Of course, you had to be in love. Preferably totally, completely, utterly, consumingly so. That was the magic prerequisite for the thing to actually *work*. The mind and the body chemistry just *so*. Loving his smells; his sounds; his feel; the texture of his skin; the taste of his perspiration; the close–up scent of his skin; the texture of his body; the ticklish roughness of his beard when he kissed or caressed her, no matter where; the sound and sight of his abandon, above, below, or beside her.

Maybe a few too many prerequisites for it to become acknowledged as a major healing remedy.

She stopped thinking about it and gave herself to Sam and the moment.

Dissonant sounds added themselves to the by–now–familiar ones produced by the bush and its inhabitants. Helen and Sam ceased their caresses and froze to listen.

"Horses," Sam whispered.

He was right. Snorting. The scrape of several sets of hooves.

Friend or foe? Mirlun or someone else? Passerby or searcher?

They dressed hastily, staying down in the grass as they did; then grabbed their guns and, ducking low, headed toward the hut and in the general direction of the noises.

Mirlun, leading four saddled horses, came toward them. He smiled thinly. "Your fake dinars fooled everybody," he said.

He told them that he'd left Lenos even before the first break of dawn, exiting the city to the east and doubling around it, such as to make it easier for them to re–enter from the south.

"There's a certain stable we need to avoid," he said. "The owner might recognize his animals and gear—and me, of course. But as long as we do this, there should not be a problem."

One of the horses had been designated as a packing animal, with a couple of elongated bags slung across its back. Large enough to hold just about all their gear.

Sam expressed his satisfaction at the arrangement. They transferred their stuff into the bags and put on the garments Mirlun had brought: short, sleeveless, sandy–colored tunics which they were to wear above their leather–strip kilts; authentic sandals of the realm, which looked much more convincing than sneakers; the kind of medium–wide–brimmed straw hats they'd already seen dangling on the backs of the *prehensi*. Almost Mexican. She put it on and suddenly felt like an actress in a Western. Indeed, the whole thing had an air of movie–set dress–up about it. Only this thing here was for real, and the authenticity of it might well determine their very survival.

Mirlun eyed them critically and commented on their still–pale skins. Sam produced something even Helen hadn't known he'd packed: a bottle of skin–bronzing lotion, which they applied to each other; sparingly, mixed in with sun–screen, which was a necessity, and without which they'd soon be fried to a crisp.

The guns. The tunics had this advantage: they provided good concealment. The Berettas went into their saddle bags, the smaller Glocks into light shoulder holsters well–hidden under the tunics. Not exactly easy to reach, but Sam appeared to be satisfied that it would do. Besides, as he pointed out, they were weapons of the very last resort. Once they used them, the game was up. The swords would have to do for effect. They were out-of-place enough, being of a very different style than what was common here. Still, until they were drawn from their deliberately worn–looking scabbards, their strangeness was not too obvious. In the manner of traveling mercenaries they wore them strapped diagonally across their backs using an arrangement that consisted of a belt, that also held the tunic together at the waist, with a strap that went from the right side straight up to the shoulder, to connect with a stiff sheath that surrounded the original scabbard, which in turn held the sword, and whose lower end was attached to the belt with a leather noose. The whole arrangement was like a 'shoulder–holster' for a sword, with the difference that it was external. They had had it manufactured according to Mirlun's specifications by a saddlery in Albuquerque. Before putting it on, Sam 'authenticated' the too–clean surface of the leather by abrading it with coarse dirt and blotching it with a variety of substances ranging from oil to red wine.

Finally, satisfied that all was a good as they could make it, their skins suitably 'bronzed'—which looked just a tad weird to her, but Mirlun appeared satisfied, so it must have been all right—they set off for Lenos.

Helen hadn't sat on a horse for a couple of years, though she used to go riding quite a bit before that. She felt comfortable enough, and the animals had been well chosen. Disciplined and yet not torpid. The saddles were constructed of leather; proper saddles, conforming to the animal's back and the rider's posterior alike. Mirlun assured her that this was the usual style. Both saddles had obviously been extensively used before.

The ride to Lenos didn't take long. They had been closer than Helen had expected. About half an hour of walking the horses and they reached the first houses: hovels mostly, the kind they'd spent the last night in. A dreary collection, scattered apparently at random throughout cleared bushland. Roads were not evident, only trodden paths between huts. There was a rudimentary sewage system which consisted of open trenches maybe two feet wide and about just as deep, which meandered without much plan between the huts, all heading downhill a gentle slope toward the ocean. The place stank to high heaven. Helen noticed even Mirlun wrinkling his nose. The people fit the slum. Scrawny bedraggled urchins, filthy and often naked; their expressions beyond despair: vacant, empty, lifeless. Adults: older girls and women, crones and withered caricatures of human beings; dressed in filthy rags, barely sufficient to conceal their nakedness, without pride or regard for cleanliness or appearance. Men: conspicuous by their absence; except for scattering of bowed old wrecks, usually crouching together near some hut or other, watching the world go by as the women washed clothes in a putrid cesspool that once might have been a charming little pond.

Helen averted her gaze from the misery and despair. She'd once gone to India, for whatever reasons she'd now forgotten, and the worst of that had been pretty much the same as here. So much misery and terminal hopelessness concentrated in one place reminded her forcefully that, no matter what her complaints about life might have been, they paled into insignificance beside…this.

The riders' passing attracted considerable attention. Everything stopped. Uncounted pairs of eyes, from the youngest to the nearly blind, followed their progress. It was like being on a stage, with the world's attention riveted on your performance. But, Helen noticed, unlike in India, there was no begging here. Nobody came up and held out their hands or clamored for help.

Probably, she thought, *because they don't expect any.*

So they rode through the outskirts of misery, and tried to ignore the sights and the stench and the silence that fell as they rode through, and which broke behind them, as possibly the only out–of–the–ordinary–misery thing of the day or the month became the topic of a thousand uninformed speculations. Helen glanced sideways at Sam, whose face was a grimace of distaste. He, too, knew that here was literally nothing he could ever hope to do; and knowing him, he was suppressing his emotional reaction with difficulty.

"I try not to let the misery of the world get to me," he'd once told her. "There was a time when I did. It nearly made me into a basket–case."

She knew what he meant. If you opened yourself—*really* opened yourself—to the terrible things all around you: the misery of poverty, the terror of the victims of violence, the terminal despair of severe illness, the pathetic misery of the ravages of old age…if you allowed yourself to actually *feel* that…

No mind had the capacity to tolerate the consciousness, the actual comprehension of the existence and the reality of such things. And so you closed yourself off and focused on your own survival, trying to retain the hope that was the burning flame lending warmth to your own life, blocking out the knowledge that for every one like you there were a thousand who did not have the luxury of hope.

They rode on and presently reached a different layer of habitation, more like that of a 'normal' city. Opulent suburban. The wooden houses, some of them elaborate and almost qualifying as 'mansions'—occasionally surrounded by expansive tracts of land, between, she guessed, one–half to one acre, but sometimes quite close to the road—reminded Helen of pictures she'd seen of ancient Roman villas; with porticos, balconies, colonnaded entrances and gardens; occasional forecourts with floors of ornate mosaics, fountains, sundials, statues of pubescent children or adults in states of occasionally explicit sexual activity or arousal; elaborate beds of flowers and shrubs, carefully tended. Here was a refined wealth in stark contrast to the abject poverty only a few hundred yards back.

Here, too, eyes followed them. The passerby—mostly, she supposed, servants of one kind or another, in the employ of the local rich–folk—though not loitering and usually on their way somewhere, still glanced at the riders, two of whom had swords strapped across their backs.

Helen bit back a grin. *We'll probably look a fearsome sight.*

Mirlun fell back until his horse was level with her own.

"I would be advisable not to evince excessive interest in our surroundings," he told her quietly. "Mercenaries are not known for their interest in local scenery."

Guiltily she did her best to conform to her role.

Beyond the affluent suburb they finally entered Lenos proper: a dense collection of, mostly wooden, edifices, many of them two or three storeys tall—some of them painted, but most showing the natural color of weathered wood—clustered around a system of winding alleys and system of broader streets almost all of which seemed to double as marketplaces; lined as they were by densely packed rows of stalls on either side—and leading right up to the town center: a rotund plaza, maybe two–hundred yards across; whose periphery was rimmed by a circle of stalls, selling just about everything, from sizzling sausages to jewelry. There were barbers, book sellers, perfume merchants, snake charmers, street entertainers, spice merchants, bakers, butchers, poultry sellers, fish mongers, cobblers, gold–smiths, copper smiths, money changers, amber carvers, sellers of a strange yellow powder which Mirlun identified as being of mainly sulfuric content, soap merchants, herb peddlers, gambling stalls and tables. An array of open vats at one stall contained an unidentifiable dark–brown liquid, which emitted a horrid stench; like mix of putrid fish and fruit, with a goodly measure of garlic and a hefty dose of vitamin B.

"*Liquamen*," Mirlun supplied.

"Huh?"

"A…sauce. It is prepared from substances derived from fish, with various spices and lots of salt for preservation."

"You *eat* that?" Sam muttered.

Mirlun smiled wistfully. "Despite the varied and often interesting foods in your world, it is *liquamen* I missed most."

Helen exchanged a glance with Sam. They both had the same thought.

Yak!

She considered the crowd of people around the *liquamen* stall, holding vessels of all kinds, from elongated crude glass bottles to pot–bellied earthenware containers, lining up to buy the vile stuff. Maybe some things were beyond understanding. Maybe this was one of them. People *consumed* this putrid shit?

Mirlun divined the thrust of her reflections. "You will have to acquire a taste for it," he said dryly. "It is a universal condiment and you will be expected to use it on almost all food. Not doing this would definitely attract attention. Especially in Lenos, where a hundred eyes watch your every move."

"Then we eat somewhere people don't look!" she snapped.

Mirlun opened his mouth to say something, but she gave him a dirty look and he shut it again. She glanced at Sam, who was grinning. He gave the slightest of shrugs. It could have meant anything: from resignation over Mirlun's attitude to acceptance of the inevitability to having to accept *liquamen* as a part of their daily diet. She grimaced and returned her attention to her environment.

In front of the stalls and across the expanse of the plaza a variety of activities attracted the attention of passerby. Troupes of gaudily dressed dancers performed grotesque mimes of occasionally disturbing intensity. A small group of musicians contrived—to her ears discordant—tunes on instruments ranging from reedy sounding whistles to banjo–like stringed instruments and what looked like bongo–drums. A bunch of women in the skimpiest of attires, some of them revealing nipples and even tufts of pubic hair, danced near the players.

"*Prostitutae*," Mirlun commented primly, not bothering to conceal his disapproval.

Helen considered the women. Some were mere children, their pubescent breasts pert and cheeky, exposed for all to see. At the other end of the spectrum over–ripe near–matrons with expansive mammaries and hips barely constrained by skimpy bikini tops and bottoms. When, in the course of their suggestive gyrations, the women raised their arms Helen saw that, like it was common even in contemporary *E1*–Europe, their armpits were all unshaven.

That's one habit I'm not going to pick up!

In this heat? You had to be kidding! They must *stink*!

Not that anybody'd notice. The place was a dazzling melange of reeks, ranging from the plainly revolting to the merely intense—though 'revolting' definitely had the upper hand. Not all of it produced by humans either. Animal droppings were copious, though the plaza itself appeared to be closed to them and thus was free of cow–pads and horse–shit. Those engaged to clean it up—a special profession it appeared, its practitioners pulling little carts of manure around to which they added using small wooden shovels—looked like they belonged to the underclass inhabiting the slums at the outer periphery. They were, Helen thought glumly, probably the ones who were considered better off.

At the far end of the plaza a small podium held a number of near–naked men, women and children in various conditions, ranging from scrawny to solidly muscular. By their poses, which had about them a universal air or profound defeat and resignation, and the way in which Mirlun carefully avoided looking at them—and when he did it was with a smoldering loathing that was almost a physical thing— Helen knew these people to be slaves. On the ground around the elevated platform milled a circle of men, gesticulating and shouting at each other. At first she thought it was a fight of sorts, but then realized that they were haggling.

Around and through all this activity flowed the remainder of Lenos' populace. Old and young, men and women, adults and children, rich and poor; dressed in plain gray and sand–colored tunics, or gaudily, like the prostitutes, in yellow, purple, red, green, blue, black, maroon, brown, or, quite often, in plain white. Because of the heat, garments were mostly light colored, not designed to keep warm, but merely to cover—and display, of course, as the case might be. Hats were in evidence, mostly of the same kind she herself was wearing. In a crowd that made for an interesting sight as the space occupied by the hats usually exceeded that of the body. As a consequence, hats often dangled on people's backs, held there by strings or bands around the wearers' necks.

And it was *noisy*! Times Square had nothing on this place. The sources of the noises were different, of course. At home it was mostly traffic, but here the noises of the peddlers combined with those of the musicians and people milling about, the grinding of the wooden wheels of carriages pulled by cattle–beast of unknown derivation and antecedents over the stone and muck ground, the clanging of the black–smith's hammer on his anvil, the neighing of horses, the shouts and bellows of team–leaders, trying to spur their sluggish cattle–beasts into more fervent activity.

A different kind of noise, maybe, but *noise*! No disputing also that the place was teeming with life and energy: fecund, basic, occasionally revolting. Whatever else Lenos was, whatever decrepitude she discerned, it was vibrant with activity and even a weird kind of purpose. A town of outcasts it might be, and some of the down–side of it she had already seen, but people definitely *lived* here. If this was a marginalized community, what might one expect to find at the heart of the Seladiënnan empire?

The travelers halted at the periphery of the plaza and dismounted, then led their horses into an alley, where Mirlun had located a stable he considered adequate for their purposes; safely distant from the place where he'd purchased the horses and gear.

"What are we going to do with our gear?" Sam wondered. "Is there any place we can leave it where it's going to be safe?"

"This is Lenos," Mirlun said scornfully. "The concept of 'safety' is allied inextricably to the force used to back it."

Chapter 13

"That," Sam said acidly, "is usually the case."

"Not in Seladiënna," Mirlun retorted, definitely miffed.

Sam regarded him for a moment, then shrugged and dropped the subject.

"Seladiënna is *civilized*," Mirlun insisted, irked by Sam's implied dismissal of his assertions. "A Seladiënna citizen does what he does because of a prevailing morality; not because he is likely to be punished if he didn't. He has agreed to accept certain precepts in exchange for the context of his society."

Sam halted their progress and made a gesture in the direction of the plaza. "So have they. Whatever society they have here: it functions, does it not?"

"It is anarchy."

"It is a society with certain unpleasant aspects," Sam corrected. "As are all societies. The social contract is never perfect, not even within Seladiënna." He looked back at the plaza, a portion of which was still visible from their current vantage point. The noises reverberated between the houses, to be swallowed by the bodies of the people moving around them, eyeing them curiously and giving them as wide a berth as was possible and discreet without being offensive. Helen had to suppress a grin. It seemed that, even if this was Lenos—or maybe because of it—heavily armed mercenaries were folks to be avoided if at all possible. She didn't think that probing questions were going to be a problem. Nobody was going to ask.

"These people have found a *modus vivendi*," Sam told Mirlun. "We may not like it and it may be lacking, but anarchy it is not."

Mirlun turned and stalked off. Sam gave her a wry look. "Our resourceful friend has some delicate sensibilities," he said lowly.

"Why do I have the feeling you're being deliberately offensive?"

"You've noticed, huh?"

"Why?"

"Because now we're here, and we've got to do the job we came here to do. Mirlun, being back home—well, almost…did you notice how he's changing? He's got us where he needs us and he's less guarded about what he does—and says. I'm just trying to get all the facts before we finally leap into the fray."

"How's pissing him off going to get us more facts?"

"It gets us more facts about those who're on our side." They halted in front of an establishment that was a combination stable and hostelry, exhibiting a curved wooden sign with the inscription *PACIVARIUS*. "Knowing your enemy is only half the game. Knowing your allies is even more important."

"You're a cynic, Sam Donovan."

"Nah! Just paranoid."

Two stable-boys materialized beside them. They were in their mid-teens, dressed in simple gray tunics, bare-footed, grimy-faced, and they reeked of horses and manure. Helen carefully refrained from wrinkling her nose. Mirlun shooed the boys away.

"Do not trust them," he said, leaning close to Helen and Sam. "Do not leave anything valuable with the horses. You will surely not see it again. Given the nature of what you've brought with you…"

"How are we going to find any place to leave this stuff without having someone go through it?" Sam wanted to know.

"I will attend to it," Mirlun assured him.

"How?"

"Threats issued by mercenaries are usually heeded. It would be better of they came from you, but your language skills are as yet not...developed...sufficiently. So, if you could just stand behind me—appear dire and threatening..."

Helen glanced at Sam whose mouth twitched. He winked at her.

"I could enjoy this."

"I bet."

They tied up the horses at a railing in front of the stable, installed there for such purposes. Helen stayed outside while Sam followed Mirlun inside, presumably to 'appear dire and threatening'. She wondered how he'd do it. Frown? Just stare at the hapless owner, clerk, or whomever, while Mirlun uttered the appropriate pronouncements?

It still was a bit like being in a movie. The whole thing hadn't quite registered at a gut level. She *knew* that she was not only in a strange town but an entirely different *world*, but somehow that just didn't want to sink in. At the moment it was still like being in...well, just a strange town. Some really far-out place on their own Earth, where there were no cars, cellphones, computers, airports, whatever—and where they ate strange foods that turned your stomach. The stench of *liquamen* still clung somewhere in her nostrils, refusing to go away. Or maybe it just all around her, so pervasive that it drenched everything in sight, the walls of the buildings, the clothes of the people.

But none of this actually made her *understand* that she was, quite literally, out of her own world. Somehow a part of her expected to travel back fifty miles or so, or maybe a hundred, and get to the little airport whence they would eventually return from this slightly bizarre holiday to the comfortable precincts of Albuquerque or wherever; where she and Sam had a house and could screw all night in a nice bed, take a shower whenever it pleased them, and do all those things they'd so much taken for granted, and which now were simply...gone.

Maybe it was sinking in after all. The feel of the sword strapped across her back—something she'd almost gotten used to—suddenly brought the reality of what and where even closer. The adults and children passing by her, deviating from their normal paths to avoid coming too close to what they must consider a threatening presence...

Me?

Threatening *whom*?

Sam and Mirlun emerged from the hostelry.

"We stay here until we've found a ship to take us north," Sam announced.

"What about our gear?"

"Mirlun told them—and I *did* look intimidating, even if I say so myself! that we'd hold them personally responsible, and that if we found out that *anybody* had been snooping around,—and find out we would! the consequences would be dire." He laughed softly. "The poor owner took one look at me, another at the dinars in Mirlun's hands, and decided to assign a special guard to watch over our rooms. All included in the price of service as it were."

"Who guards the guard?" she wanted to know.

Sam grinned. "And I'm obviously not the only paranoid one around here."

"I've been exposed for you too long."

"Ha!"

Two teenage boys helped them carry their gear inside. Others led the horses away.

They passed through a small atrium, where a man, dressed in the stock tunic of the land, stood watching them with apprehensive eyes. They climbed up a flight of narrow stairs and found themselves in accommodations of surprising cleanliness and utility.

Sam inspected the beds with some care.

"What are you looking for?"

"Bed bugs," he said laconically.

Who ever still thought of bed bugs these days? She'd always assumed that, like small pox, they had been eradicated from the face of the Earth. *Our Earth.* And even there, she suddenly realized, she'd simply never been anywhere the issue of creepy–crawlies in her bed had ever arisen.

But here…

Sam seemed satisfied.

"Looks clean."

"That's a relief."

Sam rose from his inspection of the bed and looked around. "No showers though."

"If we stick around this place that's one thing we'll have to invent."

"Definitely."

Mirlun had watched proceedings without comment.

"We should attend to engaging a boat as soon as possible," he said. "The longer we remain in Lenos the more likely that your identities will be discovered."

Sam nodded. "I suppose you're right." As he walked past her and took her hand he leaned close. "No bed bugs and no creaky springs," he whispered into her ear.

It made her feel warm all over.

Sam let go of Helen's hand as they passed through the atrium and onto the street. It would not be in tune the roles they had assumed; which were hard enough to play as it was. Helen just didn't seem the grim mercenary type. Despite the grime on her face—some of it he had rubbed there himself in order to make everything more realistic, *like makeup for a movie!* she simply didn't look the part. Her face was too soft, too gentle. None of the harshness you'd expect of what was in effect a hired killer, capable of dispatching perfect strangers—and maybe not–just–perfect–strangers—without the slightest compunction and for a few appropriately colored dinars.

Sooner or later, Sam knew, they were likely run into a *real* female mercenary, and then the shit would hit the fan. Helen might be able to fool a man. Men were easily dazzled by looks and what happened in their nether regions as a result. He'd seen the effect Helen had on Plenus, the *prehensi*. Dick–response. Plus a measure of just Helen–impact. The kind she'd made on Sam the first time they met, in another time and another world. But women would instantly know Helen for the fake she was. They'd take one look at her face, which hadd benefited from years of basic cosmetic care, and either conclude that she was a high–class courtesan from the big city, or else maybe—did such women exist? Sam wondered—a courtesan–assassin. Certainly not someone who belonged into Lenos and on a horse, with a sword strapped to her back. Though she did, Sam admitted, have the muscle–tone to use it—and her bare arms, artificially bronzed with cosmetic chemicals from another world—showed it.

He resisted the impulse to kiss her. It wasn't easy.

They returned to the plaza and made their way through the throngs of people to the other side. Sam wondered if the place was always like that. Or was this maybe some special market day?

Mirlun, when asked, professed ignorance, but ventured to guess that this was probably an everyday thing. Which was quite amazing. This city of outcasts was booming with activity and, if one ignored the grim slums at the outskirts, with disposable wealth as well. People weren't just looking at wares but *buying* them. Money was exchanged for goods—and also invested in the time-honored fashion Mirlun had explained to them: the way it had been done since thd days of old Rome. Speculation was rife, its intensity rivaling anything you'd find on the New York stock exchange. Maybe the sums involved were smaller—much smaller! but the fervor was just as intense and the relative stakes were just high. Fortunes were made and lost. The proceeds of any profits resulting from such activities often were promptly lost at the gambling tables, of which there were many; frequented, Sam noticed, exclusively by men, many of them in garb that gave away their profession: *prehensi*, or maybe mercenaries. Here they lost the dinars they'd made at their trade, and a noisy arrangement it was. A *magister tabulae* often was protected by what could only be described a 'bouncers': grim men of considerable size and usually equipped with muscles that would have put a Mr. Universe to shame. Their very presence probably guaranteed that the gamblers' weapons usually stayed in their sheaths, no matter how loudly they protested at their misfortune and accused the *magister* of cheating—which was probably the truth, but so what? A *magister* wasn't in the business of making a loss, and everybody knew it. Period. The complaints were rhetorical. Usually. Sometimes not. In such instances, as they were able to witness, matters were dealt with swiftly and without mercy. Helen gasped involuntarily as one hard-looking man ended up dead at their feet, his throat slashed from a blow by one of the bouncers' swords.

The man's comrades jumped up in anger, but suddenly the army of bouncers seemed to have doubled, and the protesters found themselves surrounded by a phalanx of very mean looking, very large, men with very sharp swords, still bearing the stains of old blood. The gamblers did the only sensible thing, decided not to gamble on their lives, and retreated to a safe distance from which they threw invectives and threats at the *magister*. The man made a dismissive gesture and paid them no further attention. The bloody corpse was removed by a foursome of scruffily-dressed individuals, who dragged it off through the crowds.

"Undertakers?" Sam wondered.

Mirlun shook his head.

"*Scavengi*. They take the corpses away and throw them into the ocean where the fish and crabs take care of them."

"A public service?"

Mirlun uttered a choked laugh. "They empty the corpses pockets and keep whatever they may find, including the clothes and footwear. Sometimes they find many dinars, though for most of the time they don't. A dead man seldom carries much money. He has either lost it at the gambling table or he has already been robbed. Nobody asks, nobody wants to know. They are allowed to do this because they dispose of the corpses. Sometimes they even cut off the hair, if it is long and might make for a good wig. Long well-groomed hair is often worth many dinars. The rich folks will pay great sums for good hair to cover up their own shortcomings: males and females alike." Mirlun's crisp

Chapter 13

tone left no doubt that he considered such practices to be of dubious merit. Sam was inclined to agree.

He caught one of the hard-looking men at the table next to the one that had just produced a corpse taking at good look at the threesome as they passed him by. Deciding that ignoring this eye-crossing challenge would probably be out of character he gave the man a deliberate stare back, then with equal deliberation turned his head to Helen.

Keeping his face as unmoved and bored as he could, he spoke lowly. "We're being observed. Be unpleasant to me."

Helen whipped around, a snarl on her face, surprising him with their reaction. Her hand twitched to reach for the grip of the sword on her back, then stopped in mid air as he made a placating gesture. She dropped her hand and stalked away through the crowd, leaving him to follow somewhat sheepishly, though having to hide his grin.

He finally caught up with her, now hopefully out of sight of their observer.

"Hey!"

She stopped and fixed him with a stare. He grinned. She smirked. "Good enough?" she said lowly.

"Almost had *me* convinced."

"What happened?"

He pulled her along. "A visual pissing contest with another of our chosen profession. I thought a distraction might be good. You did the pissed-off mercenary broad thing very well."

"Think I would have made a good actress?"

"Hollywood doesn't know what it's missing out on."

"Hollywood will never know."

Mirlun caught up with them. "What are you doing?" He appeared concerned.

"Playing the game," Sam told him. He motioned them behind the corner of a building, took off his hat and peered around the corner to see if they had been followed. He didn't see the mercenary's face anywhere, and hoped that it was because of all the right reasons.

"A mercenary will know a mercenary," he said to Mirlun. "This one was at least curious—which I suspect is not a good sign. Openly so. Or maybe he just wanted to see whose dick was bigger. I don't know. But I didn't like it."

He turned to Helen. "Whatever, I hope your pissed-off mercenary-moll routine distracted him. People in our situation aren't likely to make public scenes. Hopefully he was distracted in your antics—and your ass; which, by the way looked very fetching as you flounced off."

She gave him a dirty look.

Sam chuckled. "I have no idea about the ground-rules for this game. Are these guys willing to challenge each other openly, right there and then in the plaza, when they get pissed off? Like the Wild West, only without guns? High-noon with swords? What am I supposed to do then? Back down? That won't look good, will it? Put up and fight? And if the other guy's better—which he's likely to be, given my relative inexperience at trying to kill people with swords—then what? Am I going to shoot him rather than let him slice me up? A lot of good *that'd* do for our cover. It would be like Indiana Jones in Egypt. Besides, I don't *really* want to kill people!"

Mirlun eyed him without comprehension. "Indiana Jones?"

"Forget it." It seemed that, whatever *E1*–lings Mirlun had mind–read, they had not included fans of *Raiders of the Lost Ark*. Sam smiled grimly. The comparison wasn't that far–fetched. The setting was almost right. Life imitating the movies.

He motioned in the direction of the harbor. "Let's find a ship and get out of this town as soon as we can. I don't like it here; not when a major reward's been posted on our heads. Nothing to get people going like greed."

Lenos' port attested to the vitality of the city: an extensive arc of wharves, maybe a mile long, and every single free space was taken. Sailing ships all, from three–masted barques that were uncannily like nineteenth century clippers, through two–masted schooners, to flat–bottomed barges with roll–on–roll–off ramps and single–masted carracks. On the wharves, a purposeful chaos of activity. Goods were loaded and unloaded; traders were haggling; mangy–looking whores, quite below par the classier set in the plaza, persisted in their attempts to procure clients. The area rang from the shouting of voices, the creaking of the ship's rigging in the wind, the grinding of cart–wheels, the imprecations of sellers and buyers alike, the scraping of boxes drawn across the gravelly pavement. Dust filled the air, its musty reek mingling with the stench of fish and other putrefying sea–stuff.

"Well," Sam told Mirlun, "find us a boat."

"I am not sure how," the Seladiënnan confessed.

Sam eyed him unpleasantly. "You could begin by asking. No point in looking for us to help. With our linguistic skills we'd be goners before the day's up."

Mirlun grimaced and turned away. They proceeded down the line of ships, where he issued enquiries while Sam and Helen stood by, doing their best to look bored and generally unapproachable. It seemed to work. The wharfies and merchants gave them a wide berth, as did the whores, some of whom made moves as if to approach, but then, recognizing Helen for a female, thought the better of it. Which was a relief.

Mirlun presently returned from one of his chats and announced that he had found their transport. "It leaves tomorrow, all going according to plan, and heads straight for Seladiënna." The way he said it, it was like a prayer.

"The capital," Sam confirmed.

Mirlun nodded. "Maybe five days. Maybe more. Depending on the weather."

Helen eyed the vessel, a two–masted schooner with an elevated prow and poop–deck, with suspicion. "A week on this?"

"Traveling over–land would take several weeks," Mirlun pointed out. "The discomfort of the ship is a small price to pay for our expeditious delivery to Seladiënna."

"Let's keep on looking," Sam suggested.

"I have already paid for our passage!"

"Paid? How much?"

"Three silver dinars."

Sam did a quick calculation, considered the vessel again, which surely was a freight boat with passengers being icing on the cake, and came to the inevitable conclusion. "That's robbery."

"It includes transport for the horses."

"What kind of accommodation are we talking about."

Mirlun cringed.

Sam raised an eyebrow. "Deck–space? You mean you paid three silver dinars for a

Chapter 13   199

week's deck–space?"

He motioned to Mirlun. "Let us retrieve our money."

"The master will not agree."

"The you will tell him that if he doesn't I'll take it off him."

"What are you doing?" Helen hissed in Sam's ear.

"Playing our role," he told her. "I don't know if you noticed, but there's a man standing about fifty yards off to our left— don't look, damn it! Been watching us for quite a while. Being swindled by the captain of a dingy merchant vessel is hardly keeping in the role."

He motioned to Mirlun. "We all go there. You ask for the money back, or for a state–room—or whatever passes for it on this rat's nest. If the captain doesn't agree I'll make him."

Mirlun hesitated.

"Now!" Sam snapped.

Mirlun turned, and they followed him over a plank on board the schooner, where, amongst men carting sacks, barrels, boxes, and other paraphernalia, stood the master of it all, surveying his minions and watching the approaching strangers with a leery eye. Sam saw him motion to three hefty men, who dropped their loads and formed a guard around him and blocked their path.

Sam adjudicated the situation and decided that, risks notwithstanding, it was time to demonstrate that not only were they what they pretended to be, but they were good at it: the worst bad–ass mercenaries money could buy.

"I'm going to do some stuff," he said to Helen. "When I do, just draw that sword of yours and point it at some people, so they leave us alone. And if anybody gets to close, cut the fuckers!"

She gave him a quick glance and nodded.

Sam pushed Mirlun aside and stood before the captain's bodyguards, who eyed him expectantly. They were definitely looking forward to this. Behind them, the captain regarded his visitors with a tiny smirk.

Our lives depend on this.

Could he take these guys?

If you're quick enough.

The stuff they taught you in the service was nasty and lethal. Sam hadn't ever had a chance to use it. Pilots usually aren't in the middle of hand–to–hand combat fray.

I might be killing someone.

He looked into the eyes of the guy before him, maybe twenty pounds heavier and a head taller, with muscles like Hercules and a b.o. that was maybe even more lethal.

Weak points.

His right hand snapped out. His open fist, fingers folded into a tight edge, impacted on the guy's windpipe. The man went down with a gurgle and a bewildered expression of pain. Sam ignored him as he took a quick step to his left and hit the second man in exactly the same place. He whipped around, dodged a massive fist from the third man, grabbed his testicles under the short kilt and twisted. A yowl of pain. The man doubled over. Sam let go and brought his elbow down in a short chop at the side of the man's neck. He fell like a tree–trunk. Sam straightened and slid the sword out of its sheath on his back, held it up threateningly. From the corner of his eyes he saw that Helen was already standing there, waving her own weapon in a slow arc at the surrounding sailors. Sam took a quick step in the direction of the captain, who tried a grab for the weapon in his own belt, but never made it before the tip of Sam's sword pierced his short tunic and drew a bloody arc across the skin of his chest. The man froze. Everything froze.

Sam raised the sword to the captain's throat and nodded at Mirlun.

After Sam's brief demonstration it did not take much to make the captain return the three silver dinars. At Sam's prompting he was also relieved of the remainder of the wealth in the purse at his belt. That was robbery, plain and simple. It was also the kind of thing mercenaries would be expected to do. The captain was lucky to be alive. Someone else might just have ended the affair by slicing him up.

With the body–guards still squirming on the planks and Helen clearing a path for them by waving her blade about, Sam led the captain ahead at sword–point until they were on the land–side of the gang plank. Then he made a point of casually sheathing his weapon, before the three of them sauntered off to find another ship.

"Nicely done," he said lowly to Helen once they were out of earshot. The distant observer, he'd noted, was still there, but he didn't follow them. Maybe, after watching events on the ship, he was having second thoughts about the dangers inherent in such a course.

"It's good of you to say so," Helen replied. "Now, if only my bowels hadn't gone totally liquid…" She exhaled sharply. "You scared the shits out of me! Who do you think you are? Zorro or something? Was this *really* necessary?"

"Unfortunately, yes." Sam turned to Mirlun. "What is it with you anyway?" he said in English. "You're one of the most resourceful people I've ever met. You found us in a strange world and under the most adverse of circumstances. So, what's the matter now? You can't even organize a decent sea–voyage? In your *own* world?"

Mirlun stared back defiantly. "You should not have interfered! The accommodation was adequate. The price was fair. We had a definite means of getting to Seladiënna! Look what we have now!"

Mirlun's demeanor bothered Sam. Something had changed. He didn't quite know what it was, but it was real nonetheless. A quick glance at Helen. She also was eyeing Mirlun with an expression of surprise.

Later.

"We'll see," he said shortly as they continued along the waterfront.

Presently they came upon a small, two–masted carrack: an ungainly vessel, definitely not built for speed. The main mast slightly forward from the center of the boat was complemented by another half its height at the back. Two cabins were in evidence: one between the masts, the other, smaller one forward of the main mast.

Sam halted and considered the vessel. Activity was low. Two sailors were in evidence, lounging on the fore–deck. One of them spied the watchers and called out something Sam didn't understand.

"What did he say?" he asked Mirlun.

"He wanted to know if we had business for him."

"Tell him we might."

"Not *this* vessel!"

"Why not?"

"It is *Ladiësti*!"

"Huh?"
"It belongs to the *Ladi*."
"So?"
"They are unclean."
"That seems to be a common feature around here," Helen noted siccantly.
"They eat…" Mirlun was groping for words to express the horrendous concept on his mind, "their dead."

Sam looked closer to see if he could discern anything unusual about the two sailors. Not that he expected to see anything. Everybody around here looked 'unusual'. It would take a while to learn to sort out what might be termed 'abnormal'.

Yep. The men definitely looked no stranger than anybody else.

Eating their dead? "They kill their own people for the purposes of eating them?"

Mirlun shook his head "They consider it their religious duty."

"They eat them after they've died?"

Mirlun shrugged. "They are unclean," he said, as if that explained everything. "We do not travel with their kind. They contaminate me just by having to speak to them."

"Ask them if they are willing to take passengers to Seladiënna."

"I told you…"

"Ask them anyway," Sam said indifferently. At the moment he couldn't have cared a sparrow's fart about Mirlun's sensibilities.

"I…"

"Do you want *me* to do it?"

Mirlun called across to the ship. One of the sailors rose and went below-decks, whence he reappeared in the company of another individual, a man in his forties, of Sam's height, though heavier, who represented himself as the master of the ship. They boarded the boat. A period of brief, furious haggling, with Mirlun keeping a fastidious distance from the 'unclean' crew, resulted in a silver dinar exchanging hands—with the promise of a gold dinar to follow—in return for an immediate and exclusive passage, with accommodation and all-meals-inclusive in the forward cabin, to Seladiënna. The horses would be left behind.

"We leave tonight," Sam told the captain curtly. The sentence, uttered in the native tongue, came off convincing he thought. Almost without an accent.

"Once the land-wind springs up," the man agreed.

His name was Lobus Natois. Sam thought him agreeable enough, though the notion of the religious cannibalism remained uncomfortable. He wondered where the ritual had originated.

Without a further word they left the ship, the *Gallinis*, to return to the hostelry to fetch the horses and their gear. Mirlun started to complain about having to spend several days in the company of the unclean *Ladi*, but Sam would have none if it.

"I want to get out of this town," he said. "I don't care about 'clean' or 'unclean'. I just want us to stay alive. My instincts tell me that we're more likely to survive on the *Gallinis* than with that other rogue you booked us in with. Therefore we go 'unclean'. Period."

Mirlun shut up.

They arrived at the hostelry and announced their immediate departure. After a brief haggling they sold their horses and saddles to the owner and presently marched back to the wharves, the bags with their gear slung over their shoulders—and avoiding the plaza, where too many eyes might pry on their progress. Keeping to the back–alleys they approached the harbor—or at least Sam thought so. Given that Mirlun knew as little about the layout of this town as they…

Around a corner and another. Before them appeared six men. Their garb gave them away. All wore armor: variations on the *Lerica Segmentata*. Their swords were drawn.

Mirlun drew in a sharp breath. Behind them more sounds. Sam looked around. Another five men blocked the way they'd come.

He looked at Helen, her face pale and drawn.

"I'm sorry," he said softly.

"What do we do?"

"Shoot to kill. Pretend they're not real people."

"I don't know if I can."

"If you can't we're dead."

She took a deep breath, paused, exhaled, looked into his eyes, and finally nodded. The tortured expression on her face hurt him deeper than what he had to do now. He could close himself off from the grim task at hand; knew that it was a simple choice between lives: theirs or their adversaries'. He could not, however, close himself off from her agony. She deserved better than this.

The men approached with ominous stillness and deliberation. He reached under his tunic, at the back and extracted the Beretta with the attached silencer from its holster. Helen did the same.

Maybe fifty feet. Was there no way they could stop this? There simply *had* to be a way! Sam faced the six men, sensed Helen's back against his.

"On my mark," he said lowly.

He felt her nod. He glanced sideways at Mirlun. "Tell them to stop," he grated. "Tell them to stop or die."

"They won't believe you."

Sam took aim at the chest of one of the men in his way and squeezed the trigger. A muffled shot, echoing eerily from the walls of the building around them. The man lurched backwards, into his comrades who watched in astonishment, and fell to the ground where he lay still.

"Tell them to stop or die!" Sam repeated.

Mirlun complied.

"They're not stopping," Helen hissed behind his back. Sam looked over his shoulder.

Too damn close. He turned and squeezed off a round across Helen's shoulder, hitting a man who tumbled to the ground.

Behind him a shout. He swung around again to see them charging him.

"Shoot, damn it!" he shouted, took aim and fired off another round. Behind him he heard the 'plop' of Helen's gun. And another. Hoarse shouts of anger as the men charged with raised weapons.

Sam didn't know how many rounds he'd fired. Men died, but the others kept coming. Then the last man was upon him and brought down the sword. Sam pushed Helen sideways, himself in the opposite direction and fired at his last attacker even as he threw himself to the ground. The man stumbled and fell into another coming from the opposite direction, who lost the aim of his weapon, the blade of which ground on the gravelly pavement throwing up sparks. Before he could bring it up again there was another shot—from Helen—and he went down. Sam rolled around and took aim at the last two men—who were now running away.

No mercy this time. Sam aimed.

I've never shot a man in the back!

He leveled the gun and fired. One man screamed and went down. The other reached the corner. Sam jumped up, stomped over the corpses of their attackers and ran after him. Down another alley. The man was well ahead. Sam redoubled his effort. He arrived at another junction. The man headed toward the plaza. Sam steadied his arms against the side of the house, took careful aim and fired. The man tumbled but continued on. Sam brought the Beretta down again. The silencer now was a handicap, inhibiting accuracy and range. Sam fired again. The man fell against a wall and slid to the ground. Sam ran up to him, ignoring a few straggly youths emerging from another alley. He came up to the mercenary, who was lying half on his back, still breathing. His right arm was limp and soaked in blood from a shoulder wound. The other hand was clamped over an ugly dark patch on his abdomen. The stench of the contents of a lacerated bowl rose into the humid air.

Sam stood for a moment. The man looked up at him, his face evincing his knowledge of the fate awaiting him. He had probably witnessed it in others; maybe even caused it himself.

Sam took a deep breath, forced back the bile rising in his throat, and brought up the gun. The man stared at him without comprehension, wrapped in his personal cocoon of misery and pain, and quite unable to connect the gun with his current dire condition.

Sam shot him in the head, just above the eyes. The hollow–point tore an ugly jagged wound into the man's forehead. The hydrostatic shockwave popped the eyes out of their sockets.

Sam turned away, sickened to the core.

He looked up, at the faces of the four youths.

"*Vade!*" he shouted. "Go!"

They ran off. Sam stood for another breath, looking at the plaza maybe two hundred yards distant at the mouth of this alley. Then he turned away and ran back to Helen and Mirlun.

"Come on!" he shouted, picked up this gear bag. Helen stood there, the gun still in her limp hand, staring at him emptily.

He took it from her, tucked it into his belt, and her gear bag over his other shoulder.

"We have to go!" he said urgently. "Do you understand me? We have to go!"

She stood mutely. Her eyes were wide, the pupils eerily dilated. He knew the signs. He bit his lip and raised his hand, lowered it again. He just couldn't. He just damn well *couldn't.*

"Come *on*! Now!"

He looked at Mirlun and handed him one of his loads. "Carry this! Head for the wharf! I'll meet you there!"

Mirlun hesitated.

"Go!" Sam shouted.

Mirlun left.

Sam turned to Helen.

"Helen," he said, "do you understand what I'm saying?"

"I think so," she said tonelessly.

"We have to go," he said gently. "If we don't, we'll be caught. If we get caught we'll die."

"I don't want to die."

"That's right!" he said, speaking like one might to a child. "And I don't want to die either. So we must leave here."

She looked at the corpses. "They attacked us," she declared.

"That's right. They were bad men. They wanted to hurt us. Now they can't do that anymore."

She nodded, with exaggerated care, as if she was contemplating each and every one of his words very carefully. Her face twisted into a brief grimace of pain. "We killed them."

"We did what we had to do," he said. He shook her shoulders. "Helen, we have to go."

She nodded. "We have to go."

"Now."

She lifted her right hand and placed it on his left, which was still holding onto her upper arm. "Now," she said.

He looked into her eyes. You could usually tell where they were by looking into their eyes. She squeezed them close; kept them that way for a few seconds; opened them again; blinked as if emerging from a dream.

"I'm all right," she said softly.

"You sure?"

She nodded. "Yeah." Maybe she was.

"Come on then."

Together they continued their way to the harbor. As they left the alley Sam looked around and saw a group of men appear around the corner. Already the *scavengi* were on the job. A service both efficient and discreet, tacitly ignored by all but their own kind. They, too, Sam realized, were 'unclean'—though Mirlun exhibited none of the aversion he seemed to harbor toward the *Ladi*. He took one last look at the dozen or so figures bustling about the corpses. Like vultures. The frames of the people bore an eerie resemblance to the gaunt shapes of the birds. With function came patterns of behavior.

The thought gave him pause.

What behavior goes with our 'function'?

Killing? Again and again?

Already it was becoming something you just *did* and refused to actually feel or think too much about.

Maybe because if we did we couldn't function at all.

They had not even been in this world for three days, and already more than a dozen people had died at his and Helen's hands.

What a way to greet your new home.

The thought pursued him as he and Helen hurried through the allays and finally gained the freedom of the wharves.

14

The *Gallinis* left the harbor on the evening breeze and sailed into this world's Bay of Biscaye, called here *Mare Triang* for reasons nobody seemed to know any more. The forward cabin proved a tight fit for three persons, with its four bunks and not much other space. The space of the fourth bunk was crammed with their baggage. The captain's cabin between the masts was larger, but it was also, as they found out, the residence of Lobus Natois and his wife and son. The boat was a family affair. Living quarters occupied a goodly portion of the aft below–deck. This was the life of the *Ladi: a matter Mirlun had neglected to mention.*

The *Ladi*, Sam decided, were like gypsies of the sea. The boats were their wagons. The *Ladiësti* life style was less communal than the gypsies though. Boats traveled alone. Still, there had to be a community of sorts. Religious practices usually implied a society and required occasions for communal ritual. Presumably the occasion was accompanied by a feast on human remains. A ghoulish notion to be sure.

Lobus Natois introduced his late–teenage son, Gorlen, who was one of the crew, and the other four members of the ship's complement of sailors. He indicated a woman, who only now emerged into view, and who appeared to be his wife. Helen enquired about her name, which was 'Hotilie'. Helen smiled at her, which was returned tentatively and with obvious reluctance. Lobus Natois hesitated, almost as if expecting Helen to…

Whatever he expected, it didn't happen. Presently—slightly discomfited, Sam thought—he continued to show his passengers around the boat and its facilities. These did not appear to include a toilet. When Sam, after a side–glance at Helen, asked about the matter, the captain nodded, as if he'd been expecting the question. Maybe everybody asked it; who knew? Lobus Natois led them to the poop of the boat where hung a construction that was obviously meant to be a seat of sorts, protruding well over the side of the boat, and open to the water below. Helen grimaced as she divined the purpose of the device. Sam noted that in this instance at least modesty was catered for. A screen of planks shielded the occupant of the 'seat' from inspection from most other points of the ship.

"What comfort," Helen muttered when he pointed it out.

Mirlun kept his distance from the *Ladi* with an insulting kind of lack of subtlety. Sam wanted to tell him off about it, but Lobus Natois took him aside, lowering his voice so that Mirlun could not hear them.

"The Diënna's servant does not approve of us. This is to be expected. We do not approve of him either." He considered Sam for a moment. "*You* do not approve. But you do not reject us."

Sam shrugged. "People do as they must," he said, grappling with the unfamiliar terms. His Seladiënnan was suitable for kitchen–talk, not philosophy. "As long as I detect no evil in your souls I will not judge you. I will also not participate in your rituals."

Lobus Natois nodded thoughtfully. "You are the ones Laurentius Augustus seeks," he said in a sudden turn of conversation.

Here it was again. It looked like the whole damn world knew.

"This is obvious?"

"You speech alone betrays you."

Sam grinned ruefully and looked at Helen. She had worked through at least some of the burden of guilt adhering to her because of today's killings. It would not leave her for a long time—maybe it never would, like it would always be with him as well—but one had to learn to live with such burdens. She knew this, as did he. Earlier, as the boat pulled away from the coast and land disappeared from view, she had talked to him about it.

"I still see them dying."

He held her hand, but said nothing. Sometimes silence was best.

"Eventually I will not see them anymore."

He squeezed her hand. In silence they watched the water gurgle past the ship as it rode low swells heading north.

"Are we doing something really terrible?" she wondered.

"You know we're not."

"I know. Yet another part of me doubts."

"Good."

"You think so?"

"Certainty is reserved for zealots. Let us never become zealots."

She tucked an arm under his and leaned her head against his shoulder.

"Sam Donovan, I love you."

Now he saw her study Lobus Natois with a pensive regard.

"You knew this when we first came to speak to you," she said in halting Neo–Latin.

Lobus Natois allowed himself a thin smile. "I sensed that you were not the mercenaries you pretended to be."

"Others noticed as well," Sam said ruefully. "Our visit to Lenos was brief. But many people are dead."

"To disguise one's true nature is the most exacting of tasks—and dinars are a potent incentive for careful observation of one's neighbor."

Sam chuckled; groped to translate more English into Seladiënnan. "What is your intention with regards to the rewards offered by Laurentius Augustus."

Lobus Natois spat into the water. "May his body be robbed by the *scavengi* and left to be eaten by worms," he said disdainfully.

That was an answer, too, I suppose.

Little love lost here. Still, money was money. Larry had offered a considerable sum for their heads—preferably *just* the heads.

"I have a gold and a silver dinar I did not have this morning." Lobus Natois spoke slowly, enunciating carefully, aware and considerate of their linguistic shortcomings. "I have an easy cargo to carry, with no need to break the back of me and my men to load or unload. The monotony of the voyage is broken by unexpected human company from lands forever unknown to me. I will have stories to tell at the next *collectesi*. My daughter's children will listen to me with open mouths and marvel at their grand-father's amazing adventures."

"You have a daughter?"

Chapter 14

"I have one son and three daughters."

"Where are the girls?"

"With their spouses. *Ladiësti* boats travel far and only at the *collectesi* will I see them. Then we exchange what we have known during our journeys."

"Why do you eat your dead?" Helen asked straight out.

Lobus Natois smiled. "The Diënna's servant: he told you this?"

"Did he tell the truth?"

"He told you a partial truth. He is ignorant of the whole truth. We do not consume our dead. We celebrate our deceased by sharing their hearts and brains during the *collectesi*. They are preserved for this occasion, when all *Ladiësti* are present to partake in their minds and their *vitalis*."

"What about the remainder of the bodies?" Helen wanted to know.

"We give them to the sea. There they are out of reach of the *aquaspiriti*, like the Diënna or Plius, or any of the thousand others who might wish to avail themselves of their substance."

One of the sailors called Lobus Natois' name. The master excused himself and attended to his masterly duties. Sam turned to Helen.

"A curious people," he commented.

She gave a little shudder. "Eat the hearts and brains of the dead?"

He had to agree. It wasn't a good practice. The consumption of human flesh by humans had certain inherent risks. Recent BSE/JCD scares had brought the dangers of such activities into the open. But in this world was ignorant of such issues. The thought of the efficient distribution of the agents of something like JCD at a ceremony involving most, if not all, members of a given population…It was remarkable, Sam thought, that the *Ladi* still existed.

"What do they do?" Helen wondered. "Cut out the brains and hearts and pickle them or something?"

"Sounds about right."

"Gross! You think they have a pickled brain and heart on board right now?"

"Dunno. Want me to ask?"

"No way! I don't want to know."

"You asked!"

"Forget I did."

Together they looked out at the sea, now stretching before them apparently endless from horizon to horizon.

"Still," Sam finally said, "they seem a harmless enough folk."

"Mirlun has strong opinions."

"Mirlun is a zealot."

"Of course he is. You've only figured that out now? How could you miss it? Anybody who did what he did *has* to be a fanatic of some sort. That or crazy."

"Or both."

"Probably."

"I wonder what he meant," Sam said.

"Who?"

"Lobus Natois. When he said that they buried their dead at sea, so they were out of the reach of the '*aquaspiriti*'. Water spirits? The translation is pretty straightforward. It seems to imply that the *Ladi* believe that the sea has no sprites. Why not? I would have thought the bigger the water the bigger the spirit. Poseidon, Neptune: they weren't just spirits by gods! The nymphs of the lakes and ponds were just small–fry."

"Salt–water," Helen said.

"You think so?"

"It's what makes the ocean different from other bodies of water, isn't it?"

He looked down at the spreading ripples of the *Gallinis*' bow–wave. Some unformed notion somewhere in the back of his mind made a move as if to some forward, but then decided to stay behind the curtains after all. Still, it had an important feel about it. He struggled to tease it to the foreground, but if refused to come. Finally he gave up. It would come when it was ready. It usually was that way with unformed notions.

"What's the matter?" Helen wanted to know.

"Huh?"

"You were staring into the water."

"Just thinking."

"Wanna share?"

"I wish I could. I wish I knew what to share."

Presently Lobus Natois appeared and invited them to join him and his crew for dinner. Meals, it seemed, were a communal matter, prepared by the wife of the master for all aboard, to be consumed by the five–man crew—excluding the wife, who was reduced to serving, and presumably ate on her own.

Sam counted plates. Seven in all. He took Lobus Natois aside.

"Which one of us is expected *not* to sit at the table?"

The captain eyed him with an expression of surprise. "Your woman, of course."

Sam nodded. "I see. And what if I insisted that she did?"

"Women do not share the table with men."

"Why not?"

"How could they?"

"They sit down, just like everybody else."

Lobus Natois eyed him blankly. Humor, Sam told himself, was also a function of cultural context.

"They do not sit with men," the captain said.

"This one does," Helen said crisply, across Sam's shoulder.

Lobus Natois was scandalized. "Such practices sometimes happen with the *terrestri*," he admitted. "We consider them inappropriate."

Sam shrugged, "Just as you say. But, under such conditions, it is also inappropriate that I sit at your table."

"Because of a woman?" He didn't seem to care that the 'woman' causing all this inconvenience was standing beside Sam listening to the whole conversation.

"Because of a woman," Sam confirmed.

"I did not know that *terrestri* had such profound feelings in this matter."

"We are not *terrestri*."

Lobus Natois nodded slowly, as if to himself. "This is true. You are not even of this world" He hesitated. "That you should refuse to share my table…It is unthinkable."

"I have just thought it," Sam pointed out. "So, it is not only thinkable, but a certainty. It is without prejudice to your customs—but without her presence at the table," he took

Helen's hand, "mine is equally impossible. Such are our customs, and they are not negotiable." One had to take a stand somewhere.

A few moments passed. Lobus Natois called out to his wife, asked her to set another plate on the table, which had been placed behind his cabin. The two boards which acted as legs had been affixed to the deck by means of an angled piece of wood. This was joined to the boards and the planks by wooden pins. Two simple benches had been placed in parallel to the table's long sides. A chair for the captain stood at the head.

Lobus Natois regarded Sam thoughtfully. Sam performed a minute bow of his head. "I thank you for your gesture of hospitality."

"I admire your steadfastness," the captain replied. "I do not understand your insistence. Surely no woman can be worth such effort—except for young bucks who think of them as objects of their desire. But, for this voyage at least, we shall accede to your wishes. Let nobody say that Lobus Natois does not know how to be a good host."

"That I would never consider," Sam said earnestly.

The captain bowed and left them.

Mirlun refused to come.

"I will not dine at a *Ladiësti* table."

"Then you will have to starve," Sam said mercilessly. After having fought for Helen's right to dine at the table, against the precepts of centuries of ever–deeper–ingrained tradition, he was out of patience. "Your sensibilities are inappropriate here."

"The *Ladi* are unclean."

"*What* is unclean? Their food? Which parts of it? The preparation of the food? What are they doing wrong? Their presence? What have they ever done to *you* to offend you thus?"

"You do not understand!"

"Dead right, I don't. Truth is I don't *want* to either!"

"They are diseased; impure; soiled. How can one consort with them and not be contaminated?"

Sam considered Mirlun for another few seconds; saw nothing but a closed mind. He shrugged and turned away.

"Suit yourself. When you're hungry enough you might change your mind."

He went to join Helen and the remainder of the crew. They sat in attitudes of dazed incomprehension at her presence, apparently unable to function normally with the enormity of it all. Sam sat down. He explained that Mirlun was unable to attend because of his religious convictions. They seemed to be less bothered by this than Helen's presence. *Terrestri* and their intransigent ways they knew and had learned to, if not accept, then at least live with. The female from another world however was scary, threatening. That she should be so obviously *female* and wear garments which exhibited this—quite in contrast to the much more concealing garb of, say, their captain's wife—that was even more scandalous.

Lobus Natois intoned a brief ritualistic benediction, after which everybody tucked in. Sam carefully observed the designated pecking order and noted it down for future reference. The restraint induced by the strangers' presence was plain to see, but somehow they were all hungry enough to place the consumption of food above the distracting presence of a female at a male table—though their world must be taking a severe battering even as they ate. Furtive glances abounded. There were no secrets aboard this vessel: everybody knew who or what their passengers were. This did not, however, worry Sam unduly. Betrayal out here was impractical at best and stupid at worst. They were not planning to land until they arrived at Seladiënna—which made him think about…

"Could you take us to *Aquadiënna*?" he asked the captain. "I think the capital would be…unhealthy. Especially if we enter by boat. We must avoid attention. In Lenos we did not succeed."

"Plius would have made sure of that," the captain said.

Sam looked up from his plate. "Plius?"

"Laurentius Augustus can offer only dinars."

"Plius…"

"Offers power. You said you have been attacked? How do you think they knew you? In a crowd your disguises should have been effective enough. If they were not it is because Plius alerted those who would search for you."

"How?"

"Who knows? The *aquaspiriti* are not constrained to act as men do. Only on the ocean are their powers diminished."

"All the more reason why we should avoid Seladiënna."

Lobus Natois shrugged. "It is a small matter, though it adds to my economic burden."

"Three silver dinars. One for each of us."

"That is acceptable."

They returned their attention to the meal—which consisted of totally–gross–looking and tasting pickled vegetables; lots of *liquamen*, which smelled even worse and tasted like fermented fish piss; a stew of pickled meat and a vegetable of sorts, with a texture very similar to potato; and freshly baked bread, which was delicious. This was followed by reasonably fresh fruit; procured, Sam guessed, from Lenos' markets. Sam and Helen refrained from touching the *liquamen* but braved everything else.

Conversation at the table picked up slowly. Helen wisely said nothing and thus did not disrupt the fragile stability of the social framework. She did, however, sit very close to Sam, which occasioned a raised eyebrow from Lobus Natois, and definite embarrassment from the rest of the ship's complement.

Lobus Natois was intrigued enough to raise the matter again later that evening when Helen was out of earshot, attending to making the bunks suitable for human occupation.

"Where you come from," he began, "the women: they are all like the one you have with you?"

Sam grinned. "No."

"She is different?"

"She is different."

"You are espoused?"

"Yes."

"What is it like to have a woman who behaves in this way?"

Sam chuckled, evoking a grin from Lobus Natois.

"It is…" Sam was looking for the term, but he probably had never been told. So he adopted something from his Spanish.

"*Encantado*," he said.

"*Enchanti*?" Lobus Natois wondered. "It means that you are under her power."

"We are under the power of each other," Sam corrected him. "Customs in my world are different from yours—or from those in Seladiënna. Men and women often espouse for reasons of feelings for each other."

"You are a mature man—and you think like a young buck?" Lobus Natois seemed to consider the very notion quite scandalous.

Sam laughed softly. "Has it not happened in your world that 'mature' men think like young bucks?"

"Not with my people."

"I don't believe this."

"They are not allowed to."

Sam grinned. "That may not be as important as you think. Lobus Natois, you tell me that you have never looked at a woman with the thoughts of a young buck?"

"Only for purposes of…" Lobus Natois made a coarse gesture of universal comprehensibility. He gave Sam a confidential smirk. "Lenos is useful for such things. The spouse does not always oblige—and when she does it is not always satisfactory." He eyed Sam curiously. "Your woman: she is satisfactory?"

"Very."

"She displays her affection with little shame."

Sam considered the man and he felt a wave of what was almost pity wash over him. How could he have missed it? The questions. Across worlds, across cultures, across hundreds of years of diverging social evolution: the question remained the same, the yearning continued unabated.

Lobus Natois had discerned something in his guests that attracted his attention; something he would violently deny even being remotely interested in—and yet it was there, lurking below the surface, eating away on him; despite the rituals and the precepts, the faith, the mores, the life–long indoctrination; something more fundamental than all the foundations of his life—including maybe his affection for his son, who quite plainly was the apple of his eye. He'd seen this other thing, maybe in a gesture, a look, an unconscious movement, the sound of an utterance—and having seen it, he could not get it out of his head, knowing at some level more primal than words that here was his need also, but that he could never scratch this particular itch.

"In my world and in my society," Sam said carefully, "men and women are allowed to choose each other as spouses without interference from others, and for motives other than the need to have families."

Lobus Natois eyed him without comprehension.

From the cabin came Helen. Lobus Natois straightened; his face became an affable mask. He excused himself and disappeared even before she approached.

Helen looked after him. "What did he want?"

Sam reached out, pulled her close, and kissed her.

"What was that all about?" she said breathlessly when he let her go.

"I had an insight," he said.

"Into what?"

"The human psyche."

"Really? Which one? Male or female?"

"Funny you should ask! The male one actually."

"Is it something I want to know?"

He hooked his arm under hers and they stood looking at the ocean.

"Maybe one day," he said. "It's no big deal really."

"Want to look at our bed?"

" 'Bed'? Singular?"

"Unless you're going to start sleeping without me."

"Nope."

"Good."

"It's going to be tight though, huh?"

"You said you liked me on top!"

"I do. Mirlun's going to be scandalized though."

"Do I care?"

"Where is he anyway?" He craned his neck. It was hard to believe that you could actually lose sight of somebody on a ship this size.

She pointed. "He's been crouching behind that coil of rope."

"Probably pissed off about missing dinner," he said. "But I'll be honest: I don't care. He'll have to adapt."

"You're a cruel man, Sam Donovan," she said with mock severity, but her eyes were laughing.

"Maybe we should go and talk to him," Sam suggested.

"I think so, too."

Mirlun concealed his anger at his situation behind a mask of indifference that didn't fool Sam one bit. Conversation was difficult under the circumstances. When they announced that they were turning in for the night Mirlun declared that he had every intention of staying where he was and spend the night wrapped in the open.

Sam hunkered down before him. "Whatever you say," he said in English. "But I'm going to say this once and not again. We are here because you asked us to be here—because your Diënna asked us to be here. We have a job to do, and in my estimation taking this vessel was the surest way of making sure that we won't have our throats cut by some larcenous bastards—and this is kind–of necessary if we actually want to do this job?

"You get that? It doesn't matter if these people are 'unclean' or if they eat shit for breakfast, or if they piss against the wind when they shouldn't, or if their hair isn't cut to the right length or they believe in the big juju of the north. All *we're* interested in is that they help us to get to the place we need to get to and that they do so safely. Whatever else they do when I'm not looking—unless it's something real bad, like that they like to murder young children or rape women, or whatever other nasty stuff you want to come up with—unless it's something like that they can damn well do as they please. It's none of my business, and certainly none of yours either. So get a life and chill out, because if you don't, you're going to be starved by the time we get to *Aquadiënna*."

Mirlun sat up. "What did you say?"

"I said, they're taking us to *Aquadiënna*."

"Their presence will defile the sacred…"

"Shut up!" Sam snarled. "Just shut up! Another word from you I don't like and you'll see a side of me you really don't want to know of."

Chapter 14

"How dare you..." Mirlun snapped.

Sam cut him off with a motion of his hand. "I mean it!" he said sharply. "Cooperate. Adapt. Pretend you're in our world and that your life—and that of your Diënna!—depends on it."

He took Helen's arm and turned to go.

"Which it *does*!" he said as a parting shot.

"What do you think got into him?" Helen wondered. They were lying on one of the lower bunks, in complete darkness, with her on top of him and a blanket draped over both.

"I have no idea," Sam admitted, and he didn't. Mirlun's behavior was a puzzle. It was like being back in his world and his environment had awakened facets of his character they'd never seen before.

"A man is what he is in the context of everything else," he said. "I guess we're seeing Mirlun in his own context—and he's faced with *us*, who are like bulls in a cultural china shop, wading right across all his cherished preconceptions as if they were so much crap—which they are, of course, but that's not the point."

"Which is?"

"I think, being here, and being who we are—being as *important* as we are—we may be more of a challenge—and maybe a threat?—to his world than Larry is. After all, Larry's more or less integrated into the society."

"Mirlun's wondering if he maybe can't control us?"

"I think he's stopped wondering some time ago. I suspect the fight in the alley," he felt her tense and held her tighter, "I think that also made him realize that what he's brought with him are two people who will not lie down and submit—no matter what the cost. And we're driven by motives he doesn't understand. We spare that *prehensi*, whom he wanted killed more than anything, and we're all buddies with that 'unclean' sonofabitch Lobus Natois, who eats the dead for spiritual communion. What kind of folks has he brought to the Diënna's bosom? Despite everything she says, like how we are the ones to fix this mess for her...despite all that he's not quite sure about us. Maybe he's wondering what's going to happen after it's all done. What are we going to do once we're dealt with Larry and that damn Plius sprite. What's he going to do to control those who dealt with his demons when they're done dealing with them?"

"He does have a problem."

"Yep."

The ship pitched sideways. Sam held onto Helen as they were thrown about in the bunk. Fortunately the side facing the cabin was barred by a plank which provided lateral support.

When the ship righted again—as much as a ship would ever 'right'—Helen put her head down on his chest and tightened her hold on him. Diagonally above him Sam saw the rectangle that was the access hatch to the tiny cabin. Inside the rectangle a swaying field of stars, like projected onto a TV screen.

TV. Now there was something so totally *their* world, something that would probably never become a part of this one. Was he getting nostalgic for TV? He hardly watched the damn thing. There was too much else to do with life. Listening to music. Flying helicopters. Making love to Helen.

Of all that only one thing, the most important, was still with him.

Helen lifted her head and wriggled herself higher until their faces were level. Under the covering blanket they were naked, and Helen's movement had a definite—possibly intended—effect.

She giggled and, as her mouth brushed against his, opened her legs to make a space from him. "What if someone came?" she breathed.

"It's pitch dark in here. What could they hope to see?"

Her body shook from a little laugh. "They could hope for a lot."

His hands slipped down under the blanket until they rested on her buttocks. She slipped down, pushed herself onto him. Her sigh of contentment was one with his own involuntary groan.

The stars wheeled past the access hatch, moved by the vagaries of the ship's yaw and pitch and the passage of time as the night wore on.

Sometime, in the middle of the night, Helen declared that she really—really! needed to pee.

"Oops!"

"I've been trying to hold it."

"It's probably better in the dark."

"I don't know. Hanging out my ass over a pitch–black bottomless pit of water underneath me—it ain't this girl's idea of a good time."

"I'll come with you."

"Dead right you are! Don't think I'm going there by myself!"

Some time later, dressed to the minimum standards of modesty and Helen armed with some torn–off toilet paper from her stash, they climbed to the deck, to find one of the sailors, a certain Prodo, standing watch, holding onto the big wooden steering wheel. He greeted them affably, they exchanged a few words, then the two of them made their way to the poop where they spent a goodly amount of time trying to cope with the mechanics of what in their old world would have been a matter of minutes. The whole affair, Sam thought, definitely lacked dignity. Maybe they'd gotten too… refined?…'civilized' maybe?…to actually pay much attention to such matters, but having to dangle your ass over the side of a ship and trying to relax enough to actually be able to *do* something…He'd had a brief acquaintance with such practices before, but the prospect of several days of this…

Still, there was something funny about it all, and when they padded back to the cabin, carefully avoiding coming close to Mirlun behind his coil of rope, they found themselves giggling and holding their hands over their mouths to preserve a modicum of dignity. They could feel the eyes of the sailor at the wheel follow them as they climbed down into the cabin.

Back on the bunk they tried lying beside each other, and found that it was a squeeze. Not that they minded. Their arms finally found the right places. Their faces were just inches from each other, noses tucked one beside the other, mouths touching. Very intimate and making the PCI for that night a definite *one*.

"This bit I like," she whispered. "This is the nice part of this insane dream we're dreaming."

"Almost romantic," he agreed.

"Almost?" She tickled him.
"Stop that!"
"Almost?" she repeated.
"Completely romantic," he amended. "Totally. Definitely. Out–of–this–world."
She shook with laughter. "Yeah, right."
"Could you move your leg a bit? I need some space."
"Like this?"
"Hmmm."

Morning came with a gust of wind blowing down the access hole. The vessel pitched more vigorously. The sky was gray and leaden. Back on deck they found the crew busy preparing for rougher conditions. Things were tied down or put below–decks. Breakfast was perfunctory. Some of last night's bread. Pickled fish, which they declined. Thanks but no, thanks, not first thing in the morning.
"I'd die for a cup of coffee," Helen muttered. "You think we could…"
They had some left but now was not a good time.
"I don't think so," he said.
"I thought you'd say that."
"Sorry."
The crappy weather came from the west, which meant that it pushed them toward the coast and from their intended path. An hour later the sails were trimmed as the first serious gusts hit the ship, bringing with them whipped sheets of rain that restricted visibility to maybe a hundred yards around the vessel. Sam and Helen brought out their light waterproof parkas, to the ill–concealed curiosity of the crew, and put them on, then positioned themselves out of the way in a place where they had something to hold onto as the storm tossed the *Gallinis* about and pushed it across the waves that towered over them, looking like they would bury them anytime soon—but somehow didn't, as the boat rode through trough, over crests; and though the deck was flooded the hatches were tight and when the storm blew over in less than a couple of hours they found that hardly any water had made it below–decks.
What they did find though was that one of their bags had a tear in it. It had been pierced by the irresistible force of *Gladius Magnus* which, for some reason beyond their ken, had chosen the stormy interval to—spontaneously it seemed—revert from its on–paper–only state to that of a real live weapon.
Sam and Helen stared at the thing and called Mirlun, who appeared soon after, wearing clothes crumpled from being wrung out and immediately out on again.
He saw the sword and nodded, unsurprised.
"You expected this?" Sam snapped. "You said it would remain…as it was!"
Mirlun stared at the sword, thoughtfully. "The Dïenna must have wanted it to become itself again." He paused. "I wonder…"
"The *Dïenna* controls this? I thought it was the sword itself! You said as much."
"*Of course* it is the Dïenna!" Mirlun's expression carried the overtone of ineffable superiority reserved for those who simply *knew*. "She gives the sword its power. How else could such a thing be? *All* power resides within the Dïenna."
Sam and Helen exchanged a glance.
"What else can she do?" Sam asked casually. "There's clairvoyance and hexing

swords. Anything else we should know about?"

"No. Unless she decides otherwise."

"I see." Sam looked at Helen, who appeared as uneasy as he felt.

Later, with Mirlun standing at the railing, brooding across the comparatively placid sea, whose swells, though towering, were smooth and unruffled, Sam and Helen spoke to Lobus Natois.

"Tell us what you know about the Diënna."

Lobus Natois glanced in Mirlun's direction. "Has he not told you what you need to know?"

"He has told us what he believes the Diënna wants us to know."

"Ah, and you think that this may not suffice." Lobus Natois leaned against the main mast and considered them with narrowed eyes.

"Why are you here? To kill Laurentius Augustus?"

"What makes you say that?"

"He wants *your* death."

"We are not his friends," Sam admitted.

"Then you are also the enemies of Plius."

"It appears that way."

"Plius is more powerful than the Diënna," Lobus Natois said. "She is older, but she is female and therefore weaker." He flicked a quick look in Helen's direction, maybe to gauge her reaction to the statement. It was a testimony to an agile mind that he should even conceive of the possibility that it might not amuse her—and that she might even be so bold as to tell him exactly that.

In the event Helen held her peace.

"Plius will defeat the Diënna as soon as he retrieves *Gladius Magnus* from *Aquadiënna*. Without the sword she is nothing."

He looked at Mirlun, standing at the railing out of earshot, and leaned closer to Sam. "*Ladiësti* consensus in this matter is that the best of all possible outcomes would be if both, the Diënna and Plius, disappeared from this world."

Sam wondered if Mirlun knew about these *Ladiësti* sentiments. He probably did. Here, quite possibly, lay another reason—maybe the main reason!—for his detestation of their kind.

"Why?" he asked the *Ladi*.

"Because *aquaspiriti* should not rule men. They should serve their ponds and lakes and protect them. But they should stay out of the affairs of others."

Ponds and lakes.

"You say no *aquaspiriti* inhabit the oceans?"

Lobus Natois shook his head. "It is the one place where they cannot reach. Indeed, even their senses are inhibited. The Diënna and Plius may know what eventuates on the land, but here on the water, far away from the shore, they are as blind as you or I."

"Why should this be so?"

Lobus Natois shrugged negligently. "Who knows? Why are there no *aquaspiriti* in rivers? It is the way things are. Why should we ask questions that cannot be answered?"

"Because maybe the answer will give you a means of achieving your goals," Sam suggested.

Chapter 14
217

The *Ladi* looked unconvinced. "How could it?"

Sam groped for a suitable response to a question that didn't seem to make sense. Or did it? Wasn't he doing the same thing as the *Ladi*? He, too, dismissed a question as meaningless, just because it didn't fit his frame of reference. To him, a man from a world of science and technology, asking questions about the 'why' was usually the first step toward actually initiating a change. These people just didn't get that. They saw these kinds of questions as matters of philosophy, rather than a prelude to engineering.

Why?

Who knew? Something in their history simply hadn't pushed them to that point where it was different. For the moment that would have to do as an answer.

"What's the major difference between the ocean and a lake?" he asked .

The *Ladi* frowned at the question, probably thinking it just plain silly or pointless.

"It is much bigger," he said then.

"What else?"

"The waves are bigger. There are storms."

"Can you drink the ocean water?"

"No! It is salty."

"That is another difference."

"Yes, it is."

"So, does this mean that *aquaspiriti* cannot exist in salty water?"

Lobus Natois narrowed his eyes. "I do not know."

"But now you are interested in the question," Sam pointed out.

The *Ladi* regarded Sam with a quizzical expression.

"What if," Sam said, "that was the important difference."

Lobus Natois shook his head. "Rivers are not salty," he declared. "*Aquaspiriti* do not occupy rivers."

"Then what is the difference between rivers and lakes," Sam continued relentlessly.

"Rivers are long," the *Ladi* said promptly.

"Rivers flow," Helen added.

Sam grinned. "Exactly. Rivers flow. The water moves. As does the water in the ocean. Though we may not notice it, but there are strong currents far below us."

"How do you know this?" Lobus Natois challenged.

"I know," Sam assured him. "You feel the effects of these currents when you're becalmed but your vessel is still drifting."

The *Ladi* nodded. This he understood.

"The surface of the ocean sometimes flows like a big, slow river."

"Salinity and stagnancy," Sam said to Helen in English. "I wonder if this means anything. If someone just poisoned a pool or a lake—made it saline, say—would that destroy the resident *aquaspiritus*?"

"Which begs the question as to why it's 'resident' to begin with," she said.

Lobus Natois had listened to the exchange in an incomprehensible language without a word. Presently one of the sailors attracted his attention and he excused himself.

"Could it be that simple?" Helen wondered. "Add salt and dispose of whatever's in there?"

" 'Simple'?" Sam echoed. "Hardly that. Do you know what it would take to make a lake saline? Depends on the size, of course, and just how saline you'd want it—but we're still talking about, say, one part in a hundred, per volume, of salt to water. If we have a lake of—well, say a thousand feet across, and maybe an average of ten feet deep…"

"That's almost eighty-thousand cubic feet of salt," Helen said almost before he'd finished the sentence. "I see what you mean."

He grimaced. "How do you *do* that?"

Helen shrugged. "It just happens."

"Who needs a calculator if Helen's around?"

"I don't know *exactly* what the number is. Just approximately—give or take a few decimal places."

"It's amazing." He shook his head. "But you get my drift, right? It's a shit–load of salt for even a tiny lake. Loe Pool is much bigger than that, and Plius' 'pond' several times the size again."

"If it worked at all."

"I really think we may have something here."

"That would be good."

"Could it really be? We figured something out in a couple of days they haven't in centuries?"

"Maybe the Diënna knew what she was doing when she brought us in on this."

"Did she? You think—and this is supposing we're on the track of something real here—you really think she'd want somebody who figured out a way to actually *destroy* her?"

"And Plius."

"Yeah, but if we wipe him out that seems to imply that we'll be able to do the same to her. I don't think she'd like that at all."

15

The *Gallinis* continued to work its way north. On the third day Mirlun yielded to his hunger and, without speaking, joined them at their dinner table, where a plate was always set for him. Nobody said a word, though Sam thought to detect a gleam of amusement and triumph in the *Ladiësti* faces. Mirlun behaved unobjectionably, consumed his meal, and then retired to his usual place. So far he had not joined them in the cabin. He probably found the notion of sharing such a small un–private space with two, to him, sexually indiscreet adults disturbing, to say the least. Not that they would have done anything had he been there, but they wouldn't have suddenly slept in different bunks for his sake either. In the event, his absence made things easier and the nights considerably more relaxed and pleasant.

Lobus Natois spoke to them about salt and currents again. He appeared intrigued at the notion that they thought such factors might contribute to the viability of an *aquaspiritus*. After all, water was water, was it not? A spirit inhabited a body of water. What could salt possibly have to do with it?

"The facts are undeniable," Sam told him. "You may believe what you will, but belief should accommodate the external reality of your life. If you deny this—which of course you may—you will have to be prepared for conflicts between your belief and what *is*: in this case that being the restriction of *aquaspiriti* to stagnant bodies of salt–free water."

Lobus Natois nodded with a thoughtful mien. "Your remarks are cogent. Indeed what you say is almost self–evident. I am disturbed by just how very much obvious it is."

"That's often the case with the obvious," Sam told him.

On the fourth day another vessel appeared on the horizon and rapidly drew closer. This one was sleek and fast, with a single mast, rigged with two triangular sails in the manner of a modern *E1* yacht. It sailed hard against the wind, leaning heavily, suggesting the existence of a large counter–weighing keel.

"*Pirati*," Lobus Natois said, watching the approaching vessel, but making no move to turn away or prepare for a defense of sorts.

"What are you going to do?" Helen wondered.

The *Ladi* shrugged. "Nothing. Presently they will realize that we are *Ladi*. Then they will ask for dinars for their coffers. We will give them a suitable sum and go our way."

"They don't board you?"

"We are *Ladi*," Lobus Natois said dryly. "They, like your companion, are *fastidiosi*"—the way he used the word was like a Jew saying 'gentile'—"and won't want to get close to us."

He eyed Sam and Helen critically. "They may notice that you are not one of us. You may not find this to your advantage. Indeed, it may not be to ours either. Your cabin would be a good place to hide for the duration of this contact."

Sam and Helen thought it prudent to comply. They went below and Lobus Natois closed the hatch above them, leaving just enough of a slit to allow a sliver of light to cut into the darkness.

Once below, Sam dug in their luggage and retrieved his and Helen's Berettas, which he had cleaned and put away for the duration of the sea voyage. He didn't think they'd need them. He still kept one of the small Glocks in a holster under his tunic, but that was pure paranoia stuff. As the days went on he'd felt it to be more and more unwarranted to walk around the ship armed like this, but he'd stuck to it anyway.

Helen eyed the Beretta with disfavor.

"I'm sorry," Sam said gently. "But *pirates*?"

"Lobus said…"

"I heard what he said. I even believe what he said. But I don't believe that he has a particular angle on predicting the future or the motivations of a bunch of buccaneers."

He put her gun back in the bag. "One will do. Just in case."

She took her lower lip between her teeth and stared at the bag. Presently she shook her head, a new expression of resolve replacing the doubt.

"No," she said. "I'm not going to pike. This is you and me, both. No matter where it goes." She held out a hand. "Gimme that thing." She looked into his face. "I mean it, Sam. I feel awful—really, really *terrible*!—about killing those people. But I'm in this all the way. Consequences be damned. I'll learn to live with that kind of guilt. I'll never live with letting us down."

"You wouldn't…" he began.

"Yes I would," she said sharply. "But I won't. This is a part of that you–and–me thing. We do it together or we don't do it, right?"

Her eyes searched his face. Sam nodded and briefly touched her face with his left hand. She gave him a little smile. He took the Beretta out of the bag and gave it to her. She operated the slide, jacked a round into the chamber, and lowered the hammer again. Sam retrieved the silencers and gave her one, then screwed the other onto the muzzle of his gun.

"It absorbs recoil," he said. "Allows you to recover faster for the next shot." Mutely she nodded. She fitted the silencer to the thread, screwed it down, and gave if a last twist to tighten it in place. They leaned against the bunks and listened to the sounds from outside.

It didn't take long. A bump as the ships touched. Then, impacts, as of men jumping on board. Not just one.

"I thought these guys were *fastidiosi*," Sam muttered.

Helen stared at him, a sick feeling spreading through her intestine. Sam had been right. She just *knew* it. That's why she had asked for the gun. Sam thought he was being paranoid, but he took the appropriate actions anyway. Just in case. In that Sam kind of way she'd gotten to know so well—and to respect and pay heed to. He wasn't paranoid at all: just a survivor. Those footsteps clonking around on the deck above him proved that once and for all.

Now there was a shout. And another. Hoarse voices. She thought to discern that of Lobus Natois. The voice of a younger man. The son?

Helen looked at Sam.

"They know we're on board," she said.

"How?"

Chapter 15

"How did they know we were in Lenos?"

"Shit!" He took a deep breath. "Are you ready for this?"

Was she?

"No. Yes!"

He grimaced. "Here we go."

He made as if to ascend the short ladder to the deck. A darkness appeared across the slit Lobus had left open. The cover was pushed aside, revealing a figure, not *Ladiësti*, holding a curved sword, and grinning in triumph. The man turned his head and shouted something. Sam raised the gun and shot him in the head. The man collapsed out of view. From somewhere came a shout. Helen bit her teeth together and watched Sam work himself up the ladder using his left hand, while covering himself with his gun. She raised her own, searching for targets. A head appeared; a hand holding a sword; the upper part of a torso. The man raised the sword to strike at Sam. Helen aimed and shot him in the chest. He fell across the opening, his face staring at her from already–dead eyes. Helen averted her gaze. Sam rushed up the last few rungs and disappeared from her view. More muffled shots. Helen scrambled up the ladder and onto the deck. A pirate lurched toward her. She shot him without even thinking, looked around her, saw pandemonium. One *Ladiësti* sailor lay on the deck in a dark pool of blood. Other bodies littered the planks. Against the mast stood a pirate, holding a knife to the throat of Lobus Natois' wife. The captain and his son stood in an attitude of frozen attention.

The boarding pirates, she saw, were all dead, barring that one. He was shouting hoarse invectives and threats she didn't fully understand. Lobus Natois retorted with imprecations, mixed with suggestions to allow the wife to go. It seemed like she was worth *something* to him—even if she was a woman.

The pirate ship was already drifting away from the *Gallinis*, its few remaining crew members desperate to get away from this easy prey that had suddenly become their nemesis. The pirate holding the woman was getting desperate.

Sam stood still, like the others. Deliberately, apparently unaffected by the excitement around him, he lowered his gun and unscrewed the silencer. He held it out to Helen, who came over and took it. Sam gave her an inscrutable look and raised the gun again, aiming at the pirate and his hostage. The man flicked an uncomprehending glance at him. A shot rang out. The pirate's head exhibited an ugly jagged hole. The hand with the knife twitched away from the woman as the man collapsed against the mast.

Sam lowered the gun and looked at her again. Suddenly she understood. She remembered what he'd told her, quite some time ago. "There's only one thing to do with hostage–takers: kill them. Show them no consideration or mercy. Whatever their motives, the moment they take innocent people hostage they forfeit their lives."

Sam glanced over at the pirate ship, now a good twenty to thirty yards off starboard. He gave Helen his gun. "Hold this!" He ran across the deck and disappeared in their cabin. Lobus Natois and his son attended to their wife and mother. The captain shouted to the sailors, who began to drag the pirates' bodies to the side and threw them overboard.

Sam reappeared and hurried to the starboard railing. In his hand he held a small, ovoid object. A hand–grenade! Sam pulled the pin, drew back his arm and threw the object across the intervening water on to the pirate ship. It just made it and disappeared from sight. A moment later there was a sharp concussion, followed by screams and a fountain of water spurting up, only to collapse again immediately. Sam turned away and came over to her. He took back his gun, laid his hand on her arm for a moment, then went to speak to Lobus Natois. Helen ran to the fallen *Ladiësti* sailor and knelt down beside him. There was, however, nothing she or anybody could have done for him. She rose again and looked around the deck, slick with blood and gore. Another *Ladiësti* sailor was holding his hand over a deep cut in his arm. Helen went over to him. He eyed her with astonishment.

"Let me look at that," she said crisply.

Later.

The pirate ship had sunk. The hole blown into its wooden hull by the grenade had made sure of that. The three surviving pirates had—at Sam's insistence—been fished out of the water—and tied up against the rear mast, where they would spend a very uncomfortable journey.

"Why do you want to do this?" Lobus Natois wanted to know. "They were going to kill us. Do they not deserve to die?"

"Maybe they do," Sam agreed testily. She could see that he was upset, controlling himself with difficulty. At that point Helen realized just how much it really bothered him to have to do what he'd just done; to have his hand forced into actions he basically considered unethical. That same expression had been on his face when he used a helicopter as a weapon to hunt down and kill the two minions in Albuquerque.

"But," Sam continued, "not while I'm responsible for it."

"They have killed Jián. Now they must pay."

"Find another way to make them pay," Sam said with a definiteness that allowed no argument. He turned away from the captain and came back to her. He was angry; not least, she suspected, with himself. He probably considered the attack his fault; something he should maybe have anticipated.

"You couldn't know this," she told him. "Nobody could."

He looked at her, surprised. She smiled. She liked surprising him. Sometimes he needed to be reminded that he couldn't fix everything and have it all just so. But it was fun watching him try.

"We're up against some very resourceful people," he said.

"Not all of them 'people'."

Sam turned back to Lobus Natois, who stood in a pensive attitude, watching his crew wash the blood off the deck.

"You think Plius did this?" Sam asked.

"Plius's influence reaches far. Other ships may be searching the ocean for us." He regarded them with something approaching awe. "Plius must be very afraid of you." Pensive again, glancing at the bloody deck: "It appears that he has good reasons for such sentiments." He indicated the Beretta in the holster at Sam's belt. "These weapons, we do not know their equal. And the egg you threw into the *pirati* ship…"

"You have projectile weapons," Sam said. "Mirlun said as much."

"Nothing to compare with this." The captain pointed at the gun. "It will soon become known what weapons you carry. They will be coveted and you will be hunted not just by Laurentius Augustus and Plius."

"And yet they will avail little," Sam told him. "The projectiles these weapons use cannot be used again. Nobody in this world could produce more of them. Once our stocks are exhausted, this," he pulled the Beretta from the holster and held it in his hand, "will become a useless hunk of steel."

"Until then it is very deadly," Lobus Natois retorted. "Your world has invented some very effective weaponry."

Sam sighed. "You don't know how right you are. Trust me, you will never want to know the truth. Sometime ignorance is a blessing."

"And yet you bring knowledge to us. New ways of thinking that lead to surprising conclusions." He considered Sam from narrowed eyes. "I will pay heed to what you said to me yesterday."

"Regarding what?"

"If there is a way to dispose of the *aquaspiriti* then it must be explored."

"You're not going to do it by throwing some salt into their lakes."

"It would take a lot, yes?"

"An enormous quantity."

Lobus Natois hesitated and finally shrugged, apparently resigned to the futility of his idea.

Helen and Sam didn't watch, and indeed were not invited to watch, as the grisly ceremony of removing the dead *Ladiësti* sailor's heart and brain took place on the fore-deck. Behind their backs they heard incantations and peculiar ululations as the procedure, which took several hours, proceeded, climaxed with a chorus of mournful male voices singing in remarkable harmony, and finally came to a close. The sailor's remains were heaved over the side. The heart and the brain were considered to contain all the essence of a man. The rest was necessary to the business of living but apparently carried not a snitch of the man's *substancia*. Brain and heart ended up in a sacramental earthenware vessel, glazed and brightly painted and about the size of a cleaning bucket. Several of these were carried on each *Ladiësti* ship for eventualities such as this. The organs were pickled in a vinegary wine prepared from special grapes for this one and only purpose.

Helen didn't really want to know about all this, but Sam, her want-to-know-it-all lover, had insisted on finding out and duly communicated the gory details to her. The knowledge served to enhance her appreciation of went on behind her while they were staring out at the *Gallinis'* wake.

She could have done without it.

The trip proceeded. The weather alternated between clement and moderately rough. No sudden storms like the one earlier, but for two days the *Gallinis* labored up and down high swells on an ocean dotted with millions of cat's paws. By the time that was over, the dampness of the ocean was in every shred of clothing they wore, and Helen would have killed for something that felt dry—and *clean* for that matter! You didn't do laundry on the high seas; water was for consumption, not washing.

Yeah, washing! Helen suspected that, though her olfactory senses were probably numbed by the constant exposure to just about *everything* around here, she must surely stink to high heaven. The *Ladi* didn't seem to mind. If they ever washed while at sea they did it when she wasn't looking. Neither she nor Sam had ever been witness to anything even remotely resembling personal hygiene practices. The rains pelting down with regularity, though not with the same vigor as further south over *terra firma*, apparently suggested to nobody but her and Sam that here was an opportunity for getting rid of some of that sweat and stench.

How could people live like this?

Sam chuckled when she brought it up.

"We come from a culture which could be considered excessive in its use of showers and baths."

"Ha! Don't you breathe through your nose? Or do you just move in the wrong circles?"

Sam grinned. "I move among cowboys, honey," he said, mimicking—not very well—the broad accent of his friend Dale. "They're as ripe as they come."

It provided some amusement to the *Ladiësti* sailors when Helen and Sam stood themselves in the rain, got soaking wet, and made some effort to use the water to rinse out their salt–laden garments. Even Mirlun allowed himself to be slightly amused. He still kept mostly to himself, occupied with his own thoughts, often standing at the prow, looking ahead across the waters as if hoping to see the shores of *Aquadiënna* rise from the sea at any moment.

In the end it did. The captain, by various ways of reckoning, announced that their goal was in sight. Helen didn't understand a bit of the 'how', and even Sam, who had a background in such matters, admitted that he was perplexed—but it turned out that Lobus Natois had indeed conveyed them to their destination with an accuracy that would have made a modern–day *El* sailor using a GPS system envious.

"I don't really want to know," Sam told her.

"Really? You? Not asking endless questions?"

He made a wry face. "Don't."

"Yes, sir!" she said meekly—knowing that he knew it was fake and that would get him thinking as to why she was doing this and presently he would tell her what she wanted to know.

Helen grinned to herself. She knew it, and he knew it, too. It was a game: an affectionate one. Another way to get to know each other.

"Gai." Lobus Natois pointed. Nestled the foot of the low hills they saw a smattering of white houses. "It is a small settlement," the *Ladi* continued. "The people there live to fish and supply the Diënna with victuals and servants to keep the Mirlun and her *sacerdae* in the comforts they are accustomed to." His voice dripped with sarcasm. He pointed across the water. They discerned a couple of small dots, which might have been boats.

"There they fish. Usually there are more of them. We will berth at Gai and purchase water and victuals—which they will sell us even though they think we're 'unclean'. This is because we pay them. Is it not remarkable how deeply their convictions are rooted?" He issued a thin smile. "However, for your own sake, I think it would be better if you were not aboard the *Gallinis* when we berth. Gai is small, but Laurentius no doubt has a spy living there. Maybe more than one. I'm certain everybody knows who he is, but that may not prevent him from reporting your arrival."

"What do you suggest?" Helen asked.

"We will deliver you directly to the shore of *Aquadiënna*. But you will get wet."

The boat drew past Gai and the closer in to the shore. Helen and Sam studied the coast through their binoculars and saw nothing untoward. Lobus Natois observed them as they used the binoculars and enquired as to the nature of the instruments. Sam demonstrated and provided a simple explanations of the principles underlying telescopes. Lobus Natois was suitably impressed.

"This we *could* manufacture."

"I am surprised you haven't."

"The notion has not occurred to us."

"Surely, others from our world must have brought such ideas with them in the past."

Lobus Natois shrugged. "If they have, the ideas have not spread."

Influences were indeed at a low level, or so it appeared. The reasons? If those stranded here represented a random cross–section of the populace, the probability that it was going to be someone scientifically and/or technologically literate were low. How many people actually knew how a telescope worked—or could provide the theoretical basis for constructing one? How many of those survived to be able to do so? How many of those survivors were motivated into transmitting this knowledge?

Questions, questions.

She noticed that Sam had given up on the discussion. He gave her a wry look and a tiny shrug, as if to say "what's the point?"

She winked at him and smiled, then returned her attention to the shore.

"They must know we're likely to come here."

Mirlun, who stood at the railing a few feet away from them and started at the shore with the expression of a man in a desert finally beholding a long–sought oasis, turned around.

"The Diënna's demesnes are sacred. Even Laurentius Augustus cannot just send men there to ambush us."

"So you say," Sam muttered, clearly unconvinced. "Plius had no such inhibitions when his Minions came after us."

Mirlun had nothing to say to this. Helen and Sam continued to study the shore through their binoculars with intensity and care.

The *Ladiësti* ship drew as near to the shore as was practical. Two of the four pig–skin coracles on–board were launched to convey the three passengers and their luggage to the shallow beach. Helen and Sam had stripped down to the bare essentials in anticipation of getting very wet. Mirlun, as usual, was fastidiously over–dressed and consequently *did* get very wet. Would he never learn?

The coracles didn't make it through the surf too well and were soon submerged. Sam's self–confessed paranoia—why couldn't he call it 'preparation'?—once again paid off. She would have never thought of bringing sealable plastic liners. But Sam had insisted.

"What if we have to cross a river, get stuck in torrential rain, or have to wade through the surf?" He got didactic at this point, as was his way; a minor irritant, but if that was the worst he had to offer, she had no complaints. "Life," Sam had continued, "is easier if you take plastic liners and carry a backup gun. Never leave home without them."

At which point she'd kissed him, just to shut him up. Or maybe not 'just'.

And then *she* had thought of Ziploc bags.

Bottom line: their packs were soaked but the stuff that mattered and really had to be kept dry, was. *Gladius Magnus*, however, did get wet; it had been wrapped in several layers of cloth, which prevented it from poking through the bags and giving its presence away. Sam had thought it better to keep its existence from the *Ladi*.

"There's no benefit in letting them know," Sam had told her. "So we might as well not."

They dumped their packs on the beach and watched the *Ladiësti* sailors try to get back through the surf, which they managed with some skill, seeing that the coracles were light, could easily be handled by a single man, and floated of their own accord, though now they were submerged. The sailors simply swam and pushed the coracles ahead of them toward the *Gallinis*, which presently set sail and pulled away from the shore. Helen thought she saw someone waving and they waved back.

Mirlun stood further up the beach: soggy, bedraggled, impatient.

As they stood at the top of the barrier that separated the ocean from the lagoon that was *Aquadiënna* it finally hit her.

We've been here before.

Now they were back: the long way around, so to speak.

The expanse of *Aquadiënna* stretched before them, separated from the ocean by a strip of land maybe two hundred yards wide, its highest elevation maybe fifty feet above sea level. Not much to separate the Diënna's fresh–water habitat from the salty ocean.

A precarious existence.

"I wonder if she's aware of it," she said into Sam's ear.

"I'd be surprised if she were," he muttered, his eyes on Mirlun who stood, a few steps away from them, his face raised to the sky, his arms stretched out in an attitude of some form of prayer. "If the *aquaspiriti* are as scientifically disinterested as everybody else around here seems to be…"

At this time of day the full expanse of the lagoon was visible. Her eyes sought the place where they might have stopped on their previous visit. Maybe over there, to their right, on the lower side of yonder hill, on top of which stood a dense forest that had a hauntingly familiar look. She was certain that this was it.

"Look," Sam pointed. To their left, some distance around the shore of *Aquadiënna*, stood an temple–like edifice, surrounded by a grove of massive trees. Even from the distance they could discern the massive colonnaded entrance. The full expanse of the building was hidden by the trees.

"That," Mirlun told them, "is the Diënna's shrine—and the residence of her servants."

"Does she know we're here?" Sam asked.

"Of course she knows," Mirlun said disdainfully. "She is aware of everything in the world."

"Everything? In the entire world?" Sam probed, mercilessly. His eyes darted around here and there with an expression she knew well enough. She noted that his right thumb was hooked into his belt, near the gun. He was clearly unimpressed by the Diënna's putative omniscience and more concerned with immediacies and potential foes lurking somewhere, waiting for them.

"As far as her people have explored it," Mirlun amended, apparently unfazed by the

Chapter 15

significant distinction. "She has known of your progress ever since we came here."

So has Plius, it seems!

She considered the expanse of *Aquadiënna* and thought that it was at least half again as big as Loe Pool. She wondered briefly if there might not, one day, be another opening here.

Then it happened.

Mirlun emitted a small cry of ineffable joy and relief. He sank to his knees. Even Sam ceased his scrutiny of the environs and directed his attention to the lagoon where, with a strange tinkling sound that Helen remembered from their first visit to this place and a near–blinding halo of light, there rose, from the water a…thing.

Just a 'thing', its shape undefined, but imbued with a definiteness of existence, of something real lurking behind the amorphous facade. And then it changed, grew, until it reared above the water, several hundred feet high; reared above them, filling a part of the sky with its wavering outline…which presently became discernibly female, the features stabilizing into the outline of a luminous woman's body, clothed in a flowing garment of diaphanous gauze that did precious little to hide the 'female' features it so inadequately clothed: perfectly proportioned breasts with a high cleavage and large upturned nipples; sleek lines down to the round hips with perfect buttocks; the triangular tuft of pubic hair at the crotch; legs that flowed with the gown into an eddy on the glittering surface of the pool.

For a goddess that requires chastity of her priests she's certainly not doing much to help.

Or maybe this performance wasn't her usual get–up. Maybe intended for them? For…Sam.

Helen glanced sideways at him; noticed that, for the moment at least, his attention was wholly directed to the apparition before them.

Hey!

She nudged him in the ribs.

Sam tore loose his gaze and looked around at her. He had a slightly glazed look—which cleared away even as she watched. He grinned, self–conscious and wry, then reached out, took her hand and pulled her closer to him. Nothing was said, but the gesture, she realized, was meant as much for her own reassurance as for the apparition's benefit. Despite his definite male reactions to a very sexy and seductive female—and be it only a sprite!—he was functioning well enough to allow his brain to stay in the action; despite his hormonal responses, which must have tugged him in a completely different direction.

Was this the tactic the Diënna used on the likes of Mirlun? Maybe the sexually loaded presence was for his benefit as well. Hell, it even affected *her* in some way. If she'd had the slightest homosexual inclinations she might have gotten aroused herself. And it wasn't just the visual effects. Something more was at work; something that worked on your mind directly, around its rational defenses and straight into your unconscious where it upset the carefully maintained equilibrium of the most basic instincts, urges, drives.

Maybe she mind–fucks them—and then tells them that's the only way they're going to get it. With her.

What a perfect method of control. The wet dream of every frigid control–freak wife.

Total—and exclusive—sexual gratification without an iota of sex. The nubile temple girls Mirlun had alluded to in his descriptions—apparently the 'Mirlun' was the only male around the place—were they meant to be permanent temptations? Forever out of his reach, but always reminding him of what he could get. And then, when the Diënna considered it useful, he would get it: from her.

Which meant that Mirlun was *really* screwed up in the head. No wonder he couldn't handle the sex–thing between her and Sam; especially not with the other element thrown in for good measure: the Sam–and–Helen mind–thing, which must've really disturbed the poor benighted sod. And every time they screwed each other silly and Mirlun knew they were doing it, be it in Sam's house, the hotel, the car, or wherever they happened to have done it...

Helen decided there and then that she didn't like the Diënna; that the *Ladi* were probably right: the world might be better off without these things.

She squeezed Sam's hand; wondered what he was thinking. Feeling, for that matter. Had he figured it out yet: the truth about this whole sickening setup?

He didn't say anything, but he must have sensed that she was agitated. He pulled her closer and slipped an arm around her waist.

The apparition stabilized into an near–solid form, shrunk again until it was the size of a normal human female, detached itself from the ectoplasmic umbilical link with the water and descended to the ground just a few steps before them. The form was still that of a sexually provocative woman, with the face of a lusty angel, luscious long black hair, and a semi–transparent garment whose existence only enhanced the sexual charge.

Mirlun remained on his knees, his eyes directed to the ground.

The Diënna emitted a tinkling laugh and said something Helen only partially understood, in a voice at once demure and provocative, with a throaty catch that would have made many a Hollywood star green with envy. That voice alone, Helen suspected, would make some men weak with desire.

How about *her* man? You usually could tell when their interest was diverted. Helen had been in enough, albeit transient, relationships, to detect the signs. She glanced sideways at Sam, wondered if he was aroused.

He noted her regard and averted his gaze from the Diënna, to give her a quick wink. His right hand slipped down to her buttocks and gave her a slight squeeze.

Well, that was fine with her then. Even if the sprite made him horny, at least he still knew who he was going to be horny *with*! She hadn't realized until then that, for a few moments there, not only had she disliked the Diënna, but she had also been a tad afraid of her.

Mirlun raised his gaze to his mistress and replied in a hushed voice. The Diënna told him to rise—that much Helen understood — then directed her attention to her and Sam.

"Welcome," she said—in *English*!—and though it sounded like it had been directed at both of them, Helen knew by the inflection and her pose look that it had been meant more for Sam than her.

A tinkling laugh. "Thank you for coming to save my world. You are tired from your journey. Mirlun will take you to the temple and there you may rest until you are ready to do what needs to be done."

She performed the slightest of bows: an acknowledgement of her appreciation. Then her form fluxed and shimmered and presently winked out of existence.

Mirlun stood for a few breaths, staring at the spot where his mistress had stood. Finally, with a sigh, he turned and looked at them.

"The Diënna has spoken," he said, his voice a mix of joy and sadness. "Let me show you the way."

16

"Weapons are not permitted on temple grounds. There can be no exception." Mirlun was adamant.

So was Sam. "Then find us somewhere else to stay."

Mirlun cringed visibly. Another blow to his fragile—or maybe 'nonexistent' would be a better term—control over them.

Live with it!

From behind Mirlun appeared a number of young women, dressed in garb at sharp variance with Mirlun's preferred drab dress–up. Like their Diënna they were provocative in body as well in dress. No doubt they had been carefully selected for their roles—which made Sam wonder about the purpose of it all. Especially since Mirlun, the only male in a ceremonial role around here—and in a leading one at that—couldn't possibly take advantage of all those tantalizing offerings right under his nose.

Mirlun ignored the *sacerdae*. He inclined his head, as if to listen; then straightened and regarded them with a mix of confusion and envy.

"The Diënna has spoken. You may enter as you are."

I thought as much.

"Let's go," he said to Helen, who picked up her gear from the front steps of the temple where they had deposited them during their unexpected argument with Mirlun.

"Want to show us the way?" he asked Mirlun. This part of the pissing contest was over. He didn't expect all the rounds to go the same way.

Mirlun made a gesture which caused four of the women to detach themselves from the group of *sacerdae*. They performed precise bows before their visitors and indicated for them to follow. They passed through the expansive entrance and a vaulted foyer with ornate floors of pink and blue marble, ringed by a band of tropical plants, grown in troughs set into the floor. Beyond that, an atrium surrounding a wide courtyard where a several female gardeners tended to a luscious, carefully arranged garden of a myriad colors, at the center of which was a circular pond with a central fountain. The fountain was a representation of a beautiful woman, holding up her hands with palms facing upward, from which sprang the twin spouts of water.

The women led them around the courtyard and into another block at the back where a broad colonnaded hallway led to an array of palatial suites, into one of which they were led. It contained a low bed of a simple construction with what looked like a low mattress and an ornate throw–over. On the other side an array of wicker chairs surrounded a low square table, in the center of which stood a large basket of fruit—oranges, apples, grapes, bananas, plums, peaches—and an ornate jug with several wooden goblets beside it. On one wall hung a huge tapestry depicting a rural scene with a fanciful sky filled with colorful birds.

One of the maidens addressed them in slow, but grammatically reasonably correct, English.

"You must be fatigued from the rigors of your journey. Please allow us to tend to your every need."

Every need?

Sam glanced at Helen. She gave him a crooked grin, which, to him at least, spelled out her 'needs' quite clearly. He could not help but compare her—standing there a tad bedraggled and tired, in her inadequately–cleaned tunic, reeking of sea and ship just like himself, her dark hair matted from a week of no real cleaning—with the luscious maidens, each of them the epitome of carefully tended female charm, beauty, and seductiveness.

Seductive, no doubt. Just like that female sprite, whose potent presence had occasioned quite an involuntary arousal in him earlier. It didn't matter that his mind had remained essentially detached, and that the analytical observer had been fully active. His dick had been off in a world of its own, and there seemed nothing he could do about it. It was all he could do to hide his embarrassing condition—though he suspected he hadn't fooled Helen one bit. Just like she probably knew that right now the deep cleavages, the clearly delineated, faintly visible, nipples and clinging garments could not but occupy at least some of his thoughts. That was hormone–driven stuff over which he had little control. In the male—and maybe the female? how would he know?—the path from the visual perception of an exposed shapely female body to sexual arousal was embarrassingly short and direct. Which was why, or so it was said—though who knew if this wasn't just another Oprah–inspired crappy pop misconception—that men tended to think about sex much more often than women, with whom those same reaction–cause–and–effect pathways were more complicated. You push a button with a guy and bingo—while with a girl it was like operating a helos controls: a delicate balancing act at the best of times, and positively precarious when the wind got choppy.

But he also knew that the true *focus* of his aroused desire was the woman beside him—and that it didn't matter what she wore, or how much she needed a bath, or if she was cranky or cheerful, or if her hair was matted. *This* girl's control panel, no matter how complicated, was something you could get lost in.

Like I'm getting lost in my analogy!

"What are you grinning at?" she challenged him.

He took her hand and turned to the *sacerdae*. "We would like a bath," he said in their language.

The one who had spoken to him bowed. "As you say."

"Alone," Sam added.

She could not conceal her surprise. A look of incomprehension flickered across her even, alomost perfectly symmetrical, features. Her big brown eyes considered him for an instant. She hesitated as if to say something, but then refrained from pursuing the matter.

"As you wish," she said and bowed again.

The other three *sacerdae* also bowed and glided away, to disappear behind the flowing curtains which, Sam concluded, acted as doors in this place. Only she who had spoken remained behind.

"What is your name?" Helen asked in Seladiënnan.

"Naöme," the girl said softly.

Helen smiled. The smile lit up the room, like it always did. For that smile a man might topple empires.

Chapter 16

Or launch a thousand ships…

"Naöme," Helen said gently, switching into English, "do you have something to clean and fix…this?" She held up a strand of her tangled hair.

Naöme, the *sacerda*, issued a smile of girl–girl understanding. It was the first time Sam had seen something genuine about her behavior. Everything else had been like carefully orchestrated ritual.

"*Ulaque*," Naöme said. "I will bring you *ulaque*."

She bowed again. "Please excuse me. I will return." She disappeared behind the curtains.

"Buxom little critters, aren't they?" Helen said.

In response he pulled her closer, took her face in his hands and, very deliberately and slowly, kissed her deeply. She responded in kind, locking herself to him, mouth to mouth, body to body, flowing together and around each other, with this crazy desire to be *one*, at the same time that they were two.

I love him so…

Her tongue penetrating him deeply, caressing his, roaming around his mouth. Her hips grinding against his.

Hardness pushing into a pool of moist heat. A spasm of pleasure.

Her eyes wide open, deep brown pools he wanted to drown in.

Blue, green–flecked eyes above. A scratchy beard against her(??) face.

The sense of an intrusive presence.

They pulled apart.

Near the curtain stood Naöme, her eyes averted to the ground.

'*I love him so*'.

Not *his* thoughts…

Sam let Helen go, though he held onto her hands.

What had happened here? A sequence of words that weren't words, but a…unit…a unit of thought maybe…

Whose thought?

"You bath is prepared," the *sacerda* announced quietly. She turned and pulled the curtain aside, to reveal another suite beyond their own, at the far end of which, on a slightly raised pedestal, stood an oval marble bath of enormous proportions. Beside it two wicker–work tables, on which stood an assortment of jars and bottles. Sam decided that this qualified as the 'bathroom'. Smaller basins were positioned at one side of the chamber. At the other, behind a jointed wooden frame which supported tightly stretched sheets of a fine, dense gauze, was a toilet, remarkably like that any one might have found in a modern hotel, only that the bowl of this one was carved from pink marble, as was the bidet–like device beside it.

Naöme, without a word, stepped back and allowed the curtain to drop into place. When they looked around they found themselves alone.

Helen eyed the bath with expectancy and stepped closer to inspect it.

"Look at the size of it!" She was right. You could drown in the damn thing. "Taps!" She tried them. Water gushed forth with considerable pressure. They hadn't heard them fill it up earlier, so their requirement must have been anticipated. Nothing against the service around here!

"Hot and cold!" Helen was still exploring the taps. "Civilization!"

He regarded her fondly, found pleasure in her enjoyment of this simple, yet somehow essential, thing.

What happened back there?

Thoughts that had not been his own...

More even—thought he didn't understand what.

"Soap!" Helen straightened and held it up. She looked around herself. Satisfied that they were as private as it would get around here, she stripped and started on Sam immediately after.

He laughed at her eagerness.

"That water will be filthy by the time we're clean," she said. "Which means we'll refill it and have a nice, long, sexy underwater session." She tugged on his hand. "Come on, Sam Donovan. I want my back scrubbed—and then I want *you*!"

"In that order, huh?" he teased.

"I think you'll like it better, too."

"I like you any way I can get you."

Chuckling she stepped into the bath. "I bet you say that to all the girls." She pulled him in with her. He water was on the tepid side of hot: just right.

Helen handed him the soap. "Here, do your duty."

Later. Having found the mechanism to drain the bath—a wooden prop in a hole near one side—they changed the water, using the time it took to drain and refill the considerable volume to rub each other dry clean with the soft towels, which they'd found draped over a small wicker frame obviously designed for just this purpose.

Now they were lying in the water, Sam propped up against a side, her head resting against his left shoulder, in pleasant exhaustion and contented languor.

"I could live like this," she sighed. "Get wrinkled like a prune; make love from morning till night; and from night till morning."

"That'd be nice," he agreed.

She moved against him, expelling little pockets of water between them.

"We'll have to get out of this soon," he said regretfully.

"Don't say things like that," she muttered and turned her head to nibble on his ear. "I think we should stretch this out as far as we can."

"Oh, yes."

She raised herself off him, turned to face him, and reached down to put him inside her again. Then she laid herself against him and, wrapping her arms around his neck, rested her head against his shoulder.

"Can we go to sleep now?" she whispered. "Just like this?"

Sam took a deep breath. Helen raised her head.

"What is it?" Her eyes suddenly weren't sleepy anymore.

She looked at him closely. "What happened? Tell me what happened!"

"Who says anything 'happened'?"

"*I* say so. I *know* so."

She probably did. Scratch the 'probably'. She usually did. Which maybe made what he'd experienced earlier slightly less...preposterous.

He told her.

Helen's eyes went round. "You think this was a telepathic experience or

Chapter 16

something?"

"I think I saw *me*—like through *your* eyes. And *did* you think what I thought I thought—*you* thought...ahh, whatever."

"I thought a lot of things," she said impishly. "I have no idea *what*. But," the dimples at the sides of her mouth deepened, "I suppose something like that could have been in there. I mean, I *do* love you. Terribly. Terminally. So maybe..."

Her breath caught for an instant. "You felt me feeling you touching me? Is that what happened? Oh my!"

"Are you getting excited?"

"Am I ever! I wonder if I could..." He could actually feel her heart beating faster. Her parted mouth brushed against his, her tongue probing deeply. Her pubis pushed down on him; her breath came with small spasmodic flutters; her soft moans resounded in his head...

...and s/he was probing in his mouth and tasting him...his breath...the rough–soft surface of his tongue as it stroked hers...him inside her, pushing up to where she could clamp around him and...

...she saw what he saw, felt what he felt herself through him and him through her through him through her...

...as they spiraled through an infinite sequence of embraces...

...losing who was who...

...slipping from the side of the pool and under water, their mouths and bodies locked together in a hermetic embrace as it shook them, and they knew not whose orgasm it was—because it was his and it was hers, but neither knew which...

...coming up, gasping for breath, submerging, rolling over in the tepid water, spasming again...

...until finally, limp with an utterly satisfying exhaustion, they floated in the water, regarding each other in uncomprehending wonder at this thing that had taken them.

The marble outside the bath was very slippery indeed. The thick woolen mats probably stopped them from slipping as they emerged from the water with weak legs, holding onto each other for support, and grinning bemusedly all the way to the towel rack, where they dried each other off—again.

They didn't talk.

Why talk, thought Sam? Post–coital chit–chat...what could it possibly convey that they hadn't already communicated?

Scary, breathlessly exhilarating, humbling: all at once.

What had they done to deserve...*this*? What had *he* done? What could possibly prompt an incomprehensible fate to allow him this experience? He stopped rubbing Helen down, dropped the towel to the marble floor, and lifted his hands to cradle her face, allowed himself a long, frank, wondering inspection of her features; which she tolerated with a tiny smile and that lovely soft expression women got when they were in love and happy.

It had to be her.

Of course! Nothing else made sense. Fate wasn't out to reward Sam Donovan for anything. He had done nothing to merit rewards of any kind. Indeed, if the truth be told, he'd screwed up a great deal of things. But somehow, for some obscure reason beyond his ken, Helen loved him; and he loved her, and in this synergy of whatever there was between them, there was born this wonderful, incredible thing that he didn't even want to think about too hard, for fear that it might just blow it away like a whiff of smoke in a breeze.

"It won't," she said softly.

She knew. She always knew.

He kissed her again, lingered with the touch of their mouths for an extra moment, then picked up the towel again and finished rubbing down her legs, while she ran her hand through his hair and alongside his face, urging him to kiss her as she made soft sounds of contentment.

Dressed finally in short, light tunics, they left the bathroom. Sam's mood was so mellow that he almost forgot the belt with the holster and the Beretta. Indeed, after all that had happened it was almost like a sacrilege to strap on an instrument whose main intent and purpose was the destruction of human life.

But he did—for something else insinuated itself into his thoughts: an increased awareness of how extraordinarily precious his and Helen's lives had become. He would not risk either by dropping his guard. The world had a way of screwing around with the precious things in one's life. Fate was unforgiving. He wouldn't tempt it.

They were left alone until they finally ventured out of their suite, into the precincts of the temple. Presently, Naöme and her three companions materialized out of somewhere to invite them to partake in a banquet laid out especially for them.

"Just for us?" Helen asked her.

Naöme shook her head and smiled. "For all. You, however, are our guests of honor."

Sam nudged Helen. "Two guys and a whole lotta girls. Some men who would kill for this."

She tightened her arm around him; a warm presence at his side. One half of a being, a glimpse of which they had been privileged to perceive. Her being there like this gave him a hold on things, made him able to believe that what he remembered had really happened. Right now it was like he lived in two worlds simultaneously: the mundane reality around him—and that other place; the one he didn't understand, yet. His right hand, seemingly possessed of a life of its own, slipped lower to rest on her hip.

"Behave yourself," she murmured.

"Would I not?"

"Ha!"

They arrived at a hall open to the central courtyard, where they found Mirlun and about a dozen young women, all dressed alike in near identical garments of transparent gauze, in hues of pink and green; each apparently consisting of a single long strip of the gauze–like material, draped in artful loops and knots around their bodies, and held together by wooden clasps near the shoulders. The effect was stunning. A thing like this on a Paris catwalk would be a total sensation. It would also be terminally sexy in the bedroom. Unwrap instead of strip.

"She can't be a woman," Helen said so lowly that only he could her it, "so she expresses what she could be by surrounding herself with these girls."

"Poor Mirlun."

Said individual appraised them as they entered, and though, like the women, he bowed—albeit with considerably less reverence—he also managed to express his disapproval of the weapons in one brief glance.

Sam briefly considered saying something about it, but then decided that it would only give Mirlun an opening to an argument.

They were shown to a table. Once there, Mirlun motioned Sam to sit, while the women indicated to Helen that they wanted her to sit at another, nearby table, whose position seemed to indicate, ever so subtly, that those to be placed around it were of a lower status. Indeed, the table where he was to sit had only two places: the other one presumably for Mirlun.

What *was* it with these people? They'd been through all this before, with the *Ladi*. Not again!

"It's all right," Helen said softly when Sam took her hand and shook his head.

"No," he said firmly. "It's not. We give in even one iota to this political pissing contest and we're screwed. Remember they wanted us, not the other way around." To Mirlun he said, in English: "You must know that this is unacceptable."

"It is the place of women…"

"Oh stop it!" Sam said lowly, but with a ring of impatient menace. He let go of Helen's hand and took Mirlun aside. "If we're going to remain friends," he said, "then stop these stupid games, OK? Your customs are your own—and ours are ours. You invited us here because you want us to do a dirty job you can't do yourselves. We're not asking for much in return, are we now? So I *do* suggest that you oblige us by not being any more offensive that you absolutely have to. We might just get so pissed off that we're not going to do your dirty work—and then where would you be?"

Mirlun regarded him coldly. "And where would *you* be? Remember that by coming here you have made this world yours as well. This 'dirty work' as you choose to call it—and I call it 'noble work'!—it will be to your benefit as well. I don't think you'd want to live in a world ruled by Plius and his henchman, Laurentius Augustus. You have a profound affection for this woman of yours? You may want to have a family with her one day? How would *you* like it if your children grew up under the yoke of Plius?" he said scornfully. He issued a thin–lipped smile. "No, Sam Donovan: your threats do not impress me. I know you will do this 'dirty work', no matter what. The Diënna has seen that you will—and therefore this is what will happen, no matter what you might do to avoid it."

"The Diënna is never wrong, huh?"

"Never. She knows everything."

"Does she know *how* I am going to dispose of Plius and Larry?"

"She has not communicated this to me."

"I want to talk to her."

"She will speak to you when she sees fit."

Sam sighed. Intransigent zealots and self–important water–sprites. The details differed, but somehow it all has a familiar ring.

Human nature.

Yeah, right.

"I don't care what you think you know," Sam said firmly. "There are things I will not accede to. Anything that, directly or by implication, deprecates Helen will not be tolerated." He raised a hand to forestall Mirlun's objection. "This is not and will never be negotiable."

Mirlun took a deep breath and visibly forced himself to calm.

"You presume much, Sam Donovan. Since you have come to my world, you have done nothing but defy its rules."

"And yet," Sam retorted, "we are the ones who are meant to save it. Does that not suggest certain conclusions?"

"Such as?"

"That maybe it is *because* we break the rules of your world, *because* we do not conform to your values and your customs and your endless idiosyncrasies: *that this is why and how we are going to save your world?*" He nodded at the table. "Where shall we sit?"

Mirlun nodded heavily. "It shall be as you say. The woman..."

"Helen," Sam snapped.

"...Helen...she shall sit with us."

"And you will treat her with the respect you accorded to her when you came to recruit us," Sam added. "I'd hate to think that all that civilized behavior of yours was a put–on to deceive us into believing that we were dealing with a sensible human being."

He knew that last tirade had been unnecessary and possibly unproductive and would probably antagonize Mirlun more than he had to, but right now he didn't give a shit. The fact was that—and he had made himself not even *hint* at it! they might well not be as dependent on a fortuitous outcome of this affair as Mirlun liked to think. If—and a big 'if' it was—they could obtain enough data to get a computational handle on the distribution of the transition points.

They returned to the others. Sam took Helen's hand and led her to the head table where they sat down. Mirlun waved imperiously. Another setting was produced. The *sacerdae* distributed themselves around the three other tables. They were being discreet about it, but there were the glances, and there could be no doubt that Mirlun's standing had taken a plunge. In this twisted arrangement at the temple where 'the Mirlun' was both a tortured, constantly tempted, victim, as well as the head–honcho of the Diënna's flock, the sudden appearance of the strangers and the instant disruption of the established power–structure must surely be both disturbing and an occasion for endless speculation and gossip.

The meal was opulent—and long. Too long. Nobody should be forced to sit through a procedure like that. Not unless they actually enjoyed it—which he didn't particularly in this case. He'd had been through similar ritualistic feasts like this before and quietly advised Helen to eat as little as possible of each course. Beverages consisted of red wine, juices of berry, apricot, peach, and apple. There was also water, served from earthenware vessels, ornamented with bright semi–abstract patters which might have been yet more representations of the Diënna in various poses and contexts.

Sam, following an hunch that soon grew into a solid suspicion, leaned close to Helen.

"Don't drink the water," he whispered.

She glanced at him. "Why not?"

"I'll tell you later."

He turned to Mirlun. Conversation so far had been a trifle stilted, which wasn't surprising given the events that had preceded their meal. Maybe, Sam thought, here was an opportunity for some fishing.

He pointed at the water vessels.

"You water, it comes from *Aquadiënna*?"

"Of course."

Sam remembered what Mirlun had told them about his connection to his mistress, established through drinking large quantities of the lagoon's water.

"All water comes from the pool?"

Mirlun regarded him with scorn. "Of course not. The Diënna nourishes and heals. We do not profane her water by using it for washing and similarly base purposes."

Sam allowed himself a clandestine breath of relief. For a moment he had thought that maybe his and Helen's recent experience had been…well, 'induced' was as good a word as any.

"So, where does the other water come from?"

"The roof of the temple collects the rains into large underground tanks. It is then pumped into a smaller tank which rests above the kitchen roof and so provides pressure for the pipes."

"How does it get pumped to the roof–tank?"

"A single ox suffices to power the pump."

"Ox? You have cattle? How is this possible?"

"Not all the draft animals with the legion were castrated. There was also a group of cows with the auxiliary. These were bred, then cross–bred with a certain kind of wild cattle–beast. So we have cattle, just like our ancestors."

Sam nodded. "Interesting."

"To commune with the Diënna you, too, will have to imbibe her substance," Mirlun said.

Sam glanced at Helen. She nodded almost imperceptibly. Maybe, he thought, she hadn't nodded at all, but somehow her assent had communicated itself to him anyway. She would not drink the water. Neither would he. 'Communing' with the Diënna—or anything like her—might not be such a good idea; whatever 'communing' meant. If Mirlun's utterances were to be believed, it probably implied that the sprite thereby gained access to one's thoughts.

Maybe here was the reason why the Diënna had such a hard time reading newcomers from *E1*. Maybe the arrival had to be primed a bit, with the consumption of enough Diënna–water to soak every cell in it. A few glasses probably made little difference, but as far as Sam was concerned, even a tiny bit was too much. If Helen had access to what went on in his head: fine. But he wasn't going to have some semi–supernatural entity poking around in his head and body. Who knew where it stopped? Maybe there was even the possibility of physical dependency. Mirlun's cravings for the Diënna might well have a biochemical basis.

"You, too, will come to understand that the Diënna is never wrong," Mirlun declared with the certainty reserved for the zealot.

"Somehow I doubt it," Sam muttered.

"Of course you would," Mirlun said somewhat condescendingly. "But never in recorded history have the Diënna's prophecies been anything but accurate and precise."

"Records?" Helen's head snapped around.

Mirlun grimaced. "Of course. A recorded history is one of the frameworks of civilization."

Helen glanced at Sam.

"You have records of the incidences of the openings between our worlds?"

"Every single one the Diënna has known and predicted."

Sam forced himself to sound only moderately interested.

"There have been many such?"

"We have recorded them for almost twelve centuries. There have been many thousands."

"Many thousands," Helen murmured. "The times and the places?" she asked Mirlun.

He inclined his head. "Of course. We are nothing if not fastidious."

Indeed.

"Could we have a look at them sometime?" Sam asked.

Mirlun shrugged. "Why not? They are available for anyone to study; a testament to the Diënna's glory. In the morning I will instruct one of the *sacerdae* to take you to our library, where they have been kept for as long as they have existed."

On a platter.

Now all they had to hope was that the analysis software on their computer did the job right—that there *was* a system to these events.

The meal continued with sporadic conversation and presently drew to a close. Darkness had fallen and the servants who had catered for the occasion lit candles which were set into holders along the walls. They sputtered and smoked, and Sam thought that here was the reason why all the ceilings were slightly stained.

The evening wore on. Everybody was full to the brim. Sam and Helen excused themselves and received grateful looks from the *sacerdae*, who had been compelled to stay around until the guests chose to leave, but now looked very ready to retire. Sam wondered how *they* felt about being servants of the Diënna, compelled to chastity. For the rest of their lives? He didn't think so. None of them were older than their mid twenties. Maybe they served for some years, then were allowed, or made, to return to their homes. Chastity, he supposed, was bearable if it didn't last forever. Even so, it must have been difficult. These women were at the prime of their sexual function, and to be forced to deny nature's urgencies could not be an easy task.

Then again, who said they did?

Naöme accompanied them back to their suite, where they availed themselves of the ablution facilities and then went straight to bed. The day had been long and brought many, sometimes exhausting experiences. The wine, though they had imbibed only moderately, added its effect, and presently they were asleep, tucked against each other.

The Diënna came to Sam in his dreams. At first he didn't know it, and it was just like an ordinary dream: a sequence of, often contradictory and non–sequitur images and events, that was just accepted as–is, without the intervention of the critical faculty active when awake.

But then something changed. All of a sudden Sam *knew* that he was dreaming, and that he wasn't really standing at the edge of the endless body of still water, and that the

Chapter 16   241

apparition before him was...

What?

A figment of his imagination?

The wraith in the shape of a scantily–clothed beautiful woman—oozing sexuality with such vigor and force that even in his dream he knew that his sleeping body would be having a massive erection—swayed before him, like net–curtains in a light breeze. She spoke and yet she did not speak.

What exactly was said was the stuff of dreams and much of it could not be phrased in words. But Sam understood the meaning well enough. That he must do this soon, for Plius was gaining strength. That he must destroy Plius first, because without him Laurentius Augustus would have much diminished power and so could be defeated easily.

But how could he? he wondered. Plius would be surrounded by his Minions, which must surely be waiting for him. And even if they weren't, how could he possibly destroy Plius? He was just one man?

The sprite had no answer. It just was *so*. Several lines of possibility mapped out the future. In the one where he destroyed Plius first he would be victorious—as would she, and together they would bring a new epoch of prosperity and peace to the empire.

What about the other?

The Diënna was oddly reluctant. It must not be. That future was dark—though it also contained Plius' defeat.

'Dark'? Why dark? What kind of 'dark'? 'Bad' 'dark'? Or 'dark' 'dark'—like 'obscure' or 'unknown'?

He probed.

The sprite refused to elaborate. Maybe, he sensed, it couldn't. Maybe there was a barrier.

'Dark'?

He probed again. Which of those futures was to be?

The sprite seemed to recoil momentarily. Sam pressed harder.

She did not know. Only this: that Plius must be destroyed first. Everything hinged on this.

What if Plius was not destroyed?

That future, she insisted, had ceased to exist as a possibility. The moment they set a foot into this world Plius demise had become inevitable.

I wonder if Plius knows this.

He suspects, the Diënna informed him. That is why he was making such efforts to find them.

But if he knew that he'd be destroyed, why should he try to avert the inevitable?

The Diënna offered no explanation. Maybe she didn't have one.

Would they find them here? Did they *need* to 'find' them? Surely they must know.

They knew! the sprite agreed.

Then why not just do the logical thing? The temple seemed to lack defenses. What was to stop Laurentius' legionnaires or Plius's Minions...

The train of thought, as was the wont in dreams, was disrupted by events—as the sprite drifted closer to him, its presence growing to define the horizon of his perception. The sexual aura intensified. From it radiated an infinite promise: of unparalleled joys and pleasures, of beauty and endless vistas of a paradise he couldn't even begin to understand. His arousal became acute and urgent. The sprite, now denuded, a nubile woman of breathtaking beauty, approached and knelt before him, taking him into her mouth, her caressing tongue, occasioning an exquisite anticipatory tingle.

No!
He tore himself away.
A dream!
Just a dream!
Wake up, asshole!
His eyes snapped open.
Awake now!
I am awake. I must be awake!
He drifted.
Through another layer.
Again she was there, kneeling before him, caressing and teasing.
Sam jerked himself out of her...
...rolled over...
...came to lie on his back.
Not again!

Still his arousal was almost painfully intense. A warm mouth and tongue teasing him with tender, urgency.

The undeniable elements of waking reality. The smell of her. The sounds of skin against cloth. A low sound from her as she shifted and slowly rocked her head up and down in a steady rhythm; the source of his pleasure and the anticipatory tensing in his loins. He pulled her on top of him. A soft groan escaped her. Then her legs clamped tight around him; she spasmed and uttered a muffled cry as they climaxed and he poured himself into her.

And again they merged, riding the spiraling eddies of infinitely–layered mirror images of each other knowing the other and losing who was who and where and when—a mutual caress in which two were one and one was two and where time was shouldered aside into insignificance as they lay locked in their physical and spiritual embrace.

"What are we?"
Morning was breaking with the first chirping of birds. They lay facing each other in a close half–embrace. Helen smelled of love and love–making, of warmth and promise, of intimacy and yet more love. When he kissed her he could taste himself and her.
"Something good," he whispered.
"I think so, too."
"I *know* so."
"She doesn't like this, you know."
He didn't have to ask who 'she' was. He'd told Helen about the dream. She'd agreed that it had been more than just a dream.
"What a bitch! I'm giving you the fellatio of your life, and she's using it to pretend it was her." She giggled. "You know, I wonder if she does this to Mirlun."
"Does what?"
"Makes sure he's asleep and that he *stays* asleep, then sends in one of the girls to

add to the experience. All the while the poor benighted sod thinks his Diënna is just mind–screwing him. Maybe the girls take their turns and have fun, with Mirlun none the wiser. Have you seen how they look at him? I think they *do* this, you know?"

"You have a gutter–mind."

He felt her mouth twist into a smile. "Yeah, but you like it."

"Hmm."

She tucked herself closer.

" 'Something good', eh?"

"No doubt about it."

"Something unusual though."

"Very."

"I like unusual," she said. "If it's something like us."

For a while they rested in companionable silence.

Helen stirred against him. "If those records are everything Mirlun says they are, we may have everything we need."

"That would be an unexpected bonus."

"We might even be able to go home again."

"Still think of it as home, huh?"

"Don't you?"

"Yeah."

She sniffed. "You smell very sexy, but I think we should get into that humungous bath next door and get ourselves wrinkly like prunes."

"You just want to play games again."

"Sue me."

"Aren't you exhausted?"

"Yeah—but that's a *big* bath. If we ever get a house I want a big bath like that."

"You want a big watery sex–playground!"

"You're objecting?"

"Did I object?"

"I didn't think you would."

"Let's just lie here for a little while."

"That would be nice, too."

17

"This is unbelievable," Helen said excitedly, hovering over the crisp pages bearing meticulous record of the temporal and the approximate geographic locations of *E1–E2* transition areas for as far back as they cared to look. The script was precise, using the old Roman lettering and numerals, which, after some discussions with the chief *sacerda* looking after the library, became easy enough to decipher and translate.

Location was often vague; coordinate system on Seladiënnan maps was still based on a flat globe and the maps themselves could have been more accurate. But there was a coordinate system.

"They had almost two–thousand years," Helen muttered. "you would have thought they'd gotten it right by now."

"But we can still use this, right?"

She nodded. "Definitely. The errors are what they are and there isn't much we can do about that. But this is…just amazing."

"The anal practices of civilization," he said. "Maybe they'll be of use after all."

Helen returned her attention to the documents.

The *sacerda*, whose name was Ladaea, observed them curiously.

"Why are you studying these records with such intent?" She eyed the QTel beside the book. Helen picked it up and began the laborious task of copying the entries into a database, which would then be used as an input to the analysis program.

Ladaea watched, mystified. Sam decided that it was not advisable to elucidate their intentions.

"We are trying to understand this phenomenon, which has long been a mystery to the people of my world."

"The Diënna understands. What more do we need?"

Sam smiled at her and deliberately allowed his gaze to rest on her for an extra few moments. As expected, her attention was duly diverted from Helen's activities. A faint blush spread over her cheeks and down her neckline.

"Nothing, of course," he said gently. "It is but idle curiosity. These records," he indicated the rows of shelves bearing uncounted volumes of bound parchment, "they are truly amazing. What else have you here?"

"I'll show you." The girl, eager to please and grateful for being able to do something else but be embarrassed, turned away.

Helen gave Sam an inscrutable glance as he touched her arm.

"Behave," she said lowly.

"Just a moment!" he called after the *sacerda*. He leaned down to Helen. "This is going to take a while?"

"All morning and more," she agreed. "The more data I enter the better the predictions will be." She winked at him. "Why don't you go and distract our luscious little librarian—and make sure that Mirlun doesn't think of visiting here and maybe figure out what we're trying to do."

"I might just get him to take me for a ride around the place. Keep him out of your face." He bent down and kissed her. "I'll see you when you're done." Then he went off to let the *sacerda* show him the marvels of her library.

Mirlun had been eager enough to take Sam for a ride around *Aquadiënna*. That Helen should not be coming was a bonus, though Mirlun expressed his puzzlement at her absence.

"She is studying your records," Sam told him.

"A woman? Why?"

Here we go again!

"Curiosity. Helen has an interest in history. Yours is documented with great precision."

Mirlun shook his head and spurred on his horse. Sam followed him as they rode along the sweeping curve of *Aquadiënna*. Presently they reached the place where some months ago, he and Helen had received the sword.

The sword. He wondered if maybe he shouldn't just return it to the Diënna. It appeared to have little use and was just so much extra weight. Maybe its purpose had been fulfilled anyway. They had taken it and brought it back—and themselves with it. Maybe that's all it was supposed to do.

He put the question to Mirlun, who appeared aghast at Sam even raising the question.

"*Gladius Magnus* must remain in your care until Plius is destroyed. The Diënna says so."

'The Diënna says so.'

Sam stopped himself from mimicking Mirlun's favorite phrase and getting the guy really pissed-off. Instead he shrugged as if the matter were of no consequence.

"If Plius gets the sword he will rule Seladiënna," Mirlun insisted, piqued by Sam's apparent indifference to the issue. "You have been entrusted with its care—until the Diënna decides that you are no longer needed."

Now that didn't sound too good, did it?

Sam wondered if Mirlun was aware of how his words could be taken—of how maybe they *should* be taken.

Freudian slips?

Maybe. Something to keep in mind.

Sam dismounted. Despite the daily rains he thought the indentations…here and here…might they be those of the Range Rover's tires.

He straightened and remounted the horse, a dappled gray with a nervous prance, full of life and nervous energy. He patted the horse and, with Mirlun tagging behind, headed for the wall of trees atop the slight incline. The track: eerily familiar. And yet…

"That way lies Gai?" he asked Mirlun.

The Seladiënnan nodded. "The people come this way with their supplies."

"Helston."

"The positions roughly coincide."

They reached the forest, plunged underneath the trees. Sam halted the horse and dismounted again. He bent down and touched the ground, his fingers tracing the unmistakable outlines of tire-tracks—almost covered by the marks of horses and

Chapter 17

carts. Still...this was where he had skidded and barely caught the vehicle as they were desperately trying to get away from the Minions. The car had almost slewed off the track and into the trees.

Now I believe.

In that moment he heard her call his name.

Sam's head snapped up. "What..."

He peered around, glanced at Mirlun, still mounted on his horse.

"Did you hear that?"

Mirlun frowned with a perplexed expression. "What should I hear?"

Then, suddenly, he understood that Mirlun *couldn't* have heard—for Helen wasn't here, but back at the temple...

His heart missed a beat. The sick reality of his failure hit him like bullet.

Helen transferred the one hundred and sixty-eighth entry into the QTel's database. *That many*, she thought. *All that from just three years.*

With that kind of data, despite the errors, the analysis program should be able to generate reliable results—if any such were to be had at all; if it wasn't all random. It used a simulated neural network approach to encode the patterns and extract whatever systematic trends might underlie them—thus leading, hopefully, to reliable predictions of other elements of the pattern—meaning, in this instance, the spatio–temporal coordinates of the next members in the series.

Another two hours and she'd have so many data that the QTel, despite its amazing CPU, would be crunching away for several days to sort it all out. Fortunately, the battery life at constant operation was a guaranteed six months.

The marvels of modern technology.

She reached behind her and from a straw bag extracted the second QTel, a twin to the one on the table, and brought at Sam's insistence.

'Paranoia backup', he'd called it.

Helen took the QTel from it's specially manufactured shock and water–proof casing and placed it where it could receive the data from its twin and activated the transmission protocols. A couple of seconds later it was all done. She set the analysis program going and put QTel back its protective enclosure and into the bag; then returned her attention to the parchments, to continue her entries into the database.

It was then that she heard the thunder.

At first it was distant, yet when it came, with subsonic rumblings reverberating through the building, it triggered something—something she could not define, yet it made her raise her head, forget about everything but the sound, set her nerves on edge, triggering memories of...

Helen jumped up. She knew. The thunder of many horses pounding the ground, approaching with fatidic inevitability.

She looked around her. A panicky sensation clamped down around her heart. From behind a rack of documents emerged the *sacerda*, her face a mask of disbelief and anger.

"They approach!" she shouted in her native tongue. "They violate the Diënna's soil!"

"Who?!"

"The *legio*! They are coming!"

The legion?

So much for the 'sacred' grounds around the temple.

Would they violate it?

Somehow Helen never doubted it. Whoever was out there was after her and Sam, and they would make sure they got them.

Helen picked up the straw bag, threw the second QTel into it and ran from the library. But where to go? From the sounds of it the temple was completely surrounded. She looked around her in despair. The data! A safe place. Where was there safety around here?

She crossed the wide courtyard. Around her shouts mingled with screams of terror. Helen swallowed and forced down her building panic.

Her gaze alighted on the fountain. She took the QTel in its container out of the bag and threw it into the water, where it sank out of sight. Helen felt for the gun at her belt—then hesitated; forced herself to *think*. With that many she had no chance. And they would get the gun and that was *bad*! Helen ducked behind an ornamental shrub and relieved herself of the belt, which she pushed under the bush and out of sight—or so she hoped.

From one side of the courtyard shouts and another scream of terror. A number of black–clad silhouettes appeared, running toward her. Helen bolted, ran through the ornamental growths which tugged at her garments, slowing her down. Then she tripped, fell forward, tried to catch herself with her hands; but something snagged her sleeve, and she never got the arm forward to protect herself. The ground came at her. She might have shouted Sam's name. A sharp pain. Then nothing.

Mirlun screamed with anger as they charged out of the forest and saw the pall of smoke rising from the temple. He spurred on his horse, with Sam racing behind, sick in his heart and filled with a burning rage such as he had never known in his entire life.

They raced back toward the water, then veered aside and followed its course back toward the temple.

As they did, a nagging trace of rationality fought a battle with the overwhelming grief and fury that occupied almost all of his being. For he saw the black riders around the temple, saw their strength, knew that no matter what he did or how he did it he would never defeat them. Instead he would be killed and then there would be nobody to find her.

Find her?

How did he know she was still alive?

Because she could not be dead. Because she was not dead. Because she was…here…in his head. The reality of her existence had not gone—and it was intolerable that it should ever be otherwise. But for that he had to *live*!

Sam spurred his horse to greater speed and managed to catch up with Mirlun. He shouted at the man, but found no response. The face, set in the mask of inhuman paralysis, stared straight ahead. Sam grabbed the reins of Mirlun's horse, slowed his own mount and forced Mirlun's to do the same. The man turned to him, his face filled with loathing and anger. He reached out to tear Sam's hand from the reins. Sam let go; his hand snapped out and grabbed Mirlun's tunic and jerked him off the horse. The floor in the adjacent bathroom was strewn with ashes, scorched with indelible burn marks.

Sam turned away and made his way across to the library. He came across Mirlun who wandered the temple like a blind man. He ignored him and presently arrived at the library. The heat didn't allow him to approach too closely. The remnants of the precious documents still smoldered with a ferocious intensity. A record of the past gone forever.

One of the dire lessons of history: *you gotta have a backup!* For everything: especially documents and weapons. Preferably off–site!

Had anybody paid any heed? Maybe a few anal monks, but most people weren't half paranoid enough. The result? With the smoke over Alexandria's library went a major part of recorded human history—and the fiendish heat before him spelt the end of just about everything the Diënna's attendants and worshipers had ever jotted down.

Shit, shit, *shit*!

Maybe Mirlun was right. It looked like they *were* here for good, whether they chose to or not.

Sam turned away from the grim remainders of the library and headed for the cellars, found them un–raided, though a couple of corpses lay around the entrance. Another one lay across the entrance to one of the pantries. Sam hastened to the nook where they'd stashed their gear.

Relief! Nobody had bothered to go this far. Maybe there had no time; maybe they just wanted to do some killing and, having done so, retreated to do some more outside. Whatever, swords and bags were untouched. Sam opened one, rummaged around in the darkness, found a box of ammunition and took it with him upstairs.

He stood there, looking around. Helen was a smart girl. She would have heard them coming, drawn the right conclusions, and done the needful.

What was 'needful'? From her perspective that is. What would she have considered important—given the conditions of pressure and possible panic?

The gun! She had a gun!

She wouldn't have used it?

Please tell me you didn't try to use it!

Assuming she hadn't...

What was 'needful'?

The database and the gun: if she'd kept her wits about her she would have thought of this.

Hang in there! he thought, wishing that she could hear him.

If she'd known about the fire...

A safe place. Safe from the fire. Safe from the invaders.

Tell me...

What would he have done?

He stood, surveying the wrecked courtyard. The shrubs at the periphery, where they had been close to the fire, were shriveled and blackened. But near the fountain, its central statue still standing undamaged, pouring forth a steady stream of water, the well–tended, well–watered shrubs and plants, though trampled, had been otherwise unaffected. Sam, following a stray thought, stepped into the courtyard and ambled toward the fountain.

He saw the straw bag between a couple of bushes. He hunkered down beside it and poked around inside, felt a pang shoot through him as he saw the things she'd put in there. Her lipstick: a small leftover from their world. A comb. The QTel.

The QTel! Crushed by something heavy, maybe the foot of a soldier.

Shit!

What about the other one? Had she lost it?

Still down in his knees he peered around. Under a nearby bush he saw something. He went over there and discovered the belt with the holster and the gun.

What a girl! She hadn't lost her head.

Maybe...

He stood up; tried to put himself in her place.

Where was that QTel! Maybe more important even than the gun.

His eyes fell on the fountain and he knew—and he knew that his knowledge was a part of this thing between them, like a resonance through time where he stood where she had stood and it was like he fitted himself into the past and *was* her—or at least some of her...

...and with it came...

He jerked uncontrollably, like at the verge of a falling dream, only that it was how *she* fell and there was nothing he could do to stop it.

On uncertain legs he went to the fountain and used the wall to steady himself. Staring into its now–soiled waters he saw the QTel in its case at the bottom—just where he'd known it would be. He forced himself to calm and fished the QTel from the fountain, wiped the case dry on hois tunic, opened it, touched a key which brought the screen to life.

The analysis program was running.

He sat down to consider his options. They would get what they wanted: of that there was no doubt. He would come after Helen like a bee after nectar.

Sam pondered his two *katanas*, five hand–grenades, the two Berettas and the two Glocks. Over nine hundred rounds of 9mm ammo. Enough to fight a small war. Not an infinite one though! Even that much ammo eventually ran out.

Nine hundred rounds. Assume an average of two to incapacitate an enemy. That was a cohort. If he chose his position he could do even better. The grenades would take out even more. A pound of C4 would have been even better.

He stopped these thoughts before they went much further. It wasn't easy. For the first time in his life he actually wanted to kill somebody; in cold blood if need be. The mood he was in right now...if Frank Ricci asked him today to give him the database on ADLER and let him do his thing...Sam probably would do it.

Scratch 'probably'. He *would*. Period. Those ADLER fuckers had to be wiped off the face of the Earth. Either Earth. It wouldn't cure all the ills of the universe, but it would surely chip away on them.

"You must not do this!"

Mirlun stood before him.

"Do *what?*" Sam snapped.

"The Diënna says you must not."

"She told you, did she?"

"The Diënna knows. The Diënna sees. You must heed her words!"

Sam stood up and stared at Mirlun.

"The Diënna knows? The Diënna sees? Does she now?"

He pointed at a pathetic half-charred corpse lying nearby. The poor girl, one of the servants, probably had been trying to get to the fountain to extinguish the fire that was melting her clothes to her skin. Somebody had sliced through her back with a vicious stroke, breaking the spine and ending the girl's life.

"Then I ask you: did she know *this* would happen? Did she know they would come and do what they did?"

Mirlun stared at him from wide eyes. "The Diënna..."

"*Fuck* the Diënna!" Sam shouted. "Screw your spirit-whore! These people are *dead*! They did nothing—you hear me? *nothing!* to deserve this! All they ever did was be faithful servants of whatever it is that lives out in that lake. *She* killed them. The soldiers were just tools."

He looked around himself at the charred remnants of the temple.

"All she had to do was warn them! What was so difficult about *that*?"

"The Diënna does nothing without good reason," Mirlun said, his face closing up in the manner of a zealot whose faith was being assaulted by a disbeliever. "Her servants died for a worthy cause."

"Huh? You've got to be kidding me, right? A 'worthy cause'? What cause could be worth *this*! And do you think, if they'd known what was in store for them, they would have *wanted* to die in your worthy cause?"

"Their lives were not their own."

Sam took a deep breath and made a near superhuman effort not to strike the asshole standing before him, who could spout this errant gibberish while surrounded by the incontrovertible evidence of his own lunacy.

"Yes, they were! Their lives were entirely their own! But *she* decided otherwise, and so *she* killed them," he said. "And she endangered Helen. I will not be one of her disposable servants. I agree with the *Ladi*. The sprites must be taken out."

Mirlun was speechless just for once. Sam retrieved *Gladius Magnus* from one of the bags and unwrapped it from its cover padding of *El* clothing. He held its tip to Mirlun's throat.

"I don't know what this thing is. I don't know what devious intentions she was pursuing when giving it to us. Whatever may be, I don't want it. Besides, I think that as long as it's with me, Plius and whoever works for him basically knows where I am. And that doesn't suit me. I was a fool not to recognize that a long time ago, or I would have ditched it in the ocean when I had the chance."

"You must..."

"I 'must' only one thing," Sam grated. "I must get Helen out of the clutches of Larry Unterflug and whoever happens to be in league with him."

"The Diënna will be destroyed!!"

"Will she really?" Sam said acidly. He nodded. It made sense. That's what 'dark' was all about. The damn sprite was afraid of its own demise.

How would it happen?

Who knew? Who cared? If there was something in the contingencies of the future that configured things in such a way that his going after Helen would destroy the Diënna...

So what?

"Please don't do this," Mirlun whispered. "You will destroy the lifeblood of the empire."

Suddenly Sam felt sorry for the man. Sorry and pissed–off. But the poor fool didn't know any different, so how could one expect him to understand?

He lowered *Gladius Magnus* until its tip rested on the ground. "Mirlun," he said softly, "don't you understand? Don't you see that I would do *anything* to get her back to me; alive, breathing, unharmed? That I would do so, even if it destroyed your world?" He leaned on the sword, and looked at the blue sky, so recently polluted by the smoke of the funeral pyre around him. "Once I nearly died," he said, knowing it to be true. "Then came Hele, and though I fought it—though *we* fought it—I was forced to realize that until she came I hadn't even *lived*. It may sound selfish to you, but I do not wish to die again; for this time I would. Because I think that she and I are different faces of the same being, and that without the other we *are* dead—because we were incomplete, and would be again without the other. So you see, Helen is *my* world—and I've done enough to be obliging and try to fix up other worlds than my own. I will not make that mistake again."

"But how could this be? She is just a…"

"A woman?"

The sad thing was, Sam understood, that Mirlun wasn't really so exceptional at all. He just had a rather demanding and seductive deity. But he wasn't alone. The disease that ate away at him was the same that ate away at anybody who couldn't discern the fundamentals of human existence. Not the animal stuff, but that which made humans *different* from animals. Like love and choice. Like…

Actually, that was about it: Love and Choice. Everything else was secondary. Even friendship and loyalty and shit like that. Apart from just being alive—in a very biological kind of sense, which was the basis for everything anyway—the real distinction between humans and everything else was not language or feelings or reason or what have you.

"Love and choice," he said. "I love this woman. I choose to put her above everything. Above a whole world if it damn well has to be. And I am leaving now, and," he held up *Gladius Magnus* again, "I'm throwing this thing back where it came from."

He picked up his bags, slung them over his shoulder and started to move away. Mirlun reached out to grab his arm. Sam stopped. "Your Diënna did nothing to save those most loyal to her. Does that not tell you something? Does that not penetrate your thick skull and wake you up maybe just a little bit?"

Mirlun's hand dropped off his arm. Sam walked out of the temple and down to the edge of the lake, where he put the bags down. Then he hurled *Gladius Magnus* with all his might, and it spun out across the water and fell with a splash—and in the moment of it penetrating the surface Sam felt…something…touching his mind.

Woe. Anger. Despair.

He shook his head, and the physical sensation brushed away the mind–touch, like one might chase an annoying insect off one's arm.

Where the sword had submerged appeared a brief burst of light, and the water churned, before it settled down again to its previous placid state.

Not quite like the old Arthur story.

But wouldn't it be ironic if the last time somebody dumped the sword back in the

Chapter 17

lake he'd done it for precisely the same reason? It didn't take much of a twist to see the return of Excalibur to the Lady of the Lake in just this light.

Let's face it, it had brought Arthur and everybody else nothing but trouble, and in the end Britain was overrun anyway!

Sam pause for a moment to collect his thoughts. Plans had to be made. He couldn't just ride off into the distance and take Helen back from Larry and Plius. It wasn't going to be as easy as that. For one, it was almost certain that they'd be waiting for him—maybe not just at the end of the journey, but quite conceivably along the way.

Think!

The legionnaires had come the long way around way; avoiding Gai, presumably to prevent any possibility of premature notification of their attack. They had departed the same way. Meaning that the folks in Gai might only now, or maybe even later—depending on whether someone had maybe watched from the side of the ocean—know what had transpired here.

We arrived only yesterday.

An idea formed.

Maybe, he thought, *I am in luck.*

He and Helen would need a lot of that to survive.

He decided to approach Gai from the water–side, avoiding the usual route, passing between the forest and the shore, and entering Gai that way. The road was likely to get very trafficked once knowledge of the calamity at the temple spread through the village.

What Sam hoped for was that the *Gallinis* was still there; that something had held it up, just long enough to be still there for him.

He must hurry—which meant that he had to take a risk and use one of the soldier's horses. It would make him stand out, but he would be noticed either way, even if he walked into the village. Anonymity was impossible.

Sam rearranged his paraphernalia such that all he needed fit into one bag, barely light enough to be slung across his shoulder and to be carried in that manner should he be forced to walk, which was quite conceivable. He tied one of the swords to the bag, and affixed the other to his belt. The rest of the things they'd brought he placed in the other, which he decided to hide somewhere at the periphery of the forest on his way to Gai. He wondered whether to hide the QTel as well, but finally decided to take it with him. The truth was that he had no intention of returning to *Aquadiënna,* and what he left here he would probably never see again.

Finally, all his activities completed, with Mirlun watching him broodingly from a distance, but not approaching closely enough to speak, he slung the bags across the horse behind the saddle, mounted and, without another look back, rode off, away from the forest, taking the long, but maybe safer, way. He followed the shore of *Aquadiënna* until he came to the bridge of land separating the lagoon from the ocean. The low shrubs ended here and he would become visible to any, even the most casual of inspections.

He looked out over the sea, searching for Gai boats whose occupants might end up reporting having seen a rider cross the land–bridge. He saw no small dots. Instead…

It couldn't be!

Lobus Natois, I owe you more than you'll ever know.

He spurred on the horse and raced down the beach to where two coracles, each with a man waiting beside it, were just now being pulled out of the water. Further out lay the familiar shape of the *Gallinis*.

Sam halted before the sailors, both of whom he recognized. Some time later, wet again, he stood on deck of the *Gallinis*.

"We were just out of the harbor," Lobus Natois told him, "we saw the smoke and the fire—and the *legioni*. I considered the possibility that you might be dead—or that you might not. In that case you might well require a means to escape."

"You risked much." Sam was subdued. "I am in your debt."

Lobus Natois nodded. "That may be so, but I think you're a man who will pay his debts."

"Dinars?" Sam shrugged. "I have dinars."

Lobus Natois shook his head. "Dinars are easy to come by. No, Samuel Do–no–van, dinars we do not need. But I think that maybe—unless you kill yourself trying to rescue that woman of yours, which is likely, but maybe it can be avoided—you will be able to destroy Plius."

"You make big assumptions."

"Plius and Laurentius Augustus are afraid of you. To violate the Diënna's temple: it is unprecedented and must have been prompted by motives which are novel and intriguing. Fear no doubt figures prominently." He considered Sam through narrowed eyes. "Plius showing signs of fear is something new to my experience. It makes me think that maybe he has a good reason."

"I am not sure I can do what you hope for."

"Certainty eludes us all—just like death awaits us all. These are fundamental truths. For me it will be sufficient to know that you will try."

"First I must rescue Helen."

"You will be expected."

"I know. And I don't even know where she is." He looked up, saw the billowing sails, pushing the *Gallinis* ahead at a brisk pace.

"I think we may be able to help."

Sam looked at the captain.

"How?"

Lobus Natois grinned. "Most of us are denizens of the sea. But some of us at least live on land. It is the duty of every *Ladi* to do his stint serving our people by living among those who think us 'unclean'. How else can we know what is happening in the empire?"

"Spies?"

The captain laughed. "Traders. Craftsmen. We even own a house of pleasures in Cartaga, which is the capital's port, on the other side of the *Sela Fluver*."

"A bordello."

"Sailors and soldiers alike require such services. They are lucrative and provide channels for the flow of, occasionally useful and sometimes *extremely* useful, information."

"You surprise me," Sam admitted.

Lobus Natois performed a tiny, ironic bow. He straightened again and looked Sam squarely in the face.

"Plius will be your concern. The Diënna will be ours."
"I told you, it is not that simple."
"I know, yet we must try."
"I, too, will try. But first…"

The captain nodded gravely. "If this is your wish. I know better than to try to oppose it. We will help you any way we can. This is our bargain."

Sam held out his hand and shook that of the man who belonged to a people who ate the brains and hearts of their dead.

The things we do…

18

She wasn't out cold for long. Moments only. When she came to, there was blood dripping from a cut at her right temple. She hoped that there was no concussion. Her left shoulder hurt like hell as she had twisted around, partially because she'd snagged on a bush as she fell, partially because she tried to brace her fall. Half–instinctual reactions, over–riding what her karate instructor had tried to drum into her.

She levered herself up on one arm, groaning with the pain, for a moment even forgetting the where and why of everything. Just trying to get her brain functioning again. Amazing how pain focused everything on itself, excluding the world for a little while at least, making it a tiny universe, relatively uncomplicated, that just contained this one thing.

The complicated world outside however allowed her no respite. Footfall sounded behind her. A sickening crunch made her turn her head. Two soldiers, wearing uniforms of joined segments of black leather, approached her with purposeful stride. One of them had just stepped on her straw bag and the QTel.

Damn!

Without any further ado the soldiers bent down and picked her up, one arm each, and dragged her between them out of the courtyard. A temple servant, maybe the gardening girls, came running into the open, her tunic in flames, straight at them. The soldiers dragged her aside. The girl ran past them, heading for the fountain. The soldier on her right grunted, let go of Helen's arm, drew his sword, and, in one smooth motion, whipped around and brought it down in a vicious sweep at the girl's retreating back. The tip sliced through the burning garment. She gave a loud cry, arched her back, and fell forward to lie on her face, twitched briefly and then lay still. The soldier turned back to Helen, grabbed her arm again; then he and his comrade dragged her through smoke–filled hallways to the front of the temple, where they dumped her at the feet of another soldier.

She took a few deep breaths, then slowly got herself up, to stare at the man in front of her. Behind him stood two more of the black clad soldiers in attitudes of attention. Helen discerned differences in the man's uniform. The ornamented chest plate: a single piece of leather, molded into the contours of a male chest. Three metallic attachments to his left shoulder. Helen took a moment to discern their shape, and another few breaths to figure out where she'd seen them before.

Holy shit.

Larry Unterflug's wet dream. His own SS. The shoulder badges were almost exact copies of the symbolic lightning–SS–emblems of Hitler's elite troops.

The soldier watched her as she straightened.

"Where is the other?" he grated.

She said nothing.

His hand snapped out. The blow threw her back to the ground. This time she remembered to follow Freddie's instructions and rolled to soften the impact of the fall.

She almost rolled over all the way and jumped up again to kick this asshole exactly where he needed it.

But she didn't. She gathered herself together, still smarting from the blow to her right cheek; adding it to the list of her grievances with Laurentius and his crowd. A list that was getting longer very quickly.

Oblige him!

Damn her pride!

"Where is the other?" the soldier repeated. What was he? A sergeant or something? She decided to think of him as 'Sergeant A.H.'. As good a name as any. Maybe better.

I've been exposed to Sam for too long. That the kind of shit he'd some up with.

The thought made her smile.

God, I've changed!

Only a year ago this kind of thing would have her cowering in shock.

You're not in shock?

Of course she was, but not like she might have been. She was, at least, thinking clearly. Planning. Trying to get the best out this shitty situation, rather than bemoaning her fate.

So, what're you gonna do?

Behave. Play the weak female. That's what they expected. That's what everybody expected around here.

What a backward fucking world!

"I do not know," she muttered in her clumsy Seladiënnan. "He left."

"With the *sacerdot*?"

She gave a nod of assent.

Sergeant A.H. barked commands at his underlings. Men obeyed with alacrity. This bunch didn't fuck around. Your boss says 'jump', you jump. Instantly.

Sergeant A.H. looked at her again, a calculating expression, looking her up and down, taking in her disheveled appearance. His eyes rested briefly on her crotch.

If he touches me I will kick his balls to a pulp!

The expression changed. Brief desire was replaced by military professionalism. The asshole was a brute, but he had, she guessed, orders. These did not appear to include a license to rape her. Which meant that he was going to keep his dick under that leather-strip kilt.

What do they wear underneath that?

The thought was not edifying.

Trust me, girl: you don't want to know.

Definitely not.

Sam—are you safe??

Please, she addressed to nobody in particular, *let him be safe—and let him keep his head! Please don't let him charge in here with guns blazing.*

Because if he did he wasn't going to make it; not with a couple of hundred bloodthirsty soldiers around them.

Of course he wasn't going to! He'd be desperate, but he wasn't stupid. If there was one thing she knew about her Sam—*Yes: 'My' Sam!*—it was that he wasn't stupid. He was also a lot of other things. Just about all of them nice.

She also loved him to pieces.

Don't do anything silly because of me!
Just whatever had to be done to get them out of this shit.
"Come,' Sergeant A.H. ordered her. He turned around. Behind her she sensed more men. She looked back, and saw four soldiers surrounding her in a half–circle. She hadn't even known they were there until now.

She followed A.H. through the army, until they came to a place where stood a solid–looking four–wheeled carriage, about the size of a small stage–coach from a Western, with barred windows, and pulled by a team of two horses.

The paddy–wagon.

The soldiers herded her to the carriage and shoved her inside. The door clanged shut; a padlock of sorts was used to secure the hasp.

Sergeant A.H. actually he was probably more than just a sergeant; maybe the equivalent of a captain at least; so amend it to 'Captain A.H.'—barked more commands. There was a new movement among the soldiers. Men mounted horses, made as if to leave.

Had they given up so easily on trying to find Sam and Mirlun?

She considered her prison wagon. Two benches—*thank you for not making me stand*—both of them soiled with encrusted…what? Vomit? Excrement? Blood? Maybe all of those and more that she really didn't want to think about. She tried to find a clean spot, but there wasn't, so she gingerly lowered herself to the least offensive part of the bench. Her head was throbbing, but when she carefully touched the cut on her temple she felt a crust already forming. She didn't probe too much. Her hands were filthy and the last thing she wanted was an infection. Not in this place! No antibiotics, no disinfectant, no alcohol, no nothing.

She thought of their supplies, hopefully still undiscovered in the cellar. She also thought of the QTel she'd thrown into the fountain.

Please find it!

The library had surely been destroyed like everything else. That QTel was their last link to any possibility of not being stuck in this place forever.

The thought gave her pause. In truth, she realized, though they had talked and gone through the motions as if this move was final and definite they'd both been hedging their bets. There had always been the idea that maybe, just maybe, there *was* a way not to make this totally *final*. None of them had said as much, but they'd both known. It was like 'probably final', but not definitely so. Leaving options open.

We'll see.

The soldiers left behind the blazing temple and the dead. With the prison–mobile in their midst, departed. The wagon's wheels had no suspension; it bounced over every unevenness in the path, which meant that she finally stood up after all and held onto the bars. Her legs helped to absorb the shocks. If she'd remained sitting she would have done some serious injury to her back.

The soldiers behind her avoided eye contact, but stared straight ahead as if she didn't exist. Which was odd. Surely they were not indifferent, and even if the lot of them were homosexuals she would have expected at least a few furtive looks. But if there were she didn't see them. Talk about anal discipline.

The troop continued and presently emerged onto what was a more civilized kind of road, broad enough to handle at least two wagons like hers passing without one being forced off. The road was made of stones of remarkably equal size, closely packed together in an irregular, but solid, pattern. The wagon still bounced on the roughness, but less so. Now, however, the iron banded wheels, with only stone underneath them, made a racket that soon combined with the pain at her temple to give her a pounding headache.

She also needed to pee—but these guys seemed in no disposition to stop for anything. Well, if they could hold it, so could she. She wasn't going to degrade herself by incontinence. Her bladder was agony, but she bit her teeth together and bore it.

Finally, hours later, in a small village hugging the road, the troop stopped. The soldiers were allowed to attend to their bodily functions, which they did with a revolting lack of inhibition. Two of them eventually came and opened the door to her prison, allowed her to climb down, and then, with both of them standing guard outside the door, allowed her the use of the facilities belonging to a dingy hostelry of sorts. The owner, a little man who scuttled about like a crab and stank like he hadn't washed for years and used garlic for perfume, gave her a piece of stale bread and some rancid cheese. She considered refusing it, but then decided that she couldn't afford to get weak. So she ate the stuff, which smelled like dog's breath and tasted like shit, almost making her vomit it up. She asked for and washed it down with water, only to find that her brief respite was over, as the soldiers dragged her back to her wagon. Captain A.H. came to inspect her briefly, said nothing, and departed again. The troop moved on; the curious villagers stared after it. If Sam came this way, as surely he must, and if he asked, they would remember.

Where are you, Sam?

Evening fell. A half–moon rose from the mists over the land. The troop gave no indication of any intention to stop for the night. Did these guys never tire?

They did stop shortly after that. The place was a way–station of sorts. Well organized. Probably military. The yards were full of horses, which replaced the ones they rode. Helen was allowed to stretch her legs and to perform ablutions—which she had to do in a latrine built over a stinking black hole with more flies than stars in the sky. The experience was not edifying. She attended to the business with alacrity, bemoaned the absence of toilet paper, and returned to her paddy–wagon.

The troop departed the way–station. The journey became even more of an ordeal. Her legs were killing her, the endless noises of the wheels and the horses all around her, the rattling creaking framework of the cart, it all combined to make this into a nightmare she'd rather forget in a hurry. Right now that was difficult, since it was still on–going.

The road descended from the hills, through which it had meandered for several hours, and down to sea level, where it followed the coastline and then passed through increasingly more frequent villages and small towns, whose inhabitants, aroused from their sleep or whatever they were doing after dark, stared after them with dumb perplexity.

The moon wheeled overhead. The relentless march continued. The horses, this much she could see even in the dark, exhibited an exhaustion and listlessness paralleling her own.

Presently, in the distance, a glow in the sky, growing with every mile they traversed. An interminable time later they entered the outskirts of a large city, still remarkably active despite the fact that dawn must surely be close.

Chapter 18

Helen was aroused from her exhaustion and, in wonder, watched the city draw past. Monumental edifices in the style of what Old Rome must have been like crowded each other alongside well–paved streets. Tired and exhausted as she was, she couldn't take it all in and sat there lethargically. The carriage rumbled on, the soldiers shielding its contents from the prying looks of late passersby. Finally it passed through a wide, arched gate and into an expansive courtyard, lit by what must have been hundreds of smoke–belching torches stuck in holders on the walls. The soldiers departed. Others appeared, wearing uniforms more colorful than her former escorts, the black leather trimmed with thin white borders, making the wearers look almost dashing. The faces under the helmets however looked just as brutal.

She was taken out of the wagon. Flanked by four silent, very big, guards she was escorted into the palatial structure, along endless hallways until she was finally pushed into a chamber of a size to rival that they'd had at the Diënna's temple.

Another man appeared, wearing a more ornate uniform and an air of authority.

"Laurentius Augustus will see you at his pleasure," he said curtly. "You are to prepare by cleansing yourself, such as not to offend him. If you do, you will be punished."

He departed without a further word.

Helen looked around. At the door appeared a girl, maybe somewhere in her mid to late teens. She bowed deeply and remained in this attitude. Helen concluded that she was to say something.

"Get up," she snapped—in English. Her patience was at an end.

The girl looked up in alarm. Helen, already regretting her snappishness, shook her head and held out her hand.

"Come," she said in the girl's native tongue. "Show me where I can clean myself from this journey."

The girl hurried across the room to a curtain, pulled it aside, and beckoned Helen to follow. Behind the curtain, just like in the temple, lay an ablution room with a bath, basins, a toilet. Not quite as expansive as in the Diënna's temple, but it seemed that the basic arrangement was fairly standard in this kind of context.

"I will fetch you garments," the girl whispered so lowly that Helen could hardly make her out. She hurried away. Helen considered the bath. Taps here, too. Advanced technology indeed.

She sealed the bath's drain with a plug she found on a ledge and turned on the taps, then divested herself of her filthy garments and, when the water was high enough stepped into the bath and sank into it with a contented sigh.

The girl returned and deposited clothes on a chair, then stood in an attitude of expectancy.

"You can leave," Helen told her.

The girl considered her with an anxious expression, bordering on panic.

"I am assigned to serve."

Helen wanted to tell her that she'd rather be by herself, but didn't. She sensed that if she did the girl would probably fare badly. Dismissal might well be construed as rejection for reason of dissatisfaction. She would not want to be responsible for the consequences.

She sighed inwardly and leaned back in the bath. "What is your name?"

"Elena, *Donna.*"

Helen sat up.

Helen.

She waved at the girl, who stepped closer.

"This my name, too," she told her.

The girl's eyed widened slightly. She ventured a smile.

"How old are you?" Helen asked her.

"Twelve years."

Twelve? She could have easily passed for sixteen or maybe more. Her thin linen gown, held together at the waist with a woven belt of a coarser cloth, could not hide the luscious figure underneath. But mostly it was the face; the eyes betraying a knowledge that should have been hidden from one so young. Still, she was beautiful, with fine features, big fawn eyes, and a generous sensual mouth.

Helen leaned forward and indicated the bar of soap. The girl hastened to obey and started washing her back.

"How long have you worked in his place?" Helen asked her.

"Two years."

"Thank you, that was good." Helen straightened. "I will do the rest."

"*Donna*, I can…"

Helen shook her head and pointed at a chair nearby. "Sit down there. Tell me about this place we're in. Who is who and what people do around here."

"*Donna*?"

"Please!" Helen encouraged her. "I know nothing. If you want to do something for me, tell me about this." She smiled at the girl. "I am a prisoner," she said softly. "I am not sure of whom, but a prisoner is what I am." She paused. "We are all prisoners, are we not?"

Elena stared at her for a few moments, then nodded mutely.

"Then we must work together," Helen said, "and not be afraid of each other." She grinned. "Especially if we both are 'Elena'."

The girl finally managed to smile with more conviction and vigor. "You are one of those our master has been searching," she stated with certainty.

"Your master?"

"Laurentius Augustus, *Consil Supremus* to his Majesty, the emperor."

Helen nodded. "I am one," she agreed.

The girl regarded her with intense fascination. "Is it really true?"

"What?"

"That you are going to…destroy…the…" She appeared unable to continue the statement.

Helen gave her a wry smile. "Right now, do I appear like one who can destroy anybody or anything?"

Elena nodded thoughtfully, as if Helen had just confirmed something she'd already suspected.

"Why does Laurentius Augustus make you his prisoner? You are…old. The *Consil Supremus* and the emperor do not like old women."

Helen stared at the girl. Maybe her inadequate knowledge of the language…

But, no—why deny the obvious? It had always been that way. Certain proclivities seemed to be inextricably associated with those in power—and especially the likes of

Chapter 18

'Laurentius Augustus'.

Then she remembered something else Elena had said.

'Old'?

"How old do you think I am?" she asked the girl.

Elena eyed her critically. She was losing her awe and with it some of the timid air. "Probably at least twenty," she said.

Helen laughed.

"Be honest."

Elena grimaced. "Twenty two?" she ventured.

Helen laughed even more.

'Old' indeed.

The less savory aspects of Elena's words returned to her consciousness.

"What kind of women does Laurentius Augustus like?" she asked.

Elena hesitated. "He used to take the older ones, too—but now he is like the emperor who likes *sangra fresca*." She came closer and leaned near to Helen so she could whisper it. "Oldecus Pistor, who is our emperor and supreme to all, he likes boys even better. The *Consil Supremus* does not like boys in his chamber. They say that only two days ago, at the feast of *Titanius*, when the emperor offered him one of his *ludi*, Laurentius Augustus lost his temper and shouted at the emperor." She stood back and looked at Helen significantly. The sensation–value of this snippet of gossip must be high. The servants or slaves who had witnessed the event probably were the center of riveted attention by all their peers.

"Can you imagine?" Elena whispered. "The *Consil Supremus* defying Oldecus Pistor, who is our emperor and supreme to all?"

It must have been a ritualistic utterance of sorts. That was the second time Elena had used the phrase after mentioning the emperor's name.

"Give me that towel, please." Helen pointed. "Then I wish to run this bath again, so I do not wallow in my own dirt."

Elena hurried to obey. As Helen rose from the bath Elena appraised her frankly and critically. "You are old, but you have strong breasts, and Laurentius Augustus will like that."

Helen wrapped the towel around herself and stepped out of the bath. "Laurentius Augustus will not have anything to like," she stated with definiteness.

"Do not say such things!" the girl whispered, looking around as she expected listeners nearby. "We do not say such things."

" 'We'?" Helen echoed sarcastically.

She bent down to pull the stopper from the drain. Elena hurried over. "Let me do this. You should not do this. It is a maid's duty."

She knelt down beside Helen but the stopper was already out.

"You can clean the bath and run me a new one," Helen suggested.

"Yes!" Elena agreed eagerly. She started to get up. Helen grabbed her arm and pulled her back. "What does Laurentius Augustus like?" she asked the girl.

Elena told her; and Helen wished she hadn't asked.

"He has done this to…you?"

Elena nodded, as if it was the most natural thing in the world that a fifty–something year old pedophile swine like Larry Unterflug should practice such perversions on the likes of her. No outrage, no resistance, no apparent objection. A complete fitting into her assigned role—which seemed to be that of servant and sexual–perversion–toy.

"Of course," Elena told Helen, as if that was something to be happy about—which, come to think about it, it definitely was, "I have not been injured or killed."

Helen wanted to be sick. "Girls are killed?"

"Girls and boys," Elena agreed. "Our lords sometimes lose themselves in their passion."

Was that really how this saw brutality?

What else am I supposed to expect? If she saw it in any other way she'd go crazy.
Hell, she already is crazy. How can anybody accept this shit and not be crazy?

Depravity had a logic of its own. Once one accepted the absence of certain ethical and moral constraints, there was logical progression into these kinds of excesses. Psychopaths throughout the ages—no matter what political or religious disguise they assumed; if they bothered with disguises or excuses at all—had acted along similar lines, and would probably do so until the end of humanity. And she'd had the misfortune to fall into the hands of one such—and probably not just one. They tended to congregate. If the soldiers who had attacked the temple were anything to go by they were dealing with some seriously twisted people.

Elena finished cleaning the bath with a small rag, and ran the water again. Helen watched her quietly from behind. That was her, more than half her lifetime distant.

What was I like—then?

She tried to think back but found that memories refused to surface. It hadn't been a good time, that much she seemed to recall. A lonely time. Trying to fit in but not being able to—like it had been throughout her teens, as well as before that.

All my life.

She looked around an pulled a face. Still she didn't fit.

What did I expect? No culture shock? No nothing?

This world was *strange*. Stranger possibly than just about any place on *E1*. And it wasn't the familiarity thing; the fact that they knew its geography to the 'T'; spoke its most widely–spread language; could travel around it in a couple of days; hop on the internet and exchange email with anybody just about anywhere; know instantly about events in the most distant nooks and crannies; go to cafes and cinemas; and no *liquamen* anywhere in sight.

Of course they also had global warming, ABC weaponry, AIDS, vCJD, pollution, and overpopulation.

But they also had science; an unraveled genome; hospitals; doctors, some of whom actually knew what they were doing; Mozart; Beethoven; the Beatles; stereos; books; contraceptives; moisturizers—yeah, and *helicopters*. That damn passion of Sam's had finally infected her!

"*Donna?*"

Helen shook herself out of her reverie. The bath was filled again. She stepped into it again and gave Elena the towel, tried to ignore the girl's uninhibited appraisal of her. It didn't work.

"What is it you're looking for?" she asked the child who wasn't a child.

Elena frowned. "*Donna?*"

"Don't call me that," Helen said irritably. "I am 'Elena', just like you. It is not difficult to say."

"I must not."

Helen sighed and allowed herself to slide into the hot–but–not–too–hot water.

How do you say 'forget it' in their language? Surely, if she translated it from English it wouldn't come out just as it was meant.

She turned her head and considered Elena, standing in that infuriatingly subservient attitude; yet curious, only not daring to voice the curiosity lest she overstepped whatever imagined boundaries she perceived. At the same time she had no inhibitions about the most intimate of visual inspections.

"Why do you not have hair under your arms?" Elena asked suddenly.

There it was again. Another one of those questions she could do without.

"I remove them," Helen told her.

The girl's eyes went round. "Why?"

"Because..." Helen searched for reasons as much as words to translate the reasons into the unfamiliar language. "Because where I come from, it is customary to remove hair in such places."

Elena shook her head when hearing about such odd customs. She changed the topic.

"The other one..." she began.

"My husband?" Helen said—and caught herself.

Here's a first!

Never had she called Sam that in front of anybody. He was always 'Sam'. Sam: one half of the Helen–and–Sam thing.

'Husband', huh?

Well, that's how they would be seen by everybody else. Everything else was hidden underneath the husband–wife veneer. Whatever you made of it, unless you happened to be in the eye of public scrutiny—fueled by the need of the media to sell tabloids and crappy 'women's magazines' as much as the insatiable appetite of the public for the lurid details of lives that were none of their fucking business—the husband–wife layer was a convenient protection against prying eyes; a social shield of assumptions that few people probed much beyond.

"Your *husband*?" Elena echoed.

"Should I not have a husband?" Helen asked her.

Elena started. "Oh, no, *Donna*, I did not mean to imply that. But we all thought..."

" 'We'?" Helen interrupted.

Elena flinched. Helen decided to adopt a softer tone. The girl was easily spooked. It seemed that, while she must surely be accustomed to abuse—this much had been implied in her previous statements—she kind–of expected different from Helen; but she also expected Helen to be like the women she knew and just simply couldn't handle what she might think of as...male?...behavior patterns.

All of which seemed to imply that there just weren't any women in positions of any authority here—not at the palace anyway.

If figured.

She realized then that, when listing the virtues of *El*—parts of it anyway—she'd forgotten the move towards social equality for women. One often tended to forget that, even if one was a woman. Just like one might forget the other things that made *El* of the twenty first century a better place to live. Like at least a notion of 'social justice', the very concept of organized democracy—imperfect as it was, yet it compared very favorably indeed when comparing it to anything that had gone before. Despite the ludicrous spectacle of a US presidential election—most elections anywhere for that matter! it was better than anything previous centuries had offered.

"The servants," Elena said timidly. "When we heard that you had been captured…"

"Who told you?"

Elena smiled with just a trace of condescension. "The servants are everywhere, *Donna*. How can we not know?"

Helen looked at the girl with surprise. Maybe…

"Who did you think the other person was?"

"A great hero. Your master. Your lover maybe."

Helen chuckled. "Why not a husband?"

Elena pursed her lips. "Husbands…" She shrugged.

"Don't *you* want a husband?" Helen asked her.

"One day I would like to."

"Not soon?"

"Not soon. I would have to be a wife."

The way she said it, it didn't sound like she expected it to be particularly enjoyable.

A strange world indeed. The whole empire was held together—at least to some degree—by the cult of a sprite who, if Mirlun's pronouncements were to be believed, had once been a woman. Yet women didn't seem to fare too well in the general framework.

"I would have to get fat and bear children. I would have to bleed once every moon."

Could it be? A girl, sexually developed like this one, and she hadn't had a period yet?

"Do you not bleed?"

Elena shook her head. "No!" she said. The notion appeared to have a preposterous air. "I eat *liander* every day. I won't bleed, and I won't grow fat and have children." She stood there and eyed Helen's figure, which she could see from her position. "You must eat *liander*, too. You are not fat. You are not a mother."

A contraceptive of sorts. Screwing around with puberty, but apparently not interfering in the development of all the appropriate sexual characteristics. Maybe it even promoted them. It seemed the herbalists of this world had figured *some* things out.

"No," Helen admitted. "I am not a mother."

"Are you barren?"

"No."

"Then why are you not a mother? You have a husband."

The girl's logic amused Helen, but it was also sad. "My husband is more like a lover," she said, trying to explain the unfamiliar concept.

"So you eat *liander*."

"Something like *liander*," Helen agreed.

Elena nodded. The world made partial sense again. Still, the puzzlement persisted.

Helen leaned back. The conversation took a lull. Helen drifted off; the warm water, the exertions of the day; it all combined to send her into a doze. How nice it would be to have Sam here. The bath was big enough for both of them. They could…

She jerked and woke to her situation. It couldn't have been long. Elena still stood

Chapter 18   269

there, in that pose. The water was still warm.

Helen forced herself to get up. Elena hurried to bring her a fresh towel. Helen, ignoring the girl's looks and dismissing her attempts to help, rubbed herself down and went to pick up the garments left for her on the chair.

"I will not wear this!" she snapped, looking at the girl.

"*Donna*, you must! These are...appropriate. The *Consil Supremus* likes it this way."

"No fucking way!" Helen didn't realize she'd said that in English. She held up the gown, which was flimsy and suited for a courtesan. She might as well be naked for all the cover it provided.

She grimaced and went over to the chair where she'd left her dirty travel clothes. She picked out her bra and panties, both sweaty and dirty, and considered them. A sports bra, designed to accommodate provide a snug fit and support for her breasts no matter what the situation. Definitely not a sexual turn-on—though, and here she smiled, Sam said it was, especially on her. Custom-made, from kevlar, with a cotton lining. A bit hot for the climate, but better than running around with her ample-enough breasts flopping about.

Helen sniffed it. It definitely needed washing. She took it to the bath, which still held water, and washed it out, using the soap and rinsing it under the taps. She did the same with her filthy, reeking panties, who were also part of the custom-made set of kevlar gear. She rubbed and rubbed and with the soap they finally ended up smelling almost clean.

Elena watched the whole procedure with round eyes, but said nothing. When Helen was done, she wrung everything out as well as she could, patted the garments between some dry towels and finally put them on, and the ridiculous slut-gown over it.

"There," she said, pirouetting before Elena. "What do you think of it?"

"It is...unusual."

"It will have to do," Helen declared. She grimaced. "When is Larry...the *Consil Supremus* likely to awaken and summon me?"

Elena shrugged. "Sometimes he wakes early. Sometimes he sleeps all morning. It depends on the girls in his bed."

Yeah, right. It wouldn't just be one!

"I am very fatigued," Helen said. "I would like to rest for as long as I can."

Elena bowed. "I will ensure you are not disturbed until Laurentius Augustus, who is the *Consil Supremus*," why did they say it that way? "requires your presence."

"Thank you."

Helen went back to the adjacent suite. She took off the gown but kept on her still-damp bra and panties. They weren't entirely comfortable, but wearing them she felt unreasonably safer. She covered herself with the thin blanket and presently, and without apparent transition, fell asleep.

19

The wind was on their side, pushing the *Gallinis* first south and then east into what in *E1* would have been the English channel, but which here was a long bay, the *Baië Seladiënna*, that ended in a land–bridge maybe fifty miles wide, on the other side of which lay *E2*'s equivalent of the North Sea.

The trip gave Sam ample time to ponder his next moves and to extract from Lobus Natois information on the capital and the place where they would hold her.

Lobus Natois was clearly puzzled.

"How do you know where she is being taken?"

How do I? Do I know anything at all?

'Knowledge' was maybe not the appropriate term. But when he'd thought of a bee following nectar…the analogy was maybe more apt than he'd guessed. He could almost sense her moving along somewhere on the land to the north of him. He didn't think it was just his imagination. After what happened between them over the last couple of days he was willing to give credence to a lot of things he wouldn't have considered before. Even the whole Seladiënna thing had not prepared him for *that*.

"I will know," he told Lobus Natois.

"You have access to intelligence that is not available to us?"

"In essence this is correct. But it is not the kind you might expect."

Lobus Natois did not inquire further, but went to attend to the navigation of the *Gallinis*. Sam leaned on the railing and stared at the distant coast north of them, barely visible in the thin haze that lay over the surface of the water. The swells rose and fell with monotony, traveling in the same direction as the ship. The wind was strong enough to litter the surface with cats' paws, but stopped just short of becoming troublesome.

Something's working for us, he thought, sending it to her, yet knowing that it couldn't be this easy. But he knew she was somewhere over there, and, strangely enough, that she was probably also quite safe—for the time being at least. The soldiers would not dare touch her. They might murder and incinerate, but they probably had had orders to act in just such a fashion.

Butchering innocent women.

That tended to be the way of things. Women and children. Like Katie.

Bastards!

How was he going to pull this off?

With intelligence—and a shitload of luck!

Definitely.

They sailed through the night. Lobus Natois did not need to be prompted. The usual practice of halving the ship's sail area for the night and just coasting was abandoned on this occasion. The ship ploughed through the sea at best speed and by the time the sun had cleared the horizon they were in sight of Seladiënna, which spread to their left, its extent indefinite, losing itself in the morning mists on the hills behind it. Sam thought he could see the center, which, he knew, lay within a concentric arrangement of hexagonally arranged streets. From it reared massive edifices, turrets, cupolas, and, in the very center, a round structure of impressive proportions: the emperor's palace.

The *Gallinis* veered away from the capital, crossed the broad muddy current of the *Sela Fluver*, and presently sailed into Cartaga harbor, which looked like a magnified version of what he'd seen in Lenos; a wide arc of tightly spaced docks of various height, accommodating a wide range of ships of all sizes, shapes, and riggings. Beyond it lay storage buildings and behind them, on a gentle slope, a small city of stone buildings, all at least two storeys, arranged around a system of comparatively regular streets.

The *Gallinis* coasted to a low dock near the entrance of the harbor where Lobus Natois with a deft hand managed to steer it to an amazingly smooth berthing. Lines were thrown across and fastened by men at the wharf. The sails were furled and tied to the masts. The journey was at an end.

The *Ladiësti* bordello was near the wharf, which, so Sam found out, actually belonged to the *Ladi*. Lobus Natois expedited Sam's way there in *Ladiësti* sailors' garments—which stank, but Sam ignored that as well as he could.

Once inside the bordello, which they entered through a back–door, he was conducted to a smallish room on the top floor. Lobus Natois informed him that it was one of those rooms reserved for visitors, which were frequent; their purposes varying from trade to espionage. Sailors deposited Sam's two traveling bags and the wrapped-up swords in the room and left him alone. A young woman appeared and declared that she had been assigned to attend to his every need. He considered her garments and decided that 'every need' did not include the main business of the house. The girl either was not on that kind of duty, or she must be classified as 'non–active' support staff.

Sam expressed his desire for a bath and was conducted to a small chamber, which contained a tiny bath of the style that required the user to sit in. No taps here, he noticed. The girl, whose name was Maia, announced that she would see to the filling of the tub—which happened in due course when two other, amazingly strong, girls appeared with buckets of hot and cold water. Several return trips later, and after refusing Maia's offers to help him with his cleaning activities, he was finally left alone to attend to making himself human again.

Lobus Natois appeared soon after he'd returned to his room and guided him downstairs and through a kitchen, to a small room, where they were awaited by five men, all wearing the same non–descript short–tunic–of–the–day and sandals. He introduced them and Sam promptly forgot their names. He recovered them during the conversation, but until he had, he was careful not to get himself into socially difficult positions. On *E1*, some cultures were *very* touchy about names forgotten. Others didn't give a shit. He didn't know where the *Ladi* stood.

The men were agents. Pure and simple. Their function was to do whatever it took to promote *Ladi* interests in a world that was basically unsympathetic to their cause. This included, Lobus Natois told Sam, the procurement of intelligence, low–level political machinations, the disposal ('disposal'?) of enemies, the protection of *Ladi* sailors and the members of this establishment alike.

Sam regarded the men with new respect. These suckers were organized and, if his impressions were correct, probably ruthless and efficient as well. Not a peacenik in sight. They were the protectors of their people, and they were going to make damn sure that they did what they were supposed to do.

Lobus Natois was remarkably open with Sam, but he also withheld nothing from his own men. Sam was asked to display his weapons, which were handled—after he'd secured them—and discussed at great length. They seemed to accept his assurances that the technology required to *keep* them lethal was beyond their capabilities, but that didn't stop them for eyeing them with envy. The things they could do! Sam could almost see their minds at work. Serious toys for some serious action. With such weapons in their hands—and their hands alone, and here lay the catch! what could they not do?

One of the men, a certain Garmen Distil, to whom adhered an air if definite authority, finally handed Sam back the Beretta and nodded with an air of regret. "It is as you say," he surrendered the 9mm round as well. "We have not the means. To learn to use these weapons would expend more of the…"

"Ammunition," Sam supplied.

"The am–mu–ni–tion…it would be wasted in practice."

"This is true," Sam agreed. "I would not wish to waste a single shot."

"You are skilled in the use?"

"That he is," Lobus Natois agreed. "As is his woman."

Garmen Distil's face was skeptical. "His woman?" he echoed.

Lobus Natois made a wry face. "I have been a witness to her capabilities."

"I need to know where she is," Sam interjected.

"In the palace," Garmen Distil said.

"You know this?" Sam asked him.

"She was delivered last night."

"Your intelligence travels fast," Sam said dryly.

"Our spies are placed for optimum effectiveness."

"Can they be more than just sources of intelligence?" Sam wanted to know.

"They are female," Garmen Distil admitted. "It has proven impossible to smuggle men into the inner precincts of the palace. Laurentius Augustus is an excessively cautious man. He does, however, expect little danger from women."

In other words, he underestimates them almost as much as you do.

Sam refrained from voicing his thoughts, but he caught a quick glance from Lobus Natois, which made him suspect that the *Ladiësti* captain knew exactly what he was thinking.

I suppose I've made my position in this amply clear.

"How does the intelligence leave the palace?" Sam wondered.

Garmen Distil hesitated, reluctant to divulge more about organization than he had to.

"You want something and I want something," Sam snapped. "There is no danger that I will betray you."

Garmen Distil looked around the table. Finally he nodded. "The women relay it to certain of the *pedeservi*, who cannot penetrate as closely to Laurentius Augustus as the females, but roam the kitchen and hallways, and are allowed to enter and exit the palace. In this manner we are informed."

Pedeservi? Foot–servants. Footmen.

"How closely are the *pedeservi* investigated when they enter and leave the palace?"

"It depends on the mood and dispositions of the guards on duty at the time. Searches are usually more thorough when entering—in order to insure the absence of weaponry. Did I mention that the *Consil Supremus* is excessively cautious?"

"Indeed," Sam muttered.

That scrapped two of his ideas. The first one was to enter in lieu of a *pedeservus*. That notion probably had been harebrained to begin with. But the second plan, namely to smuggle one of the Glocks into Helen's hands, so that, even if he could not get her out, she might contrive to do so herself...

Not a good idea. This could get her killed.

But at least she won't be helpless.

And help she would need. Whatever Larry had planned—and Lobus Natois had told Sam more of Larry's known predilections than he had really wanted to know for his own peace of mind—it wasn't nice and the moment when Helen needed to a gun to shove into his gut might well come sooner rather than later...

If she was able to use it! How would she function when it came to that kind of crunch? Would she be able to look a man fully in the eye and shoot him point–blank? Even if it was Larry: maybe especially if it was. Because he wouldn't just be some anonymous attacker in a street or on the high seas, but a human being; extremely dislikable maybe, but *human*. Could she do this? Should he place her into a position where she had to make that decision and where, if she failed to pull the trigger, there suddenly would be a gun in Larry's eager hands? And the bastard would have a total hard–on and at that point might do just about *anything* to her.

Besides, he couldn't risk smuggling the gun in. If they found it...

Unless they only found meaningless pieces—*if* they found them as they might be small enough so they could be hidden even from a more–than–just–casual search.

The plan gained more substance.

He would do it. The thought of leaving her completely unprotected, with him unable to even get close, at the mercy of this Nazi fucker and his bunch of thugs: that was intolerable.

"How many messages could you get into an out of the palace in a single day?"

Garmen Distil eyed him curiously. "Maybe a dozen," he ventured. "Possibly more."

Impressive. It meant that, if all went well, he could have all the pieces in her hands within a day. He knew that she could assemble a Glock. They'd practiced.

"Here's what I want you to do."

20

They came for her after only a couple of hours of sleep. Elena woke her and urged her to hurry. The *Consil Supremus* did not respond well to being kept waiting. Helen decided to oblige, even though she felt like crap. Two hours sleep left her feeling drugged and torpid. She splashed cold water into her face and, threw on the flimsy gown. On the other side of the curtain two big men in the stock black–leather uniform waited for her. She realized that she was being treated quite unlike a normal female would have, whom they would probably just have dragged along the hallways; by the hair if need be. Indeed, the two men appeared ever so slightly confused by their new situation, though they hid it under masks of indifference. Their sideways glances gave her the creeps. It might be better to stay in Larry's good graces than to be thrown to these brutes and their mates as a plaything. Elena had hinted that such things were common enough.

The guards led her through an array of echoing hallways defined by endless rows of columns, through the usual open–plan type of architecture, where rooms and private were defined by partitions and curtains. They halted in an expansive room, adjacent to a spacious courtyard with ornamental plants, pebbled paths, and several small fountains and statues of heroic figures, depicted in attitudes of battle, others in states of acute priapism; usually in the company of other, smaller, males or females who displayed similar dispositions, but invariably appeared submissive. None of the discreet genital representations of the Roman statues she remembered from her own world; this was full–on statuesque soft porn.

Helen turned away, to find herself confronting a middle–aged man of about her own height. She knew him to be Larry Unterflug and to be in his mid–fifties, but he looked older and more decrepit that she would have expected. A flaccid face was punctuated by a pair of heavily–bagged eyes, and framed by lank, artificially curly, severely graying, hair, combed over the top of his head to hide the fact that not much was left there. He wore a toga–like garment of expensive looking cloth; possibly silk. It was rimmed with an ornate band of shining fibers that might have contained real gold.

His light–blue eyes, whose white had long been threaded with red veins and turned a jaundiced yellow hue, regarded her with what she considered an unhealthy expectancy.

"Well," he said in an unmistakable mid–west accent. "So here you are. One half of my nemesis—or so some would like to think."

He allowed himself an extended inspection of her, grinning broadly when he took in the bra and panties.

"Modest, are we? Well, we'll see about that." He motioned to a nearby chair. "Sit."

She hesitated.

"Sit," he said sharply. He gave her a crooked grin. "You're not in Kansas any more, baby." He cackled at his own joke. "Here what I say goes—and don't you fucking forget it." Sharper now. "So sit the fuck down or I'll *make* them sit you down—and you won't like that."

Helen sat. Larry let himself into a chair opposite her and leaned back luxuriously. He nodded at the men standing a couple of steps behind her.

"These fuckers can't understand a word we're saying. You get that?" He grinned and made a sign at them. "That's right, isn't it, you stupid motherfucks?"

Behind her she heard the sounds of a quick burst of dutiful laughter.

Larry glanced at her. "See? No English. Only this gibberish they call a language." He sighed. "You know how nice it is to be able to talk to someone in English and actually have then *understand* you?"

He waved a hand at her. "Come on. Say something. Any damn thing. I just want to hear someone talk in a decent language."

When she said nothing he narrowed his eyes. "Last chance," he said, his voice chilled and all the fake joviality gone. "Let me make this clear—in case you haven't figured it out: I am God. Get it? You are nothing." He grinned unpleasantly. "Actually less than nothing. I could have you killed by a mere twitch of my fingers." He raised his right hand and made a motion, bringing his thumb and index finger together. Behind her Helen heard a shuffle.

Larry looked up, shook his head, waved negligently. Scraping steps, retreating.

"That's all it takes," he said to her. "You so much as *look* at me the wrong way and I twitch my fingers. Get it? You have no idea what these fuckers like to do to women. Believe you me, you don't wanna get the *Consil Supremus*—that's me!—pissed off. Bad idea!"

"I get it," she said coldly.

He grinned. "She spoke!" He eyed her eagerly. "I like your voice." He snorted. "Mind you, I'd like *any* voice speaking English. Talk to me some more!"

"What do you want me to say?"

"You could start with your name."

"Helen."

"Helen what?"

She was going to say 'McCormick', then started saying 'Donovan', then switched to 'McCormick' again.

"I don't know why Plius thinks a woman's going to be any trouble to me, but he says you are, and so you've gotta be. What's the name of the guy you came with?"

"Sam."

"He have a last name? Come on woman, don't piss me off! I'm getting tired of dragging it out of you word by word!"

"Donovan. Sam Donovan."

Larry eyed her shrewdly. "You're fucking him?" He nodded. "Yeah, I guess you are. Well, no matter. I'm not choosy. Can't be in this godforsaken place. I don't give a shit if your Sam fucked you over backwards and sideways. I'm kinda tired of these dark–skinned bitches." He winked at her. "You've got a decent white skin at least. Bit of a tan, but that's just the sun. Should be a nice change." He leaned forward. "Can you have kids?"

"What?!"

Larry laughed. "Simple enough question. Can you or can you not?"

"What's it to you?"

Larry got up faster than she'd expected he could. He took a couple of steps, towered over her and snapped out his hand. Without thought her own came up in a blocking motion from the jujitsu drills. She twisted.

Behind her, quick footsteps. Hands clamped down on her arms, pinning them to her side. Larry, his sore right hand dangling at his side, slapped her across the face with his left, making a fist as he did. It threw her head aside. She tasted blood where her teeth had opened up the inside of her mouth.

"Bitch!" Larry hissed and slapped her again, this time a backhand.

Helen bit back a scream. Larry reached under her chin and forced her to look at him.

"Don't—you—ever—defy—me—again."

He reached down and tore open the gown. "And the next time you show up here, you show up like you *should*—which is like *this*."

He hooked a finger into her bra and tugged. The material held, so he just pulled it down off her breasts and to her waist.

He grinned and feasted on the sight of her. "Nice," he said hoarsely. "Real white skin." He nodded. "Nice."

He motioned to the men who lifted her up by the arms until she hung suspended with her feet off the ground. Larry pulled down her panties and reached between her legs, grinning all the way. What he did there hurt like hell, but the pain was nothing compared to the humiliation. She wanted to kick him but controlled herself. They'd kill her—after doing unspeakable things. If they did she'd never see Sam again, and the very thought of that was intolerable. She would do whatever it took to survive. He'd want that more than anything—and so did she.

Larry nodded at the guards, who let her down to the floor and released her arms. She stood before Larry, too proud to cover herself.

"I'd rather have you cooperative," he told her. "After all, you're going to be the mother of my sons and we're gonna make sure *some* decent blood is injected into this shithole. So, we can do this the hard way or the easy way. You cooperate and you can be the closest thing to a fucking empress once I get rid of Oldie Piss. Or you don't, in which case I'll fuck you anyway and you better believe it! Except you *won't* get to be empress, but I'll keep you like a breeding hen and your kids will never know their mother." He shrugged. "Take your pick. Think it over. And don't think that, whoever this 'Sam' is, he's going to make one fucking bit of difference. Because you see, I'm just about the head–honcho here. *The man*, as the niggers say. And Mr. Sam Donovan isn't going to make a shred of difference to that."

He looked at the men behind her.

"Take her back to her quarters," he ordered, in heavily accented Seladiënnan.

To Helen he said, in English. "I give you a day to figure out what's what. And that's fucking *generous*—and I'll do it only because you're a white woman and I'd rather have you on my side than against me. But when you come here tomorrow, you better do it willingly, because if you don't then I won't give a fuck." He reached out, laid a hand on her left breast, and fondled her nipple. She forced herself not to squirm under the touch.

"Nice," Larry said hoarsely. "I like them like that. You and me, babe," he said. "We can show these greasy fuckers what a pure child looks like. So let's do it and let's do it right."

He waved at the soldiers who grabbed her arms. A sharp command from Larry made them release her. He looked at her significantly and held up the thumb and forefinger of his right hand. "Remember: easy or difficult. Shouldn't be too hard, eh?"

As they walked her out she grabbed her panties from the floor, sensing Larry Unterflug's grinning regard as she did. They accompanied her back to her suite, past the gazes of curious passing servants and functionaries who made sure that their interest was not too obvious. But news of her disheveled condition would soon circulate in the local gossip mill. As she walked along she pulled up her bra again. Her panties she clutched in her hand.

She was going to get the bastard for this. Oh, how she was going to get him for this.

Larry Unterflug wasn't bragging. He was 'the man' and he had an army to do his bidding. Sam was just one guy.

It's not fair.

Who said life was fair?

I love you, Sam. Please be careful!

She arrived back at her suite. The soldiers stationed themselves outside the curtains. Helen went straight to the bathroom and was sick into the toilet. Then she ran the bath and sat herself into it.

Elena appeared.

"You *did* defy the *Consil Supremus!*" she muttered. "Don't you know that it could bring your death?"

Helen regarded her tiredly. "Be silent!" she snapped. "I have had enough of your admonitions."

Elena regarded her uncertainly. She was holding something in her hand. It was a piece of cloth wrapped around something. She held it in Helen's direction.

"I am to give you this," she said.

"What is it?"

"I do not know. Athena gave it to me. She did not tell me what is was, only that you are to have it."

"Who is Athena?"

"She organizes the girls for the *Consil Supremus*."

" 'Organizes'?"

"She ensures they have eaten *liander* and that they are clean and of good cheer. The *Consil Supremus* does not like surly, unclean girls."

"I bet," Helen muttered to herself and took the cloth. She unwrapped it and suppressed an exclamation. It was a piece of parchment in which, in Sam's unmistakable large capital–letter print, were written the words: "1 of 8. Be brave. I love you." The parchment had been rolled around another couple of objects, one of which was a spring and the other a tubular device, which Helen recognized as the barrel of one of those Glocks Sam had made her fire until her arms ached, and then made her take apart and put together again until she could have done it in pitch darkness, under water, and without looking.

She glanced at Elena who was observing her intently and got out of the bath, forgetting about modesty.

"What else did Athena say to you?"

Chapter 20

Elena shook her head. "Nothing. Just that I was to give this to you."

"And that you were to say nothing to anybody about it?"

Elena nodded.

"Will you do this?"

Elena nodded.

"Why?"

Elena regarded her from wide eyes. "Will it hurt the *Consil Supremus*?"

What was she to say?

When in doubt, tell the truth.

Maybe Sam was right...

"I hope so."

Elena nodded softly to herself.

"Ilya was my best friend," she said softly and hurried out of the room.

Helen stared after her.

Ilya?

Has she been wrong about Elena? Maybe submission was not complete, despite all appearances...

Helen hurried to conceal the spring and barrel under the mattress of her bed, then went back to the bathroom and dried herself off. She put the bra and panties back on. Whatever tomorrow brought, right now she still could do as she pleased. Elena returned and brought her another of those flimsy gowns, which Helen put on and then lay back on the bed to await further developments.

A sudden idea. She summoned Elena by merely calling her name, knowing by now that it would cause her to be alerted, maybe by other servants or guards.

Elana appeared. Helen, in hushed whispers, requested parchment and a writing stick, which was like a pencil without the wooden sleeve. Elana appeared dubious.

"Just the writing stick then," Helen said. She would write on the parchment Sam had sent.

Elana, still dubious disappeared and returned some time after—and with yet another missive from Sam, this time containing the slide and a full magazine. How he'd contrived to get it to her she had no idea, but now she had *two* pieces of parchment and she made good use of them, scribbling as tiny as she could, and telling him everything she thought he might find useful. She didn't bother with descriptions of the layout of the place. If Sam had managed to get people to help him to smuggle these things to her, he would know everything about the layout he needed to know.

She only hoped that he wasn't thinking of breaking her out of here. That would get him killed for sure.

He was probably beside himself; maybe—no, *surely*—blaming himself for what had happened to her. Which wasn't his damn fault! He was alive only because he *hadn't* been there. Laurentius wouldn't be much interested in Sam Donovan. Couldn't make any racially pure babies with him!

Helen hesitated as a thought struck her. The notion made her so dizzy that she just sat down and needed a moment to recover.

Think.

Her last period...

Shit! She *was* late! She'd taken the last of that batch of pills...when?

On the *Gallinis*, some days before they reached *Aquadiënna*? One...two...She counted them off on her fingers.

A day late. Maybe two. Which might mean nothing at all, of course. With all that excitement it was maybe of little surprise. It had happened before. During one particularly stressful, and sexually inactive, stretch of her life she'd been so stressed out of her skull that her periods had been coming only about thrice a year, and so irregularly that she'd been getting to think about early menopause. At the time that had frightened her, though kids hadn't really been on her agenda. They never had been. You screwed up too badly with them, and she really didn't want to do that. There was enough shit happening in life without adding to it by bringing a child into the world and then messing it up.

Since then things had changed.

Was she 'late' or just stressed?

She called Elena and gave her the folded–up note she'd written. "Can you give this to Athena? Ask if she can get it out of the palace." Elena looked doubtful. "*Favor?*" Helen said.

Elena winked at her and departed. The guards, as usual, allowed her to pass freely. Helen smiled. Sam would mutter stuff about lax security, but he certainly wouldn't complain.

She lay back and touched her belly. She'd been very good about the pill, but it wasn't fail–safe. She smiled a dreamy smile. Maybe with everything...especially that wonderful thing between them...maybe this was the way it was meant to be.

Don't get your hopes up too high.

'Hopes'? Was she actually *hoping* for this?

Maybe not, but she caught herself thinking that it would be nice if it were true.

21

Sam got Helen's message late in the afternoon. He had just returned to the bordello—which bore the colorful and un–subtle name *Palatius Priapi*—from an exploratory outing into Cartaga, when one of the whores handed it to him. He folded it open and, with trembling hands, read the compressed, barely readable message. When he was done he went to find Lobus Natois.

The *Ladi* nodded, unsurprised, when Sam communicated some of the contents of the message.

"Laurentius Augustus has been known to express his disdain for the people and their institutions."

"And they still allow him to continue in his position?"

Lobus Natois chuckled mordantly. "Why not? He manipulates the emperor, who is his puppet, and he has the services of the army, whose leaders he rewards—or punishes, as the case may be. He needs little more. The *Senatus* is defunct. They are just a group of meaningless functionaries." He shrugged. "Once it was different, but these are dark times." With a grimace. "Of course, to the *Ladi* it made little difference who has in power. We were always considered outside Seladiënnan society. This has been our burden for a thousand years."

"I must help her."

"You are doing what you can."

"It is not enough."

"It is all you can do."

"I have to get into the palace tonight. Tomorrow it will be too late."

"She is an unusual woman. She may be the death of Laurentius Augustus."

"That is of no use if she, too, is dead."

"You cannot help her," Lobus Natois declared with finality. "The guards in the palace have bows and cross–bows. They can kill you from afar."

True enough. Even a kevlar flak jacket covered only so much of you. A strategically placed shot and that was that.

He needed a plan.

Give me a fucking plan!

Several issues here: how to get in, how to survive while in there, how to find her, how to get out alive—both of them.

A few explosions would be useful. A pound or two of C4 would have been helpful at this stage, but that hadn't been on his shopping list. The grenades wouldn't do the job. They made a lot of noise and killed people, but he wanted some serious destruction.

"How about some…" How to translate 'sabotage'? "Internal disruption?" he ventured.

Lobus Natois frowned.

"Do you have a map of the inside of the palace?" Sam asked him.

"We have such things," Lobus Natois agreed.

Sam stood poring over the palace map. The place was extensive but not labyrinthine. Three levels, all surrounding the huge central courtyard which seemed to be an architectural feature for just about everything of significance around here, from the homes of the wealthy to temples of sprites and imperial palaces. The area, according to his *Ladi* informants, was a luscious park, with another small building in the center which served the emperor as a retreat and was accessible only to an extremely small group of select servants and imperial guards. Rumor had it that it contained a shrine, though others claimed that the central room contained a deep pool. It was certain that there was a place to burn things. The retreat had been constructed some two hundred years ago; long after the palace had been built—and after the appearance of the *Plius Filii*: a fact Lobus Natois insisted was important; while Garmen Distil dismissed it as insignificant.

"Nothing is insignificant," Lobus Natois declared. "Everything connects with everything else. A shout upon the high seas may cause a storm somewhere else years later. Every action has consequences."

Sam regarded Lobus Natois with surprise. Here was an interesting parallel to a fairly modern scientific idea, uttered by a semi–cannibalistic denizen of a very unscientific world. An odd parallel. Or maybe the consequence of a latter–day mathematician stranded here? Who knew? If and when he had the time he might be able to investigate this mystery.

There were places in Oldecus Pistor's *Sanctum Supremum* where servants had never gone. Some might have, but these were probably the ones that were never seen or heard of again. This happened at regular intervals which the servantry of the palace had learned to predict with some accuracy. Everybody dreaded being sent into the *Sanctum Supremum*, even on the most innocuous of errands. A young boy or girl taken there was considered lost forever. The moment of their taking was considered the instant of their death—or worse; though nobody dared voice, or had any idea of, what 'worse' implied. It was dark thing that lurked in the back of people's minds and filled them with dread.

Children went inside. Smoke emerged from a vent. The children did not emerge again. The facts spoke for themselves. Since almost all of the victims were slaves nobody cared much. That they were also human seemed to concern few, not even the men with Sam. For them, too, the distinction between slave and non–slave was significant. Somehow, despite the fact that they, themselves, belonged to an ethic group considered apart they did not seem to see a connection between themselves and those led to a grim demise in the *Sanctum Supremum*.

Sam was going to say something about it, but held his tongue. This was a different world and people saw things in a different way. Who was he to try and impose his views? It would be a waste of breath anyway.

Garmen Distil informed him that Laurentius Augustus visited the *Sanctum Supremum* on frequent occasions. Apart from the emperor maybe only the *Consil Supremus* knew what truly went on in there—and *why*.

Sam tried to dismiss the *Sanctum Supremum* from his mind. It wasn't easy. Indeed, it was impossible.

"I need a distraction; a large distraction," he said by way of trying to distract *himself*.

"A feigned attack?" Garmen Distil suggested. "It appears infeasible."

Chapter 21

"It will have to be more than a feint," Sam told him. "We have to think on a large scale. Whatever happens, it must distract their attention completely. Something approximating a catastrophe that diverts every possible effort and all available resources into dealing with it. Chaos would also be useful."

Garmen Distil was openly skeptical. "It cannot be done." He grimaced. "I am unable to understand why such an effort is to be expended to rescue a woman."

Sam looked up from the map. "Your lack of understanding is no concern of mine." He was getting quite fluent in this language. Words flowed much easier and required less careful control. Maybe he wasn't saying things with grammatical accuracy, but his broken Seladiënnan seemed to be understood well enough. Certainly, Garmen Distil, had no problem getting the message of Sam's testy reply.

"Fire," Sam said. He looked at the map again. "A fire that'll engage the full attention of the soldiers—but will harm not harm innocents."

"Who is innocent?" Garmen Distil asked. "A feast requires the shedding of blood."

Sam eyed him and returned his attention to the map.

"The guards: where are they quartered?"

Garmen Distil pointed at the map, at an area adjacent to the palace. "The barracks for all military personnel."

"Outside the palace?"

"Only the emperor and the *Consil Supremus* live and sleep in the palace proper."

"That's a lot of vacant rooms," Sam muttered in English. Garmen Distil gave him a questioning glance. "Many rooms for such few people," Sam translated.

The Seladiënnans shrugged in unison.

A plan began to form in Sam's head. "A fire would be a good distraction," he said. "The barracks: what material are they made of?"

"Wood."

"Excellent! Two men should be able to do this easily."

"How?"

These guys obviously had no skills in terrorism.

"You fill a small vessel with lamp oil and attach a…" he searched for the word. "A piece of twisted cloth, which is soaked in oil and can be lit. It sticks in the vessel, which you throw. It breaks. The…"

"*Wiech*," Lobus Natois supplied. "I understand! The *wiech* ignites the oil. Such devices were used in former times for purposes of siege."

"Exactly. Make them small enough and they provide an excellent source of incendiary material."

Garmen Distil's eyes were bright with the thought of it. A new tool for terrorism—and Sam had just provided him with it.

Why didn't they figure that one out by themselves?

A classic case of blinkers.

I may have just changed history.

Tough.

"We also need a fire inside the palace," he said. "How high up are the lowest windows? Could someone throw a small vessel into the lower rooms?"

Garmen Distil, getting the spirit of it all, nodded. "It is possible."

"Good. How many men could you engage to do this for me?"

Garmen Distil thought. "Twenty."

More than enough.

Now for the other part of the unformed plan.

"I need a uniform. It would be preferable if it fit me—even better if it also belonged to an officer of reasonably high status. I have noticed that they wear capes. That would be useful to conceal my weapons."

"You intend to disguise yourself?"

"Who will question me in the confusion? They will be preoccupied with more weighty matters. I need to know exactly where Helen is. And I need to reply to this message."

"There is no surety that she will receive this."

"Do what you can do."

They produced the uniform two hours later. The owner, they informed him, was dead. Sam didn't want to ask, but yielded to temptation.

"He chose the wrong house of pleasures."

"What was his rank?"

"*Centurio*. He frequented our establishment—as well as another, belonging to the Goths, in Venida Unter. His habits were eclectic. The girls were happy to deliver him to oblivion."

Very lethal 'girls'! "Will nobody come to look for him here?"

"His body has been taken to the wharf. When they find him it will be assumed that he was attacked and robbed."

"Will they not be concerned about the missing uniform?"

"Robbery victims seldom retain their clothing. Uniforms such as this are disassembled and their segments sold to mercenaries and *prehensi*." Garmen Distil grinned. "The disposal of a *centurio* is not a rare event. They are not popular and know the risks associated with visiting Cartaga. This one was arrogant enough to come alone, and declaring his alliance by wearing his uniform, thinking himself safe after previous visits. He was a fool."

Nice way of putting it.

Sam inspected the uniform: a modified, lighter–than–usual *lerica segmentata*, completely black; a kilt of leather strips; heavy sandals, thong–tied to the lower legs; a short sword in a scabbard; a helmet; a cape, just long enough to hide the guns. The helmet would keep his face concealed during the hours of darkness. He would have to avoid bright lights though. The whole thing was risky, and the plan sucked, but it was the best he could come up with. He'd have to make it up as he went along.

"Let us start on those fire–pots," he said. "Night is approaching and we don't have much time."

"*This* night?"

"Tomorrow it will be too late. Tonight I will see Helen again."

And so it would be.

~·~

Helen got Sam's message as dusk was approaching and all around the palace servants and slaves placed lamps into holders along walls and lit them. Elena came

Chapter 21   285

to Helen's quarters and brought candles which were placed into three free–standing holders distributed around the room, each holding four of the thick, about ten–inch tall candles.

Helen watched Elena light them with an already–lit candle in a hand–carried holder designed apparently especially for this purpose. Elena disappeared again and returned maybe half an hour later with a tablet containing Helen's supper. The usual fare. A salad; baked fish; the potato–like vegetable; liquamen; fresh fruit; an assortment of sweets; wine; water. Not a bad dinner, except that the liquamen stank to high heaven. Helen fastidiously put it as far away from her as possible as she sat down at the table to eat.

Elena stood close to her and pushed a small wad of cloth into Helen's hand.

Joy!

Helen unwrapped it. The last parts of the gun, which she could now finally assemble. Another spare magazine. That gave her a total of thirty rounds.

Was she going to do this?

Eagerly she unfolded the parchment, suppressed an exclamation when she realized that he'd gotten her message and was *replying*! He told her how much he missed her and that—and somehow the sentence didn't make any sense and stood out by its stilted way of putting things—there would be no need for her to undergo any ordeals in the morning.

What 'ordeals'?

Strange way of putting it!

Unless he was being cryptic. Helen thought about the weird phrasing, then decided that he'd been trying to tell her something, and the only thing he could possibly have meant was that she would not be here in the morning. Meaning that something was to happen tonight to get her out of here.

How? The place was littered with guards. He wasn't going to waltz in here guns blazing?

Sam, don't be stupid!

She wished she hadn't told him about Larry and his ultimatum!

She stood up and went over to the bed. She wasn't hungry anymore. The notion of Sam doing something totally stupid and reckless just because he was beside himself with concern...

She lay down on the bed, extracted the other bits of Glock from underneath the thin mattress and, very quietly such as not to attract attention, snapped them into place. When it was done she gently shoved a magazine into the grip and jacked back the slide, chambering the first round. That done she tucked the gun back under the mattress and lay back, staring at the vaulted ceiling with its ornate, semi–abstract reliefs, trying to *think*.

The fire–bombs, as Sam thought of them, were small pots, normally used for holding liquamen, about five inches across, glazed, with two–inch–long flared necks for pouring the vile stuff into smaller containers such as bowls, into which the eaters dipped just about every item of food in sight; bread included. The containers had been filled with a particularly light and volatile kind of oil, extracted from a kind of bean, called *ygarba* by the Seladiënnans. *Ygarba* oil was toxic to human consumption, but its cultivation was a major industry, since it was used in lamps everywhere. The other source of light were candles, fabricated mostly from bees' wax; bee–keeping being another widespread industry.

The bombs' cloth wicks were also soaked in *ygarba*. Garmen Distil expressed his surprise at not having thought of thus miniaturizing an old tool of war for urban purposes. Sam said nothing. If it hadn't been that he needed to save Helen he would certainly not have introduced the idea. But, he guessed, sooner or later *someone* would have figured out the obvious.

Timing was an issue. Everything had to happen in a precisely synchronized manner. Chaos would be maximized if all went wrong at the same time. But how do you time such a clandestine operation in a place where precision time–pieces had apparently never been invented? There had been no need for it. Time–keeping of this kind was necessary mainly for the purposes of navigation and the determination of global longitude. There was no such need in the empire. Shipping was confined to the coasts of Seladiënna. Nobody went anywhere else. For general time–keeping, basic astronomy was quite sufficient. For his purposes, however, it was completely useless.

"Count," he told the men as they separated. He indicated the pace of the counting by example. "When you reach a thousand, initiate the attack." He guessed at the pace he'd indicated he was looking at half and hour or so. Enough time for everybody to get into place.

The men dispersed. Sam started counting himself and ducked into a tiny alley to change into the *centurio* uniform, using one of their flak jackets to pad the extra space and to provide extra protection. The belt holding the sword also acted as a strap for the holsters which held the two silenced Berettas and the remaining Glock, plus the spare mags. He'd emptied six boxes of ammo, that being another three hundred rounds, into a leather purse, which he affixed to the belt; as he did with his five remaining hand–grenades. The thin nylon rope that had been a part of his providential equipment he slipped over his head and one shoulder. The cape hid that and the armory. Just. There'd better be no wind to blow it about!

As he kept on counting he left the *Ladi* and the alley and strode through the streets toward the palace. It was the first time he'd been in Seladiënna proper, and if the situation had been different he might have had the time to admire the architecture around him, which surely rivaled what Rome's must have been like, with its impressive edifices lining the concentric hexagons of broad avenues, which, even at this time of the night, were littered with people, stalls, gambling booths, mimes, whores, musicians—all of them combining to make a racket that would have done Lenos proud.

The more the better. More people meant less attention to his own person. He strode through them with the air of someone heading toward a destination with a definite time–table and purpose. Which was the truth, of course. The rank implied by the uniform meant that the occasional soldier or lower–ranked officer saluted him but did not care to stop and talk, and that people in general gave him a wide berth.

Eight–hundred and ninety–five…eight–hundred and ninety–six…

Ahead, the central ring of avenues around the looming palace, amazingly unprotected, its entrance beckoning from behind an expansive flight of about fifty steps, at the top of which stood a guard of a dozen legionnaires at attention. Buckingham Palace was more protected than this. The swath of parkland between the street and the palace was only about fifty yards wide and unfenced. Patrols of pairs of legionnaires marched in sedate lock–step, but he could see that they were not truly attentive. A certain edge of caution was absent. The same applied to the guards at the entrance. They stood at attention, but they were relaxed. The guys who ran this show—and those at the front–lines—were obviously so arrogant that their security had suffered in accordance.

Maybe, Sam told himself, they were right. Nobody here seemed disposed toward revolution. The *Ladi* were a discontented ethnic minority of no apparent significance.

I shall introduce you to urban terrorism, Sam thought. The grim irony did not escape him.

Of all people…

Nine–hundred and seventy…

Shouting. A commotion ahead. Men running in the general direction of the barracks. The guards at the entrance crane their necks but remained at their posts.

More shouting. Soldiers emerged from the palace and ran past their comrades. Sam spied smoke and finally flames pouring from several low–level windows of the palace. The guards were getting restive. Sam strode up the broad steps and motioned.

"Vade!" He'd practiced that one word until Garmen Distil declared that it was uttered in the correct manner and without apparent accent.

The guards hesitated.

"Vade!" he repeated, louder this time.

The guards ran off in the direction of the building confusion. Sam, without hesitation, passed through the colonnaded entrance and entered the huge hall beyond. He saw several guards heading across the wide floor and forced himself not to look up at its vaulted ceiling but strode straight toward a hallway at the far end, ignoring the men's salutes as he swept past them. He marched down the hallway. More people passed him. Most of them were servants who did their best to avoid him, though many stood aside and bowed their heads in brief gestures of submissiveness.

Sam was curious to know how long they'd stand there after he had passed, but that would have been out of character. Besides, it has hard enough trying to focus on finding his way through the endless hallways. He came to a broad flight of steps, which was what he'd been looking for. He took it two steps at a time; as fast as he could without dislodging his cape and thus exposing his armory. It was, he thought, difficult to believe that he hadn't been challenged yet.

Don't question luck when it smiles on you.

One of his father's favorite sayings.

At the top he turned left, following the passage which skirted along the periphery of the vast central courtyard that spread out below on his left. Between trees that must have been as old as the palace the outline of the *Sanctum Supremum*.

Coming toward him were two soldiers. He saw the badges on the left shoulder– segments of their armor. Their swords were drawn and they were in a hurry.

Officers!

Sam had no illusions about being able to bluff his way through any encounter with them. As he walked toward them he reached behind his back and pulled out the silenced Berettas. By the time they were upon him he had them pointed. A couple of seconds later they were dead.

Sam stopped and looked around. He thought he saw a figure duck around a corner, but couldn't be sure. He forced himself to calm and re-holstered the guns as he went. From a distance, muffled by walls, he heard shouting. The smell of smoke wafted to him.

A shout. He looked into the courtyard and saw two guards stare up in his direction. Without thinking he pulled out one of the guns. He used the banister to rest his arm as he aimed. The first shot hit one man in the shoulder. Sam forced the gun down and fired at the second man, hitting him in the chest. The first man shouted something. Sam aimed carefully and shot him again. The man lay still.

Sam turned away and continued in a hurry. He had to be almost there! He came to a passage leading to his right; flanked by rows of columns, illuminated by rows of oil-lamps attached to each third column. The passage ended at a large open door which led to a balcony. From his position Sam could see the lights of the city through the opening. About halfway along, on the left, stood two guards in attitudes of attention. Sam squared his shoulders and advanced down the passage with a brisk step. The guards watched him approach. He halted before them, steeled himself to the gruesome necessity of what he had to do, the reached behind him, pulled out the Berettas and shot them both. They barely had time to look surprised before their bodies crumpled and collapsed the floor.

From behind the heavy curtain an exclamation. He glanced up and down the passage, ascertained that nobody had witnessed the event, and pushed the curtain aside—to find her arms around his neck, squeezing the life and soul out of him.

She let him go and stood back. In her right hand dangled the Glock.

"You're *crazy!*" she whispered, but he knew that she didn't mean it. Like himself she had tears in her eyes.

"Oh, Sam."

He hugged her to him again, wishing he wasn't wearing the uniform, and holding those guns. Nonetheless the moment was heady, filled with a giddy relief that made him positively light-headed.

Footfall outside. Shouts and commands. No time to escape or to hide.

Guards burst through the curtain, leveling crossbows. Sam interposed himself between them and Helen and raised his weapon. As one they fired. The projectiles penetrated the leather armor as if it wasn't there, only to he stopped by the kevlar of the flak-jacket. Their combined impact threw him backward against Helen. She caught him, he regained his balance, raised the gun and fired—again and again. The men, briefly paralyzed by the sight of man hit in the chest by several cross-bow bolts and still functioning, reacted too late. Four died on the spot. The fifth and sixth managed to recover from their unpleasant surprise, rushed forward, and prepared to stab him.

From behind Sam a report. One of the soldiers reeled back, an ugly hole in the center of his chest. Sam fired at the other, who died beside his comrade.

Sam glanced at Helen. "Don't mind me," she said grimly. "I've had enough of this crap."

He considered her garments. No protection at all. She was wearing the kevlar bra and panties, but they were rudimentary.

A frightened woman's face poked through the curtain.

"Vade!" Helen shouted at her.

The face disappeared.

Helen looked after her. "I hope she'll be all right."

"If she keeps out of the way, she should be," he said, struggling to get the *lerica* off him.

"What are you doing?" she wanted to know.

"Help me with this."

"What..."

"They'll shoot at you, too!" he grated. "I didn't come here to have you die while we're trying to escape!"

She didn't try to object anymore. They lost precious time while the flak–jacket came off him and the armor back on. It was *very* loose now. Its original wearer had been considerably more voluminous than Sam.

Sam poked his head through the curtain. "Let's go."

His target had been the balcony. The rope would let them down. But suddenly that path was blocked. A dozen guards appeared. Four leveled crossbows. Sam jerked back. The guards discharged their weapons. Bolts whizzed harmlessly past. As the archers reloaded the others ran forward with raised swords. Sam fired the Berettas. The men fell before they could reach them. The archers were almost done reloading. One leveled his crossbow. Helen shot him: a lucky hit at that range. Sam shot the others.

More hurrying footsteps.

"Let's go!"

They ran, away from the balcony, toward the inner courtyard. Behind them came at least a dozen guards. Several cross–bow bolts missed by disturbingly small margins. Sam undid one of the hand grenades and, as they reached the end of the passage and turned left, pulled out the pin and rolled the grenade into the soldier's path, then ran after Helen.

Behind them a loud concussion. The screams of wounded men. Sam bit his teeth together and ignored what he'd done.

They reached a staircase leading to ground level and ran down it, to end up at the periphery of the courtyard. Hurried footsteps crunched on pebbled paths. From the foliage of the artificial forest burst four soldiers. Helen gave a shout and emptied the magazine of her Glock in their direction. The only one she didn't hit, reeled back with Sam's bullet in his chest.

Helen ejected the empty magazine and shoved in the second one. She even had the presence of mind to pick up the empty one and stuff it into a pocket of the flak jacket.

From behind them more footfall and loud voices. Also from their left and right. Their options looked grim. Helen glanced at Sam, who nodded. Together they ran along the pebbled path, toward the *Sanctum Supremum*. They came around a corner and to an entrance—with a door!

A door? In this place?

The mere existence of this layer of isolation added an unexpected touch of the sinister. And there was more. Sam couldn't place his finger on it, but he sensed it anyway. An odd pressure building somewhere on his brain.

Helen regarded him uncertainly. Maybe she, too, felt the oppressive touch.

He examined the door. A padlock in an ornate hasp locked the door. It didn't look too solid. More ceremonial than anything. Sam hesitated for a moment, then motioned Helen away, stood back himself and blew the thing apart with a couple of shots.

He kicked the door open and stepped inside. Helen came after him. They pushed the door close; found an internal latch; pushed it into place, and stood to look around.

From outside the door came the noises of hurrying footsteps; the sounds of men talking. They stepped back and looked at the door. Sam motioned to Helen who kept the Glock trained on the door while Sam reloaded the Berettas' magazines, and then the one from Helen's Glock. He handed her the other spare as well, which gave her forty-five rounds of ammo.

Outside, the number of people appeared to be increasing, but nobody had yet made any move to break down the door. Sam thought he should have been comforted, but found that he wasn't. The strange oppressive feeling was deepening, pushing down on him like a leaden mental weight. He looked at Helen and knew she was feeling the same. If people didn't come in here it was probably for a good reason.

"They're waiting for somebody," Helen said.

Yeah.

Larry maybe?

The emperor?

What was it that scared the shits out of these people and made them wait?

They have us trapped, and they know it.

That was another reason…

"Let's see what's in this place," he said.

"But…"

He shook his head and looked around himself. "What are we going to do? Wait? Might as well see why this place is spooking them."

The room they were in was a lobby of sorts. A semi–circular wall against which stood a row of statues depicting…what? Weird gargoyle–like things. Misshapen creatures carved from black marble hunching on pedestals of pink marble.

A single opening in the middle of the semi–circle led into a darkness. Sam brought out his Mini–Maglite and turned it on, adjusting the beam to focus as narrowly as possible. With Helen at his back they advanced into the gloom. Sam swept the beam about. A single vast room, with a vaulted ceiling. Most of the space was taken up by a large pool, before which stood a pedestal and on that an ornate framework of metal, topped by a heavy grate. Underneath it was a large metal tray, probably for catching ashes. The whole assembly was blackened and charred by many fires. Above it, in the center of the vaulted ceiling, was an opening. The vent for the smoke, Sam guessed.

He flicked the beam back to the burning–place and stepped closer.

"Where are we?" Helen whispered.

Sam directed the beam to the metal pan underneath the grate, discerned what he knew were tiny human bones. He turned the beam elsewhere.

"You don't want to know."

"I don't?"

"Trust me."

"Oh no!" She made a little choked sound.

"Oh yes…"

He took her hand and together they stepped closer to the pool. He shined the beam into it. The light reflected off water strangely gray and murky. Sam let go of Helen's hand and hunkered down. As he did he noticed that the pressure which had been building up between his eyes was increasing. Now it was like someone had grabbed his head between two hands and was squeezing tightly.

He fought the sensation and forced himself to look closer at the water. The layer immediately underneath the surface appeared to be clear, but further down there was the gray murk, like...

It reminded him of something, but what?

He sensed Helen kneeling down beside him.

"What is it?"

"I don't know."

She reached down toward the water. His hand jerked out and pulled hers back.

"Don't!"

She leaned forward.

"What is that stuff? It looks like...I don't know. You ever had an aquarium?"

"No."

"I did. Once. It went bad. The goldfish died. We didn't empty it. Forgot because we went off on holidays. When we came back the water was full with this stuff. A kind of stringy fungus."

Sam held the light as close to the surface as he dared and peered into the murk. Now he thought he could discern a structure to it. Like a dense web of strands, running this way and that, filling the pool as far as they could see.

It reminded him of...

He looked again. Associations formed in his head.

Aquaspiriti.

What were they? How did they come to be? What was their physical basis? How did they fit into the universe they knew?

He'd asked himself these questions before, but now, as he peered into the water—and the pressure on his brain increased as he had a notion that maybe...

He felt Helen jerk him back.

"They're opening the door!"

Sam said nothing. He stared at the water, because, though he didn't fully understand it, he suddenly *knew*. Facts assembled in his head to form a picture of...

From the entrance lobby came a crash.

"Sam?"

Sam rose. Another crash. From the sound he concluded that they had breached the door. Hurried footfall. A flickering torch appeared at the entrance.

Sam turned around and shined the torch at the approaching men, discerned three: a man in a light–colored tunic; behind him to guards, holding back, trying to keep in his shadow.

"That's Larry," Helen whispered.

Larry Unterflug blinked in the beam of the flashlight.

"Turn the fucking thing off!" he shouted.

Sam pointed the Beretta at him; held it where Larry could see it.

"What is this thing?" he grated.

"Get the fuck away from there!"

The men beside Larry moved like lightning. Their hands, hidden behind their backs so far, whipped forward, to reveal small crossbows which they leveled at Sam and

Helen.

"No!" Larry shouted, but it was too late.

The guards brought the crossbows into line. Sam and Helen fired simultaneously. The echo of the shots, though muffled, reverberated through the cavernous space. The guards' shot went wild as they collapsed. The projectiles arced high and out of sight. Sam thought he heard them splash into the pool.

Larry Unterflug screamed. The pressure on Sam's head suddenly increased. He tumbled, tried to support himself against Helen, only to find that she, too, had sunk to her knees, whimpering softly.

"Stop it!" Larry shouted and came running at them.

Sam allowed himself to drop to the floor, rolled onto his side, brought up the Beretta, aimed at Larry Unterflug's chest, and squeezed the trigger.

Larry stopped like he'd run into a wall. A gurgling sound escaped his lips. Sam fired again. Larry reeled backwards.

Sic transit gloria, Sam thought dryly.

The former ADLER man, who had become the second most powerful man in the Seladiënnan empire and was well on his way to being its emperor, collapsed on the stone floor where he lay still.

The pressure in Sam's head was killing him. With his last ounce of will be unhooked another hand–grenade from his belt and pulled the pin, then chucked the egg into the pool—before throwing himself across Helen, who lay there, moaning softly.

The explosion was a non–event, dampened by the mass of water in the pool. All Sam felt was a faint shaking of the ground. The pain in his head became a last stabbing spear of agony, so bad that he screamed—as did Helen—and the men outside, from where resounded a chorus of outcries, screams, moans, and near–inhuman howls.

Then it was all over. The pressure was gone. The headache was still there, but now it was bearable.

"Come on!" he muttered hoarsely. He got up and dragged Helen after him.

"What…"

"We leave now or we'll never leave." If he was right the people outside would be even more severely affected than they were. He only hoped that the effect extended well beyond the *Sanctum Supremum*. In fact, he was banking their lives on it.

Helen tumbled after him as they ran out of the *Sanctum Supremum* and into the lobby, where men were rolling and writhing on the floor holding their heads. Some functioned well enough to shout weakly. Sam and Helen ignored them and sprinted along the pebble path.

Soldiers appeared to intercept them. They, too, were still dazed. Those who raised their weapons died on the spot. The remainder looked after them apathetically, too fazed by the psychic blast from the thing in the *Sanctum Supremum* to do anything decisive. Sam lowered his weapon. Mercy was not on his agenda—but neither was needless killing. From his peripheral vision he saw another soldier raise his sword.

Damn you! Just leave us alone!

He shot him in the chest.

Our lives or yours. Tough choice.

They continued.

More men arrived as they reached the stairs and raced up. Some of those didn't even have the coordination to get down the steps, but lost their footing and tumbled down. Others were more coordinated. A cross–bow bolt hit Helen in the chest, but the flak–jacket saved her life. Sam thanked providence and himself and whatever Powers–There–Might–Be for his earlier foresight.

They came to the hallway at the end of which lay the balcony.

Men closed in from behind them. Sam shoved Helen toward the balcony and lobbed a grenade around the corner. He didn't even listen to the screams anymore after the thing had gone off.

The balcony!

The rope!

Sam fumbled to get it off him. The damn thing took forever to undo loop by loop. Men entered the passage. Helen emptied the magazine of her Glock. Sam gave her the Beretta and she emptied that one, too. The men, wise to the lethal potential of their quarries by now, stayed well back and behind cover.

Soldiers appeared below the balcony. Sam tied the rope to the railing and dropped his last grenade on the men below, ducking out of the way as it went off. He ripped the hem off her thin gauze garment, tore it in two and wrapped it around her hands.

"Down you go."

She hesitated, but then grasped the rope tightly. He helped her over the railing.

"Don't look down. Just use it like a brake to slow your descent."

She grimaced; then pushed herself off and let herself down the two floors to street level. Sam covered her with his gun. When he saw that she was down he looked around for some more cloth for his own hands.

Not a scrap of cloth in sight! Sam cursed. Glancing along the hallway he saw that they were trying to sneak up on him. A few precise shots wounded at least two and forced the others to retreat into cover. He stuck the Beretta into the holster and climbed over the railing. He grasped the thin rope the way they'd taught him in the service, how to do it when your hands were all you had, holding it at right angles to increase grip and handing yourself down inch by bloody inch, avoiding slippage at all costs.

But course the rope *did* slip and it cut into his palm and fingers and then they were slick with his blood and so he dropped the last nine, ten feet or so and nearly sprained his ankle in the process. Helen fired off a few more shots at the guards appearing on the balcony. From their left Sam saw half a dozen or so come toward them.

Shit! Was this never going to end?

He held his gun with both hands in an unsteady grip slippery with blood and fired. His aim sucked, but somehow he managed to hit several of them. Then there was a shout. The guards halted and turned their attention to something behind them. More shouts. Guards collapsed. About a dozen men in tunics, carrying crossbows and swords, set upon them and slaughtered them without mercy or quarter. Three of them came running toward Sam and Helen.

Helen shouted something. Sam aimed at the balcony and squeezed off a couple of shots. A guard doubled over, toppled over the railing, and landed on the street with a sick thud.

"Come!" one of the *Ladi* shouted. "There will be more!"

They dragged Sam and Helen away from the palace walls, helping Sam whose ankle had suffered some damage and wouldn't carry him very far. The men picked him up and dragged him along as they hurried away from the palace and into the anonymity of the city. Looking to one side Sam saw that the barracks, just a block or two off to their left, were still smoldering and smoking. The chaos had abated somewhat, but it was still keeping them busy. That and the pandemonium inside the palace, courtesy of Sam and Helen.

The citizens of Seladiënna ignored the *Ladi*—for *Ladi* they had to be—and their companions. They merged into the crowd and presently—with Sam being helped along more discreetly so that it wasn't so obvious—and along circuitous routes, they made their way back to Cartaga and the bordello. They entered through a back door and presently found themselves alone in Sam's tiny room.

The door closed behind them. Sam and Helen stood, looking at each other, weary beyond description, both physically and mentally. They embraced and it was just heaven holding her. He found himself choked up, his eyes hot and wet; and so were hers, and they wiped the tears off each other's dirty faces and laughed and cried, but it was mostly happiness—though in the background there lurked all the bad stuff that had happened and they'd had to do; but it faded into insignificance when compared to the reality of their just being alive—and together again.

They took off armor and flak jacket and Helen carefully unwrapped the pieces of her torn gown from his mutilated palms, got out the medikit, and carefully cleaned it all up and bandaged it with sterile hi–tech dressings.

Someone knocked on the door. Lobus Natois poked his head into the room.

"We will leave you to rest. If you wish to clean up, the whores have prepared a bath for you to use."

Sam nodded and dragged himself up. He looked at Helen. The reek of sweat, cordite and blood clung to them like a disease.

"Let's get this stench off us," he said softly, in English.

She hooked her arm under his and helped him as he limped on his sore ankle—and it was nice leaning on her, and her holding him up like that, because *something* good had to come out of the bloodbath he had started tonight. The memory of it was still fresh; yet already his mind was wrapping a protective cocoon around it so that it didn't cripple him. But he knew that one day he would have to deal with it—and also that it wasn't over by a long shot. For what he had glimpsed in the *Sanctum Supremum* had scared the living daylights out of him—and he really had no idea how to deal with what it all meant.

22

Helen was dreaming. Laurentius Augustus had sent for her and she was being escorted along endless gloomy hallways to his lair. As she entered he took one look at her and made that motion with his index finger and thumb. The guards jerked her away and dragged her off to the *Sanctum Supremum*, where a grotesque ghostly gargoyle hovered above a pool of churning black oily waters. The soldiers pitched her headlong into that dreadful water, and the last thing she knew was that she screamed as she flew into the ghostly shape and plummeted into a deep, black hole...

Helen jerked and jumped up, unable to breathe, wanting to scream and scream until she couldn't scream anymore.

An arm clamped around her. She fought it with the force of desperation.

"Helen!"

She jerked out of the semi–trance. The arm became Sam's. She felt his breath at her right ear.

"I..."

"Come on," he said gently. "Lie down. We're together."

Reluctantly she complied, fearing that it might mean that she was going back to that dark abyss. But it didn't. Sam ran his bandaged hands through her hair and murmured soft, soothing endearments. Her breathing and heart slowed down to something approaching normality.

"Shit!" she muttered.

He said nothing, but just held her. She turned to face him and clung to him as if her life depended on it—which it well might—and kissed him deeply and passionately; finding, as always, a satisfying response.

They'd been too tired and fatigued last night to do anything but fall asleep—but now, despite the nightmare, she felt herself flushed with a deliciously familiar heat. She yielded to the pull of this thing; felt herself sinking into it, received in a warm embrace, just like she took him into her and felt him slide in with a perfect fit, and herself around him, and him into her, in the same whirling, dizzying embrace she–he–they had experienced before—surrendering to it in an endless moment when she was him and he was her and she was herself *through* him, having given up her identity, only to regain it from his perspective, because he was her, and so it went...

...opened her eyes, saw her own face, glowing with the rising climax...

...his face...

...as she–he closed her mouth over his/hers to stop themselves from screaming...

...her–his hands on her buttocks, squeezing and pushing...

...*us* inside *us*...

...*us* around *us*...

...*we* kissing *us*...

...*we* breathing *our* breath, caressing *our* tongue, rocking with *our* climax that didn't want to end...

Then...

....separation.

She didn't know if she liked it. Then again maybe it had to be. Biologically necessary: without a doubt. Cognitively as well. When they were like...this...though they saw more than either had ever seen, knew more than either could possibly know by themselves...it somehow left them blind to the basic elements of external reality. The world became the you–I–*we* and nothing else seemed to exist. The ordinary five senses, usually major instruments of personal identification and individual separation, provided no clues as to who was who anymore.

But separation, she decided, also had its uses. One had to cope with he real world after all. Besides, it was also just...nice...to know him like she could, to touch and smell him, to kiss him, knowing *who* was kissing *whom*, and indulging in the sheer pleasure of the *knowledge* of their togetherness. But in those...moments...there was just...well, things just *were*. The very idea of separation, of a dual identity, came meaningless, an inconceivable existential absurdity.

Does that scare me?

A little. But she was also willing to let this go where it wanted to go. They'd explore this thing together, whatever it was, wherever it took them.

She made a contented sound and slipped higher so she could kiss him, savoring the sensation of their perspiration–slick skins sliding against each other.

She raised her head to look at him. "I have to tell you something."

"Hmm?"

"I'm late."

He didn't ask what she meant.

"Are you sure?"

"Not yet. It's only been a few days. Three at most. Could be bogus. But I *feel* that it isn't."

"Oops!" He was grinning.

Good.

She'd known that he would, of course.

He told her anyway—with few words but lots of body language. This time they didn't...meld...but it was dizzy stuff anyway—and when she finally collapsed on top of him, totally out of breath, content, satiated, languid—just crazily, dizzily *happy*, she suddenly realized that she was crying...with relief and the unbelievable knowledge that they might be having a baby.

She sniffed and wiped her eyes. "I'm sorry," she whispered.

"It's all right." His arms closed around her, and she snuggled into the embrace.

"We'd better get our ass into gear then," Sam said.

"Hmmm," she said drowsily. She wriggled herself into another position. "Looks like we've done what we came for."

"Not quite."

"Eh?"

"Larry was only part of the situation. As long as Plius is about and kicking." He paused. "At least now we know what to do to finish him off."

She raised her head again. "What do you mean?"

"Do you know what was in that pool?" he asked her.

She shuddered. The mere memory was too much. She'd tried her best to push it aside and lock it away somewhere in the back of her mind.

"I tried, too," he said. "But we can't."

"What was it?"

"I think," he said carefully, "it was a brain. Not one as we know 'brains'—but made from networks of filamentous fungi. There are algae that tgenerate action potentials, just like neurons, only slower. Add synapses and bingo! Give it the right environment—water with very specific chemical characteristics..." Gently he stroked Helen's back. "I don't really have a theory of how this all works—all this paranormal crap, which seems to be a given in this world, and maybe in ours as well, but not quite as obvious or predictable. Maybe it's just that focused paranormal activity *needs* a biological basis of some sort. Like a brain. And who says the brain's got to be animal? Why not a giant fungus? Maybe this is what we've got in this world: evolution creating giant fungus–brains with amazing psychic capabilities."

"And that thing in the pool?" she wanted to know. "What's it got to do with Plius? I thought Plius was based in that dragon–lake."

Sam shrugged. "What if someone took a bit of Plius from the lake and grew more of him in the pool? Maybe it just became an extension of his main brain—you know, like some dinosaurs had little brains in their extremities."

"You're saying Plius made them do this?"

"It's a scary thought. If it's in that pool, why not in some other lake as well: like the Diënna's?"

"Because there's already someone else in the lake?" she suggested.

"Exactly. Still, Plius may try in the future."

"We've got to stop him."

Sam took a deep breath. "The *Ladi* want to wipe out the Diënna as well."

Who cares?

"It'll shake the foundations of the whole society," he said.

Helen found that she was getting used to them having this silent parallel stream of communication. It was like like...she just *knew*. You couldn't tell the difference between the thoughts that were your own and those that weren't.

Where was this going?

One of his bandaged hands slipped up her back; the fingers of the other ran through her hair.

"Don't be scared," he said softly.

"I'm not."

"I know."

"Then why did you say it?"

He grinned. "Just to make sure."

"How are we going to destroy Plius?"

"I don't know—but we'll have to try. I wish..."

...we had more explosives.

"Ten or twenty pounds of C4 would probably do the job nicely," he said. "Even in a big lake like that. It'd be like someone planting small charges in your brain. The hydrostatic shock alone will probably do the job where the main explosions cannot reach. I think that's what killed the brain in the pool."

"You think it'll re–form?"

"Yeah, maybe. A few sacks of salt would stop that pretty quick though."

"You want to bomb the lake and then poison it?"

"Succinctly put. But how?"

Later, socially respectable—though Helen felt that they weren't really, because she, for one, still felt so horny that nobody could possibly miss it!—they found out that the issue was even more difficult than they had anticipated.

"Plius has surrounded *Lacus Draconis* with legions and his Minions," Garmen Distil told them. "Approach is impossible. It appears that he is very afraid of you."

"He has good reason," Sam told him. "We have destroyed a part of him already." He explained in simple terms, that he regarded whatever had been in the pool as a part of the body of Plius, specifically his brain, which had now been destroyed—possibly causing the *aquaspiritus* considerable discomfort; whatever that meant in such an entity's context.

Garmen Distil was impressed, particularly when Sam explained his idea that maybe it wouldn't take much at all to disturb the delicate chemical balance of any given lake sufficiently to make the continued existence of the 'brain' impossible.

Lobus Natois uttered a small exclamation. "So you think we may be able to eliminate all *aquaspiriti*?"

Sam glanced at Helen.

What have we started?

He'd told her about the Diënna's adamant insistence on the removal of Plius *before* they tackled Laurentius.

Had the Diënna known? Had she seen a branch of the future in which they had discovered what they knew now and communicated it to the *Ladi* with their implacable detestation for all *aquaspiriti*?

If she has, then her fate is sealed now.

Sam's look told her that he knew this, too.

Have I thought this—or Sam?

How, with this connection between them, could she know exactly which were 'her' thoughts? How did she know that she was not sharing his—or vice versa?

"It doesn't matter," he said to her in English.

The *Ladi* regarded them with puzzled expressions.

Helen smiled at Sam.

It doesn't.

"They are ours," he said softly. He turned to Lobus Natois. "Yes," he agreed. "It is possible that much less is required."

She sensed the brief turmoil within him.

This is as it must be.

This world would never be the same again.

"You may enhance the effect by using other substances." He proceeded to explain what basic chemistry he knew of. The Seladiënnans knew sulfur and phosphorus. Helen, like Garmen Distil and Lobus Natois, listened with wide eyes as Sam explained the lethal toxicology of these substances.

"You have *vinegar*? You make soap from oils and fats?" he asked. "If you do this…"

he proceeded to explain how apparently innocuous chemicals, when combined in appropriate measure, produced various unhealthy substances. His clumsy Seladiënnan made it difficult, but the message came across clearly enough.

Lobus Natois was in awe. "You are," he whispered, "indeed the ones to end the tyranny of the *aquaspiriti*."

Sam shook his head. "Think before you act. This is what I ask of you. Remember that profound changes disturb people. Whatever you do—after we have done what we need to do to destroy Plius—be careful. I have seen the dark side of the Diënna and I bear her no affection—but the people of the empire do; and no matter how much you detest their treatment of your kind, if you act hastily and without thought, you may destroy everything that's good along with everything that is not."

Garmen Distil smiled almost condescendingly. Lobus Natois however was thoughtful and nodded at Sam's words. Helen realized that in the two men both sides of the revolutionary coin were represented.

Will they do it right?
Probably not.
Still, they have to try.
As always.
Four thoughts.
Whose? Ours!
Sam reached out and took her hand.
How will we destroy Plius—if we cannot even approach his lair?
"I found the QTel," Sam said softly, in English.
Her eyes snapped to meet his.
Crazy! Do–able. Maybe.
"Where is it?"
"In one of the bags."
"I'll go and have a look at the data."
"Let me know."

She let herself out of the room and returned to their own, feeling oddly…alone, almost desolate…as she closed the door to the room behind her. She found the QTel and sat down, forcing herself to study the results of its analysis.

⚛

Sam found it hard to focus on the issues at hand. Helen's disappearance from the room left an odd empty space—and not just in the room. Ever since they'd come together again it was like…

He still sensed her presence, at a level too subtle to define. But there was something about her physically just *being there*. More even than used to be the case.

He didn't like to give it a name, but the words 'telepathy' or 'empathy' *did* spring to mind. It was unavoidable that he'd think about it in those terms.

Labels.

Nothing, however, that came even close to conveying those dizzy, completely absorbing experiences they were having while making love. It was like…

He froced himself to attend to exigencies of the molment.

"Remarkable," Garmen Distil said. "For a woman."

"Remarkable for a man as well," Lobus Natois added. "If the women of this world were like this…"

Sam laughed. "They are like this," he said.

"They do not have such courage and valor."

"They are not given the opportunity," Sam said.

Lobus Natois regarded him with a pensive mien. "You are dangerous people."

Sam shrugged. "We came prepared with the superior weapons of our world—and we know how to use them."

Garmen Distil grimaced. "This is true. But you bring more than just your weapons. You are agents of change. Already, though few know you, the whole city knows of your exploits; of the man and the woman who defied the might of the emperor, his *Consil Supremus*, and their master, Plius. You, Sam"—he pronounced it like 'sum', as they all did—"Do–no–van, have assumed the position of a romantic hero—like Odysseus or Theseus—whose obsession with his romantic impulses"—making it sound like it was some mental aberration or illness—"led him into the lair of an invincible foe, armed with magical weapons given to him by agencies unknown but surely benevolently disposed—to emerge with the fair maiden intact and many of his enemies lying dead at his feet."

He allowed himself a crooked grin. "That Laurentius Augustus is dead…it elevates you a living legend, created within a single night."

The notion of being a living legend tickled Sam, but it also made him vaguely uncomfortable. "Compared to the task of destroying Plius, what happened last night was simplicity. I fear that your 'living legend' may find himself unable to live up to his fame."

Their serious faces told him that they shared the assessment.

"Unless," he added "Ariadne finds a thread that will allow us to penetrate into Plius' lair and do to him what we did in the *Sanctum Supremum*."

Looking at the men it was clear that they didn't understand a word of it!

So much for the excessive use of metaphor.

"Helen is trying to find a way to make it possible for us to destroy Plius." he told them.

"The woman?"

What *was* it with these guys?

"Helen."

"What can she do?"

"She knows things I don't. Some of them might decide whether we destroy Plius or not."

Could one possibly make this any clearer?

Lobus Natois nodded slowly. "It is difficult to understand, but understand it we must."

Sam grinned. "Learn to live with it."

He turned to the door. "We need some time to think about this."

"Time is yours," Garmen Distil told him.

Sam left the room and went to join Helen.

She looked up as he came in.

Chapter 22

"We're going to do it, huh?" he said.

"We'll have to hurry."

"It works that well?"

"Better than the Diënna ever *could* predict it."

"*That* good?"

"Let me put it this way: with those data the algorithm predicted the opening in Cornwall, location and time within a few miles and hours—and the one in Spain better than Mirlun did initially. Of course, spatial location's more uncertain than temporal, though it looks like the algorithm figured out *some* kind of pattern." She pointed at a tiny map on the QTel screen. The resolution didn't make it easy to read. Helen used the scrolling keys to roam across the map. "These circles represent the approximate locations from the temple records. Big errors here. The crosses inside are the locations the algorithm's pin–pointed if it were to fit some internally generated function to the data. See how all the crosses lie within the circles? Not always in the centers either. But they all *fit*!"

"Which means there's a definite system to it all," Sam said.

"It looks like it."

'How about the times?"

"Same thing," Helen told him, "only one–dimensional."

Sam nodded. "Amazing…So: when and where's the next one?"

"About four days."

"*That* close!"

"They happen a lot."

"Surprising not more people get sucked across."

"I should say: they happen a lot at the *moment*. The things go in six–ish year cycles. We're just about at the peak now. In a couple of years there'll hardly be any, before it picks up again." Helen looked thoughtful. "Besides, maybe these…passages…maybe they aren't all…*big*. Maybe some are just tiny openings and don't last long at all."

Sam thought that she might have a point. The one in Cornwall, the one where they'd gotten the sword, that was huge—and it had lasted for the best part of…what?…an hour? Maybe more. With the lost time on their watches—and what had caused *that*? it was difficult to tell.

An hour relative to *what*?

Anyway, the big one had certainly lasted for longer than the one in Spain, which had been much smaller and had disappeared pretty soon after they'd made the transit into *E2*.

A correlation between size and duration?

Why not?

All of which meant…

Helen nodded, divining his thoughts again. "I have no idea if it's going to be big or small, and if we can use it at all. Also…about 'where'…We'll have to work that one out. Somewhere in the Netherlands…*our* world's Netherlands. Near the North Sea."

"Not *in* the North Sea, I hope."

"I don't think so. I hope not."

"You and me both."

"Let's look at a map. Maybe we can pin–point it."

"I've used the last *known* locations in *E1* to get some more precision. That's the best we can do."

"So we have to rely on Mirlun's overlaid maps."

"Looks like it."

They dug out the, by now somewhat tattered, map. Helen smoothed out the rumpled bed and spread it out over the cover. If Mirlun's drawings were accurate—a big 'if'—they would have to be about…

"That's a long way to go in four days."

"The next one after that is in ten days."

"Where?"

She didn't have to check. She knew. Helen and numbers.

"London–ish. I don't know if London goes that far north."

"If it does it's not going to be any good to us. We can hardly…" He shook his head. "Just imagine."

"I don't want to."

"At any rate, that'll give us just under a week."

"*If* we can find the place and be there on time. *If* it's are big enough and last long enough to get us there and through."

"And if not?"

"Then we'll have to wait for another twelve days and it's going to be *really* out of the way."

"Where?"

"Italy."

"Forget it."

"Yeah."

"You wanna do this then?"

"You don't think it's crazy?"

"So crazy it just might work." He paused. "What's the next one after Italy?"

"About a couple of weeks later. Somewhere in southern Germany again. A few days after that there's another in eastern France." She glanced at the QTel's screen. "Then—you won't believe this! there's one at *Aquadiënna*. Well, practically there."

"When?"

She looked at the QTel again. "In exactly…eighty–two days."

Their thoughts were one. *Home? Home!*

23

The *Ladi* were frankly incredulous. Their attitude, Sam thought, was symptomatic of the differences between Seladiënnan Earth and their own. They simply weren't able to grasp even the most rudimentary aspects of statistics; the whole notion of predictive mathematics; the very idea that a device manufactured by men—albeit very clever ones—should be able to predict reliably what only an *aquaspiritus* could possibly understand...

"Your reverence is misplaced," Sam told them. "You must decide what you really want. You denounce the *aquaspiriti* and yet, in your hearts, you are in awe of their powers, as if they were gods."

"We know they are not gods," Garmen Distil replied testily.

"Then act as if you knew it," Sam said in the same tone. "I do not believe you do. You *want* to believe it, but yet they have a hold on your every thought."

Garmen Distil pointed at the QTel in Helen's hand. "It is more unbelievable even that men should have created such devices and have such knowledge as you say."

"And yet they have," Sam said. "We call it," he hesitated, then decided to translate the term, "*scientia*; and it is what its name implies. It has limits and its use brings many dangers, yet when used properly it is powerful indeed."

"I understand nothing of this," here Garmen Distil cast a curious hooded sideways glance at Helen, "and I cannot believe that…"

"You cannot believe a woman could understand it?" Helen said crisply. Sam noticed with interest that, after all this time, she was finally beginning to lose her temper.

"It is likely," Helen snapped, "that most of your women, if they were given the chance, would understand a great many things better than you do! It is well known that women are of superior intellect to men most of the time."

Ouch!

Garmen Distil opened his mouth to say something, but she cut him off. "Be quiet! You bore me. Your mind is narrow and limited, and your words make so sense. I wonder if they make sense even to you!"

Gastel Distil's face contorted in sudden livid anger. Before Lobus Natois—who like Sam, had been watching the scene with mild amusement—could do anything, he took a quick step. His hand snapped forward with an open–handed blow at her face. Helen's reaction was instantaneous and quite instinctive. Her left arm came up, deflected the blow. She performed a small turn to her left and jabbed her right elbow sharply into Garmen Distil's rib–cage. He wheezed and doubled over. Helen stepped back nimbly and assumed a balanced fighter's stance. A quick glance at Sam, who kept a carefully neutral face, but she knew anyway.

Lobus Natois observed the scene with sudden concern.

Garmen Distil straightened. He looked at neither of them and left the room without another word.

Lobus Natois' face was grave. "It was not wise to do this. Garmen Distil is a proud man. He will not forget such an insult."

"It was Garmen Distil who issued the insults," Sam grated. "He has done so repeatedly, despite sufficient evidence to prove that his opinions require revision. Now he suffers the consequences."

"He will not forget," Lobus Natois repeated.

"He should control his desires," Helen told him.

Lobus Natois, though he was more flexible—or maybe just more used to Helen—than Garmen Distil, still found it difficult to find himself addressed by any female as if she were his equal. The contents of her statement made the situation only worse.

Sam, too, was taken aback by Helen's comment, but realized almost immediately that she was probably—definitely!—right. Garmen Distil's subtle and not-so-subtle barbs at Helen, be it in her presence or absence, had been occasioned by a complex set of motivations, not all of which were social. Helen, as Sam knew only too well, had a potent and profound sexual appeal. Its wasn't confined to Sam. Harry likewise had been terminally smitten—as had poor Mirlun, who had had to suffer through extensive exposure to what must have been excruciatingly tantalizing torture.

Add Garmen Distil to the growing list. And Lobus Natois, who was writhing with personal discomfort at this very instant, not knowing where to look, or what to say. His mouth was open but no words came out.

Sam gave Helen a wry little grin.

Bad girl!

She bit her lower lip, trying to stop herself from smiling. Contrite she was not.

You're guilty, too!

Whose thought?

Guilty? I?

Definitely Sam this time.

"We have four days," he said, by way of changing subjects. "How can we get to where we need to get in such a short time?"

Lobus Natois, grateful for the diversion, looked dubious. "It is almost impossible." He glanced at a locally produced map. "Maybe a hard ride. If fresh horses can be found when they are needed. You will get no sleep as you'll have to ride through the night." He hesitated. "You *will* return?"

"We will," Helen promised. Lobus Natois glanced at Sam, who nodded. "We have made a bargain," he said. "We are both in your debt. The debt will be repaid."

Lobus Natois exhaled and seemed to relax.

Sam traced a finger over the roads drawn on the map. "We will have to leave the road about…here…" He looked up. "We will need a guide. Someone who knows the country around there."

"We will find one. When do you leave?"

Sam and Helen looked at each other. Another night in the bed would have been nice. The temptation was great. They could leave in the early morning. There would be enough time.

Maybe.

"We leave tonight," Sam said.

Lobus Natois nodded heavily. "We will make preparations."

Their guide was a young man called Olger Hastronius Gabil, an open faced boy, somewhere in his late teens, with curly dark–blonde shoulder–length hair, whose otherwise likable appearance was slightly marred by what Sam thought was an unhealthy zeal shining from his wide hazel eyes. He bowed stiffly before them and announced that he would be honored to lead them wherever they needed.

"We shall call you Olger," Sam said pleasantly.

The youth bowed.

"Please stop genuflecting," Sam told him. "It is unsettling."

"Of course," said Olger, bowing again.

Sam bit back a comment. "Why have you been chosen to lead us?"

"I was born in the regions you plan to visit."

"I thought you were *Ladi*," Sam said.

"I am half–*Ladi*," Olger amended. "My father was *Ladi*. My mother was *Garmandi*."

Sam enquired as to the origins and identity of the *Garmandi* and was told that they originated from a segment of the Legion's auxiliary, who had acted as carpenters and builders of siege scaffolds and engines. It seemed that they were one of the ethnic groups which had retained an identity of sorts, despite all the forces that went against such a thing. *Ladi* and *Garmandi* got along, if for no other reason but that the latter were excellent ship–builders and both were considered not–quite–respectable on the grounds of certain traditions: both rejected the Seladiënnan submission to the *aquaspiriti*. As a result the *Garmandi* had separated from the bulk of Seladiënna in their own manner, settling in the city of Urkuli at the coast of the North Sea, where certain species of trees, ideal for the construction of ships, grew in great abundance.

Urkuli, from what Sam gathered, was small, but very prosperous. Its business was building superb ships. It was as simple as that. Eight yards with ramps to construct the vessels, turning out up to twenty ships a year. More if they were smaller. Olger's father had come to Urkuli and decided to settle there. Olger was vague about the motives. His mother may or may not have played a part in it.

Romance among Seladiënnans? A man picking his place to live because he was smitten with love for a woman? Olger seemed to be unaware of the implications of what he told them; or if he was, he wasn't telling. His sister, who apparently was older, might have known and felt free to talk about such matters; but his sister had chosen to leave the ranks of the *Ladi*—another remarkable feat for a woman!—and was now was espoused to a Seladiënnan farmer who lived somewhere in the south.

Soon after they packed and departed Cartage toward the east. A waxing half–moon, a cloudless sky, good roads, and dark–adaptation of their eyes made the journey possible. Sam had been afraid that the roads might be watched, but the *Ladi* spies had reported that all soldiers had been assigned to guard the palace, for fear of a renewed intrusion.

Idiots.

If Larry had still been alive he would have figured out that, having retrieved Helen and blown up the thing in the pool, Sam had no reason to enter the palace again, but would do everything to get out of the capital a.s.a.p. Oldecus Pistor, it appeared, was not as perceptive as his now-deceased *Consil*.

Or just paranoid—which can be a survival trait.

The night ride continued. The roads across the Seladiënnan empire were studded with strategically placed way-stations providing exchange horses even for a traveler in a hurry. Horseback couriers, the fastest messaging system around after pigeons—whose efficacy was diminished by weight restrictions, a limited set of destinations, as well as other logistic problems—made good use of these. The stations were well-maintained and provided 'service' even during the hours of the night. Which was just as well; not all horses possessed the stamina of the military breeds and after fifteen to twenty miles or so they needed to be replaced.

Sam and Helen also suffered from sore haunches, and Sam was worried about the effect of the ride on Helen's possible pregnancy.

She waved his concerns aside. "The baby will be fine."

"You're sure then."

"Don't you feel it, too?"

So, fate had taken a hand in the planning of their lives yet again.

They rested briefly and continued. Sam lost track of where they were. Their existence were the sounds and smells of the ride, the motion of the horses underneath them, the wind blowing across their faces, the night-time countryside passing by them.

Dawn. Another waystation. A brief respite and off again.

The countryside changed. The road passed through flat plains, dotted with scattered farms. Curious eyes followed their progress. The road veered toward the water and followed it for a while, then turned back inland, to pass through low, rolling, densely forested hills and then back onto a plain.

On the evening of that day they decided to take a rest. They had made good time. The QTel, who acted as their one and only time-reference, told them that they had more than two days—and Olger estimated that they should reach their goal in a day or so.

The room in the waystation was reasonably clean. Sam, despite their exhaustion, insisted on inspecting the bed, and found it apparently free of undesirable life forms. This surprised him, but an inquiry with Olger revealed that the *Garmandi* had long discovered that certain plants provided a good protection against insects.

"Maybe they're using Pyrethrum," Helen suggested. She sighed. "Let's just go to sleep." She massaged her sore butt. "I'm going to lie down and let you massage me until I fall asleep."

They tried it. The massage inevitably, predictably led to other things. They went to sleep with Helen draped across Sam, her breath coming evenly and gently stirring the hairs on his chest.

They arrived at Urkuli on the evening of the next day. Night was falling and the day of their planned departure was almost upon them.

Urkuli, lying by the sea on a flat plane, with the scaffolds of the ship-yards rearing taller than the houses, provided them with another night's rest. By now they found it hard to walk with their legs together, like normal human beings did

Olger found them a hostelry where they ate, then retired to their room and re-arranged their gear. They were returning to *E1*, and into the Netherlands somewhere. It would probably be advisable not to look like a bunch of extras from *Spartacus* or *Gladiator*.

"What about the guns?" Helen wondered.

Good question. If they were picked up by Dutch cops—which was possible, depending on where they came out and what their situation was—it wouldn't be advisable to be caught with their armory. On the other hand, Sam really didn't want to leave the guns in Seladiënna either. They'd screwed around with this world badly enough.

"We'll leave the guns before we make the transition and take the ammo," he said. "We'll ditch that as soon as we get home."

It was the best they could do. The knives and swords—none of which had ever been used—they would give to Olger. If he was smart, he could made a mint selling them.

"We didn't think we'd use our passports and credit cards again so soon, huh?" Helen held up the ziploc bag with their *E1* mementos.

"We didn't take pictures either," he replied pointing at the digital camera.

"Busy, busy, busy."

Sam emptied the ammunition into a couple of small leather bags. They separated out what they would take and what would be left behind. Helen critically inspected their clothing. They had kept almost all of what they'd brought. At the time that had seemed like excess and useless baggage, but they'd hung onto it. Now that turned out to be providential.

They went to sleep and rose in the early morning. The QTel told them that they had maybe ten hours.

Time to find the place. That was something they could have used Mirlun for. They could be many miles away from the actual place of the event. In that case, or even if they were close and it didn't stay open for long enough, they were stranded here.

"Take your best guess," Sam told Helen.

"I hate this," she admitted. She looked at him.

Together.

Yes.

With Olger in tow they rode off. The map and the QTel coordinates provided their initial guide. Some hours later they passed through a shallow basin between low hills. At the bottom was a lake. More of a large pond, Sam thought. It wasn't very deep; as they rode over the top of the surrounding elevations he could see the bottom, even at the center.

They rode on and stopped to allow the horses to drink, then continued.

All of a sudden they looked at each other.

Stay.

Olger watched them curiously as they rode back into the depression and dismounted.

Helen studied the QTel. "Three and a half hours."

"Let's get ready."

If they were wrong about this...

They pretended they weren't and made final preparations; changed into *E1* clothing; unloaded the guns and took the remaining ammunition.

Sam gave the guns to Olger. "I want you to take these back to the capital." The youth listened with attention. "I want you to give them to Lobus Natois and tell him to keep them for when we return."

"I will do this," Olger assured them.

"The swords and knives are for you," Sam said. "Sell them or keep them. Do as you wish." He smiled. "Unless we are wrong and we are not going anywhere at all. In that case we will reward you in some other way."

"I need no reward," Olger said. That gleam of the fanatic occupied his eyes again. "The destruction of Plius and the Diënna will be all the reward I need."

"Why do you hate them so?" Helen wanted to know.

"Men should be ruled by men," Olger declared.

Sam found that he couldn't really disagree; though he didn't think the issue warranted zealotry.

"What do you think will happen when the *aquaspiriti* no longer rule?"

The youth's eyes lit up. "Then we shall be free."

And then the real work starts.

Was there any benefit at all in pointing this out?

He caught Helen's shaking her head minutely.

I guess not.

Time passed.

The computed instant arrived.

Nothing happened.

No fog. Nothing that might have indicated that anything was out of the ordinary.

Gloom settled over them. Maybe they'd screwed up after all. Maybe *we* were wrong.

Another hour passed.

Helen and Sam looked at each other.

From Olger came an exclamation. They turned and saw a tuft of fog appearing in the clear air, maybe two hundred yards further down around the pond.

"Go!" Sam shouted.

Without looking at Olger they ran.

The fog grew in size, its outlines sharply delineated, but wavering, as if shaken by a breeze.

They reached the fog and plunged into it without hesitation.

Visibility zero.

Underneath their feet, the clod of Seladiënna.

Ahead...

They redoubled their efforts. Holding onto each other they just ran forward toward the familiar noises of...

...cars. The roar of traffic...

What would happen if one got stuck in one of these openings when it collapsed again?

Hurry!

They stepped into emptiness, tumbled, fell a foot or maybe two and landed on hard gravel. They let go of each other and broke their fall but rolling over and coming up again.

The roar of the traffic was deafening compared to the silence at the pond they'd left behind. Sam looked up.

A few yards further and they would have been smack in the way of the cars. Sam glanced at Helen who was getting up. She wrinkled her nose.

What a stink!

Looking behind them he saw that the fog was fading away, leaving them a clear view

over the houses spreading all around them. The outskirts of a very ordinary European
E1 city.
 Traffic, suburbs, air pollution.
 They'd made it back.

24

"A hotel. A bath. Making love until we're completely exhausted. Sleep. Food. In that order."

Yes.

She took his hand and together they climbed down the incline of gravel that elevated the highway above the surrounding land. Alongside the highway ran a street, along which were arrayed uniform mass–fabricated houses for those who didn't mind or couldn't afford to be choosy about living alongside a highway's constant noise.

God, the place stank! It made her nose itch, and her eyes felt like they had sand in them.

They continued walking, attracting the curious, but fleeting, attention of passersby on foot, bicycles, and occasionally cars. About a mile further on they came upon a shopping center where they found taxi–cabs. The driver of the one they flagged down regarded them with a critical expression. Well, he should. Sam did look a tad wild and so must she—and their tattered *E1* outfits…The less was said the better.

"Do you speak English?" Sam asked the cabbie, a fat Dutchman who had evolved into his profession, fitting into the driver's seat like he was born for it.

"Of *coarse*," the cabbie said disdainfully.

"What is the name of this city?" Sam asked.

The cabbie looked at him askance and then shrugged with a very continental kind of gesture. "Scheveninge," he said it like only a Dutchman could, permanently throat–infected as they were.

"Could you take us to Amsterdam? A good hotel?"

"Can you pay?" The tone of voice made it clear that the cabbie was none–too–sure about that.

"You take VISA?"

"Of *coarse*!"

Sam handed him his VISA. The cabbie looked at the back, saw Sam's photo and compared it to the man leaning into his vehicle.

"OK," he said and handed Sam back the card.

The cabbie was mercifully quiet during the trip. Maybe his English wasn't *that* good. Maybe he was just naturally taciturn. As long as he didn't ask dumb–ass questions.

"Yoo vant ze Hilton?"

"That will do nicely," Sam said and settled back beside Helen. She leaned against him and presently found herself dozing off. When she woke up they were in Amsterdam, and the cab was pulling up before the wide portals of sheer luxury.

God, I'm so pathetic…

Sam's arm around her tightened. "No, you're not."

It still works…

In the darkest corners of her mind she had feared that leaving Seladiënna might choke off this thing between them; that maybe they would end up basically isolated again. Not that it would make a difference to them. They were what they were and nothing could change that. But...

Anyway, it didn't matter. He'd known. That's what mattered. He would always know. This was a part of what they were. Nothing that depended on other worlds or realities. This was *theirs*.

The cabbie processed the VISA and drove off. The doormen at the Hilton regarded them with suspicion, but did nothing to stop then from entering. They got themselves a room—which, so a diffident but forcibly polite concierge advised them, was very lucky as the hotel was normally fully booked. The credit card exchanged hands again, and was subjected to an electronic check, which required Sam to enter his PIN, after which the concierge became almost effusive in his willingness to oblige.

They were shown to their room, apologized for the non–availability of a tip—the bellboy favored them with an expression of muted disgust—and went straight into the shower where they cleaned themselves; then to the bed where they made love and fell asleep with their limbs entangled.

It was getting dark when they awoke. Sam glanced at the bedside clock. Almost ten. Helen lay on her back, looking devastatingly beautiful in the half–light, her hair in a tangle across the pillows, one of her legs still draped over his. Maximum PCI.; it couldn't get any higher than that. He slid closer to her and kissed her nipples, ran his tongue over her breasts and down her belly. He paused there, thinking of their child that might be growing inside her. Before him appeared the image of Katie, and how she'd looked when she emerged from Frances' womb: a tiny blood–stained human being, starting off on her way through life. His child. A unique human being, created in a never–to–be–repeated instant of time and combination of genes.

Then there was Katie the day before she died. An exquisitely lovely little girl, just waiting to get out into the world and put her mark on it.

Katie hugging him tightly.

Katie calling him 'daddy'.

Katie' still face—after...

No! He refused to go there.

I won't forget you, my love. Never!

He kissed Helen where her belly merged with her pubic mound, savored the salty taste of the soft curls. Her hips shifted. Her hands ran through his hair. A small contented sound.

Three again.

I'm sorry Katie. For not being a good father. For being late. For all the times I should have been with you and wasn't.

Her hands urged him on. He buried himself in her warmth, the strong musk of their love–making. She arched her back; her hands tightened, urged him even deeper. Guilt for past sins was obliterated by the overwhelming present.

Helen moaned. Her legs clamped around him.

...{ ! }...

A dizzy descent—into her—into himself—into *us*...

...his tongue inside her...

...his hands holding her hips as she arched and spasmed around him...

It's all right, daddy...I love you...I trust you...Look after my sister...

Chapter 24

After more than ten years, he finally wept.
Helen held him as the grief poured out of him like a flood.

Morning.
"We really should get something respectable to wear," Helen said, eyeing herself critically in the mirror. She glanced around at him. "You OK?" she said softly.

Sam nodded. He'd told her about last night. He didn't understand a damn thing about it, but he guessed it was OK. Whatever it had been, he hadn't felt as guilt–free as he had in years.

"We can stay in," she said. "I don't mind."

Sam stood. "No. We have to get things done. Nine days isn't that long. We've got shitloads to do."

So they went shopping. When they returned to the Hilton the door–men did not give them that certain look anymore. They decided to leave for England as soon as possible and flew out of Amsterdam later in the afternoon, landing at Gatwick shortly after. Helen busied herself with the QTel. Once in London, at a small hotel near Kensington, they did the paranoia–thing and procured two more identical ones and transferred data and the analysis program to both. One they kept, the other Sam mailed to his bank in Albuquerque with instructions to add it to his safe–box in their care.

"This is much better," Sam said to Helen.

"You realize what we've got here?"

"A ticket to every gate between here and Seladiënna."

"Scary thought."

Instead of hiring a car they bought one: an old Land Rover that definitely had seen better days. They also bought a large trailer, which cost almost as much as the car. Then Sam procured three pre–pay cellphones, had their accounts charged up to a sufficient level, and used one to call Frank Ricci.

"Hey! You're alive! We thought you'd vanished off the face of the Earth."

Sam chuckled. "We did. Kinda."

"Kicking the shits out of them ADLER fuckers I hope!"

"Yeah. Now I'm after bigger fish."

"What'd'ya need?"

"I'll pay for it this time."

"Pay? Fuck you, Sam. If you gonna start like that you gonna piss me off. Don't get me pissed–off!"

"We might need a safe phone."

"Gotta a number?"

"Disposable cellphone OK?"

"Everything's fucking disposable nowadays." Frank cackled.

Same gave him the number of one of the phones he hadn't used yet and disposed of the one he'd just spoken into in the next public trash receptacle.

"Why?" Helen wanted to know.

"When you're talking with the likes of Frank you never know who's listening in."

The other cellphone rang when they were sitting in a cafe at Piccadilly Circus.

Sam listed his requirements. From other end of the line came a bark of laughter. "You *are* going to war!"

"I'm trying to finish one."
"When do you need this stuff?"
"Seven days—max."
"No sweat. Somebody'll call you at this number."
"OK."
"Happy hunting."
"Thanks, Frank."
"Lemme know if you survive it."
"You'll be among the few to know."
Sam killed the connection and looked across the table at Helen.
"Now, where are we going to get a couple of Microlights?"
"Mircolights?"
"Powered hang gliders, but with seats."
Helen grimaced.
"Doesn't sound very confidence-inspiring."
"The flyer of choice in a world without landing strips."
"And how am I going to learn to fly one those?"
"You'll do fine."
She looked unconvinced.
"For anyone who flies helos like you did, a Microlight is a push–over."
"Ha!"

They found a local club in Stevenage, not too far away from where they expected the transition point to appear. The club rented a flat grassy area from a nearby farmer as an 'airfield'.

Sam bought two second–hand, near–new Microlights, from a lot of three who'd been left behind when a former member had lost his enthusiasm after a unfortunate accident.

The craft basically consisted of a large three–blade carbon fiber propeller, powered by a small two–stroke engine, mounted in a cage behind a seat into which the pilot strapped himself. The whole assembly was mounted on a three–wheeled, T–shaped aluminum chassis. It was designed for use either with a para–wing or, alternatively, with a hang–glider wing. Sam bought two of those, opting for a type that weighed next to nothing and collapsed with minimum effort; as well as the frames required to attach them to the chassis. He also had the tiny wheels replaced by fat ones, which tolerated rougher ground. They added to the drag, but it was important that their craft would not get stuck or flip during takeoff or landing. Larger fuel tanks were another issue. They might have to stay in the air for quite a few hours at a time. One of the club's members had a workshop and knew his business, replacing the one–and–a–half gallon tanks with bigger ones holding almost seven.

"That'll give you a good eight hours flying time," the man commented. "What're you trying to do? Circumnavigate England?"

Sam laughed. "Something like that." But he didn't say any more. The man forbore to ask since Sam paid him well.

Sam taught Helen how to fly the fragile devices. After some initial doubts she took to them like a bird to the air.

"I told you so."

"I know."

"Why don't you believe me when I tell you these things?"

"I..."

He laughed. "Remember, I'm almost Mr. Infallible."

She gave him a demure look. "Mr. Right you are—but infallible you are not."

Three days before D–day Sam got a call on the cellphone. There was a locker at Paddington station. Where to send the key to? Sam gave them the address of their hotel. That same evening the concierge gave them a plain envelope with Sam's name on it. Inside was a key with a plastic tab on which was a number. They took a tube to Paddington station, retrieved a couple of bags from the locker and returned to the hotel.

Sam looked at the lethal stuff spread out across their bed. Several plastic–wrapped slabs of C4, time–triggers, two special–issue and highly illegal Berettas with fully–auto capability and high–capacity magazines. Two–thousand rounds of ammunition. A *katana* for Sam and a *wakisashi* for Helen. Where Frank had gotten hold of these at a moment's notice was one of life's great mysteries. Sam guessed they they'd probably been stolen to order. Whoever had done the job had known what he was doing. The *katana* and *wakisashi* were from the same set and would have made a samurai proud to be their owner.

"You'd think we were heavily into terrorism." He shook his head. "If anybody catches us with this we're in deep shit."

"What scares me," she said, "is how easy it is to get this stuff—if you have the right connections."

They bought a couple of packets of large zip–loc bags and added them to the arsenal. They would need them for the final drop. Sam resolved to be especially well–behaved on the roads between now and D–day.

They inspected the projected site of the event—which was going to take place in broad daylight. It turned out to be in the middle of a field of wheat. The farmer would not be pleased at them driving over his precious crop.

More time spent waiting and practicing Microlight flying.

Finally the wait was over. They went to the lock–up where the club stored their spare flyers, disassembled the two Microlights, packed them onto the trailer, fastened them securely, and drove off.

Time minus a couple of hours—or so the QTel had projected. The land Rover stood parked at the side of a narrow English country lane, near a gate providing access through a hedge onto the field. A few cars came past, but nobody paid them much attention. One helpful gentleman offered help if they needed it, but they declined politely. He smiled and drove away.

Time...

Sam used a crowbar to crack open the gate's locking mechanism and joined Helen in the car.

"How long?" he asked her.

"Anytime."

Sam went over their preparations, wondered if they'd forgotten anything important. If they had, he couldn't figure it out.

A police car came down the lane and stopped behind them. Sam watched the two cops talk to their controller, then get out of their car. They approached the car from two sides.

Sam rolled down the window. "How are you doing?" he said to the cop on his side, while Helen beamed her best full–frontal smile at the other.

"Any trouble, sir?" the cop asked.

Sam shook his head. "We're just waiting."

"Waiting?"

"For some friends. We lost them when we came off the motorway. They'll probably get off at the next exit and turn around."

The cop nodded at the trailer. "These yours?"

Sam nodded.

"Where you going with these?"

"Friend's place near Cambridge. He's got a farm. Nice and flat to take off and land." Sam made it up as he went along.

The cop nodded, apparently satisfied. "Can I see your driver's license please?"

"Sure."

Sam produced his New Mexico license. The cop raised an eyebrow. Sam produced his international license. The cop inspected both, then seemed satisfied and handed them back. Despite his relaxed mien Sam noted that his eyes were furtively searching the car. At another time he would have appreciated the man's alertness, but today he'd really wished they'd just leave.

He felt Helen tense.

Shit! Not now!

Don't appear in a hurry!

He leaned back and grinned at the cop. "Anything else?"

The policeman eyed him curiously. "Are you a cop?" he asked.

It shows?

"I used to be a US Coast Guard pilot."

The cop nodded, satisfied that his instincts hadn't let him down. He'd sensed something odd about Sam and decided that this was what it was. Just as well. Otherwise he might have kept being nosy. The portable radio at the cop's belt squawked. He operated the mike at his lapel. Something was up; somewhere. The cop tipped his cap and motioned to his partner, who had a very hard time getting his eyes off Helen.

Thinking with your dick, Sam thought. *The downfall of many a good cop.*

"Have a good day, sir."

"Thanks. See you."

Sam leaned back. The cops drove off. Sam waved after them, even as he turned on the engine.

"Hurry!" she said urgently.

There was no time to open the gate nicely. Sam jammed the Rover into gear and drove off, ramming the gate open and entering the field. Above it lay a broad thickening blanket of dense fog.

"Good timing!" he muttered.

The Land Rover labored across the growing wheat. They approached the bank of fog and drove into it. Already the process had assumed an air of familiarity, something

Chapter 24

they'd almost gotten used to.

The fog closed around them. The Land Rover's engine howled in protest as Sam revved it in low gear and the 4–wheel–drive lurched across the furrowed field, with the heavy trailer lumbering behind.

From the fog emerged the shapes of trees. Massive pines, standing close together with barely enough space between them to drive through.

"Shit!" This was a contingency they hadn't considered. The Land Rover lurched through the forest, the trailer jumped and bounced behind them. Sam hoped that he'd tied everything down well enough. He didn't want to stop and look, fearing that he mightn't be able to get going again once he did.

Behind them the bank of fog disappeared between the trees. The Land Rover bulldozed its way through the undergrowth. Ahead, mercifully, the appearance of an open space. Finally, miraculously, the Land Rover burst into an large open meadow in the center of which was a small lakelet. On the opposite side of the water a gap in the trees through which they saw the rolling countryside beyond.

Sam kept going, circled the lakelet, almost got stuck in a boggy patch, but just managed to extricate the trailer. They came to a rocky area, which provided all the traction he needed. The Land Rover complained but kept on going like the reliable work horse it was. They reached the cutting and continued until they were out of the woods, and presently stopped at the edge of a gently sloping hill.

Sam turned off the engine. "We made it!"

"Just."

"We made it," he repeated. He pointed at the slope. "If that's reasonably smooth we'll have the ideal take–off ramp."

They got out of the car and took off their too–warm *E1* clothes. They had dressed for the occasion. The sweatshirts and track–pants came off. Underneath they wore T–shirts and shorts, much more humane in the sultry air of Seladiënna.

"We'll put the micros together tonight," Sam said. "Then we'll check the runway. Tomorrow morning we'll take off."

25

Sam did a test–run with one of the Microlights, just to see how it bounced around on the fat wheels. It was rough but the thing wouldn't flip. Still, it was going to be close. The gentle incline and a comparatively smooth surface would help the takeoff.

Night fell. They were ready for the morning and retired into the car. They didn't light a fire. It might keep off animals, but it might also attract humans, if any such lived around here. They'd rather deal with wolves, or even bears, than people.

They kept alternate watches, but in the event nothing much happened. The one kind of animal Sam had been worried about, bears, didn't show. They were the ones that might have destroyed the assembled Microlights; less from malice than curiosity. A pack of wolves came strolling, but when they skulked around too closely and persistently for comfort a burst of gunfire sent them running.

Morning came. Sam and Helen decided not to set fire to the car to avoid attracting attention. With a bit of luck nobody would come here, and if they did it wasn't likely that the old Rover would be anything but a puzzling curio to them.

Helen was the first to take off. Sam ran beside her, holding one wing–tip, until she was going faster than him and the lift was billowing the wing. The chassis bumped and jumped, but in the end she lifted off and cleared the low growths at the bottom of the hill. She went into a turn and slowly orbited above the site, while Sam fired up his engine, and, after a hair–raising careening downhill, joined her in the air. Without the wind blowing up the slopes from the north they wouldn't have made it. Even so the Microlights were laboring hard to gain altitude.

"I'm glad that's over," her voice said in his ear. Their helmets had a built–in low–power two–way with a range of a couple of miles in direct line–of–sight. He checked his compass, made a guesstimate correction for the wind, which blew from the north, and headed off south west. He'd thought of trying to head directly toward Plius' lake, but it was too risky. He needed the coast for orientation; the coast and the *Sela Fluver*. It was a longer way, but they should have enough gas to do this and more; maybe even to fly all the way to Aquadiënna and wait it out there somewhere until the transition point opened there for them to go back home: this time, he hoped, for good.

Meanwhile, and despite the uncertainty of everything, the flight across what was essentially an alien landscape that had never known anything on the wing but birds had a magic all of its own. Helen, too, seemed to enjoy it—after she relaxed somewhat from trying to focus solely on her flying. The wind blew steadily, the sky was laden with gray cloud, but it didn't look threatening. Nonetheless Sam kept a jaundiced eye on the weather. He didn't want to be caught out in one of those torrential downpours. Their fragile aircraft would plummet like rocks. They needed to prepare well in advance; find safe landing strips; secure the Microlights against possible winds.

The day wore on. The coast came into sight. Far ahead, in the mist, the unmistakable outlines of the great hexagonal layout of Seladiënna. They veered aside, heading inland, to intersect with the *Sela Fluver*, which they followed north. Behind them the inevitable afternoon cumulus was building up. They circled an expanse of seemingly flat grassland, with nobody in sight to observe them. Sam descended to almost ground level to for a closer inspection of the surface. It still looked good. He circled into the wind and came in for the landing, bumped over unevennesses but, thanks to the fat tires, didn't tip and finally came to a standstill.

He jumped out of the seat and helped Helen to get herself into position. She came down somewhat harder than she should have, bounced too high. He shouted for her to do another circuit. She revved the engine and circled again, then finally set down and came to a halt not too far away from him. Sam ran to her. They pulled the Mircolights together, collapsed the wings and tied them together. They had hardly finished when the afternoon torrent came gushing down. They took off their clothes to take advantage of the free shower. No hank–panky this time though. Sam was twitchy; the Beretta stayed in his hand for just about every minute they were on the ground.

With the ground soaked, immediate take–off was impossible. Maybe they should stay here; wait out the night and do the needful in the morning. On the other hand, the day was still several hours long.

Let's do it.

Let's.

Sam dug out the C4, which he'd already placed into zip–loc bags, and those into yet another, and another and another. Four layers of zip–loc should survive a fall into water and protect what was inside. He uncovered both of the bombs and set the timers. This, too, he had tried before. A flick of a safety switch, the near simultaneous depression of the starter button. One hour after that: *boom!* That was the plan.

He took Helen through the drill. They did a dry run, with one the triggers disconnected and the timer set for one minute. It all seemed to work. Doing it through the layers of plastic made it a bit clumsy, but it was doable; with one hand, so the other could keep of flying the Microlights.

"I can do them both," he said.

She gave him a dirty look. "And I couldn't?"

"Oops!"

They tested the ground and found a strip that was drying fast. Sam walked along its length. Since the wind had died down they needed spee; no bouncing and getting bogged down.

They waited another hour before making the attempt, using the time to pack their gear into packs, which were affixed to the rear of their seats. Sam dithered over the decision whether to pack away or wear their weapons. In the end he decided to wear the shoulder–holster with the Beretta and four spare magazines; as well as the *katana*, which he fastened to his belt with a strip of duct–tape around the scabbard and another around the grip and looped twice around the scabbard to stop the sword from falling out. Helen decided against the guns, but affixed the *wakisashi* to her own belt in a similar manner. On the other side she carried the QTel in its water– and shock–proof case.

When it was all done, Sam gave Helen her bomb and she took off. It went well enough; she made it into the air just before the end of their of runway. Sam followed her a few minutes later.

Heading further along the *Sela Fluver* they veered north–west. They climbed as high

Chapter 25

as seemed sensible and necessary to have a good view over the countryside. In this manner they spotted *Laco Draconis* from many miles away.

"Plius, here we come," Sam muttered.

From his ear–phone came a dry laugh.

They drew closer to the basin that held the lake, and as they did it became clear that Plius was very serious indeed about protecting himself. The hills around the lake were a solid encampment of soldiers. The sprite wasn't taking chances.

But now it knew!

It knew and it fought back. Not with physical weapons for its enemies were circling high above, little dots in the sky, flying above it like noisy birds. Instead Plius reached out with its mind—or whatever took the place of that. The pressure was familiar. Sam had felt it before, in the palace, at the pool. Only that had been but a tiny version of the massive brain that lay beneath the waters below.

"Fight it," he rasped as a band seemed to tighten around his head.

He placed the bag with the bomb on his lap and told Helen to do the same.

"On my mark," he said. "These things have to go off as simultaneously as we can make it."

She indicated that she was ready. The strain in her voice told him that she suffered the same pressure he did.

"Are you all right?"

"I'll manage."

"Ready?"

"Count."

"Three...two...one...*now*!"

He flicked the switch and pressed the button. A red light winked on, a small LED display began to count down. Sam started the timer on his wristwatch.

00:59:55...

He looked below. The Microlights were drawing into position.

"Drop it!"

No reply. He looked over to her, but couldn't see her face.

"Helen!"

No reply.

Her Microlight started to descend.

"Helen!" he shouted, trying to stay level with her as she slowly spiraled down.

Helen! Stay with me!

Sam? What is it?

Drop the load!

Sam?

Drop the load!!

Sam!!

Drop it!

"Drop it!"

Sam!

Reaching out; trying to touch her; push that infernal creature out of her mind. For the briefest of instants...

...{ }...

The bag detached itself from her Microlight and plummeted, disappearing from sight.

As Sam watched in horror, Helen's Microlight turned into a steep downward spiral. At the same time Helen's presence in his head gave way to a terrible silence. An instant later a vise gripped his own head. Something tried to pierce his eyeballs and push into his brain. Vision became a blur, shot through with sparks and lances of light; exploding stars replaced the scene high above Plius' abode.

Then the sight of Helen plunging away from him refocused his attention and pushed the agony into the background, where it throbbed away unrelentingly.

Helen!

"Helen!!"

Sam tilted the Microlight forward and plummeted after Helen, going into a steep spiral dive of his own. Above him the wing–fabric fluttered, flapped, and made a racket that nearly drowned out the engine.

They were still over the center of the lake and Helen's descent looked like it was going to end right in the middle of Plius' filamentous fungoid brain. And when she hit the water, strapped in as she was, and probably near–unconscious, she would sink like a stone, together with the Microlight.

Helen!

He didn't know if he shouted her name aloud, or if it was just his mind, or if he did anything at all and wasn't just imagining it, like one might in the throes of one's worst possible nightmare.

What he did know was that he let go of his own bomb, which disappeared from sight into the lake below, passing Helen's out–of–control Microlight a few seconds before splashing down.

That was it!

Dizzy from the pain in his head and the unrelenting spiraling descent, some sane part of his mind warned him that this was a bad idea that would do nothing for Helen and only serve to kill him as well.

So what? Why live in a world where she was not?

But when? *When?*

Think!

Focus! If you don't she's dead.

He craned his neck to follow her path. The fabric of her wings fluttered; the Microlight jerked erratically as the airflow broke into chaotic eddies. The craft, no longer supported by orderly air flow, dropped like a stone.

Sam, without thinking, hit the emergency release of his harness and launched himself forward into the void. The Microlight clipped his legs and the sword, jerking him around, but mercifully doing nothing more. Sam, his body following the conditioning from endless parachuting lessons, stretched himself into the airflow and dove almost straight down, angling himself slightly toward Helen's Microlight.

A couple of seconds before he hit the water he brought forward his arms, breaking the airflow, spinning his body around, just in time to hit the water with his now–bent back. The impact knocked the wind out of him. The sword twisted at his hip, the hilt digging painfully into his abdomen. His mouth opened involuntarily. A gush of water. He closed it and swallowed convulsively, forced his arms and legs out, brought his descent into

Chapter 25   323

Plius to a halt.

He opened his eyes, looked up toward the surface, started to swim up. The helmet restricted his visibility and mobility. He tore it off him and it floated up.

A dark shadow came down above him. The shock of the impact was a concussion in his ears.

Helen's Microlight!

Already it began to sink; not straight down, but at a slant, the wings acting as brakes and gliding surfaces.

Helen!

Sam could see her, sliding into the deep only a few yards distant. Above her, the Microlight's wing—which, while slowing her descent, would drag him down into the depth if he came into its reach.

So what? Where she goes...

Sam swam with wide strokes. He crossed the distance to the Microlight, grabbed onto the frame and, as the machine continued to descend, used it to drag himself to where Helen sat imprisoned in the harness.

He found the emergency release, pulled her out of the seat and—in a moment of lucidity, where he saw exactly what he had to do—dragged her *down*, toward the rear of the deadly wing above them.

The Microlight sailed over them and into the abyss of Plius' brain, wherever it was.

Sam, his lungs now on fire and his vision blurring and distorted by bright dancing motes, held onto Helen's collar as his free arm stroked desperately, trying to generate enough lift to get them to the surface.

Later he would realize that it was probably the air trapped in their hi–tech jackets which provided the extra lift they'd needed; despite the extra weight on him, consisting of the Beretta and four spare magazines, as well as the sword. But there was no space for such reflections now—and when they finally broke through the surface and his lungs filled with air and he coughed and coughed, there was only one thought on his mind. For Helen was not breathing, and in his mind was a dreary void, because Plius' pressure had gone and apart from himself he felt...nothing. Nothing at all.

For ordinary human beings that might have been 'normal', but after the last few weeks...

Helen!

He took a beep breath, rolled over, brought her above and in front of him, so she was facing upward, scissored his legs to keep them afloat, wrapped his hands around her chest and *jerked* them tight. And again. And again.

Her weight and that of his gear were dragging him down. He let go of Helen with one hand and undid the clip holding the holster in place, wriggled out of it and let holster and contents sink into the depth. Immediately he felt more buoyant and returned his attention to Helen.

Don't leave me!

You said you wouldn't leave me!

He continued the spasmodic tightening of his arms.

Please!

...{ }...

Helen?

Another contraction.

I'm here.

Her body spasmed. Her chest heaved. With the next tightening of his arms an arc of liquid spewed from her mouth.

The spasms lasted for a few racking, irregular breaths. At one point he almost thought she was gone again, but he knew better because he *felt* her presence.

I'm here.

She coughed again. Another spasm shook her.

Sam held on.

I love you.

And I you. How could you think I'd leave you?! How could I leave our baby?

HerHisTheir thought[s]…

Never had it been so clear, this being–in–the–other's–mind. Was it the immersion in this lake, where somewhere underneath there lurked an immense brain of unbelievable power?

Why was it silent now?

Maybe it's listening to us.

Then it must know it is doomed.

If Plius was capable of listening into their communion, it gave no indication of it. Maybe it simply did not have the concepts required to appreciate its imminent demise. In a world where the concept of high explosives and timing electronics was simply unknown, how could an entity like Plius even *believe* what it might be gleaning from their thoughts?

But we know—and we have to get out of here!

Sam glanced at his wristwatch. Just over fifty minutes; and then a shockwave would propagate through the water that would kill not only Plius, but possibly them as well.

Helen was still weak, and though she tried to help to stay afloat her efforts initially were feeble at best. They were in the middle of the lake and the shore was a long way off. And there, Sam reminded himself, waited Plius's Minions and an army of assorted soldiers.

Their survival therefore depended on luck and careful timing. Sam didn't like their chances. He was particularly skeptical of his assumption that with Plius' demise there would be some magical effect on his minions and followers, who would hopefully lose all interest in them once their master was history. So far, it was, at best, wishful thinking. And even if it was true: they had less than an hour to reach the shore.

On the plus–side: Helen was alive and so was he; and Plius' presence had, for the moment, faded into imperceptibility. Why, Sam did not know, nor did he care. Everything in him was focused on *keeping* her alive. The feel of her living presence was with him physically and in his mind, and it lent him the strength he needed to see this through.

Every now and then he looked over his shoulder to see how far they had to go. At the shore he could now discern the figures waiting for them. With every scissoring stroke of his legs they became clearer.

"Twenty–three minutes."

"Let me swim. I can do it!"

"You..."
Let me!
"All right, but..."
"You worry too much!"
"Get used to it."
She laughed. It felt good to hear the sound. He let go of her. She turned around. For a few moments they treaded water as they held onto each other, putting everything they had into their kiss. Then she let go of him and swam toward the shore in long, smooth strokes. Sam looked after her for a few moments then started after her. She made it through an excursion into death and she would make it through whatever lay ahead. He was so proud of her, it hurt.

The figures on the shore formed a clump at the place for which they were heading. Sam looked at his watch.
"Ten minutes—give or take!" He tried to judge the distance to the shore.
"Can you swim faster?"
"I'll try."
The drag of their jackets, light and water–resistant as they were, was a definite liability. A while ago they had helped to save them. Now they might kill them.
"Take them off."
A minute of treading water as they helped each other out of the jackets.
"The sword?" she asked.
"No!" The swords were their last weapons. Everything else had gone to the bottom of the lake, presumably tearing some holes into Plius' brain. If they got out of this alive, they'd need *something* to fend off the wildlife, two– and four—legged. It wasn't going to be as easy as it had been, but there was no armor on this world that would put up a great resistance to the *katana* or *wakisashi*.
They resumed their progress with increased urgency. Sam kept checking his watch and measuring the distance to the shore and those waiting there; most prominent among them the towering figures of at least a dozen Minions: terrifyingly familiar from what seemed an eternity ago. The thought of facing them was daunting. Still, they continued to forge toward the shore.
Presently their feet touched ground; at the same time as the last seconds of the timers ticked off. They rose and faced the mob at the shore. The soldiers had lowered the vicious–looking pikes they were holding, pointing them in their direction. The Minions stepped forward as one. Sam realized that they'd never have the time to undo the duct tape from their swords—and, even if they did it, would make precious little difference. Unless they'd worked this out just right they'd be dead.
He glanced at his watch—held his breath, glanced at Helen, nodded once.

A low sound, a sub-sonic vibration, followed an instant later by a mental scream that tore through their minds and those of everyone on the shore. Men dropped their weapons, shrieked and fell to the ground, clapping their hands to their heads and screaming, screaming, screaming.
Sam heard himself screaming, too. Beside him a loud wail from Helen, who turned to grasp his arms, her fingers digging into them with the strength of one possessed. They

collapsed onto their knees in the shallow water, holding onto each other as if their lives depended on it.

And then it was over—just like that.

The pain disappeared with a suddenness that was almost as shocking as its onset.

The screams ceased. Men stopped writhing and lay still, whimpering, moaning, sobbing.

Sam looked at the Minions, who had stopped moving, and stood still, their heads raised in an attitude of listening, or maybe waiting. Waiting for something that would never come. A command from their master perhaps. Some guidance as to what to do next.

Sam took off the duct–tape holding the *katana* in its scabbard and withdrew the weapon, pointing it at the Minions. From his peripheral vision he saw Helen do the same with her smaller weapon.

But there was no need. The Minions just stood there, apparently oblivious to anything but the never–to–be–heard–again voice of Plius, and when Sam and Helen eased past them onto dry land, it was as if they didn't exist.

Some of the soldiers stirred, but they, too, ignored them.

In the distance stood a group of saddled horses, tied to some of the scraggy trees that grew by the lakeside.

Sam and Helen headed straight for them, picked two and mounted. The animals, apparently unaffected by recent events, tolerated their attention without demur, and obliged readily when prodded them in the flanks and urged them away from the place.

Looking behind them, Sam saw that nobody made a move to follow them.

They stopped when they felt safe, whatever that meant.

They looked around the hills ringing *Laco Draconis*. Somewhere, there would be a pass out of here, and after that pass there would probably be a road leading to what, for lack of a better term, they thought of as 'civilization'. A civilization the face of which they had just changed beyond recognition—only that nobody knew it yet. But after the other part of their job was done, it *would* be noticed, and this world would never be the same again.

"I think we should follow this track," Helen said, pointing at the ground. The feet of uncounted men and the hooves of many horses had left their mark in the tall grass.

They followed the track, only to arrive at a large encampment. Avoiding it would have been impossible, and so they decided to brave it and rode straight through, followed by the zombie-like attention of its occupants: soldiers in the black uniforms of Plius' army, or whatever it had been. Now it was a bunch of aimlessly wandering, blank–faced idiots.

They left the camp behind.

"Whatever they were," Helen said, "I hope they will gets their own minds back."

Sam hoped so, too. Most of these people probably were not intrinsically evil. Few people were. But, as history had demonstrated again and again, a lot of people were capable of committing evil deeds when appropriately conditioned or pushed.

Were such people to be considered guilty of what they had done or not?

Was he—was *anybody*—really in a position to judge them?

About an hour later they arrived at the pass: a broad gap in the hills, which led to a steep decline on the other side. At the end of that grade there lay a verdant plain, and in the distance they saw the regular outlines of several obviously-cultivated fields, and among them the tiny shape of a building.

They reached it just before nightfall, now exhausted beyond belief.

The farmer who greeted them at the door eyed them with initial suspicion, but when he realized that Helen was a woman all that changed.

Sam introduced himself as 'Samus' (a name he concocted on the spot) and Helen, more sensibly, as 'Elena'.

The farmer, after another hesitation, gave his name as 'Portil'. Presently his wife joined him, told them she was 'Atena', and a short time later they all were seated behind a table, partaking in the couple's simple meal. Portil commented on the strange events of that day, when he and Atena had been assaulted by a strange and painful sensation, which lasted only a few moments, but left them incapacitated for much of the rest of the day.

"Plius is no more," Sam said laconically.

The couple stared at him open–mouthed.

"How can this be?" Portil asked. "Plius is most powerful."

"Even the powerful can fall," Helen told him.

Portil nodded thoughtfully, and placed his arm around his wife's shoulder. It was an oddly tender gesture, which Sam had not expected, and it touched him deeply.

"Then we are finally free," the farmer said.

"Of Plius? Yes."

"That is all we require. The Diënna can once again bring light to our lives."

Sam said nothing, but glanced at Helen, who shook her head minutely. This was not the time to discuss the politics of *aquaspiriti*.

Sam and Helen announced that they were extremely fatigued from their recent journey. Portil appeared disposed to ask more questions, but Atena clearly was not. Thanks to her, Sam and Helen soon were fast asleep, wrapped in a blanket, lying on a soft though somewhat prickly bed of straw between the bales in the farm's small barn.

26

On the next morning they awoke to the strange sight of a long procession of dark-clad soldiers filing down from the pass to *Laco Draconis* and along the road south, which passed the farm-house at a distance of about a quarter mile. Even from afar it was clear that they were a dejected lot, their movement and sluggish progress betraying their complete loss of purpose.

Portil appeared glad to see them go, watching them broodingly as they marched past.

He looked at Sam. "Whoever killed Plius, he will have our eternal gratitude."

"That is good to know, " Sam told him, but said nothing more.

They were served a typical Seladiënnan breakfast, but without *liquamen*, which apparently currently was in short supply.

After this they attended to their swords and the scabbards. The blades, having been immersed in water and left without attention until now, had begin to exhibit the first spots of rust. The scabbards had been soaked and were beginning to dry out, and warping in the process. They would take a while to dry, and so Sam and Helen focused on cleaning the swords, dismantling them, drying the handles over the farm-house fire, and coating the metal parts in a mixture of *yarba* oil used for the lamps and oil of lavender, which was one of the products of this particular farm.

When asked, Portil told them that the sale of lavender oil was their main livelihood.

"We go to the capital twice a year and sell it on the market," he said proudly. "Then we go and buy whatever we need."

He took them out into the fields to show them his lavender paddocks. Sam was impressed by their extent, organization, and the care lavished on them, and said so. Portil was pleased and showed them the press he'd built to extract the oil. Sam complimented him on his craft.

When the swords had been cleaned and oiled—not without some curious looks from Portil—they wrapped them in thick swathes of cloth, to protect them while the scabbards dried. To stop them from warping too much, Sam requested some straight planks from Portil and tied the scabbards to them, then left them out in the sun, which took care of the drying with a vengeance.

Sam and Helen decided to stay at the farm another night. The main reason was the procession of soldiers along the road. They really had no desire to join them; for who knew? Maybe some of them *did* remember who they were and resented their interference in their lives. The only alternative, traveling cross-country in a strange land, seemed like a really bad idea. They needed to get back either to the capital, or somewhere else they could contact the *Ladi*, who would hopefully assist them to get to the next transit point home.

So, they were stranded until the soldiers had gone from *Laco Draconis*. Since they felt bad, however, about abusing hospitality of the farmer couple, they decided to offer the only thing they could in return: their labor. Several times that day Sam attempted to suggest such a course to Portil, as did Helen to his wife. There had to be chores they could do, unskilled in such matters as they were.

On the third such occasion, when Sam suggested that maybe he could tidy up the barn, which was in some disarray, Portil paused and raised a hand, forestalling anything else Sam might have wanted to say.

"There is no need for you to offer your services. You have done enough, and we are honored to have you as our guests. It is but a small service, compared to that you have rendered to Seladiënna."

When Sam stared at him, he smiled.

"We are simple people," he said, "but we are not fools, and we know what's going on in the Empire. When we were in the capital but a few days ago we heard the tale of the strangers who appeared here from the other world, carrying strange and powerful weapons. They were not afraid to face even the Emperor—or Laurentius Augustus, who now is no more. A man and a woman—and it is said that the man burned down half the palace, and killed many soldiers, just to free his mate from the clutches of Laurentius Augustus."

"And now you come here, and now Plius also is no more!"

Portil shrugged. "Coincidence? I think not. You carry no strange weapons but the swords, which are of a kind I have never seen or even heard of. Yesterday my wife called out to me and pointed at two strange birds in the sky, over the lake. They did not flap their wings as birds do, but made a strange buzzing sound. Then they disappeared behind the hills, and later we felt Plius' death–scream. Then you arrived on horses belonging to Plius' soldiers. Your speech is adequate but full of odd sounds that tell me that you are from far away indeed.

"I do not know how you came to be here. I do not know how you destroyed Plius. But you did, and it was more than anybody could have done."

He performed an little bow of profound respect. "Our house is your house, for as long as you wish it—for our debt to you can never be repaid."

It was a long speech for Portil, who appeared more disposed toward short pronouncements and questions.

"You will require victuals for your journey," he added. "We will provide whatever you request. Please do not insult us by not accepting what you need and we can give."

Later, Sam found out that Atena had given Helen a similar lecture.

"They will be happy to help us," Helen said. "I think we should accept without any more protests."

Towards the evening of that day the stream of soldiers thinned to a trickle, and then no more came. The mood at the dinner table was jolly and relaxed; their guests appeared relieved, not just for the final departure of the soldiers, but also because the implicit secrets of the night before had been, at least partially, cleared up.

Sam reassembled the *katana* and *wakisashi*, and was relieved to find that everything fit together just fine. The scabbards also had dried out and were straight enough to accommodate their blades without jamming. The swords and the QTel in its case was all they had left from their own world, and it felt strange. Sam had never fully appreciated just how much all those things they'd taken with them had provided a kind of link with their own world: a link now almost completely severed.

Helen had tried out the QTel and, to their relief, found it to be functioning as it should. When Helen had it display the transition calculations, it also reminded them, however, that they did not have an unlimited amount of time. Besides, there was the issue of the Diënna. The *Ladi* would be making plans to dispose of her as well, and that might not be such a good idea.

So, on the next morning, they departed the farm at first light, and set off south; well-provisioned but acutely aware that, armed only with swords, their situation was inherently more precarious than it had been so far.

Portil and Atena had also given them a dozen tiny glazed, stoppered vessels filled with the aromatic lavender oil they produced on their farm.

"Sell them," Portil told Sam, "and make sure you don't sell them too cheaply."

The road was dotted with way-stations at irregular intervals, but usually not more than two hours' ride apart. They stopped at the second one they came across: a small house with an enclosed paddock containing a few horses; a small room with two tables where guests could sit and eat victuals provided by the owners. Sam put Portil's advice to the test. The station-master's wife recognized the jars, enquired politely about the health of Portil and Atena, and made her husband pay what Sam considered a reasonable fee for one jar: feed for their horses plus several coins that would exchange for service at two more stations, in addition to a night's lodgings. From the woman's demeanor Sam concluded that she probably got the better end of the deal.

Helen agreed. "Next time we won't let them go as cheap as that!"

Two days later they reached Seladiënna. They might have gotten there faster, but found it necessary on several occasions to leave the road and hide in order to avoid running into small groups of soldiers. Their uniforms were those of the Emperor's regular army.

Despite their caution, at a way-station only half a day from Seladiënna, they ran into a small troop of soliders. To their relief the men took no note of the two riders. Those snippets of conversation between their commander and the station-master which Sam and Helen were able to overhear suggested that they were after other quarry.

"They're mopping up Plius' followers," Helen said.

"I wonder what's been happening at the palace."

They found out, when they finally reached Cartaga and were greeted with enthusiasm at the *Palatius Priapi*. It seemed that Oldecus Pistor, his position weakened by his excesses and inattention to matters of state, deprived of the support of Laurentius Augustus and, above all, Plius, had met his demise just the day before: not by palace intrigue or power struggles that did him in—but the hand of one of his boys, whom he'd beaten and abused and who, in a fit of anger and pain, picked up a sharp knife, ran into the emperor's gut and twisted it about a bit for good measure. The boy was killed on the spot, of course, but Oldecus Pistor survived him for less than an hour. It was rumored that only death finally cut off his screams.

The empire was now without a head: an eventuality inconceivable only days earlier. Confusion might have reigned, had it not been for group of members of the near-defunct *Senatus*, who saw the opportunity and, with a speed that suggested some degree of prior planning, and managed to rally a significant fraction of the army behind them. They imposed martial rule and started the mop-up of what might have been left over from Plius' force.

Sam and Helen didn't care.

"Where is Lobus Natois?"

"At *Aquadiënna*," they were told. "Facing those who are defending the Diënna."

Apparently there was a stand–off. The *Ladi* who had come, armed with sacks of salt, sulphur and other substances presumed to be toxic to the Diënna, had run into a solid phalanx of local citizens, organized by Mirlun himself.

"No rest for the wicked," Sam grumbled.

"Or for the just," Helen agreed.

They left for *Aquadiënna* the next morning, accompanied by two *Ladi* guides.

27

Lying off the shore were several *Ladi* vessels, among them the *Gallinis*. Surrounding Aquadiënna was a small army of locals, armed with every device that might conceivably be used as a weapon.

Sam and Helen had been conveyed to the Gallinis in a small boat, which had set off from Gai, a town now deserted by every able man; left to women, children and the aged. No one interfered with the movement of either the *Ladi* or their other–worldly guests.

Lobus Natois extended them an effusive welcome.

"You have kept your bargain!"

"You doubted it?"

"Men often say one thing and do another. Even men who say they have honor."

Sam nodded. "This is true enough."

Lobus Natois smiled. "I am glad to see that my assessment of you was correct."

They stood at the railing, gazing at the motley collection of defenders on the beach.

"Blood will be spilled," Lobus Natois said darkly. "I see no way to avoid it."

"Maybe not."

Sam broached his proposal. Lobus Natois initially rejected it outright. Sam insisted, argued, cajoled—but refrained from implying any threat. He needed *Ladi* good–will: not fear and, ultimately, resentment.

"Withdraw the ships. If I cannot persuade the Diënna you can return and do what you have to. But if we can avoid blood–shed and social catastrophe we must try to do so at almost any cost."

"The *Ladi* will not accept this."

"Be persuasive!"

"I know not if I can."

"Yet you must."

"Despite the service you rendered, the *Ladi* will not be able to accept your suggestion. It was not a part of our bargain."

Sam laughed. "I know. But this is the way of life. Surely, you are experienced enough to know this."

Lobus Natois regarded them for another few moments.

"I will see what can be done."

He turned to a sailor and ordered a convocation of the assembled ships' captains.

"Let us go and talk to Mirlun," Sam said.

"How?"

"We'll sneak around the back."

They returned to Gai and from there rode to the temple.

They never reached it, but were stopped by a group of men, wielding pikes and pitchforks.

"Find Mirlun and tell him Sam and Helen are back," Sam told them.

The defenders said nothing, but stood there in silence, their weapons leveled at Sam and Helen.

Diënna, thought Sam, *if you value your continued existence, send me Mirlun!*

There was no response, but Mirlun appeared a short time later.

"You have returned," he said tonelessly. He wore a simple gray tunic and laced sandals, and he walked with a stoop.

"We have returned to speak to the Diënna," Sam said.

Mirlun regarded them both for a few moments. Then his eyes went blank. A few moments passed. "She will not speak to you," he declared with definiteness.

"She will—if she wishes to survive," Sam corrected.

Mirlun frowned.

If you do not, Sam thought, addressing the sprite again, *we will not only let the Ladi do what they came here to do but help them do finish it. But if you speak to me, we may yet find a way to make it come out advantageous for all.*

He received only silence.

Sam waited a few moments, then turned to Mirlun. "Persuade her."

"You destroyed her." Mirlun cast a dark glance at Helen. "Because of *her*."

Sam shook his head. "No." A thought came to him. It had been nagging at him for some time, refusing to become clear. But now…

"The Diënna," he said to Mirlun, "saw darkness in the future that is now. I've often wondered what she meant. What kind of 'darkness'? Did she see her extinction? Was she just unable to see anything at all and concluded that the cause for this must be her extinction?"

He continued in English.

"I thought so, too, but now it occurs to me that there's another possibility. The Diënna is what she is. She lives in the certainties of the things she sees. She sees the strands of future possibilities and chooses the one that suits her best. In a way she doesn't really *decide* at all. Instead she selects the path that assures the persistence of her goals. Like," he glanced at Helen, "a machine. A chess–playing computer, which evaluates all possible paths and decides on its next move based on an evaluation of the path of least damage—or best return, whichever the case may be."

"Don't we do this, too?" she said.

"To an extent. We killed people because of decisions designed around the goal of personal survival. But as humans we live with uncertainty—for most of us cannot see—or compute—the future; at least not in the way the Diënna or a chess–playing computer would. We therefore have to live with the agony of uncertainty and the necessity of choices based on guesses, values, ethics… Stuff like that. Something the Diënna doesn't. Though she's been imbued with aspects of humanity, yet ultimately she's fundamentally alien from us. I don't know how because I don't even begin to understand her basic nature—but I think the facts support this idea."

"I don't understand," Mirlun said.

"What Sam is trying to say," Helen elaborated, "is that the 'darkness' the Diënna foresaw had nothing to do with her extinction—or maybe it had, but not the way Sam thought it did. In this future there is a moment—*this* moment maybe—where the Diënna can *not* see past the point we're at now. For what happens depends on her decision, and so maybe she actually can't see past this point—not until she's actually *made* the decision."

Sam nodded. "Or maybe she can only see *some* futures. We have theories in our world, about predictability and unpredictability, about the likely and the unlikely, about simplicity and complexity, and how in certain situations the minutest disturbance can amplify into the most diverse set of incalculable changes. In such situations the future branches are so manifold and complex that it may seem like there was no future here at all: not if you're used to perceiving a clear and finite set of branches."

Mirlun scowled. "This makes no sense. The Diënna has faced such situations before. She would know how to deal with such things."

"Maybe," Sam pointed out, "she was never *forced* into a such a future. Maybe she always avoided the branches that contained instances of similar 'darkness'—and chose, insofar as she was able to, those which were 'open' or unafflicted by such dire content. But we forced her hand. She inhabits this future with us. Now she must make a choice based not on some optimized future path, but with the same uncertainty afflicting all of us."

He stepped close to Mirlun and looked into the *sacerdot*'s tortured eyes. "Make her understand. For this is certain: that if she chooses to deny my demands she will indeed sink into eternal darkness. We will see to that—and if we don't the *Ladi* will. Sooner or later. They know how to destroy the Diënna—and in the end they will succeed. The only way to avoid this is for the Diënna to make the pact."

"A pact with the *unclean*?" Mirlun protested.

"Such is life," Sam said mercilessly.

"What are your demands? Tell *me*—for she will not speak to you. You have betrayed her."

Sam shrugged. "Suit yourself. Here are the demands. The Diënna has to cease meddling in human affairs and stop using her influence to brand the *Ladi* as outcasts. She will instead make it known—through *you*! that she considers them just as 'clean' as anyone else in the empire, since they were material in the destruction of Plius.

"Next: there will be no more *sacerdae*. The Diënna is not worthy of being entrusted with the care of those whom she sacrifices as she did. The 'Mirlun' may continue to act as the Diënna's ceremonial attendant, but that's it!"

"Those conditions are intolerable!"

"Maybe—but they are as they are, and they are not negotiable. The Diënna knows we can move freely between our world and Seladiënna. We have destroyed Plius. If she does not comply with our demands we will destroy *her*. If *we* don't, the *Ladi* will. This is fact. Certainty. She can avoid her destruction only by compliance." He motioned. "Now go and commune with your mistress. Don't delay too long. If you do, people will die, and ultimately so will the Diënna."

Mirlun turned and, with heavy steps, went into the scorched temple.

Sam and Helen waited, watched by the vacant-eyed peasants.

"You think she knows?" Helen said.

"Of course. She doesn't need Mirlun to communicate. That's just the mummery that goes with rank. Gods don't talk to people except through priests. It's a time-honored ritual, invented by priests, of course, but the gods of this world no doubt have found it useful to relay their orders through their official spokesmen. I mean, how often does the

US president talk to the ordinary folks?"

She slipped her arm around his waist and pulled him closer. "You think she hates me?"

"I don't think she much likes either of us."

Mirlun approached.

"The Diënna accepts the terms of the agreement," he grated.

"I thought she might," Sam said dryly. "Remind her every now and then that the *Ladi* will be watching her closely. If she chooses to renege on her agreement, her extinction will be the consequence."

"The Diënna understands that," Mirlun replied, his voice thick with loathing.

"Good." Sam looked at Helen. "Let's go and tell the Ladi that they can put their water–polluting plans on hold—for the time being at least. I hope they are as capable of seeing reason as the Diënna."

Fortunately they were.

28

"Shall we try for the gate in France? I don't want to wait around another two months."

They were sitting aboard the *Gallinis*, looking out over the ocean's lazy swells. The wind had died down a few hours ago, and it was sweltering.

"If it doesn't work," Helen continued, "we can always come back here in time for the next one."

"Why not."

The *Ladi* declared their willingness to help. "We need you to get us to somewhere… here." On the map before them Sam indicated a place about halfway up the coast of 'France'. "From there we ride; following this river to about *here*…" He pointed at a small dot on the map. "This is a settlement?"

"Illus," Lobus Natois supplied. "A small town of no great significance. Still, we have connections there. I will announce your arrival to our…representative…and ask him to provide with whatever you require."

To Sam's quizzical look he smiled. "Doves fly faster than any man can travel."

Maybe here.

"That will do us well enough," Sam said.

"You are impatient to leave us."

Sam shrugged. "We are creatures of our world. This much we have determined. Also, the longer we stay, the more likely it becomes that we are discovered. I am not confident that those in authority appreciate our presence—despite what we've done for them. Unpleasantness might be the result. This we should avoid."

Lobus Natois nodded. "We will help you any way we can."

On the evening of the same day, the *Gallinis* detached itself from the *Ladi* fleet and headed south.

They weathered one storm and spent a day becalmed. One morning four days later, they pulled into a small bay into which discharged a river that may have been the one on the map. The *Ladi* again demonstrated their scarily efficient organization. They were met on the shore by a man, holding two horses, who apparently had been waiting here for over two days for their arrival.

"This may be the last time we speak to each other," Lobus Natois said with a melancholy air.

Sam grasped his hand. "Thank you for your willingness to consider our ways of solving your problems."

Lobus Natois grimaced. "If the Diënna fails to honor the pact…"

"Then do what needs to be done," Sam agreed. "But for now, have patience. She, too, needs to adapt to very strange new circumstances."

They said their farewells. The *Gallinis* pulled away from the shore. With their guide, one Nilfit Gasti, they rode east, following the course of the river. The country was flat, the horses' endurance remarkable, and their progress encouraging.

At nightfall they came to a road and traveled on it for a mile or so until they came to a way–station. There they stayed the night, and with the first light of dawn set out again, cross-country. It would, assured their guide, save them much time.

They came to another road.

Nilfit Gasti pointed. "Follow it and you will be in Illus by nightfall. Once there, ask for Lothorio Regasti, who will aid you in any way he can. As for me, I am long overdue for my return home." He bowed. "It was an honor to be of service to you."

They rode on. Presently in the distance they saw the outlines of Illus.

Their appearance caused some interest, as is the way of things when strangers come into small towns. Illus consisted mostly of white–washed single storey houses, arranged in a haphazard pattern around a system of dusty streets that had apparently grown in an organic fashion. The people moved with the unhurried mien of those who have all the time in the universe and who are in perfect synch with the rhythms of the world around them.

They stopped an old man shuffling along, supported by a crooked stick.

"We are looking for Lothorio Regasti. Can you help us?"

The old man grinned up at them from a toothless mouth and pointed his stick, then shuffled off without another word.

"That was useful," Helen muttered.

They continued in the general direction the man had pointed and enquired with another passerby. This one was middle–aged, powerfully built, and moved with a stride more purposeful than the old fellow.

"I will guide you," he declared.

"That is very kind, but…"

"I will guide you," the man insisted. "Lothorio Regasti is expecting you and has asked everybody to inform him of your arrival."

Why doesn't he blow a fanfare? Sam thought. Lothorio Regasti appeared to be a man of some significance in this town. And a *Ladi* to boot? An undercover agent in a prominent position?

It turned out that Lothorio Regasti was the equivalent of the local bank: the one who juggled the finances for the town, which was based around the production of wines. As such he was an important man and folks obliged him.

He received his visitors with polite curiosity. "Lobus Natois, who is a man I respect, has asked me to provide you with all the help I can."

"It is little," Sam advised him. "We need a bed for the night and, tomorrow, two horses that will carry us swiftly to a place not far from here."

"And then?" Lothorio Regasti prompted, unable to conceal his curiosity.

"Has Lobus Natois told you who we are?"

Lothorio Regasti nodded. "He was oblique rather than explicit, but it sufficed."

"We wish to go back to our world."

"Ahh, so it is true. Folks may move back and forth as they please—if only they know the 'where' and 'when'."

"We hope that our estimates are correct," Sam said cautiously.

Lothorio Regasti rose from behind the table at which he'd been sitting. It was loaded with parchments and features a small cradle for holding writing implements.

"I will show you to a hostelry. You will be afforded the best. The *Ladi* have much to thank you for. This is but an pitiful contribution from us."

The hostelry was pleasant enough. Bug-free, too. They were accorded the luxury of privacy in a normally public bath. Lothorio Regasti made sure that even the water was clean. A man of influence indeed.

That night in their room—after a walk around the town and under the unsettlingly curious, though benign, gazes of the citizenry—they studied the map.

"If we don't get this right we'll have to go all the way back to Cornwall," Sam said.

"We got it right last time."

"Luck?"

"Maybe. But we both *felt* that it was going to be there, didn't we?"

"I thought so."

"So did I."

"Mirlun knew."

"Mirlun's body held the Diënna's water."

"We also have something more than ordinary people."

We do indeed.

Was *that* what it was?

They lay down on the bed and spent some considerable time not thinking much at all.

Later, lying there in pleasant languor, he placed his hand on her belly.

"Definitely," she said.

He kissed the back of her neck where an erratic swirl of downy hairs reached down almost to her shoulders. Helen called it her 'feral throwback'. Sam thought it was charming and utterly fascinating.

"A girl," she said.

Her stroked her belly. Helen wriggled herself into a closer fit and made a contented sound.

"You know it's true," she murmured.

As always, she was right. The child inside her, despite its embryonic nature, already was a definite psychic *presence*. Whatever that meant. So much was…different…now. Their sojourns in Seladiënna had left their indelible imprint on their minds; changed them forever. And with that came this odd…awareness…of someone who wasn't even 'someone' as yet—who could not be, because the embryo didn't even have the semblance of a brain at this stage of development.

But there was *something*.

Familiar.

Sam drifted off to sleep and dreamt of Katie—who smiled and laughed and hugged him and made him whirl her around like a dervish—and her giggles and laughter echoed through his mind…

Morning arrived.

Helen studied the screen of the QTel. "About six hours."

"Off we go then."

Breakfast was brief. The horses were ready. Lothorio Regasti offered them the use of a local for a guide. They declined politely. There wasn't much distance to cover; maybe two or three miles, heading east. If the calculations were right again, and if their maps were reasonably accurate. The area around this part of the country was obviously of less interest to Seladiënnan cartographers than others. The maps were lacking the detail accorded to other parts, especially those corresponding to the southern UK and around the capital.

They'd never seen much of the capital, Sam reflected. Or of anything else. Come to think about it, they hadn't used Helen's digital camera more than a few times, and that had been on the *Gallinis*, where there had been time to spare. They'd been so busy thinking about other things that they'd completely forgotten to take it back with them on their first return. Everything had been hurried and urgent, leaving no thinking space for anything but getting the job done. Their initial naive notion of acting as explorers and observers...

Sam smiled at himself and their folly.

Nice idea, but...

We've been far too involved to be observers.

And yet...

He looked around the room. Already the prospect of going back to their own world was putting a distance between them and their environment. The familiarity that came with the implicit acceptance of what *was*—simply because there was no time to be detached—was giving way to the alienation resulting from critical observation. The room's decor: non–existent, not even the slightest trace of anything that wasn't strictly necessary. The bed: if they weren't high–PCI people it would have made for an uncomfortable night.

Give me decent inner–spring mattress anytime.

Or even a futon. Anything but horse–hair. The very thought of sleeping on a base of hairs of dead animals...

The smells: already, from the kitchen of an eating place nearby, wafted the scents of Seladiënnan cuisine. Maybe a trace of fresh bread—but that would have come from the bakery just a few houses down. Mainly it was meat frying—and those doughy patties they threw into the same pan to soak up whatever oil they poured into it. Animal mostly. Cholesterol city. With it came the pervasive scent of spices he'd never quite been able to identify; and, of course, the ubiquitous reek of *liquamen*. Indians and curry? Ha! Seladiënnans and *liquamen*! It came out of their pores like an exhalation and surrounded them like an olfactory halo.

Sorry, but it just ain't me.

Us.

For a moment he felt a twinge of guilt. Looking back over his actions since they'd come to this place, he found that now, in the aftermath, the judgments and decisions he'd made appeared less obviously justified than they had been then. The same went for his—and Helen's—dismissal of the Seldiënnan ways of life as unsuitable for them.

The price of 'difference'. We are who we are.

It was no judgment on the people here; just one about their own preferences. What could be wrong with that?

He looked over to Helen, who was pulling her khaki T-shirt over her. She smiled at him. She knew what he was thinking again. Looking devastatingly beautiful—as always. His gaze slid down her torso, followed the contours of her body. She smiled even broader and ran her tongue along half–parted lips. Terribly suggestive, but there

Chapter 28

was no time for anything more than kissing her. Briefly, all–too–briefly.

Let's go home.

Home: to global warming—*Is it going to be like here one day?*—a depleted ozone layer, air and water pollution, global pandemics, US presidential elections, terrorists, Hollywood, third world mass–starvation, internet, ADLER, helicopters.

Home.

Are we just too culturally sclerotic to adapt to this world?

Think of what we have here!

No pollution. Well, not car exhausts anyway. Or nuclear power stations for that matter. *Any* power stations.

And no electric lights, but smoking oil–lamps.

And no helicopters…

Call me pathetic, but I miss Meg and Suzie.

Their flights in the micros…it had brought back the taste of something he realized now he'd come to take for granted. The simple joy of flying. Not just in your dreams, but with your earthly body. Next to making love to Helen it was the one thing that, each time, lifted him above his own limited self and made him believe that maybe all the shit was worth it after all.

"You're full of crap," she said, pulled him to her and kissed him. "You know much better than that," she whispered.

Well—maybe…

"Shall we go?"

"Let's."

Illus was well behind them. Around them a flat plain of vineyards, stretching right to the hills in the east.

"We're close," she said.

He didn't feel a thing, but he trusted Helen implicitly. She sensed stuff he couldn't. Sometimes, when they were…joined…he thought he did, but not right now.

They pulled up the horses amidst the vines and looked around. Helen consulted the QTel.

"There's no need," Sam told her. He pointed. The fog was almost upon them.

He turned his head. It was behind them, too. And to their left. All around in fact.

"You're getting good at this!"

"I had always hoped that I might be useful one of these days," she said demurely.

The sky above them disappeared as the fog enveloped them and shut out the world.

"Now where do we go?" Helen wondered.

An excellent question. Sam realized that here were some questions he'd never even thought about. Like where was what? How could you tell which side was which world? Or did that make any sense at all? After all, both worlds were on all sides and yet…

"Shit!"

She brought her horse closer to his. "Let's just go." She pointed. "Thataway."

They made the animals move.

It took a long time. The fog seemed to go on and on.

Wrong way?

Please not!

Did he sense a coolness—a lessening of the ubiquitous Seladiënnan humidity?

They prodded the horses to more speed.

Without warning the fog ended. They emerged into brilliant sunshine. Endless flat fields. A short distance away a long row of willows betrayed the existence of a creek or stream. A subtle, acrid scent pervaded the air. Gas fumes. From somewhere distant familiar sounds. Less than a mile off the familiar shape of cars rushing along some French highway.

They looked at each other and smiled.

Home.

They dismounted, unsaddled and unbridled the horses and let them run off. The saddles they left where they were. They went to the stream, which was murky with a greenish–brown color. When they looked around they saw that the bank of fog had disappeared.

There they hid the swords, in between the twisted roots of an old willow. Sam looked around and noted salient landmarks. They'd come back for them later. It was too dangerous to leave them here. Besides, they were the last objects that connected them in some intangible way with their adventures.

When they were done they stood still for a few moments, listening to the water of the stream gurgling over the rocks and along the willow roots at its banks.

They embraced and kissed; held each other for a while. Then, hand in hand, they headed toward the highway.

Epilogue

These days, the baby stretched her belly taut; her movements drew bumps across the surface.

"Behave yourself," she told her after a particularly vigorous stir and patted the place where an elbow or foot had tested the elasticity of her skin.

From somewhere inside her came a wordless reply, followed by another physical sign of the girl's aliveness: a solid mental presence, adding itself to Helen's and Sam's joined awareness; wanting attention, and reveling in it when it was bestowed—which was almost always.

It was all a part of that thing which had started the day they got lost in a fog in Cornwall. Now it was a threesome, and even Sam was beginning to accept what Helen had known for a long time. He'd resisted it, of course; thinking that his occasional visions of Katie talking to him were just wish–fantasies, symptoms of not being able to let go. Psychologists, he'd told her, would have a field–day with all the labels they could stick on him.

But Seladiënna—which seemed far away by now, though in other ways it was there, close, all the time—had demonstrated that there were indeed things between heaven and earth that made sense only if you accepted the possibility of some truly far–out notions.

Sam still wasn't willing to accept reincarnation, but what the hell! If an *aquaspiritus* could capture the essence or whatever of a human being and effectively *become* that person—albeit inflicted with much of the sprite's crotchets—then why should not a new–born baby become a similar…vessel? And the way Sam and Katie had been…

Why not?

The third presence in their mental communions was quite definite, possessed of a distinct personality that could not be explained with the relatively blank mind of a truly 'new–born'. This girl had been around before, and she was looking forward to being born.

More than that! Helen sensed anticipation of something more specific. The girl wanted to meet Sam. *Really* meet him: face to face.

How could the undeveloped mind of a fetus have a concept of 'daddy'? Yet this is what Helen felt.

Toward Helen the girl also had definite attitudes. Here, too, was anticipation, mixed with simple, open affection and a notion that all this was just like she wanted it to be.

"Yeah, we're going to be a strange family," Sam said.

Snoop!

"Sue me."

"We were strange before we started a family. Lisa is just going to continue the tradition."

Sam laughed and took her hand.

Together they walked to Suzie.

Big day, today.

Decision day.

Commitment day.

They climbed into Suzie. Sam had bought the helo back from Dale, who told them that he'd known they would be back and that he had bought it only for safe-keeping, awaiting their return.

"I love it when I'm right," he had told them.

Maddie had given her husband a firm nudge in the ribs. "Behave yourself."

Sam had flown Suzie to her new abode, just across the border in Mexico, where he quickly acquired a solid clientele for his services, both as a tutor and a skillful pilot for those times when you really needed one—which seemed to happen a lot. Already Sam and Suzie had attended to several naval emergencies and ferried a number of urgent patients to nearby hospitals.

It was good to see him doing what he liked to do. And she did, too, of course—though right now it was a bit difficult, with Lisa kicking and prodding away and everything becoming just a tad tedious. The sooner she was out and about the better.

Suzie lifted off the concrete pad and headed out to sea. About a mile out Sam hovered. Helen slid open the tiny window on her side of the canopy bubble. She picked up the QTel and held it up. It was the one they'd mailed to Sam's bank, the last one to hold the database. The other one they had erased.

Of course, they could have just erased this one, too: push a couple of buttons and presto! Everything gone for good.

But it wasn't enough. Not enough...ceremony. This was, after all, the moment of their commitment.

To what?

To their world of course. No hedgings, no maybes, no ways out. They belonged *here*—not into some parallel universe. No matter how shitty this world might be, it was theirs. Here they would raise their children—and they would make sure their children knew that it wasn't such a bad place; it was worth fighting for, hoping for, persisting for.

Their experiences in Seladiënna would forever be a part of them, but that world wasn't *theirs* and never could have been. It was simpler in many ways, but simplicity itself was not a virtue: just another way of doing things, and not necessarily a better one.

And once you looked past the simplicity there were, in hindsight, many mysteries which they had never had an opportunity to investigate during the time of their sojourn there. Like the strange magic of the sword, and...

Helen shrugged it off.

It doesn't matter.

Sam touched her leg.

She looked at him and saw him smile.

Now.

She leaned over and kissed him briefly but with passion. Suzie swayed as his attention was diverted by her action. He stabilized it and grinned at her.

Now.

Helen held the hand with the QTel out the window and opened her fingers. Gravity and the downwash from the rotors tore it away. She saw it tumble over and over—and then it disappeared from her of her sight in the blue waters below.

THE END